Close Relations

Also by Deborah Moggach

You Must Be Sisters
Close to Home
A Quiet Drink
Hot Water Man
Porky
To Have and to Hold
Driving in the Dark
Smile and Other Stories
Stolen
The Stand-In
The Ex-Wives
Changing Babies
Seesaw

Close Relations

DEBORAH MOGGACH

HEINEMANN : LONDON

Close Relations is a work of fiction.
Names, characters, places and incidents,
are either the product of the author's
imagination or are used entirely fictitiously.

First published in Great Britain 1997
by William Heinemann
an imprint of Reed International Books Ltd
Michelin House, 81 Fulham Road, London SW3 6RB
and Auckland, Melbourne, Singapore and Toronto

A CIP catalogue record for this title
is available from the British Library

ISBN 0 434 00285 2

Typeset by Falcon Oast Graphic Art
in 11.5 on 14 point Palatino
Printed and bound in Great Britain
by Clays Ltd, St Ives plc

For Kate Harwood

PART ONE

One

You had a problem? Gordon Hammond was your man. He was a jobbing builder, a man with a van. He was good with his hands, cheerful and reliable. He was his own boss, beholden to nobody; he was not the sort to knuckle down under someone else's orders. No job was too small for Gordon in those days. This was forty years ago, when he was just starting in the business and struggling to make ends meet. He had a wife, Dorothy, to support. And then his daughters were born, one closely followed by another, and though you could scrape by on £10 a week, especially with a wife like Dorothy who could conjure up a meal out of nothing, you still had rent to pay and as time progressed money to put down on a house.

Gordon called his business Kendal Contractors, for he had a romantic streak and it was on a holiday in the Lake District that he had proposed to his wife. He stayed a one-man band for years and he worked all the hours God gave him. While he hammered and plastered, the Russians sent the first sputnik into space, 3,000 anti-war protesters marched on Aldermaston and Christian Dior, a man unnoticed by Gordon alive or dead, died. For Gordon was busy.

By the late fifties the two daughters had arrived, and though people thought that he and his wife were trying for a son next time, a strong young lad to join the firm, Gordon said he was proud of his daughters and wouldn't want it any other way. His tone silenced any further questions, even from his wife. By 1959 another daughter had been born. She was born on February 3, the day Buddy Holly was killed; if it had been a boy, Gordon would have called him Buddy but as it was another girl they called her Madeleine. In that year the Mini car was invented, heralding the start of the swinging sixties. It was a decade that passed Gordon by as if it were happening in another country. He kept his head down; he was busy elsewhere.

In 1960 he and Dorothy bought their first home, a maisonette in Chislehurst. They even made a down-payment on a caravan but there was precious little time for holidays, Gordon being rushed off his feet and having to hire an ever-increasing work-force to cope with the demand. Word of mouth did it. He boasted that he had never advertised his services, there was no need for it, he kept his customers because no job was too small, small led to big, one recommendation to another. There was always a demand for a reliable builder who gave a fair estimate, turned up when he said he would, did a first-class job and cleaned up afterwards, not one of those cowboys–wally jobs on the cheap and the next month the ceiling falls in.

In those days the world was a hopeful place. The Russians thrust Gagarin into space, Kennedy was elected President and in 1963 Martin Luther King had a dream. The housing market was booming too. By the mid-sixties Kendal Contractors had a ten-strong work-force of chippies, plasterers and plumbers, in addition to a fluctuating number of labourers Gordon called in on a casual basis. Flat conversions, local authority work, private speculations – in those days property developers were two a penny and in partnership with a firm of local architects he ploughed his profits into some terraced housing in Putney, divided them into flats and made a larger profit which he ploughed into another speculation. And so on.

He put the girls into a private school, St Agnes, in Croydon. Though he winced at the size of the fees, his heart swelled with pride as he wrote the cheque. He bought a larger house, detached, up the road from the maisonette. The

2

Vietnam War ended; the Watergate hearings began. In 1974 Gordon moved his family into their final home. It was a five-bed Tudor-style property in Purley, woods out the back, garaging for two cars and a dream kitchen at last for his wife, bless her. By the time Nixon had resigned Gordon had built an office extension on the side of the house, there was even room for a small yard for storing materials.

So the girls went to school, benefiting from the sort of education neither he nor his wife had enjoyed. While they did so, his wife, Dorothy, sat in the office and answered the phone. Over the years she had taught herself book-keeping, she discovered that she had a flair for figures, and though they had their ups and downs, particularly when the property market collapsed in the late seventies, there was always work for a good builder, for if people cannot afford to move house they have to adapt the place they are living in, and by now he was the oldest-established builder in the neighbourhood.

The girls grew up. Louise was the first-born. She was blonde and pretty and vague; from infancy she charmed those around her. She daydreamed her way through school, preferring to play with her dolls in a rehearsal for motherhood. Everybody loved Louise and she accepted this with the equanimity of the beautiful. Even her sisters' intermittent bouts of jealousy were disarmed by her obliviousness to their existence, for those who are favoured by nature have an innocence about them, a protective envelope that seals them into their own sunny climate. She grew up into a willowy teenager with long silky hair. Lovelorn young men laid siege to the house; bricklayers hung around on payday hoping for a glimpse of her. In her sisters' eyes she always seemed to be disappearing, roaring off in some sports car leaving emptiness and a smell of exhaust behind her. She enrolled in secretarial college but she never completed the course, she was far too disorganised. By that time, however, it no longer mattered for she had fallen in love with a young venture capitalist and soon she was ensconced in a flat in Chelsea, pregnant with her first child.

3

Prudence, the middle sister, was the intellectual. 'Always got her nose in a book,' boasted Gordon. With Louise it was 'bees round a honeypot'. Not a reflective man, he spent little time analysing his daughters and, when asked, summoned up the same phrases throughout their teenage years. He set each daughter in the mould of his own catchphrase. Prudence was the quiet one, the bluestocking. Prudence, whose self-esteem was low, considered herself plain but when removed from Louise's proximity her face gained in definition. It was a face one could gaze into with pleasure, like a painting of a Dutch interior.

Prudence was the only sister to go to university. She led a separate life inside her head and on graduation day it gave her a shock to see her parents in the audience, so alien did they seem in the mock-medieval hall. In their different ways all three sisters grew away from their parents but it was Prudence who was educated out of her background. Though she knew her mother and father were proud of her, the very shininess of their pride showed up their incomprehension of what she so easily took for granted. They had worked so hard to get her there, and in doing so they had lost her.

She remained a dutiful daughter, however, the peacemaker between her father and her unruly younger sister and the one to whom her parents turned when Louise moved away to her new house in a favoured part of Buckinghamshire. Prudence was the reliable sister, one of life's baby-sitters, who held the fort whilst others were having fun. If she rebelled against this she did it in such a well-mannered way that nobody noticed. Her parents were too busy with the daily dramas of the business and their two grandchildren. And Maddy, her younger sister, though a loyal ally – she would fight to the death for Prudence – had never got on with her father and absented herself by moving away from home and finally out of the country altogether. Meanwhile Prudence got a job in publishing, bought a flat in Clapham and lived there with her cat for company, and a row of African violets, the spinster's houseplant, on the window-sill.

From an early age siblings are assigned their roles and through the years they settle into others' expectations. Louise was the beautiful earth mother and Pru was the clever one. Maddy was the tomboy. When their mother recollected their childhood the same scene repeated itself. Louise sat in the garden, tucking up her dolls on the lawn. Pru lay on her stomach reading a book. And along charged Maddy, vroom vroom, pushing her toy bulldozer over Pru's pages, vroom vroom, pushing it over Louise's dolls. The yells! Maddy was a fierce, sturdy little girl. Sometimes her sisters wondered if her destiny was to act the part of the son her parents had never had, and maybe secretly desired. A truculent girl, she grew up at odds with her surroundings, 'a square peg in a round hole,' her father said. Even the name she was given, Madeleine, didn't fit; she never grew into it and remained Maddy from an early age. Photos showed her with a round face and pudding-bowl haircut, glaring at the camera and standing halfway out of the shot.

Despite her glowering, somewhat humourless exterior, she was deeply loyal to her sisters and fought with anyone who criticised them. She was a strong girl, good at sport, and won swimming trophies which her father proudly showed visitors. When he did this she grew red-faced and abrupt; her father considered this rude but her sisters knew she was simply embarrassed. When she was sixteen she dropped out of school. Her father was furious; hadn't he slaved away all these years to get her into the best school in Surrey? But she left anyway and went to live with a group of people in Stockwell who were running an adventure playground. For years she all but disappeared from view. She met Prudence from time to time, but she seldom saw Louise because she disliked her husband. He was a handsome, caddish man called Robert about whom Prudence, too, had mixed feelings but she was more tactful about showing it.

During the late eighties Maddy travelled a great deal, backpacking, and for a while she lived in Canada where she worked with disadvantaged kids. Though she had never

5

been a student there was a studently feel to her life – footloose, impermanent, at odds with not only her upbringing
but with the Tory government, the felling of the rainforests
and the conspicuous consumption of many people including
Louise's venture capitalist husband. Her face remained curiously youthful, like a nun's unmarked by the passage of time.
By the age of thirty-three, when she left to work in Africa, she
could still be mistaken for a girl of twenty. 'You must have a
picture in your attic,' said Prudence, who was feeling her age.
Maddy, however, didn't understand; she had never heard of
Dorian Gray.

Gordon, too, was feeling his age. That day in September, his
granddaughter's sixteenth birthday, he and Dorothy were
driving down to Buckinghamshire for the lunch party.

'Sixteen,' he said. 'Seems only yesterday she was a baby.'

'Seems only yesterday the girls were babies,' said Dorothy.

It was true. His daughters were three great creatures,
practically middle-aged. It seemed only yesterday that they
were playing together in the garden. They seemed to have
grown up while his attention was momentarily diverted. It
was as if he had nipped out to buy the evening paper and
come home to find them women. They had mortgages and
opinions. Maddy was in Nigeria, speaking Ibo or whatever,
how about that?

Birthdays always gave him pause for thought. His granddaughter Imogen was sixteen – practically capable of breed-
ing herself. They drove towards Beaconsfield. Dorothy sat
beside him, a parcel on her lap. She had bought it, she saw to
that side of things.

'What is it?' he asked.

'Wait and see. It goes with her big one, from her parents.'

'Why won't anybody tell me?' he whined. He swerved out
to overtake a lorry.

'Gordon!' Dorothy clutched the door handle. 'It's a secret.'

A secret – the story of his life. Girlish giggles behind closed

6

doors. A houseload of females, mother and daughters, closeted together. Mood-swings, whispers. *Don't tell Dad, he wouldn't understand. He's just a man.*

'Gordon! It's a thirty-mile zone.'

Gordon was a restless, impulsive man. He drove too fast, he smoked too much. He was probably a stone overweight if he ever thought to stand on the scales. His wife was always nagging him about his health; he was sixty-five, he should have more sense. But it was his drive, his own blind energy, which had got him where he was today. It was part of the package.

In fact he resembled a parcel. He was a short, sturdy man – Maddy was the only daughter who had inherited his physique. He was getting bald, no denying that, but the extra weight was all solid, he spent his days on the go, he was as fit as a bull. There was a pugnacious set to his jaw, a forward thrust to his stocky body. But he was a cheerful man, too, a whistler. None of the young lads who worked for him whistled, they didn't have the tunes any more, but he had a repertoire of standards which used to get on his daughters' nerves. He was a robust man, he liked a drink and a joke; he was a man of action rather than a thinker and though he grumbled about the business he was happiest haring from one site to another, bawling out orders and bantering with his lads, he was a male animal through and through.

Women were by and large unfathomable. He should be used to them by now, he had had enough practice, but to tell the truth his daughters had always bemused him. Their preoccupations seemed beyond him, in another dimension entirely. And why couldn't Prudence and Maddy each find themselves a man, get married and give him some more grandchildren before it was too late?

His wife, now she was a different matter. He could rely on Dorothy. She twittered and fussed, like all women, she couldn't tell one end of a car from the other, but her femininity was of the old school, it was comprehensible to him.

They had been married for forty-four years, they held no secrets for each other. His childhood sweetheart had become a plump matron of sixty-three; when he looked at her properly, which wasn't often, it gave him a mild shock. His familiarity with her hadn't caught up with her age. Her hair, tinted now, was set in the same soft waves she had set it in for years. They were old companions, they had weathered their storms, they understood each other. If people had asked him about his marriage – which they didn't, it was too settled an institution and besides, nobody of his acquaintance talked in that language – if they had asked he would have replied that he and Dot rubbed along, what else was there to say? Conversations about relationships always made him fidget.

So Gordon Hammond and his wife drove through Beaconsfield in their Mercedes estate car, its back heaped with bags of cement. They passed the Queen Anne homes belonging to captains of industry and TV personalities. Set behind grass verges, the shops in the high street displayed designer clothes and photographs of desirable properties. The prosperity of the place – the width of the street, the manicured lawns! This was the heart of the Home Counties, sealed off from the brutish outside world. Nothing terrible could ever happen here, that was the message. Intruders beware! Wealth breathed from its renovated façades. Soon Gordon would be sitting down at Louise's table. It made his heart swell, to think that his daughter's sweet face had gained her entry into this priviledged world. She had always been his golden girl, touched by the Good Fairy's wand. The reward for her beauty was two healthy children, a handsome husband and a life her sisters must surely envy.

He braked at a zebra crossing. Dorothy jerked forward. In the back of the car, paint cans shifted.

'Gordon! One of these days you'll give me a heart attack.' She replaced the package on her lap. 'Unless you have one yourself first.'

*

8

Six miles from Beaconsfield, in a fold of the hills, lies the village of Wingham Wallace. Set amidst rolling pastures and beechwoods it is in an area of Outstanding Natural Beauty. The village itself was recorded in the Domesday Book and its core remains – a pub, rows of cottages and a church dating from Norman times, with Victorian additions. The beauty of the village has been enhanced by age and wealth, the first needing the second for its own preservation. Within easy commuting distance of London, the place has attracted those high-fliers who wish for rural relief at the end of a demanding day. It is also convenient for Heathrow Airport, a mere thirty minutes' drive away. As a result of this several of the larger houses are inhabited by people so rarely glimpsed that they have become rumours. The smaller cottages have long since been gentrified, too, and their outhouses converted into garages that are too short for the 5-Series BMWs whose bonnets jut into the lanes and cause the passing traffic to swerve.

At its heart, however, this is still a real community inhabited by real people. Pebble-dashed council houses prove this, and bunches of youths who gather at night in the bus shelter, shifting restlessly like heifers, their cigarettes glowing in the dark. There is still a primary school – just – and a store-cum-post office run by a man called Tim, who does all the work, and his depressed wife Margot. And how could the rich live without the local people to service their households, cleaning and gardening and minding the place when they are away in the Caribbean?

On Sundays the church is well-attended, mainly by women with carrying voices and organisational skills who make jam and who campaigned successfully against a proposed development of starter homes which would have ruined the views and brought down the property prices. The vicar has long since moved into the next village; he now has five parishes in his care and the vicarage itself was sold back in the sixties. In a village of desirable properties it is one of the most enchanting – a Georgian house burdened with wistaria, grand but not imposingly so, with sunny rooms

9

overlooking a walled garden and a view of the Chiltern Hills from the master bedroom. Successive owners have improved the place, adding *en suite* bathrooms, a Smallbone kitchen and that essential accessory of the seventies, a conservatory. When Robert and Louise moved here with their children, six years ago, there were no more improvements to be made. This suited Robert. He hated DIY and said he had better things to do on a Sunday than stand on a ladder covered with dust.

This particular Sunday was their daughter Imogen's birthday. It was one of those early autumn days that already possess their own nostalgia; like petals packed into a bud, the dewy garden held within itself the future memories of a perfect day – the sort that makes England in general, and Wingham Wallace in particular, a satisfactory place to live. Robert's and Louise's visitors, of which there were many, remarked how it always seemed sunny at the Old Vicarage, as if one of Louise's many skills was to create her own weather for her guests.

Today's lunch was to be a family occasion – Louise's parents and her sister Prudence. Unaided by her adolescent children she was cooking the meal. She was hampered by the dog, an overweight labrador called Monty, who lumbered to his feet whenever she moved and who stood in front of the kitchen units, strings of saliva hanging from his jowls, whining as she unleafed the salami from its wrapping paper.

Louise was forty-two and still beautiful. In fact age had improved her, revealing the bone structure beneath her soft face. Twenty years of marriage had also strengthened her character, sharpening the edges that had been blurred when she was younger. Robert was a demanding husband, easily bored. He expected her to amuse him and to be a sophisticated hostess when their guests came to stay. She had always wanted to please him – too much, according to her sisters. They suspected that deep down she felt that her background and intellect were inferior to his and that she had to stay in trim, mentally and physically, to keep up with him. They despised this lack of self-confidence, this female compliance. Didn't Robert realise how lucky he was to have her?

Louise carried some muddy lettuces in from the garden. Her son had appeared. His face was bleary with sleep. He leaned against the sink eating a bowl of Nutty Cinnamon Shapes.

'Jamie, it's twelve o'clock.'

He raised one eyebrow. It was a new mannerism, caught from his father. 'Chill, Ma.'

'They'll be here in a minute.'

'It's only Granny and Grandad.' His withering tone, too, resembled his father's voice. She hoped that he wasn't growing up to be a snob. Jamie was eighteen. Next year he was going to university. He was tall and bony, with thick fair hair. Judging by the number of phone calls for him he was becoming attractive to girls. This wasn't improving his character. They spoiled him. One would have imagined that in these post-feminist times this would be a thing of the past. But then Louise had spoiled her son too. Her sisters had always accused her of being slavish with men.

'Budge up,' she said, dumping the lettuces in the sink.

Imogen came in, yawning. 'Where's my black top?'

'Is nobody going to help me?' asked Louise.

'It's my birthday!'

Jamie, still eating, sauntered away into the living room. Sound bloomed from the TV.

'Why does he always leave the room when I come into it?' asked Louise.

'Because he thinks you're boring.'

'Gap year my foot. Gap from what?' She pointed to the potatoes. 'Scrape these, will you?'

'That's sexist. What about Jamie?'

'He's not here. Where's your dad?'

'He went to buy some lemons.'

'That was hours ago.' Louise thought: the trouble with the country was that you spent the whole time running out of things and the rest of the time in the car.

11

Her daughter popped a slice of salami into her mouth and wandered off. She paused to pat the dog. 'How's my sweetie today?' she crooned. It often struck Louise that her children were nicer to their pets than they were to her. Yet neither the dog nor the rabbits had ever lifted a finger to help them, they had never been bored rigid by playing card games with them, nor had they nursed them through the night. Imogen had a sugary voice that she only used with Monty. When Louise pointed this out Imogen showed no surprise. 'But he's so sweet,' she said. 'So if I rolled on the floor with my legs in the air you'd be nice to me?' asked Louise.

Imogen was a small, wiry girl. Her hair was dark, like her father's, but she hadn't inherited his good looks. The person she most resembled was Aunty Maddy, a fact that her brother pointed out when he wanted to upset her. Like Aunty Maddy she was no intellectual; she was a direct, loyal girl whose slow responses irritated her father and caused Louise to jump to her defence. Robert wanted dazzling children. When Louise pointed out that success could be measured in quieter, more internal ways – didn't niceness matter? – he said that niceness was the most tepid word in the English language and should be banned. Besides, Imogen was never nice to *him*.

Upstairs, Louise brushed her hair. The arrival of her parents always filled her with trepidation. She could trust neither of the men to behave themselves; they brought out the worst in each other. Her father's pride in her and her lifestyle made him look foolish and Robert, who had a cruel streak, goaded him on, much to Louise's and her mother's embarrassment. Gordon was a simple soul. He was putty in his son-in-law's hands and became a caricature of himself – legs akimbo, rubbing his hands like a north country mayor in a play by J. B. Priestley. Louise despised him for this and then hated herself for despising him; she hated Robert turning her father into an object for his own amusement and hated herself more for finding it amusing. For her husband could always make her laugh.

12

It was a quarter to one. Louise went downstairs. Where was Robert? Trust him to disappear when she needed him most. He would breeze in, late; he was never late for his friends, only for her parents. Sometimes she suspected that he was jealous of her family. He had no brothers or sisters. He had been brought up in some style, a lonely little boy on whom lavish amounts of money were spent but who was shamefully neglected. His mother had been too busy marrying her various husbands to take any notice of her son, who had been sent off to boarding school at the age of four. When Louise and Robert were quarrelling he brought up this fact, embellishing it with pitiful descriptions of himself sobbing in the dormitory, clutching a sodden teddy bear. This always did the trick, reducing Louise to tears. The bastard.

There were two composers who made Prudence cry: Brahms and Schubert. Other composers could, with certain passages – Bach, during the slow movement of his double violin concerto, the violins soaring up and entwining, making love to each other with such tenderness it seemed they must break. It was Schubert and Brahms, however, who spoke to her heart. Not the symphonies – Prudence found symphonies windy and self-important, there was a look-at-me feeling about a symphony. She was a chamber music person; there was a spareness and precision about a string quartet that suited her. Prudence needed order. It was essential to her life, it was the structure upon which she depended.

As she drove out of London the road blurred. Brahms was playing – her cassette of the Piano Quartet No 2. On their first date together she had taken Stephen to a lunchtime concert at St John's, Smith Square. The Brahms had been played then, the Lindsay Quartet had performed it. For months afterwards whenever she read the name *Lindsay* she had felt a foolish jolt of electricity. During the concert she and Stephen hadn't touched each other. She had kept her hands in her lap, resting on her handbag, like a dowager, but she had felt the heat of Stephen down her right side. Her skin had been drawn towards the magnet of his shoulder and his thigh. It was the strangest sensation, as if her soul were being removed into his body.

Later, when the whole thing had started, he said that he had felt it too. They had lain in bed, and with the luxuriousness of all new lovers they had gone back over the preceding weeks, charting their progression into intimacy moment by moment. 'Did you feel that then, really?' 'What about that time when we bumped into each other next to the photocopier?' They described each other's clothing – 'You were wearing your white blouse' – all those months of working together in the office were rerun, their own tender videotape, as they lay under her duvet. Hindsight made their most mundane conversations charged with significance. It was during the Brahms, he said, that he had felt his soul removing itself from his wife and finding its home in Prudence.

Her Metro was a mess. Her box of Kleenex was buried under a tea-towel, a box of fisherman's lozenges (empty) and a packet of Silk Cut (also empty). She pulled out a tissue and wiped her nose. People's cars are often a surprise. Those who lead orderly lives can have chaotic vehicles, and vice versa. Those whose lives are disintegrating can drive around in spotless cars smelling of air freshener, with a single hardback road atlas on the back seat. Cars, supposedly an extension of our personalities, in fact reveal something more interesting – the contradictions that lie within us all. Prudence kept her flat tidy but in her car she became a different person, liberated and powerful, in control of a destiny which in normal life eluded her. She drove fast too – fast and skilfully. Yet she looked like the sort of woman who bicycled around London with a basket full of Kit-e-Kat. Which she did do, too.

Stephen was her editorial director. He had a wife, a Dutch woman called Kaatya. He also had two sons. Prudence's affair with him, conducted for the most part with little physical contact, at lunchtimes, had been going on for a year. Prudence wasn't the sort of woman who fell in love with other people's husbands. The revelation of her own capacity for deceit had been one of the more painful experiences of the past twelve months. She drove along the fast lane of the M40; she turned up the Brahms. Stephen had given it to her two days earlier. 'Our first anniversary,' he had said, lifting her chin towards his face.

She rummaged for a cigarette and lit it. She was the only Hammond sister who smoked though she hid the fact, out of some vestigial childish cowardice, from her parents. She didn't look like a smoker; she wore navy-blue cardigans to work, white blouses, flat shoes. It surprised some of her authors when she took them out to lunch and lit up. She smoked; she committed adultery. She thought how none of us are what we seem. Explore deeper and a person disintegrates, just as newsprint, when viewed close-up, disintegrates into tiny dots. How could you trust a word when it was just a collection of spots? Yet her life consisted of working with words, she had to believe in them.

At times she believed that she only existed in other people's expectations of her. When she was a child, for instance, her parents had assembled the dots to create Prudence, the nice, steady sister, the middle one, the swot. These dots clotted together to become her personality. But she knew better. She knew that she was a shifting collection of atoms trying to shape themselves out of chaos. Stephen didn't suspect this; neither did her sisters. Only her cat knew the truth; she could see it in his eyes.

The front of the Old Vicarage was knotted with wistaria. It had been planted many years ago, before the arrival of Robert and Louise. Its thick branches were twisted around each other like lovemaking limbs; their marriage had lasted so long that nobody could prise them apart, even if they had thought to do so. To the right of the vicarage rose the church, St Bartholomew. In its graveyard, beneath the silence of the yew trees, stood headstones. They slanted this way and that,

15

as if blown on by the breath of God. Depending on the mood of the onlooker the mellow brick house and the ancient place of burial suggested either the permanence of love or its transitoriness.

Louise, hearing cars arriving, stepped out of the front door. Later, months later, she remembered that moment. A leaf from the wistaria spiralled down in front of her and came to rest on the gravel. She looked up, beyond the knotted limbs of the trunk. Did it have some sort of blight? The leaves were dying already; they usually didn't fall until October.

It was five to one. The cars arrived – her parents' estate car followed by Robert's BMW. They stopped in the driveway. As they did so Prudence's car appeared along the lane and drove through the gates. Louise hurried to greet them.

'Hello!' called her mother. 'We've all come together.'

'Glad some people do.' Robert grinned at his wife. 'Just kidding.' He shook Gordon's hand and kissed his mother-in-law.

Gordon pointed to the house. 'Should get that guttering seen to.'

'Gordon –' Dorothy said.

Robert smiled. 'Want to fix it while we're having lunch?'

'Don't, love,' said Dorothy. 'He will.'

'One of my lads lives out this way. I'll get him to drop by –'

'Come on!' said Robert.

Robert carried two Tesco bags. A new superstore had opened four miles away. Though he had only gone out for some lemons he had missed the village shop, which only opened briefly on Sundays, and had driven to Tesco with the pleasant sensation that he was both doing his duty and skiving off helping with lunch. Once in the superstore he had succumbed to impulse buys, he was a man who seldom resisted temptation. He had picked up exotic, whiskery fruits from Penang and a bottle of such extra-virgin olive oil that he had practically remortgaged his house to buy it. He had headed to the wine section where he had been seduced into buying various obscure New Zealand vintages. How could such a boring country produce such interesting wines? Maybe, once they had finished polishing their Vauxhalls and filling in their crossword puzzles, they had nothing better to do. Then he had lingered at the magazine rack and leafed through the more lurid Sunday tabloids, admiring the girls' breasts and the catastrophic lives of lottery winners.

Robert went into the house with his parents-in-law. Louise paused with Prudence. She looked at her sister's reddened eyes.

'You all right?'

'Blame it on Brahms,' said Prudence.

'Only Brahms?' Louise hated it when Prudence cried; she did it so seldom. Prudence was the one she relied on, who would always be there. The trouble was, other people thought so too.

'How's everything with . . . you know?' she asked.

'Same as ever.'

'That's why you look so awful.' Louise accompanied her to the front door. 'Listen, I don't want to sound like an older sister but shouldn't you –'

'No.'

Louise looked down the hallway. Sunlight slanted onto the tiles; it shone onto the rear portion of Monty as he wagged his tail, greeting the guests. A champagne cork popped; Imogen laughed.

Louise stood there, seeing it through her sister's eyes. She felt a wave of hatred for Stephen, a man she had never met, for Prudence kept him a secret and their parents didn't even know about his existence. Stephen wasn't entirely to blame, of course, but it is easier to put the responsibility onto somebody unknown, particularly if he is so visibly making your sister unhappy.

The dining room was square and masculine. Its french windows opened into the conservatory where geraniums glowed

17

blood-red in the sunshine. There was a marble fireplace; there was a grandfather clock and a large mahogany table which Robert had inherited from one of his uncles. They ate salami and tinned artichokes, Imogen's favourite starter. Robert poured out more champagne. He was a generous host; he looked at home in this room, doling out wine and chatting, a man at ease with himself and his possessions. Today he wore a striped silk shirt from Turnbull and Asser and a plum-coloured cravat; he looked exactly what he was – a City whiz-kid who had loosened up for the weekend.

'So how're you doing, Pru?' he asked. 'How's the literary scene. Discovered any geniuses?'

'Well, I'm working on a book called *My Favourite Microwave Recipes*. It's written by that newscaster, what's his name.'

'Yeah, and really written by you. Why don't you tell them? I would.'

'It's what I'm paid for.'

'Don't be such a wimp,' said Robert. 'You're wasted in that place. You should be managing director by now.'

Prudence shrugged. She was immune to Robert's flattery; to his attractions too. He had a handsome, wolfish face and thick black hair. He was a small man – it always surprised her that he was shorter than Louise. At some point in his child-hood he had contracted TB and spent months languishing in bed, that was probably the reason. Like many small men he had grown up to be intensely competitive. He played tennis in a London club, thrashing what he called merchant wankers and boasting about it afterwards to Louise. Prudence was both fascinated and repulsed by his hairiness – dense black hairs on his slender arms. She pictured him in bed with Louise, gripping her like a monkey. When other people were talking a muscle twitched in his jaw; there was a restlessness about him, an impatience to be amused. Next to him Prudence, in her floral dress, felt like a head teacher.

Jamie had inherited his father's restlessness. His leg was jiggling under the table. His grandmother was talking to him.

'So what are you going to do in your year off?' she asked.

18

'Try to find a job.'

'Should be easy, with your A levels.'

'Not round here.'

Jamie was bored with the country; he had grown out of it. His days of tadpole-collecting were over and though he sometimes joined the local youths in the bus shelter they seemed like bumpkins to him. Like most adolescent boys he was unwillingly drawn into family gatherings and looked as if he would rather be doing a hundred other things. The question was: what?

Louise came in, carrying a platter. It contained a large salmon strewn with herbs.

'Look at that,' said her father. 'Is there nothing this girl can't do?'

'Woman, Dad,' said Louise. 'I'm forty-two.'

'A moment's silence.' He tapped his fork. 'Let us gaze upon this masterpiece.' On these occasions Gordon was inclined to grow flushed and jovial. It embarrassed his daughters but amused his grandchildren, who were at one remove. Louise sliced into the flesh of the salmon. Gordon raised his glass to Imogen. 'To the birthday girl. Sweet sixteen! You'll be giving me a grandchild before your aunties, unless they pull a finger out.'

There was a silence. Louise glanced at Pru, then she laughed hastily. 'I thought I was starting the menopause last week. Then I realised I'd just left my diaphragm in, all through my period.'

Prudence laughed. Dorothy indicated the teenagers: 'Louise!'

Robert turned to his father-in-law. 'Some potatoes? So how's the business doing?'

'Worked off our feet,' said Gordon.

'I wish he'd take it easy. Haring around London like a twenty-year-old. He won't admit he's getting older.' Dorothy turned to Louise. 'You tell him. He never listens to me.'

'He never has,' said Louise.

'And what's that supposed to mean?' demanded her father.

19

'You've never listened to Mum,' said Prudence, joining in.

'Oh-oh, they're ganging up on me.' Gordon turned to Robert. 'Same as always.'

The doorbell rang.

'Shit,' said Louise. 'Send them away, whoever they are.'

Robert left the room. They heard murmurs in the hall, the surprised tone in Robert's voice. There was the bumping, dragging sound of luggage being brought in.

A woman came in. Though she was thirty-seven she looked younger. She had a no-nonsense, tanned face. It was bare of make-up. She wore jeans and a T-shirt and when she entered the room she paused, startled, as if she had emerged from the darkness to popping flashbulbs.

'Aunty Maddy!' cried Imogen.

Forks clattered onto plates. Her sisters hugged her.

'When did you arrive?'

'I've come straight from the airport.'

'Why didn't you tell us?' asked Louise.

'Are you all right, love?' asked her mother. 'You look so thin.'

'Wicked tan.' Jamie grinned at his aunt.

'We would've come to the airport,' Louise protested.

'She always was a law unto herself,' said her father.

Maddy looked at the teenagers. 'You're so enormous!' She hadn't seen them for four years.

Robert dragged forward another chair. Maddy, who didn't like kissing, who shrank from any show of affection, turned to Imogen and said gruffly: 'Happy birthday. See? I got back in time.' She looked around. 'I didn't know it was going to be, well, everyone.'

'Shall we go home then?' asked her father.

'Gordon.' Dorothy shot him a warning look.

'A letter would have been appreciated,' he said. 'Just one.'

'Dad.' Prudence frowned at him.

Louise gave Maddy a plate of food and a glass of orange juice – her sister didn't drink alcohol. They asked her questions: why had she decided to come back to England? How long was she here for?

'I don't know,' said Maddy. 'I just wanted to come home.'

Maddy had been working for an aid organisation in Nigeria. She had worked in a remote village helping to drill bore-holes and teaching women to read. Her letters had been infrequent and her life there was mysterious to her family. Like all people who have returned from living abroad she didn't know where to start; the experience was both too familiar and too amorphous to be made digestible for others. Besides, she was not by nature a talkative person and she felt exposed with her parents there. For years she had lived in places that were incomprehensible to her family and she felt grateful that even her sisters' curiosity was limited and would peter out after a few days. She needed to keep something to herself, otherwise her family consumed her. That was one of the reasons she had had to get away from them in the first place.

They gazed at her. Dorothy was right; she was thinner. Her face had sharpened; her arms looked muscular. Though far from a glamorous person, to the teenagers she was exotic – only yesterday she had been sweltering under an African sun.

Maddy couldn't eat. She was still living in another time-zone and was filled with airline food. She got up and pulled a wooden object out of her baggage. She gave it to Imogen. 'Happy birthday.'

'Gosh,' said Imogen. 'What is it?'

'An Ibo fertility truncheon.'

Imogen paused. 'Wow.'

Robert burst out laughing. 'So if they don't shag you, you can beat them to death.'

Maddy said: 'I thought – you could make it into a lamp or something.'

'Thanks, Aunty.'

'Don't call me Aunty,' said Maddy. 'It sounds so . . .'

'Auntyish,' agreed Prudence.

Louise pointed to the salmon. 'Eat up.'

21

Gordon indicated her plate. 'Bet you didn't eat that in Wogland.'

'Dad!' said Prudence and Louise together.

Gordon raised his hands. 'Only joking. I employ one of them myself. First-class chippie –'

'For God's sake –' said Maddy.

'– very sunny disposition.'

'Nothing's changed, has it?' said Maddy.

'– and he's got a lovely sense of rhythm,' said Gordon.

'Can't you stop him, Mum?' demanded Maddy. She turned to her father. 'We're human beings, Gordon –'

'So I'm Gordon now? What's wrong with Dad?'

'Know your problem?' said Maddy. 'It's ignorance and fear –'

'He's only winding you up,' said Louise.

'Forgot the Thought Police was back,' said Gordon. 'Better watch what I say –'

'Anybody different from you –'

'Jesus, Maddy!' Robert raised his voice. 'It's Imogen's birthday. Can we postpone the lecture about race relations?'

There was a pause. It reminded them of the debris settling, after a minor explosion. The grandfather clock struck three.

'I'm sorry.' Maddy turned to Imogen. 'I'm terribly sorry.'

'It's all right,' replied Imogen. 'You sound just like Mum, with Dad.'

'What?' said Robert.

'They're always having rows.' Imogen looked at her father. 'You're incredibly racist.'

'I'm not!'

'Sexist too.' Jamie joined in. 'When Janet Jackson came on TV –'

That wasn't racism,' said Robert. 'That was lust.'

'Shut up, everybody!' shouted Louise.

There was a silence. In the hush, they heard the sound of a lorry arriving.

*

There is something about a horse that stills the heart. She was a grey mare, heart-stoppingly beautiful. She pricked her ears and gazed at them with her liquid brown eyes, could she really be as intelligent as she looked? She was 14.2 hands high, the perfect height – just taller than a pony, just a horse but not alarmingly so. She was six years old, still darkly dappled like a rocking horse. In the years to come she would grow whiter.

The lorry had driven away. The horse stood on the gravel, her nostrils expanding like sea anemones as she breathed in the air of her new home. Louise held the rope of her head-collar. She put out her hand and stroked the horse's muzzle; it felt velvety, like a raspberry.

'Where'll we put her?' asked Louise.

'In the kitchen,' said Maddy.

'What? Robert'll have a fit.'

'Don't be a sissy.'

Louise laughed. Suddenly the years fell away. After all this time one word could reduce them to giggles.

The others waited in the dining room. Robert called out: 'What's happening?'

'Wait! Don't come in!' yelled Louise through the kitchen door.

'We're not ready!' called Prudence.

Their mother smiled. 'Nothing's changed, has it.'

'Instant regression,' said Robert. 'How thin is the veneer of maturity. They're always like this when they get together.' He knocked on the door. 'What on earth are you doing in there?'

Suddenly they heard the muffled neigh of a horse. They jumped. Louise opened the door.

It was a large kitchen. The horse stood in the middle of the floor. Her tail and mane were plaited with red ribbons.

'Happy birthday, darling,' said Louise. 'She's called Skylark.'

Imogen stepped up to the horse. She looked as if she were sleepwalking. Her mother passed her the rope. For a moment she was beyond speech.

'She's the most beautiful ... the most ... oh, Mum ... Dad ...' She gazed at the horse. Her eyes filled with tears. Just then there was the sound of soft thuds.

'Ugh, gross!' said Jamie.

'Her first dung.' Imogen gazed at it, entranced.

'Want to embalm it?' asked Robert. 'Louise, I really think –'

'We'll clear it up,' said Prudence.

Imogen flung her arms around the horse's neck. She buried her face in the fur, breathing the scent.

'Love at first sight,' said Gordon.

'Steady on,' said Robert. 'Any closer and we'll have to call the Horse Helpline.' He went to get his camera.

Imogen lifted up her face. It was radiant. 'This is the most wonderful day of my life.'

The shutter clicked. It was a moment of pure happiness – pure, distilled joy. For months afterwards, whenever she smelt horse dung, Louise would remember it. Later she would frame the snapshot and put it in her bedroom. When their lives had changed out of all recognition she would look at it and feel a blade through her heart.

Maddy, standing apart from the rest of them, felt confused. One minute they were quarrelling, the next laughing. She had forgotten the tumultuous ebb and flow of family life. She felt buffeted one way and another like a stick in a stream. She had forgotten how to cope with it. How peaceful it had been to live abroad, even in a war zone. For years she had been amongst people to whom she was not related, with whom codes of manners and distance applied. Most of them didn't even speak the same language as she did; apart from the Nigerians, her closest European colleagues had been a French doctor and a Swedish project manager. She watched Louise sweeping up the droppings. Thrust back, jet-lagged, into the intimacy of family life she wanted to crawl away and pull a duvet over her head.

Gordon's heart swelled with pride. Imogen led the horse outside. Through the window he watched her saddling up with casual expertise. He had a granddaughter who could buckle a bridle, who could talk with authority about fetlocks and gymkhanas. The sun shone on the yellow, rag-rolled kitchen units. Here he was, in the autumn of his years, surrounded by the fruits of his loins. For over forty years he had worked all the hours God had given him to arrive at such a moment. It was worth the wait.

His heart thumped. Pain shot along his arm. He sat down heavily on a chair.

Dorothy looked at him. 'What's the matter, love?'

'Nothing.'

Gordon took a breath – once, twice, breathing deeply. At the time, he just thought his heart was bursting with pride.

The three sisters sat on the lawn eating birthday cake. The sun was sinking; clouds were building up over the church spire. At the end of the garden was a vegetable patch, its poles trousered with runner bean plants. Beyond it lay the paddock. Imogen cantered round on her horse. Her hard hat rose and fell as she passed the brick wall. She wore the new hacking jacket her grandparents had given her.

A ladder had been erected against the house. Gordon stood on it, fixing something or other. He could never sit still. At the foot of the ladder stood Dorothy. From time to time she passed him a tool.

Maddy lay on her back, looking up at the clouds. 'I'm sorry. I've forgotten how to do this.'

Louise said: 'It comes from being amongst all those savages.'

Prudence listened to their father whistling. 'Nothing's ever going to change him.'

'Or her.'

Prudence licked her fingers. 'Wouldn't it be interesting if something happened which really shook them up?'

'It won't.' Louise, lying on her back, turned to Maddy. 'Where are you going to live?'

'Somebody's lending me a flat.' Maddy's friends were

mostly unknown to her sisters. Maddy was not a social sort of person; neither Pru nor Louise could remember her ever holding any sort of party, or if she had, she hadn't invited them. From what they gathered, her friends worked for the sort of good causes that made Pru and Louise feel guilty.

'How's work?' Maddy asked.

Pru said: 'We were taken over in the spring. Maybe I wrote to you about it. A big German media group.' She didn't bother telling her sisters the name; neither of them would have heard of it. 'They're going to move us into a state-of-the-art monstrosity down by the river. It's all accountants now, they keep talking about the bottom line. Everybody's very jittery.' She lay back and closed her eyes. 'Mmm, it's so peaceful here.'

'Everybody says that,' said Louise. 'They come down from London and fill up here, like a garage. Robert does too. Then the next morning he buggers off again.'

'He always wanted to live in the country, didn't he?' said Maddy.

'That's because he's hardly ever here.'

The three women lay on the grass. The sun slipped behind a cloud.

'How are you two getting on?' asked Prudence.

'Oh, fine,' said Louise. 'It's just . . .'

'What?'

'Nothing. We're fine.'

Her sisters were silent. A long marriage is closed to outsiders, even to sisters. It seals off a couple from the world. It is only when the marriage is in trouble that the curtains open for a moment and people glimpse the astonishing drama that has been playing on the stage all those years. At that moment they can step inside with their consolation and advice – '*To be honest, I never liked him*', or '*I always thought she was selfish*'. Two things can then happen. The marriage can split apart for ever, baring its soul and loosening its secrets into the world, or the couple can make it up. When this happens the curtains are closed again and those who have offered their advice feel foolish, especially when they have been frank about the

26

person's spouse. The words hang embarrassingly in the air, everyone tries to pretend they have never been said.

Prudence was a discreet woman; she didn't like to pry. Besides, she had never lived with a man and felt unqualified to offer advice. Maddy, on the other hand, wasn't that interested anyway. She turned on her side and pressed her ear to the ground. She could hear the faint, rhythmic thuds of the horse cantering around the paddock. It reminded her of the village where she had lived. The old men could remember when messages were sent, miles through the bush, by their fathers banging their staves on the earth. How simple, how satisfying, this method of communication seemed. How preferable to words, so treacherous and prone to misunderstanding. In Maddy's opinion, if people communicated with knocks the world would be a better place.

'Imogen says she's never going to get married,' said Louise.

'Don't worry, she will,' Prudence replied automatically. Then she thought: why should she? We all want people to marry. We think it will solve them. We have been brought up to think that this is the end of the story. In fact the entire romantic fiction list at her publishers, one of the few imprints that made a healthy profit, was based upon this lie.

She thought: I want to marry Stephen more than I have ever wanted anything in my life. I want it so much I feel sick.

It was cold. Maddy went into the house to find a jacket. She glanced through the front door. Robert was washing his car in the driveway. The dog stood watching him. Suddenly Robert swung round, grinning. He turned the hose on the dog. Monty yelped and ran away. Maddy watched as the dog shook himself in a glittering cloud of spray. As she turned back Robert caught her eye. He smiled.

Maddy glared at him. How dare he? She moved away, abruptly, out of his line of vision. Upstairs she could hear the thump of music. She went up to Jamie's room and knocked on the door. She had always been fond of her nephew and niece; in fact, she preferred teenagers to adults.

Jamie was taping a cassette for one of his friends.

'Can I borrow a sweater?' she asked. 'I'm freezing.'

He opened his cupboard. His room was the usual adolescent chaos but Maddy didn't notice; she was blind to her surroundings and she could live in chaos herself. She could live out of a suitcase, it made no difference to her.

Jamie passed her a sweater. 'Africa sounds great. I want to go there.'

'You'd like it. You're the only person here who would.'

'Why did you come back now?'

Maddy pushed her head through the sweater and pulled it down over her shoulders. 'Because I needed to start my life.'

'So why did you stay so long?'

'I just – didn't fit here,' she said. 'England didn't fit me.'

'I know what you mean.'

'That's because you're eighteen. With me, it was more than that.'

'Why?' he asked.

'Because –'

She stopped. Her father's face had appeared at the window. He waved at them, through the glass, and started hammering at the gutter.

When someone is in love with a married man, evidence of family contentment is too much to bear. His own home life, of course, is beyond thinking about. But the domestic lives of others are painful too, being a shadowy reminder of his. Oh the easy intimacy, so casually taken for granted by those enjoying it! Prudence tried not to be affected by her sister's house but so much stopped her in her tracks – scrawled notes stuck to the fridge, shopping lists with items on them such as Coco Pops, that only people's children want . . . Below this, a layer below, lay the evidence of the past, things that belonged to a younger Jamie and Imogen and that no doubt littered the boys' rooms in Stephen's house – abandoned roller-skates,

28

battered boxes of Cluedo. Prudence didn't envy Louise's marriage – she herself wouldn't want to be married to Robert – but the sight of their bedroom filled her with self-pity.

She had gone upstairs to fetch a magazine. Louise was a magazine-addict and had kept a copy of *Elle* that contained an interview with one of Prudence's authors. Their bedroom was a large, corner room, its walls washed peachy pink. Robert's and Louise's clothes were strewn over the chairs; the disordered intimacy made Prudence feel like an intruder. *Master bedroom.* The words rebuffed outsiders. Master bedroom with *en suite* bathroom. The phrase implied a life of sensuality behind closed doors, of frequent couplings and sluicings. Prudence gazed through the door. The towel-rail was hung with lace knickers and black stockings; Robert liked to buy Louise fancy underwear for her birthday. Louise's bedside table was heaped with magazines. Robert's side was piled with heavy new hardbacks – the latest brat-pack American novelist, a weighty volume called *Plunder and Plenty: The New World Order*. The chest of drawers was crammed with photographs of their wedding, their children, and snapshots of parties with friends of theirs that Prudence had never met.

As she stood there, thunder rumbled outside. It started to rain. She went to look out of the window. Down in the driveway she could see the abandoned hosepipe next to the BMW. Robert sat inside his car. From this angle she could see his legs. She remembered thinking, vaguely, that he must have got into his car to escape the rain. If she had really thought about it she would have realised that he could have easily run into the house – that nobody, a few yards from their own front door, would choose to take shelter in their car.

In fact, Robert was making a phone call. He kept his head bent, as if he were rummaging in the glove compartment. But Prudence couldn't see this from her angle and besides she was too busy speculating about her own painful and unsatisfactory state of affairs to think about those of anybody else.

*

29

Later, she gave Maddy a lift to London. It was still raining. The oncoming headlights blurred and smeared as the windscreen wipers slewed to and fro. They didn't talk; somehow, after three years' separation, there was too much to say. Maddy told her sister the address of a flat in Tufnell Park, the place she was going to stay. When they arrived, Prudence unloaded the luggage and helped her with it to the door.

She drove home to Clapham. It was eight o'clock. On Sunday evenings she felt a loneliness that stretched beyond Stephen. In the houses lamps glowed behind closed curtains. Attic rooms bloomed with the nervy flicker of TVs. Everyone in the world was utterly alone, all those people who believed themselves companioned, they lived alone and they would die alone. Yet simultaneously Prudence felt that she was the only person who was really lonely. This sensation was peculiar to Sunday nights.

She arrived in her street, Titchmere Road, and parked her car. It was a long road of red-brick Victoriana, those claustrophobic façades and surprisingly spacious interiors that are characteristic of Clapham. Commuters used the street as a rat run, a short cut from the southern suburbs to the City. Various traffic-calming devices – humps, narrowed bits – failed to calm the traffic in the rush hour; in fact, just made it more impatient. In twelve hours Prudence herself would be joining them; only twelve hours to go before she could rejoin the human race.

She climbed up to her flat. It was on the first floor. The man upstairs was engaged in his nightly spring-clean, an operation which seemed to consist of dragging heavy items of furniture across the floor. She had a recurring fantasy that Mr Witherall, a timid bachelor, was in fact a serial killer and that every night he had to clean up the evidence and conceal dismembered limbs behind the wardrobe.

She went into the kitchen. Her cat, Cedric, brushed against her shin. Long ago she knew a man who used to brush her cheek with the knuckle of his hand. He had married and gone to live in Vancouver. On the draining board sat the morning's washed-up cup and plate, exactly where she had left them. Her African violets sat moistly in their pots. Her flat had the stilled, Marie Celeste air of all flats belonging to single people; sometimes, in the past, she had found this comforting.

She went into her living room and switched on the lamp. A pile of manuscripts lay on the table, waiting for her. The top one was called *Commuter or Computer: Work in the Second Millennium.* Upstairs there was a thud. Mr Witherall had felled his latest victim.

She looked at the answerphone. It said '1'. She switched it on.

It was Stephen's voice. *'Listen, she's taken the boys swimming.'* His voice was low and urgent. *'If you're back before five, phone me. I'll come right over. We can have an hour. Oh darling . . .'*

Prudence was a methodical woman. Before she did anything she walked across the room and closed the curtains. Then she sat down on the arm of the chair. She gripped her stomach; the noise was wrenched out of her guts. Coming from this composed person it was a shocking sound – a howl of animal pain.

Two

Beveridge and Bunyan had been established in Bloomsbury since 1933. It was an old family firm, though the Beveridge side of it had long ago ceased to exist and remained but a ghostly presence. There was an other-worldly air about the premises too – a pair of shabby Georgian buildings near the British Museum, reputedly haunted by an eighteenth-century poet of unrecognised genius who, Chatterton-like, killed himself in the attic amidst a welter of rejection slips. Once this part of London was the hub of the publishing business. Every other building housed an imprint – Deutsch, Nelson, Hamish Hamilton. Behind mahogany desks sat editors of the old school, gentlemen of letters who peppered their memos with Latin quotations, took their authors out to epic lunches at Bertorelli's and who could be spotted at four-thirty weaving their way back through Bedford Square before issuing forth to their clubs. Only their ghosts remained. They themselves were extinct; their successors had been merged, rationalised, bought-up and despatched to post-modern office blocks rising from no man's lands of orbital loop-roads and security gates, situated in unappealing parts of London miles from the Garrick.

Beveridge and Bunyan had held out longer than the others. Over the years it had resisted change and stubbornly stayed on in Bloomsbury. The place had a certain musty charm. There was an office cat. The editor in charge of religious books still insisted on using a typewriter. In the lobby, under a faded photograph of Mr Beveridge and Mr Bunyan, sat the

32

receptionist Muriel. She was a bewhiskered matron who had been there for ever and whose wall was stuck with postcards sent by holidaymaking members of staff. She ran the switchboard; she knew all the gossip – people's ailments, their problems with their children. It was Muriel who first heard the rumour of a buy-out by Unimedia, through various hush-hush calls from Frankfurt to their chairman Arthur Bunyan.

Unimedia was a German-based communications empire. It owned newspapers and TV stations; it owned paper mills and software companies in Europe and the United States. It already had a majority shareholding in another publishing group, the result of a takeover bid in the early nineties. It had been sniffing around Beveridge and Bunyan for some time, for despite its air of gentility B&B in fact made a healthy profit. This was due to publishing various standard legal textbooks and a series of EFL course books that were used in schools throughout the developing world. So in April the company was bought up and the last of the Mr Bunyans, a man whose heart lay in fly-fishing, retired to his home next to the River Test.

Since then the place had been shaken out of its long slumber. The first swathe of redundancies and early retirements had removed various old time-servers. Prudence had mixed feelings about this. Though she was sorry to see her colleagues go, their jobs merged or their positions taken by corporate suits who seemed to regard books as just another commodity – though she was sorry to see this, she also found it invigorating. Coming from her background, she had always resented the old boy network. Publishing used to be full of them; privileged, patronising, invariably male, they had kept the best jobs for themselves, relegating women to the lowlier editorial posts or, if the girls were pretty, the publicity department where they could charm journalists over spritzers at lunchtime. Didn't they realise that the world had changed? One of them, Prudence's former managing director, had once boasted: *'I've only been into my wife's kitchen twice, and once was to put out a fire.'* Her new MD was a coarse

Australian called Alan Watkins who cracked jokes and who chain-smoked in meetings, setting off the alarms. He had fought his way up from nowhere, like her father, and though his ruthlessness dismayed her she also found him refreshing.

It was Monday morning. Unlike most of Britain's workers Prudence longed for the arrival of Monday. For two days, throughout the interminable weekend, she hadn't seen Stephen. She couldn't phone him; he couldn't phone her. Yesterday's painfully frustrating message had been a rare occurrence. Each week the shutters came down. He was closed away with his family in Dulwich, in a house she had never seen and that she tried not to imagine.

She knew his routines. He played football with his sons on Saturday afternoons; he went to Sainsbury. He was a husband. The word grew in her like a tumour. *Husband* . . . a rounded, smug word, a word describing a man who belonged to somebody else. She told herself it was just a collection of letters, a gathering of dots, but she couldn't convince herself. Like all married people he spoke so casually of *we*. *'We had to go to this boring residents meeting, I wished I was with you.'* He tried to be tactful, to imply that his marriage was unhappy. *'We had an awful row on Sunday morning.'* Though he was trying to reassure her, it was the *we* that cut into her heart. Sunday morning . . . croissants in bed . . . sheets rumpled by the previous night's lovemaking, though he promised her that sex between himself and his wife had ceased.

He called his wife *she*; so did Prudence. Never by name. The verbal courtesies of a married man speaking to his mistress occurred so naturally that she sometimes suspected he had done this before. He strenuously denied it. He said that until he met Prudence he had been faithful to his wife but even this hurt her. 'Faithful' was such a beautiful word. She had looked it up in her *Shorter Oxford Dictionary*. *'Faithful: firm in a fidelity or allegiance to a person to whom one is bound by any tie; constant, loyal, true.'* Her heart, sinking, had barely been cheered by *'Conscientious in the fulfilment of duty'*.

Prudence approached the office. Despite the traffic roaring down Museum Street there was a shiny, rinsed feeling in the air. Last night's rain had washed the pavements clean. In a few minutes she would be seeing Stephen. Her spirits rose; suddenly the street had the bustling optimism of a Frank Capra movie. Luigi, who ran the snack bar opposite, trundled in a trolley of fruit-juice packs. A woman polished the brass plate of the occult bookshop on the corner. Outside Beveridge and Bunyan a green van was parked on the pavement. It said Fox Gardening Services. A woman unloaded plants from it.

Beveridge and Bunyan occupied two houses, knocked through to make them interconnecting. Prudence's office was on the ground floor – a narrow, partitioned-off space with a window onto the street. Trish, her secretary, was pouring boiling water into the cafetière. Trish was a bouncy, uncomplicated girl; she lived with, and supported, a flabby young man called Don who Prudence suspected was gay.

'So did you persuade him to go bungee-jumping?'

Trish shook her head. 'He's such a wimp. How was your weekend?'

'Went to my sister's. The one in the country.' Prudence suspected, rightly, that her secretary considered her life spinsterly. 'My little sister arrived from Nigeria.'

'Want a Hobnob?' Trish offered her a biscuit. She popped one into her mouth and opened the diary. 'Editorial at ten, jackets at twelve and lunch with Elspeth Wilmslow.' This was an author who was writing a book about paint techniques. Prudence suspected there were enough of these already. 'Shall I book Pièro's?'

'No, the Groucho. She's coming all the way from Huddersfield. She might want to bump into someone famous.'

Prudence looked at the pile of manuscripts on her desk. She was halfway through editing – well, rewriting – the book of pasta recipes. She was also working on a *Wither Britain Now*-type monograph by a *Guardian* columnist, which might do well if its publication coincided with a Labour win at the

35

next election. On the other hand, it might not. At times she felt that every book in the world had already been written countless times and was simply being reissued, disguised under another title. This didn't dismay her; not on Monday morning, not when she was waiting for a tap on the door.

A tap. She swung round. Stephen stood there. He wore his green corduroy jacket. Her chest folded within itself.

'Morning, Trish. Pru. Has Bill shown you the mock-ups for the authors' cards?'

'Not yet.' She looked at Stephen's clothes. She longed to buy him something new. She couldn't even buy him a pair of socks. 'Alan wants to see us both at four.' She turned to her secretary. 'Trish dear, could you photocopy these?' Why did she call her dear? Because Trish was bathed in her happiness.

Trish left. She was not a curious person; she suspected nothing.

Stephen said: 'I'm sorry.'

'I'm sorry.'

He shut the door. They collided, bumping against the edge of the desk. After two days they always felt awkward with each other, especially in the broad daylight of the office. The hiatus of the weekend set them back to being acquaintances. His interlude of family life made him strange to her, all over again. It usually took them until Tuesday to recover their old intimacy. Prudence rubbed her cheek against his, shyly. He smelled of the aftershave his wife must have given him. It seemed to have a stronger aroma on Monday mornings.

'I didn't dare go out in case you rang,' he whispered. 'I sat there for an hour. Then they came home, all smelling of chlorine.' He drew back and touched her hair. 'My love, I wanted you so badly.'

'Did you really?' She hadn't smoked a cigarette yet; she wanted to keep her breath fresh for him.

'Shall I tell you which bits?'

Prudence froze. A face had appeared at the window. It was the gardener, from the van. Prudence jumped back and busied herself, riffling through her mail. The woman didn't

36

seem to have noticed them. She was replanting the window-box. She pulled out the summer bedding – white geraniums – and flung them out of sight.

'I can't bear it,' said Prudence.

'I want to run my finger down the inside of your thigh,' Stephen murmured, standing on the other side of the desk.

'I want to suck your fingers, one by one . . .' she said.

'I want to take your breast in my mouth . . . I want to be inside you, now . . .'

Prudence picked up a letter. Her hand trembled. 'I want to lie with my arms around you all through the night . . .' She stopped. Trish came in. Prudence said: 'See you at four then, in Alan's office.'

'And could you run me up a budget for the bulimia book?' he asked.

He left. Prudence sat down heavily in the swivel chair.

Stephen Miller was a charming, weak man of forty-six. He had always been susceptible to women. He liked talking to them; he liked the sort of things they talked about. He sought out their company. In this respect he was unusual for an English man of his class – upper-middle, public school. They responded by finding him endearing, though he was far from handsome. He was a soft man, chubby in fact, with sandy hair and freckled hands. He had a dry, amused way of talking, as if nothing much mattered in the end, life was a baffling business. He wore bow ties and scruffy corduroy jackets which devoted girlfriends, in the past, had repaired for him. He had been to Oxford. He was well-read, there was something of the absent-minded schoolteacher about him which had lulled women into thinking they were safe in his company. He was a romantic. If he forgot someone's birthday, because he was forgetful, he made up for it by an extravagant present the next day, because he was extravagent. In his publishing career he had frequently been bailed out by a devoted series of assistants – underpaid, over-educated women who

37

covered up for him and took the blame. They didn't resent him for this because he thanked them profusely and took them out to lunch.

Stephen liked lunch. During it he invariably drank too much, charging it to the firm of course, and all afternoon his secretary had to make excuses for him and tell callers he was in a meeting. There are many such men as Stephen, supported by invisible women. This is because, even in the the last years of the nineties, there are still women who willingly do so.

Prudence was an intelligent woman. Love had not blinded her to Stephen's weaknesses. He had been her boss for three years now; on occasion she, too, had bailed him out. He was the editorial director, responsible for the trade lists at B&B – fiction, children's and – Prudence's section – general non-fiction. He had slid into the job through a combination of flair and charm; he was particularly good at wooing authors from other publishers. He was also close friends with the Bunyan family, having been at All Souls with one of the sons where they had performed together in amateur dramatics.

Under the ruthless new ownership, however, Prudence feared for him. Their new MD, Alan, had a more hands-on approach than his predecessor. He liked to know what every-body was up to. He involved himself in every detail down to the consumption of petrol in his staff's company cars. He summoned them to meetings – Prudence and Stephen had one that afternoon – where he watched them shrewdly through a veil of cigarette smoke and asked them to update him on their projects.

Prudence was thinking about this when she left the office for lunch. She was also remembering the last time she and Stephen had made love – a snatched hour in her flat ten days earlier. It was almost impossible for him to get away in the evening without arousing suspicion. Most of their love-making consisted of fumbles in doorways or in his car, with the windows steaming up as if the two of them were teenagers. Except teenagers seemed to be at it all the time.

'*What we've got is sex-free adultery,*' she had complained to him, the week before. '*Like alcohol-free lager.*'

She was remembering his tongue nuzzling her pubic hair when she stepped onto the pavement. The gardener's van was still there. She gazed at it fondly, for it was imprinted with her erotic memories. The gardener leaned against it, eating a samosa. Prudence smiled at her. She hadn't seen this one before. She was just about to cross the road when the woman said: 'Hey, are you an editor?'

Prudence stopped. 'How can you tell?'

'You look like one.'

Prudence was silent. She didn't know how to take this.

'Wait a moment.' The woman was tall and striking; a jewel winked in her nostril. Her hair was bundled up in an ethnic turban. She swallowed the last mouthful of samosa, wiped her hands and reached inside the van. She took out a mud-streaked folder and shoved it in Prudence's hand. 'Will you read this?' It was more a command than a question.

'What is it?'

'My novel.'

'Goodness.' It was heavy. Four hundred pages at least. 'I'm non-fiction.'

The woman laughed shortly. 'We're all non-fiction, aren't we. If you think about it.'

'I mean –'

'My address is on the inside.'

The woman strode off. She got into the van, slammed shut the door and started the engine.

It was called The Birches, the house in Purley. There was a birch wood at the end of the garden. Silver birches, they reminded Dorothy of her eldest daughter Louise – slender, graceful, bending to the will of the wind. The wood was thin, however; just a belt of trees. Beyond it was the local comprehensive, a series of ugly modern buildings that were revealed each autumn when the leaves fell. Raucous shouts rang out at

39

lunchtime. The pupils climbed into the wood and left behind a litter of sweet wrappers and worse. Depending on the season, the wood seemed either like a barrier sealing her home safe from the outside world or a sieve that let it all in. Whether this disturbed Dorothy varied according to her mood. Sometimes she welcomed the yells and laughter; they seemed the only sign of life in the hushed, respectable neighbourhood. Even with the windows closed she could hear them; they cheered her when she stood in the empty house.

There was no one moment, of course, when her daughters had left home. It had happened gradually. For years they had left their things in their rooms; it had taken a long time for them to depart entirely. But they were gone now, they had been gone for almost two decades, and the house seemed huge without them. The bedrooms had reverted to just being bedrooms. Sometimes relatives came to stay. Sometimes even the grandchildren came to stay. But it was no longer a family home; it was a large house, with Gordon and herself rattling around in it. Now and then she grew restless. She told her husband that they must move somewhere smaller and more suitable but he wanted to stay put.

Besides, they were too busy. At this moment, for instance, Gordon had seven jobs on, one of them the refurbishment of ten thousand feet of commercial premises down by the Elephant and Castle. In addition to this he had constant calls from his regular customers – maintenance, emergency repairs. He was up at six, out of the house by seven. Like all builders his own home remained full of half-completed tasks. When the girls were small it had taken him four years to put in a proper kitchen; she had had to nag him to get it done and finally threatened to walk out. He hadn't taken her seriously, he never took her seriously. And she hadn't walked out, had she? She was still here.

It was lunchtime on Monday. Dorothy sat in the office extension. One window overlooked the front yard; the other overlooked the garden. She was typing up the estimate for a new job. In the front yard, two of the lads were loading panels of Gyproc onto the van. Gordon breezed in.

'Got the Selwood Avenue invoice, love?'

She gave it to him. 'I've left off the VAT.'

'Thanks, pet.' He pocketed it.

She put on the kettle. 'She seemed very quiet yesterday.'

'Who did?'

'Prudence.'

'She's a quiet girl.'

'Shouldn't call them girls.'

'They are, to me.' He lit a cigarette.

She fetched two tea-bags. 'How do you think Maddy looked?'

The phone rang. He picked it up. 'Kendal Contractors . . .'

She looked out of the window. At the end of the garden, on an old stretch of hard standing that had once been a garage, sat the caravan. It had been parked there for years, quietly rotting.

'. . . in the woodwork, you said?' Gordon was talking on the phone. 'Well, rot's a fungal infection, give it a sniff . . .'

Through the woods, the schoolchildren shouted. They echoed through the years. If she narrowed her eyes she could see her daughters playing in the caravan, playing houses.

'. . . it gives off, well, a fungal-type smell . . . slide in a knife and see if it gives . . . I'll send one of the lads around to-morrow . . .'

She remembered their holidays, parked in the sand dunes near Hythe. Maddy was shouting, she could hear her. Why was Maddy always angry? Nothing Dorothy said could comfort her.

Gordon put down the phone. 'I'm off.'

'Gordon! There's a sandwich here.'

But he had gone. All that was left was a cigarette, smouldering in the ashtray. He never stubbed them out properly.

Through the trees the school bell rang. The voices ceased. In the front yard, the lads drove away. Dorothy sat there in silence. Yesterday, for the first time in years, she had seen all

41

three of her daughters together. It had been a curious sensation. Oh, it was lovely, of course, that Maddy was home and that they had all gathered together, briefly, as a family. But it had been painful too. The undercurrents had risen to the surface, nothing had changed. Maddy contradicting her father; Gordon rising to the bait. Prudence the peacemaker looking diminished, as she always did in her sister's house. And yet, at the same time, her daughters seemed like strangers. By seeing them together, she realised how unknowable their lives had become – even Louise, to whom she felt the most close, with whom she had domestic life and the grandchildren in common. Her own role as a mother was long since over. Her role as a grandmother was almost over too; Imogen and Jamie no longer needed her.

Dorothy sat there with her pile of invoices. Was this all there was to it? You raised children, you made a home, you kept the business ticking over. And in the end you were left alone with a husband who fidgeted to be somewhere else.

Dorothy was not a rebellious person. She had been brought up by strict parents. Her father had run a haulage company, her mother had raised a family. Dorothy herself had followed in her mother's footsteps; she had just accumulated more money on the way. Suddenly she envied her daughters their freedom. Even their unhappiness seemed an adventure, a voyage into uncharted waters. Her grandchildren were growing up in a world that was largely incomprehensible to her. She had sat here in this suburban street; over the past years her main contact with the outside world had been the lads, her surrogate children, jostling into her office on payday and bringing tales of treacherous girlfriends and custody battles.

She gazed at the caravan – curtained windows, shabby cream bodywork. What a symbol of freedom it had once seemed! All of a sudden she had an impulse to hitch it to the car and drive away – anywhere, anywhere but here. Chester. Aberystwyth. Somewhere she could see before it was too late. Drive off to a new life and see if anyone noticed.

She didn't, of course. Instead, wrinkling her nose, she stubbed out Gordon's Marlboro. She thought that in all their years of marriage, her husband had never asked if she minded the smell of his cigarette smoke.

'The thing about adultery,' said Prudence, 'is that you have to snatch your moment and it's always the wrong time of day. Like two in the afternoon, sitting in a freezing car. Or a quick grapple in the photocopying room at half past nine in the morning. The person they're living with gets all the good times – the evenings, the nights, oh, the nights . . . the sunny Sundays in the park. As if they don't have enough of them anyway. Seems so greedy of them.'

'Give him up then,' said Maddy. 'Seems stupid to me.'

Prudence sighed. If only it were so simple. It was Wednesday evening. They were sitting in the basement flat in Tufnell Park, the place that had been lent to Maddy, eating takeaway pizza.

'Ditch him and find somebody else,' said Maddy.

'You don't understand.'

'No. I don't.'

'If you were in my position –'

'I wouldn't get into your position,' said Maddy.

'No. Everything's black and white to you, isn't it.' Prudence looked around. 'Aren't you going to unpack? It looks awful. Shall I help?'

'What's the point?'

'Well, to make it look nice for yourself.'

'But I don't mind.'

'There must be some other reason,' said Prudence.

'What reason?'

'You can never find things.'

'But if I don't need them I never look for them anyway.'

Pru gave up. She looked out of the window. From this sub-terranean viewpoint only a strip of the street was visible – the pavement, the wheels of parked cars. Somewhere, children

43

shouted.

'I always feel like this when I've been to Lou's and Robert's,' she said. 'Do you?'

'Feel what?'

'Like this.' Suddenly she yelled. '*Men!*'

Maddy closed the pizza box. 'In the village I lived in, all the woman had clitoridectomies.'

Prudence gazed at her sister. She got up and paced around the room. 'I'm going to ring him up. Now. He'll just be putting the boys to bed, having *quality time* with them. His horrible wife'll be cooking supper, lamps lit, gin and tonic waiting. I'm going to phone him up and blow the whole thing apart.'

'Don't be daft. Course you won't.'

'How do you know?'

'I'm your sister,' said Maddy.

Prudence smiled. How quickly they had slipped back into their old relationship. She admired Maddy – she was simple and direct, there was something morally upstanding about her. But she also irritated Prudence. Despite her adventures in foreign countries, despite her physical bravery, she was so untested.

Prudence made her way past the slumped plastic bags belonging to the owner of the flat, past the detritus of someone else's life amongst which Maddy seemed content to live. She went into the kitchen. A batik hanging failed to cover a damp patch on the wall. She looked through the window. Even in the dark she could see that the garden was a mess. She thought, irritably, that if she had this place she would make it nice. She had always wanted a garden. 'You should do something about it out here,' she called, searching for some coffee. She could only find a jar of Nescafé. Prudence, who liked real coffee, suddenly felt lonely. She longed for Stephen so much that her legs felt weak. She loved her sister, but in matters of the heart Maddy was no use at all.

Prudence drove home. She wondered what Stephen was doing now. In fact, from the clues she had gathered about his wife, Kaatya wasn't the sort of person to fix him a gin and tonic. Prudence had said this to Maddy because her sister made her speak in clichés, she didn't encourage subtlety. From what Prudence had heard over the past months, clues she had picked at like a scab, Kaatya was a neurotic, self-absorbed person who didn't look after Stephen at all. She was always going off on courses, leaving Stephen to cope with the boys and do the cooking. She was restless and impulsive. *'Now she wants to live in Normandy,'* he had sighed one day, making Prudence's heart lurch. Kaatya was moody, sinking into glooms that made her family creep around the house speaking in whispers. The next day she would suddenly dig up the garden to lay a patio. *'I never know what's going to hit me when I get home,'* said Stephen, running his hand through his hair. Kaatya seemed to keep the three males of her household in a constant state of wary anxiety. They sounded bemused by her wilful femaleness. Prudence thought she sounded a pain.

Back in the flat Prudence made herself a pot of real coffee, freshly ground, and switched on the gas-coal fire. How cosy her living room looked. *She* would make him a gin and tonic. She looked at the manuscripts she had brought home. She ought to read a treatise on environmentally sustainable industries but suddenly she wasn't interested.

She lifted up the top folder. Rubbing off the mud with her finger, she read the title: *Playing with Fire* by Erin Fox. She should have given it to Liz, who dealt with novels, but something about the gardening woman had intrigued her. *'We're all non-fiction, if you think about it.'* Prudence thought: if only we weren't. If we were fiction I could rewrite Stephen and make him leave his wife. I could create a man to fall in love with Kaatya and the boys would like him even though they still loved their father and we could all live happily ever after.

Prudence set her gold-rimmed cup and saucer precisely in the middle of the table. The cat jumped into her lap. She withdrew the manuscript from the folder and opened it at page one.

Three

The General Stores in Wingham Wallace was an old brick cottage with living accommodation above. It faced the village green. Years before, there had been a butcher's shop next door, and a hardware shop up the road towards the church. The older residents could even remember the days when there had been a ladies' outfitters called Meryl Modes in a building that had since been flattened to create the pub car-park. These shops had long since gone. They had been re-absorbed into the cottages, leaving no trace except enlarged ground floor windows – in one case, regrettably glazed with bottle-glass. The hardware store was now the weekend re-treat of a City solicitor whose intruder lights froze the local courting couples in its beam. This was just another irritant for the villagers who had seen their shops disappear and public transport reduced to two buses a day.

Now, only the General Stores remained. In summer it did a brisk trade in ice-cream but the rest of the year it struggled to survive, relying on the elderly locals collecting their pensions and the other villagers dropping in for things they had forgotten to buy at Tesco. The owners, Tim and Margot Minchin, had moved in five years earlier. Their lives had already been bedevilled by bad luck. This was another blow, for the superstore was erected only ten minutes' drive away, between the village and Beaconsfield. Once it was built even their most loyal customers deserted them, seduced by the miles of aisles crammed with everything anyone could need, and a lot else. How could Tim's wizened bananas compete? It was a vicious circle, for the less business he did the less cash he had to invest in stock, so the shelves emptied and the shop began to have a third-world look. That spring there had been yet another blow. Tesco had introduced a free bus service which lured away his last remaining customers, those too poverty-stricken or dilapidated to run their own car. And on top of it all he had to cope with Margot.

Tim was a small, weedy man. Margot was huge. Since their tragedy six years earlier, a tragedy of which they never spoke, Margot had put on an alarming amount of weight. They never spoke of this too – what could you say? Tim blamed the various pills she had been prescribed at the time – anti-depressants, Prozac – upon which she had grown more and more dependent. He knew that she ate too much – comforting, sweet things like cake and chocolates – but he had no idea of the extent of her addiction for she spent increasing amounts of time upstairs, leaving him to run the shop. Over the past year she had retreated from the world. To his customers she had become creaking footsteps across the ceiling and the murmur of daytime TV. He had long ago given up talking to her about the problems with the business, she became so upset. *'What are we going to do?'* she would wail, tears sliding down her cheeks and settling into the creases in her neck.

Tim was a gallant man. To him, women were to be worshipped, as he had worshipped his mother. They were to be protected. When he was a boy he had made swords out of planks of wood and pretended to be a crusading knight, rescuing damsels in distress. Nowadays his favourite recreation was to take part in Civil War re-enactments, fighting for the Royalist cause. Once he had worshipped his wife. In those days she'd been a big, fruity woman with a ringing laugh. When they'd made love he had marvelled at the ripeness of her body; he had sobbed with gratitude, burying his face between her breasts. That was long ago, however. Nowadays he simply kept her safe, shielding her from the nudging giggles of schoolchildren and the financial problems

47

of the shop that had once been their dream. And his need to worship at the temple of womanhood – that need, so powerful within him – was channelled elsewhere.

On Friday he was slotting copies of the local newspaper into the rack. He always remembered, later, what he was doing when she came into the shop. The door opened; the sunlight dazzled him. She greeted him and picked up a basket.

Today her hair was piled on top of her head. It gave out a golden glow, like a halo. She raised her eyebrows and paused, as if trying to remember what she had come in for. She always did this. She inserted her finger into her nostril – not picking it, she wouldn't do that. Thoughtfully exploring it. She wore jeans and a white T-shirt saying *The London Marathon*. Her husband ran in it each year; he was that sort of competitive creep. He didn't deserve her little toe.

'Saw your daughter riding by yesterday,' said Tim.

'She's in seventh heaven,' said Louise. 'All through school she's itching to get back on her horse. Not that she ever does anything in lessons anyway. Got any anchovies?'

He looked at the cans. 'No, but I could get you some.' *John West Salmon . . . Tuna Chunks in Brine . . .* the words danced.

'Remember what it's like to be in love? Wildly in love?'

He moved to the counter and wrote *anchovies*.

'You dream about them? Your heart thumps when you see them?' She flung a tin of tomatoes into her basket. 'You get goosepimples just thinking about them?' She reached up. When she raised her arm, her breasts moved beneath the T-shirt. He looked down quickly, and replaced his biro next to the till.

'Well, that's what she feels about her horse.' She pointed to the potatoes. 'Two pounds please. Mine have got some disgusting sort of blight.' She laughed. 'Story of my life.'

He picked up the potatoes; his fingers felt boneless. He could see her shoes – the scuffed gym shoes she normally wore. Not surprising – she was only coming to the shop. She wouldn't get dressed up for him. Sometimes, when her

48

London friends were visiting, she wore delectable high-heeled shoes. His favourite were her grey suede ones with the ankle strap.

'Better, really.'

'What is?' he asked.

'I mean, a *horse* doesn't leave the lav seat up or criticise you in front of other people. A *horse* doesn't tell you you're getting fat.'

'You're not!' he said loudly.

She turned to him with a dazzling smile. 'Tim. You are nice.' She moved away. Her T-shirt was hitched up on one side; it revealed the shape of her bottom – womanly, round.

'Where's the peanut butter?' she asked, looking at the shelves.

I'm sorry, it's –'

'I know.'

'I'll get you some.' He picked up his biro.

'This place used to be humming,' she said. 'I got all my gossip here.'

'I don't know how long we can go on.'

'Don't say that!' When she frowned, a crease appeared between her eyes.

'Post Office Counters, they're threatening to close us down.' He stopped. 'I shouldn't bore you with this.'

'It's not boring –'

'They want to take out a franchise in Tesco.' He took her money. Her beautiful hands were grubby; she must have been gardening. 'And now I hear they're planning to build a Safeway out near the old A40.'

'Well *I* shan't go there.'

'Margot's in a bad way. She wants us to close down.'

'You can't!' Louise protested. 'Coming here's the most exciting thing I do all day.'

There was a silence. 'Is it?' he asked.

The doorbell jangled. He jumped. James, her son, came in. His bike lay on the verge outside, its wheels spinning.

'Mum, I've got it!' he shouted. 'I've got the job!'

49

'That's wonderful!' Louise hugged him.

'I can start on Monday. It's a doss. I just walk up and down bunging stuff onto the shelves.'

'Where is this?' asked Tim.

'Tesco,' said Jamie.

There was a pause. Louise picked up her carrier bag. 'Come on,' she said to her son. And she left.

At six o'clock Tim turned the sign to CLOSED. Above him he heard Margot's heavy footsteps. He paused, listening. Then he went across to the shelf next to the frozen foods. He knelt down and removed the sack of Bar-B-Q Briquettes. He reached behind it, easing his hand around the plastic-wrapped baking trays that nobody had bought for years. He drew out the wallet of photographs.

You have to be careful with photographs. You must not surrender yourself to gluttony. Upstairs, Margot was breaking up a Toblerone and putting one piece after another into her mouth. Down in the shop, however, Tim practised self-control. He knew, from experience, that if you look at a photograph too often the meaning drains from it. Like sucking the fruit juice from an ice lolly, you are left with frozen water. For this reason he didn't open the wallet often; he needed to preserve that jolt of joy. This evening, however, inflamed by the first proper conversation he had had with Louise for weeks, he succumbed.

Tim was known to be a keen photographer. The year before he had won second prize at the village fête for his study of a chaffinch feeding her young, an artistic composition of hinged beaks. It wasn't unusual for him to be seen on his day off with his Olympus strung around his neck. But this tender hoard was his alone.

He drew them out slowly, sensuously, delaying it. One snapshot showed Louise letting the dog out of her car. Wearing her padded jacket – it was winter – she held open the door of her Space Cruiser. The dog was a blur, half out of

50

shot. Another, overexposed on a sunny day, showed her at the village pageant. She stood there, maddeningly half-obscured by Arnold Allcock, who ran the pub. Another, shot over her garden wall, was a far view of her kneeling at her lawn-mower. It had broken down. At the time Tim had longed to go to her rescue, but in doing so, of course, he would have had to reveal that he was spying on her in the first place.

'What are you doing?' Margot's voice rang out querilously. Tim climbed to his feet. 'Just cashing up,' he called.

Prudence was known for her temperance. Her personality had been forged, to some degree, by the personalities of her two sisters. Louise was the vague one; the girl who forgot her homework books, the woman who couldn't map-read and who collected parking tickets whenever she drove to London. Maddy was the impulsive one who blurted out home truths and who decided, on the spur of the moment, to pack in her job and go to Nigeria. Somebody had to keep things in order and that role had been taken on by Prudence, the sensible one in the middle. When her family was quarrelling, Prudence had learned to keep the peace. She had learned to conceal her own feelings in the cause of general harmony. Having reined in her impulses for so long she sometimes forgot that she had them in the first place.

For a year she had resisted the urge to see where Stephen lived. She had tried to blank off that part of his life – the part that began when he left the office each day. But the imagination is a powerful organism. It swells and festers, like a boil that has to be lanced. Sometimes she thought that she was going insane. *36 Agincourt Road, Dulwich.* She had found the street in her *A–Z*. She had inspected it so many times that her thumb had blurred the print.

On Friday she went out to dinner in Camberwell. She hadn't wanted to go. She knew her hosts had arranged a spare man for her, a fact that would be glaringly obvious both

51

to her and the man in question. They would be seated next to each other and watched, beadily. On the last occasion the man, whose name she had mercifully forgotten, had spent most of the evening telling her all about the wonderful things he could do on his Apple Mac. He had also spilled wine on her dress. *Hell is other people*, said Jean-Paul Sartre. Hell was sitting next to a man who wasn't Stephen. When she got home she would be gripped by such loneliness she would feel as if she were dying.

Sometimes the man asked her out; sometimes she went. The evening would be spent sitting in one of those Italian restaurants near Leicester Square that are listed in *What's On in London*, the sort of restaurant nobody she knew ever went to, the sort that still served veal in mushroom sauce. The man would order house plonk and tell her how he never saw his children now his ex had moved to Hull. Panic would rise in her, panic for the whole human race.

All things considered, she preferred staying at home. She was also becoming engrossed in the gardening woman's novel, which she had begun reading the night before. But she went to the dinner party in Camberwell, just to prove to herself that she had a life. During the meal she was seized with the certainty that Stephen was ringing her at home. She heard his voice, speaking on the answerphone in her empty flat. *'She's gone out for the evening . . . the boys are staying with friends, I could come over now . . . are you there, Pru? . . . oh my darling . . .'*

On either side of her the dinner guests chattered. They were talking about how often their cars had been broken into – a favoured topic in Camberwell.

'. . . we take the radio out, of course, but they still smash the window . . .'

'. . . last time they took all the tapes except *Queen: The Classic Collection*. They left it on the roof.'

'How embarrassing! So now your neighbours know you like Queen.'

'I don't. It belonged to the au pair.'

52

Suddenly Prudence saw Stephen so vividly it took away her breath. He had got no reply. He had remembered she was going out to dinner, so he had driven to her flat. At this very moment he was letting himself in with his key . . . he was getting into bed, waiting to surprise her . . .

As soon as she could politely do so, after the first round of coffee, Prudence said her goodbyes and left. She drove home fast. She jumped the lights; she took a left corner so tightly that she narrowly missed a cyclist. She speeded across Clapham Common and down her road, jamming on her brakes at each hump.

Her flat was dark. There was a smell in the kitchen; she had forgotten to put out the rubbish.

It was then that she could bear it no longer. She got back into her car and drove to Dulwich. By the time she arrived at the end of his road it was half past one.

She switched off the engine and sat there. So this was where he lived. Her stupid heart thumped. It was a street of large, red-brick houses with front drives. They were obscured by trees. The street lamps illuminated the branches; they illuminated the pavement upon which he had walked for the past seven years. It was the strangest sensation to look at a road that was so familiar to him and sickeningly, unknowably familiar to her.

She turned the car round and drove through the neighbouring streets, acquainting herself with them. She drove past a parade of shops – a Thresher, for his whisky; a place called Animal Crackers where his sons no doubt bought food for their gerbils. She knew about the gerbils. She felt like a thief, crawling at walking pace through the streets. She felt she was betraying him by spying on his life; from now onwards she would have a secret from him. It struck her as unfair: *he* didn't have to spy on her, he didn't have to feel like a criminal.

Finally she plucked up courage to return to Agincourt Road. She drove past 36 and stopped. The hall light illuminated the number. It was like the other houses – a comfortable,

Edwardian, family home. The downstairs windows were dark. Upstairs, however, a light glowed behind a blind. This must be their bedroom – the master bedroom. The next window was plastered with what looked like football stickers. This must be Dirk's or Pieter's room. In the driveway two cars were parked – his company car and a battered 2CV that no doubt belonged to his wife.

Oddly enough, Prudence felt nothing. Now she was here at last, parked outside the place she had imagined so painfully, she felt blank. Thinking about it all these months had sucked the flavour from it. All she felt was that she shouldn't be here; it was nothing to do with her. It had no connection with the Stephen she knew. The only shock was seeing his Ford Granada parked outside.

She drove home. It was only when she slotted in the Brahms that the tears came.

'They can't close it down!' said Louise. 'The village will die. It's more than a shop. It's where everybody meets. Old ladies who can't go anywhere else.'

'Market forces, my dear,' said Robert.

'Don't market forces me! It's all right for you, you're hardly here. He can't afford to buy the stock, everybody goes to Tesco. Soon there'll be – oh, a packet of tea-bags and a box of bootlaces. Like Eastern Europe.'

'You been to Eastern Europe lately?'

'You don't care. Oh why did I marry a Tory!'

'Your father's more Tory than me. He reads the *Daily Telegraph*.'

'Well *I'm* going to keep going there.'

'You can afford to. Know why? Because you're married to a venture capitalist.'

'God you're cheap.'

'No. I'm expensive. That's why –'

'Oh, shut up!'

Robert grinned and left. He was off to play tennis.

54

Louise was cleaning out the rabbit's hutch. She dug viciously at the dried droppings in the corner. Boyd, the rabbit, sat hunched in his sodden sleeping compartment. He glared at her. Nobody liked Boyd. He was the last of their dynasty of rabbits, a moth-eaten old buck who had fathered hundreds of babies, fluffy darlings the children had crooned over and then forgotten. Jamie and Imogen had grown out of their pets. Though Imogen's bedroom was plastered with Save the Whale posters she ignored Boyd; he could be dead for all she knew.

But Boyd didn't die. Like many belligerent octogenarians he clung stubbornly to life, refusing to go gently into that good night, sticking it out and making life a misery for anyone who ventured near. Nobody did, except Louise. She scattered sawdust into the hutch. She tried to shunt him into the clean side – she couldn't pick him up, he was surprisingly powerful and would scratch her arms to ribbons. She pushed his rump. He turned round and bit her. She yelped. Ears flattened, he hunched himself further into his corner. He growled. Boyd was the only rabbit she had ever known who growled. Robert said he was a Pit Bull terrier in disguise.

Louise, kneeling at the hutch, heard the sound of an engine approaching. That would be the blacksmith. It was Saturday; Imogen had spent most of the morning grooming Skylark and preparing her for this visit, as if preparing a bride for her groom. This past week had transformed Imogen. Where her horse was concerned, there was no problem with droppings. The moment they fell onto the stable floor Imogen darted forward with her spade, her face radiant. She was a young girl in love.

'Do you want sugar – er –'

'Karl.' The blacksmith nodded.

Imogen put the mugs on a ledge. The blacksmith flexed himself against Skylark's back leg. He lifted it up, wedging it between his thighs. With a pair of pliers he wrenched off the

55

old shoe and flung it aside.

'She likes you,' said Imogen, 'she usually fidgets in here.' She gestured around the stable. 'I ride her for miles. I feel so free! The birds don't fly away when you're on a horse. It's, like, you're part of an animal too.'

'We are animals,' he said. 'Just animals, with clothes on.'

'I suppose we are.'

'Trouble comes when we forget it.'

She watched him working. He had curly black hair, damp with sweat. He wore a singlet; when he moved, she could see the muscles shift under his skin. She could see the bushy black hair in his armpits. Around his hips was slung a leather apron. He was pressed against the flanks of the horse, peeling off pieces of hoof as if he were peeling the rind off an apple.

'I saw a heron yesterday,' she said. 'And a fox.'

'Know Blackthorn Wood? There's a badger's sett there.' Karl had a ripe, local accent. 'Pal of mine showed me. He's into wildlife photography.'

'Badgers! Wow!'

He leaned against the horse, grinning. 'Yeah. Wow.' He turned away and hammered in a shoe. 'Have to go at dusk. They come out and play. Thing about badgers, they don't lumber around, like folk think. They're really light and graceful.'

'Wicked!'

He looked at her. 'How old are you?'

'Sixteen.'

'Ah. Thought you were older.'

Imogen glowed with pleasure. 'Really? How old?'

'Then you say something dumb like wicked.'

Imogen flinched. 'It just means great.'

He reached over for his mug and drank a draught of tea. 'Should enlarge your vocabulary when you grow up. That's what your mum and dad pay for.' He put back the mug and reached into his box of tools. 'Bet you go to private school, right?'

'It's not my fault! I didn't want to go. Anyway, I hate school. I'm hopeless at everything except netball.'

He grinned. 'Don't get angry with me. Save it for your parents.'

She smiled at him. He didn't notice; he pulled Skylark's leg between his, braced himself against her and started filing the hoof.

'Where exactly is this badger's sett?' she asked.

'Maybe I'll show you.'

'Do I have to get older first?'

He looked up at her, under his oily hair, and grinned.

Louise watched the van drive away. Beside her, Imogen rinsed out the mugs.

'Mmm, very Lawrencian.' Louise leered. 'He can take my shoes off any day.'

'Mum! Don't be disgusting.'

Louise laughed. 'It doesn't stop at forty, you know.'

Stephen was trying to read a manuscript. Kaatya was hauling the furniture about. She was a volatile, black-haired woman. Tonight she was dressed in leggings with a child's skirt over them, and a shrunken jumper on top. Her perspex earrings rattled. She glared at one of her collages, hung on the wall. She took it down. Then she yanked an armchair across the room.

'Kaatya, come and sit down,' said Stephen.

'I don't like this here!'

'You liked it once.'

She pulled the coffee table across the floor. 'No, you did.'

'Kaatya!'

She pushed the coffee table against the chair. 'Don't mind me. Just read your intellectual book.'

'Actually, it's a poorly constructed, derivative, and totally unconvincing little thriller by that man you fancy on *Europe*

57

Tonight. Just because a chap can read an autocue he thinks he can write like García Marquez.'

She yanked the table back. 'What are you talking about?'

'It doesn't matter.'

Kaatya went upstairs. He heard her call: 'Dirk, get out of that bath!'

Stephen tried to concentrate but he kept reading the same sentence over again. Pieter, his older son, came in from the other room, where he had been working at Stephen's computer.

'She seems in a tizz.'

Stephen ruffled his son's hair. 'Women.'

Living with Kaatya was like living with Mount Etna; one never knew when she was going to erupt. Even when dormant, she smouldered. This bonded Stephen with his sons.

Pieter, carrying his books, went upstairs. Though he was thirteen he already seemed like a little old man. Stephen's sons were quaint, formal boys. They had a wary look to them. Sometimes their mother shouted at them. Sometimes she flung her arms around them and smothered them with kisses. How could a chap know where he stood?

The trouble was, they could be wary with him too. Though sometimes united, blokes together, by Kaatya's moods, they could also be alienated. Kaatya lived by no discernible moral code. She had no compunction about corralling her sons when she was quarrelling with Stephen. *'How can he treat me this bloody way?'* she would wail, clutching her sons under her wing. *'How can he be so cruel, your own father?'* She pressed their heads against her. They stood there, three black heads, foreign people with their foreign names, and he felt like a visitor in his own home.

Stephen tried to read the sentence again. His eyes wandered. Did she suspect something? Over the past months he had often wondered this. He had been careful – no whispered phone calls from home, no incriminating evidence in his jacket pockets. He had only stayed overnight with Prudence

58

six times during the past summer, each occasion prepared for with a watertight alibi.

He just felt that it showed. Like all men in love, he believed it must be as glaringly obvious to others as it was to him. That was love's transforming magic; that was what the poets wrote about. Prudence was in his heart and in his bloodstream. Even *Playing with Fire*, the manuscript she had given him to read, sat in his briefcase like a bomb. Kaatya was a wilful, self-absorbed woman but she wasn't stupid. Besides, she was experienced in sexual matters – far more experienced than he was. Before they met she had had scores of lovers back in Amsterdam. She, too, when she was twenty, had had an affair with a married man. It seemed inconceivable that she couldn't guess what was happening. But if that was the case, he would know. Kaatya wasn't the sort of person to keep things bottled up. She plunged straight in and never mind who heard the ensuing row – her sons, fellow shoppers in the supermarket checkout. There was a fine carelessness about Kaatya. In fourteen years of living with her he had grown used to public showdowns. Used to them, but still cringingly embarrassed.

Stephen went upstairs to say goodnight to his sons. Pieter lay in bed, holding up his book so he could read it in the light. Thick black hair sprouted from his armpits. Stephen stared. His own son was reaching puberty! He knew this, of course – Pieter's voice seemed to have broken overnight – but the hair gave him a jolt. How fast the years had passed! Soon he would be a grandfather with his life behind him.

Stephen went downstairs and opened the back door. He breathed deeply. Outside, the leaves were falling; the scent of autumn was in the air. Across the gardens the church clock struck ten. It was a Thursday evening in September, just another evening in a leafy London suburb. As Stephen stood there, however, he felt as light as a husk, drifting towards death. Prudence, too, would one day die. Separated by five miles of slumbering streets they were voyaging alone when they should have been clinging together. How could either of them bear it?

He longed to jump in the car and drive to Titchmere Road. He would let himself into her flat – how neat and cosy after the chaos of his own home, with its broken dishwasher and scattered homework. Prudence would welcome him into her arms. He would bury himself in her and be safe. Like a child, he would shut out the terrors of the night. Sometimes he imagined this so vividly that it astonished him to find he was still in his own home. Surely it must show on his face.

Stephen poured himself a whisky – his third but what the hell. The problem was, he couldn't bear to hurt anybody. He loved his sons. When he thought of leaving Kaatya he felt a physical pain in his chest. How could he break up his family? He had never really been unfaithful before – just a couple of drunken incidents, hastily regretted, at sales conferences. His relationship with Prudence was different. He loved her. He loved her intelligence and clarity. He loved her grey eyes and her big feet and her scent of Floris carnations. He loved the way she served him tea in delicate china cups. He loved the way she was utterly unlike Kaatya. She was English, she understood what he was talking about. They could talk for hours – about work, about books, about everything. She released words in his head. Kaatya was artistic; she lived on her impulses, like an animal. Prudence was a thinker. Not exactly an intellectual: a thinker. He loved her brain as much as her body.

Kaatya came downstairs. Stephen started, guiltily, and turned the page of his manuscript. Kaatya had showered; she wore his towelling robe. She squatted beside him, slid her hand under the pile of paper and massaged his balls.

'You come to bed?' she asked. She was jealous of his work. Words, meaningless words, they took him away from her. 'You staying here, sweetie?'

Stephen put the manuscript on the floor. He nuzzled her neck. She smelt of sandalwood. She liked rubbing herself with exotic oils. 'No, I'll come with you.'

He got to his feet, swaying slightly. One too many scotches. She took his hand and slipped it inside her robe. She moved his finger to and fro over her nipple. Kaatya was a woman of strong sexual appetites. As time went by they seemed to increase, rather than diminish.

Stephen cupped her breast in his traitor's hand. Then he withdrew it. 'I'll lock up,' he said.

Across Britain the wind blew. Rain lashed the windows of bedrooms where couples slept, clasped together. Autumn was approaching; there was the scent of mortality in the air. Men and women gripped each other, flesh against flesh, seeking the comfort of a living creature. Their dreams spiralled away like the leaves blowing above the roof-tops, but their bodies lay locked together.

Louise lay next to her sleeping husband. She was still dressed in her suspender belt and stockings. The clasp dug into her skin. Outside, the rain flung itself at the window as if someone were throwing gravel. Easing herself from under Robert's arm she sat up. She slid open the little tabs, rolled down her stockings and unhitched the suspender belt. Robert liked her to dress up for bed, to truss herself up like a turkey in the corsets he bought her. It took an age to get these garments on, hopping about on one leg in the bathroom, twisting round to fasten all the tiny little hooks down the back. The worse thing was when she caught sight of herself in the mirror. Her limbs ached from gardening, her nails were dirty, but she still performed her dogged preparations for him because it gave him pleasure. Robert was a sensualist, a sexual epicure. In the lamplight he would sit on the bed, waiting for her. When she emerged from the bathroom, naked except for corset, stockings and high heels, he would look at her body as if it were disconnected from her altogether. Sometimes she felt aroused by this. Sometimes she just felt silly, a middle-aged mother shielding her stretch-marks with her hand.

Despite these erotic aids there were certain routines to their lovemaking. After all, they had been married for twenty years. There were various positions which suited them, various touches which aroused them. That was why Louise felt uneasy. She pulled on her nightshirt. She slid back into bed and gazed into the darkness. Recently Robert had introduced something new into their repertoire. It wasn't gymnastic – some technique he had seen in one of his magazines – it was more subtle than that, more pleasurable, in fact. He turned her on her stomach, lay on top of her and, whilst caressing her between her legs, breathed into her ear. He whispered, he licked, he breathed – pleasure shot like quicksilver through her body. It was as if, through the secret whorls of her ear, he tickled her very bloodstream.

Where had Robert learned this? He had never done it before. Louise lay beside him and gazed into the darkness.

Imogen lay in bed, listening to the rain. Around her head rolled the words, spoken in that Buckinghamshire lilt . . . *We're just animals, animals with clothes on* . . . Karl straightened up and grinned at her – white teeth, tanned face, curly black hair. She had rerun this moment so many times during the past fortnight, her own tender video replay. He stood there, stocky and virile. His hand ran over the horse's flank, stroking her coat, calming her . . . such strong hands, their palms callused and cracked . . . She closed her eyes. The hands ran over her body, calming her as she lay quivering beneath them . . . he pulled her down, into the straw . . .

Did he really want to take her to the badger's sett or was he only saying it? He thought she was just a kid, a spoiled rich kid. She lay there. She ran her hand over her body, the way he would do it. He had grinned at her as if it was just the two of them, alone in the world. As she lay there, listening to the rain, she remembered a joke they had giggled over in primary school. *Her name was Virginia. Virgin for short, but not for long* . . . How babyish they had been. Surely Karl could see that she was grown-up now. She had grown up for him.

*

62

Thirty miles away, in Purley, the houses were dark. Sealed into their homes, the residents slept. People went to bed early in Ravenswood Close. Out in the street only the cars were awake, the red lights pulsing on their dashboards, for this was a neighbourhood that lived in fear of intruders. Dorothy turned, in her sleep, and slipped her arm around her husband's chest. Beneath his pyjamas his heart pulsed . . . tick tock, tick-tick tock . . . the bump of its beat was irregular. Dorothy, however, slept on, oblivious to the delayed detonation beneath his ribcage.

Outside in the shrubbery there was the scent of decay. Tick tock, tick tock . . . downstairs the clock ticked, out of synch with her husband's heartbeat. Downstairs the alarm was set, the doors bolted. But no Neighbourhood Watch could keep one intruder out of their home. The countdown could be measured in heartbeats. The thief waited, weeks away, waiting for the moment when it would glide in through their walls and change their lives for ever.

Four

Prudence was sitting in her office correcting a manuscript. She was alone. Last night's storm had scattered twigs over the pavement. The awning over the occult bookshop was skewed. Prudence, too, was feeling mutinous. She scored a red line through a paragraph and wrote *pretentious* in the margin.

There was a tap at the door. Stephen came in. He smiled at her and dumped a folder on her desk. It was *Playing with Fire*.

'I finished it this morning. You're right.'

'Extraordinary, isn't it?'

'Is that what women do together?'

'I prefer men,' said Prudence. 'When I get the chance.'

He sat down. 'I'm sorry. Dirk's got tonsillitis.'

'Your son's always getting tonsillitis. It's your fault for having him born under water.'

'That was Kaatya's idea.'

'Everything's Kaatya's idea,' said Prudence irritably. 'Haven't you got a mind of your own?'

'She was the one giving birth.'

'Must be because she's Dutch. All those canals.'

Trish came in. Stephen said hastily: 'Talking about dykes – think we should publish this? Has Liz read it?'

Prudence nodded. 'She thinks it's great.'

Trish asked what it was.

'The novel the gardening woman gave to me,' said Prudence. 'Erin Fox.'

Trish picked it up. 'What's it like?'

64

'Sort of post-feminist lesbian pornography,' said Stephen.

'An inter-racial Sapphic soap opera,' said Prudence. 'Rather extraordinary.' She had read its 550 pages in three sittings, it was compulsive stuff. Rough and ready, that was to be expected, but with a confidence in its own voice one rarely encountered in a first novel. There was an epic sweep to its story, which ranged from London to Paris to Bombay and back. 'And, er, a highly erotic use of language.'

Stephen laughed. 'It certainly puts the lingo into cunnilingus. And, in addition, it would make a handy bedside table.'

'Sounds brilliant,' said Trish. She picked up her coat. 'Can I take it to lunch?' She took the manuscript and left. There was a silence.

'I'm sorry,' said Prudence.

'*I'm* sorry.'

'I feel so guilty.'

'*I* feel so guilty –'

He stopped. Trish rushed in. She collected her handbag and rushed out again. Prudence pushed her hand through her hair.

'Listen, Steve,' she said. 'All my life I've tried to be a nice person . . . I wasn't jealous of Louise. I worked hard and pleased my parents. I tried to save the rhino and remember people's birthdays . . .' She paused. 'And now, know what I feel like? A murderess. I sit at home, willing the break-up of a happy family with two boys who've never done any harm to me and who love their father –'

'We're not a happy family. Kaatya and I –'

'Shut up! She's got you, hasn't she? She lives with you. You and me, we have this half-life, this non-life, two hours here, two hours there, snatched moments, creeping in and out!' Her voice rose. 'Nobody can see you, I've known you over a year and you don't know anything about my life, you haven't even met my sisters!'

'I did, once –'

'Oh yes – Louise saw you from her car.'

65

'I want to meet them.'

Prudence paused, panting. She should be offering him happiness, not guilt and blame. If she went on like this their love would drain away and they would be left with nothing.

'All right.' She raised her head and looked at him. 'Now Maddy's back, I'll ask her to dinner. I'll ask this Fox woman, to celebrate her novel. I'll cook a meal. Just once, we'll have a real evening, like real people. Can you manage that?'

Stephen nodded. He hung his head like a boy, hauled up in front of a headmistress. Then he raised his eyebrows and smiled at her, wheedlingly, from under his sandy fringe. Today, however, she was in no mood to be charmed. She disliked him as much as she disliked herself.

Her phone rang. He lifted her hand, kissed it, and left the room.

'Tuesday,' said Prudence. 'Can you come?'

'Yeah,' said Maddy.

'It'll just be him . . .' She felt shy, saying *him*. 'Him, and the woman whose novel we're buying.' She gazed into the flames of the fire, searching for the right words. 'The thing is, he can only get away for four hours.'

'So?'

'So – can you, sort of leave quite early? If you see what I mean?'

'Why?' Maddy paused. Then she said: 'Oh. Okay.'

'And be discreet. Please! In front of this Fox woman.'

Prudence put down the phone. She gazed at the flames of her gas-effect fire. Eternal flames, like eternal love. The thing was, could they be trusted? People flung rubbish onto these coals – tissues, cigarette ends – and nothing happened. These objects were never consumed by the flames; they just lay there. Was this the impermeability of love, its stubborn resistance to whatever rubbish you flung at it? Or was it just a sham – a fire that looked like a fire but was no such thing? There was something eerie about the flames, something

66

denatured. Like Stephen and herself they sprung into life for a few hours here, a few hours there. There was no smouldering, messy normality to them.

Prudence yawned and got up. She turned off the gas tap. There was a soft *phut* and the flames disappeared.

Maddy was immune to charming men. Prudence had good reason to be nervous about introducing her sister to Stephen. Maddy was a direct woman; she saw through any attempt at gallantry or flirtation – in fact, she never noticed them in the first place. This in turn led to Maddy being considered charmless. She wasn't; she just didn't play the game. The sparring between the sexes didn't interest her; she didn't have time for stuff like that.

In the past this had led to trouble. On the few occasions that Prudence had introduced Maddy to her boyfriends her loyalties had been divided. On the one hand she was irritated with her sister – why couldn't she wear some make-up, why hadn't she made an effort? She felt irritated when Maddy looked restless and then suddenly told the assembled company about genocide in Ruanda. Yet she admired her sister for caring about the world, for being so uncompromising. The man in question suddenly looked unattractively belligerent; couldn't *he* make an effort, for Prudence's sake? Prudence would squirm with embarrassment, feeling trivial for wishing Maddy wouldn't sit there with her legs planted apart. And then she would think: if Maddy is so caring, why can't she care about me? If I were a starving Bangladeshi she would help me. I'm her sister; I love her more than a Bangladeshi would. So why can't she adapt, just a tiny bit, to please me?

She remembered a particularly spiky evening with a man she had liked. During dinner Maddy had launched into the scandal of child prostitution in Bangkok. 'They're kept in pens,' she had said, 'and continuously raped from the age of eleven.' This had effectively sabotaged any hope of sexual activity later on in the evening. In fact, it had effectively sabotaged the relationship, for after Maddy had left she and the man had had a row about immigration controls and she had never seen him again. The next day she had rung her sister, who hadn't realised anything was wrong.

'Don't you ever suffer from compassion fatigue?' Prudence had asked. 'Like metal fatigue in cars?'

'How could I?' Maddy had replied. 'With the world the way it is.'

The problem was Maddy was a wonderful woman. She was generous, truthful and loyal. She cared deeply about things that most people chose to ignore. Prudence loved her. But she also loved Stephen. Contemplating Tuesday evening she felt exhausted before it had even begun.

Maddy, meanwhile, was trying to find a job. The trouble was she didn't know what to do. She had been lent the flat, rent-free, for a couple of months. Its owner, a paediatrician, was away in Romania working in an orphanage. When she returned Maddy would have to find somewhere to live. Before that happened, she had to find some work.

She sat in the kitchen, the *Guardian* appointments page open on her lap. Her attention wandered. She gazed out at the garden. *You should do something about it*, Prudence had said. It was a small garden, overshadowed by a tree of some sort. The recent storm had wrenched off a branch; it lay on the ground like a severed limb, the torn flesh shockingly white in the gloaming. There were some bramble bushes, a patch of lawn with two rotting footballs on it, and a concrete patio strewn with rubbish. A gas cooker stood outside the back door.

For the first time in her life Maddy saw why people did it; why they turned their backs on the world and dug their little plot. Her experience in Nigeria had defeated her; she felt burned-out. What was the point of it all? She had never felt like this before; it alarmed her. During her first few days in

England she had told herself that she needed a holiday; she would have a break, forget about it and start again.

But it was deeper than that. She had told nobody, not even her sisters, about the events of the past few months. Confiding in people had never come easily to her. She felt shamed by what had happened; there seemed no point to the last twenty-one years for her beliefs had been shaken to their foundations. She gazed at the collapsed trellis along the garden wall. No, they had been more than shaken. She had a horrible suspicion that they had evaporated into thin air.

On Tuesday, in her lunch-hour, Prudence walked to Soho. It was a beautiful day. Though it was mid-October the pavement cafés along Old Compton Street were crammed with people leaning back in their chairs and inspecting passers-by through their dark glasses. She felt uncharacteristically skittish. She smiled at a street-sweeper and wiggled her fingers at a taxi that stopped to let her cross the road. She passed the Algerian Coffee Stores, breathing in the aroma. She heard the wind chimes tinkling outside the Thai restaurant; they danced to her dancing heart. She was shopping for Stephen. She was going to cook for him and sit there with him, in the company of other guests, around her dining table. How normal this sounded to normal people: how extraordinary for her! Even her qualms about Maddy had vanished in the sunshine.

Stephen's wife was a vegetarian. Prudence went to Bifulco and bought a joint of beef. She hadn't cooked such a thing for years but tonight she was going to be a woman feeding her man. She queued for vegetables in Berwick Street market. How marvellous were the fruits of the earth, heaped up in their diversity! Her guests would leave early; she and Stephen would pounce on each other. Cabbage leaves were arranged around a mound of potatoes; they cradled them like the hands of a woman cupping her sweetheart's balls. Prudence smiled at the stall-holder. He called her *darling*.

Prudence bought cheese and artichokes and warm Italian bread from Lina Stores. She walked back towards the office. Everyone cherished their lunch-hour but over the past year she had felt proprietorial about hers; this segment of day belonged to her and Stephen. Unable, except on rare occasions, to see him alone, her hour with him was packed with such emotion it took her most of the afternoon to recover. She imagined a prisoner must feel like this when released into the fresh air for one hour out of the twenty-four.

She and Stephen had their favourite places – a bench in Russell Square, various pubs situated at a discreet distance from the office. Happiness transformed them into tourists, for lovers have nowhere to go and find everything curious. They wandered into art galleries and sniggered at the installations. They browsed in the sort of second-hand bookshops visited by American professors; leafing through the volumes, they caressed each other beneath their coats. They pointed up at buildings – pediments, crenellations – looking upwards as people do in any city but their own. They even gave money to buskers. They didn't dare hold hands; they walked along so close to each other that when they bumped together, hip to hip – they were the same height – they felt they must give off sparks like dodgem cars. This was their hour.

Tonight, however, she would have him for longer – a whole evening. It was the first time in nearly a month. She walked into the lobby. Muriel greeted her with a conspiratorial smile; surely, after all these months, she must have guessed something was up? Prudence went into her office and dumped down her carrier bags.

Suddenly she was flooded with joy. Something momentous was going to happen that evening, she could feel it. Little did she know that the momentous event would happen not to herself, but to somebody else.

The doorbell rang. Stephen stood there holding a bottle of champagne. Prudence threw her arms around him: 'Darling!

70

I didn't think you'd make it.'

It was true; he had let her down so often in the past. He dumped the bottle on the floor; he undid her blouse and slid his hand under her bra.

The doorbell rang. She jumped back and buttoned herself up.

It was Maddy and Erin Fox. Maddy said: 'We met on the doorstep.'

Prudence, flushed, introduced them. 'This is my sister Madeleine – Maddy. Erin, this is Stephen Miller, our editorial director.'

Prudence hadn't seen Erin since the day she had thrust the manuscript into her hands. What a magnificent woman she was – tall, powerful, with a strong nose and hair tied in tiny braids. She wore a long velvet dress and boots. When she moved, her jewellery rattled. Maddy was wearing jeans, as usual.

'We're all very excited about *Playing with Fire*.' Stephen filled Erin's glass. 'Has Liz told you the schedule?'

'We're having lunch next week.' Erin's voice was deep and forceful. She didn't seem like a first-time author; she seemed to take the publication of her novel as perfectly natural.

'And we'd be delighted if you could come to our sales conference,' said Stephen. 'You know, meet the publicity people, chat up the reps. Tedious but necessary.'

'Doesn't sound tedious,' said Erin. 'I want it to sell.'

'Music to my ears.' He passed a glass of champagne to Maddy, who shook her head. She didn't drink. 'You'd be amazed how many novelists are too precious for the rough and tumble and then start whingeing that their books aren't on the bestseller lists. Since Unimedia took us over we've got a lot more muscle sales-wise. We're moving into a spanking new building down by the river . . .'

Prudence turned to Maddy. 'I'll get you some orange juice,' she said, and went into the kitchen.

Maddy followed her. Prudence opened the fridge. 'What do you think of him?' she whispered.

'Bit pompous, isn't he?' said Maddy.

'He's nervous. Oh, do be nice to him!'

They sat down to eat. Prudence had opened out her dining table and lit the candles. However, Erin made the living room seem cramped. She was such a splendid creature, blazing with confidence and tossing back her braids. Behind her, the ornaments on the mantelpiece looked niminy-piminy. During the first course she did most of the talking. She cast a spell over the three of them. Prudence surrendered herself gratefully; it threw the balance of the evening and diverted the spotlight from Stephen and her sister.

'You seem to be as footloose as Maddy,' Stephen said, tearing a leaf off his artichoke.

'I lived in the Himalayas for a while, photographing the Kalash tribe,' said Erin. 'The women are wonderful – strong, tall, fierce as tigers.' She pointed to her necklace. 'They gave me this. They do all the work while the men sit around playing flutes. The men are utterly irrelevant.'

'Sounds just like our editorial department,' said Stephen.

'Then I came back and started a film co-operative in Hackney, working with Muslim women. I made a documentary about a man who had two wives.'

Prudence stiffened. Was Maddy going to say something tactless?

Stephen said hurriedly: 'And the gardening business?'

'I started that with my lover but we split up last year; she went to live in Wales. It's just something I'm doing at the moment. Next year, who knows?'

'Who knows?' said Stephen. 'I like that.' How casually she had mentioned a female lover! His life in Dulwich seemed suddenly suburban.

'Our tragedy is that we define ourselves according to a gender, to a skill,' said Erin. 'Most people are three-quarters asleep – they neglect so many parts of themselves.'

Prudence carried the dirty plates into the kitchen. Stephen followed her, carrying the bottle of vinaigrette. 'Just using this neglected part of myself,' he said, indicating his hands.

72

He put down the bottle and moved close to her. 'Actually, there's another bit I'd prefer to use –'

Prudence pushed him away. 'She's quite something, isn't she?'

'Very evangelical. And quite humourless. I can see her filling the Albert Hall.'

Prudence was relieved. For a moment she had thought that he was attracted to Erin. Men were often attracted to strong-minded lesbian women; they had a missionary zeal to convert them. She carried the vegetables into the living room.

Before Stephen could follow her Maddy came into the kitchen. She dumped down the bowl of artichoke leaves.

'I'm so glad to meet you at last,' he said. 'I've heard a lot about you.'

'What are you going to do about Pru?'

'Er – what do you mean?'

'She's so unhappy,' said Maddy. 'She's got so thin! I hardly recognised her –'

'Look –'

'She's bloody lonely too. Sitting here, waiting for you to ring –'

Stephen glanced at the door. 'Look, I don't think we should –'

'Are you going to leave your wife?'

Stephen paused. 'It's more complicated than that.'

'Not for her it isn't. She's the only person I mind about.'

'It's all terribly –'

'She's too nice. She's always been too nice –'

'*I'm* too nice. That's the problem.'

Maddy stared at him. 'Nice?'

Prudence came in. She stopped and stared at them.

'Maddy –' she began.

'He says he's too nice.'

'Please, Maddy! Don't spoil everything.'

Maddy picked up the dish of potatoes and went back into the living room. Prudence turned to Stephen.

'I'm sorry,' she said.

73

'Blimey.'

'She's very loyal. Once she got her nose broken fighting for me in the school playground.' She took his arm. 'Come and help me dish up the meat. I've cooked you some beef.'

Erin, it turned out, was a vegetarian. Prudence apologised and grated her some cheese. Erin didn't mind. Later, when Prudence reran that evening – she did so many times, with a fascinated curiosity – she realised how an egocentric person can liberate those around them. Nobody suffers from embarrassment because it is simply not noticed. To a deeply English person such as Prudence it was a relief. She felt absolved from her own hot self-consciousness.

Erin was telling them about her life. It turned out she had a daughter called Allegra, who was now nine.

'I wanted one, so I had one,' she said, munching a potato.

'Just like that?' asked Stephen.

'I had to fuck someone first.'

'Er, yes,' he replied. 'But did he know why?'

Erin shook her head.

'Who was he?' asked Prudence.

'An architect. Out of work, of course. They all are.'

Stephen laughed. 'Well, at least he didn't have trouble with *one* erection.'

Prudence burst out laughing. Maddy stared at Stephen. 'What an appalling joke,' she said. Prudence sat there, rigid.

Erin speared some beans. 'He did have trouble, now you mention it. But then I put on a tape I use.'

'You use?' asked Stephen.

'Just some music,' said Erin.

The three of them gazed at her, awe-struck. The flat seemed suddenly constricted and spinsterly. What sort of music? Something only lesbians knew about? None of them dared ask. Prudence carved some more slices of beef; she remembered her only brush with Sapphic pleasures. A girl in her class called Jemima, who had come to stay the night, had inserted a Tampax up her and said, *'Now you'll have an orgasm.'*

74

Stephen, though hypotised by Erin, wanted her to leave. He wanted to go to bed with Prudence. He only had a couple of hours before he had to go home. Erin hadn't laughed at his joke – not a bad one, in the circumstances – and he disliked humourless women. That was the main problem with his wife, but she had her foreignness as an excuse. Now he thought of it, Kaatya and Erin had a certain amount in common – vegetarinism, flamboyant clothes, a high-voltage quality to them. Stephen swabbed his gravy with a piece of bread. He didn't want to think about his wife.

'Is this your first novel?' asked Prudence.

Erin nodded. 'I'd always meant to write one but I'd never had the time.' She spoke as if she had fitted it in between breakfast and dinner.

'Well, I hope it won't be your last,' said Stephen. 'We like our authors to go on producing.'

'They're not cows,' said Maddy.

Stephen laughed. 'Oh, I could name you one or two.'

Prudence stiffened. Was Maddy going to flare up? It was like being with their father all over again. But Maddy didn't seem to hear; she was talking to Erin. Prudence gathered up the plates.

She had made a rhubarb fool. Stephen had said it was his favourite pudding. As they ate it she was conscious of a gathering tension in the air. Maddy and Erin were discussing the crippling effect of World Bank loans on developing countries. Prudence wasn't interested; she felt the wires between the four of them, stretched so tight they hummed. Was it Maddy's hostility to Stephen? Her sister's face was flushed; her eyes were bright. This could simply be caused by political zeal. Maybe the tension came from Stephen, who was longing for the guests to leave so that he could tear off her clothes. Twice he had looked at his watch – the adulterer's nervous tic. She hated him for it; she hated his watch. And, just for a moment, she hated her sister for her fierce and mistimed loyalty. She looked at Maddy and thought: what a ball-breaker my sister is. And then she hated herself for even thinking it.

The trouble was it was true.

'I'm sorry,' said Stephen. He rolled off Prudence and lay, gazing up at the ceiling.

'It doesn't matter,' she lied.

'Your sister certainly knows how to –'

'I know.'

They lay there, miles apart. 'As evenings go, tumescence-wise, that little scene in the kitchen was on a par with my Aunty Madge telling you about my potty training.'

'But I've never met your Aunty Madge,' said Prudence.

He got out of bed and picked up his boxer shorts. 'That's why.'

'That's not why.'

He paused, one leg in and one leg out. 'You will, one day. I promise.'

Prudence lay there, watching him as he got dressed.

His eyes flicked to her bedside clock. 'I'm sorry,' he said.

'Sorry I made us leave,' said Maddy. 'Thing is, he's shagging my sister and wants to give her one before he gets back to his wife.'

'He'd better hurry then,' said Erin, 'he looked half-asleep already.'

'I shouldn't have told you, I suppose. Seeing as you're their author now.'

'Who cares?' Erin parked outside Maddy's flat. She switched off the engine. 'It's you I'm glad I met.'

There was a silence. The street was empty, as if it lay under a spell. Nothing stirred – not a leaf, not a piece of litter.

'Really?' Maddy's throat closed up.

Erin nodded. Maddy concentrated on the parked car in front. She felt Erin's hand cupping her face. She turned. Erin kissed her on the mouth. Her lips opened Maddy's lips; her tongue met Maddy's tongue. It was a deep kiss, long and warm. Maddy sat there, rigid.

Erin drew back and smiled. 'Relax,' she said.

She pushed back Maddy's hair and kissed her again. Maddy felt the strangest sensation. It was as if her body unclosed. It was as if, after a lifetime asleep, she had finally woken up like a princess waking from a spell.

Erin touched her mouth. 'I've been longing to do that all evening,' she said, her voice low and thrilling.

Maddy opened the door and climbed down from the van. 'Night,' she said shakily.

'You've got my number. Ring me.'

Maddy hurried to her basement steps. Behind her, the van revved up and drove away.

Five

'She didn't!' Louise clapped her hand to her mouth. 'Poor Stephen!'

'It's not funny.' Prudence choked back her laughter.

'Good old Maddy,' said Louise. 'Remember Hans, that German boy? She asked him if his father was a Nazi?'

They had reached Russell Square. Prudence grabbed her sister's wrist.

'There he is!'

In the distance, Stephen was making his way to the snack bar. They could see him through the trees.

'Is that where you have lunch?' asked Louise.

'Sometimes.'

'Bit cold, isn't it?'

Prudence nodded. 'We freeze to death. Adultery's bad for the circulation.'

It was Friday. They were meeting Stephen for lunch. Prudence had arranged this, hoping it might defuse Tuesday's disastrous evening with Maddy. Stephen was bound to be charmed by Louise. Everybody was. This was the reason, in fact, that she had been reluctant to introduce her boyfriends to Louise in the past. Louise wouldn't have stolen them. Of course not. But it had sometimes seemed prudent not to risk it.

On the other hand, she liked showing her sister off. Today Louise had been shopping. She wore a new blue jacket from the Nicole Farhi shop in New Bond Street. Her hair rose and fell as she walked. Men gazed at her. They seldom wolf-whistled – her beauty was too upmarket for that. After she had passed, however, they found themselves humming. There was a sheen to Louise. She looked like a woman who had been spending her husband's money, a woman who didn't have to pay her own parking fines.

They walked towards Stephen. He sat on one of the plastic chairs, with his back to them. Prudence hadn't seen him all morning; he had been in meetings. As they drew nearer she noticed something odd; cigarette smoke wreathed up in front of his head.

She said: 'Stephen?'

He turned round in his seat. He didn't get up.

'This is my sister, Louise –' Prudence stopped. 'What's the matter?'

Stephen took a drag of his cigarette. 'They've made me redundant.'

Louise glared at her husband. 'Don't you dare call it market forces! He's got to clear his desk by next week.'

Imogen rummaged in a carrier bag. 'Got my tights?'

Louise pulled out a Sock Shop bag and gave it to her daughter. She had just arrived from London. Robert was mixing gin and tonics; her children were hovering, looking at the carrier bags.

'Did you go to Red or Dead?' asked Imogen.

'Yes, I went to Red or Dead.' Louise turned to Robert. 'They've sacked ten of them, even the old boy who packed the parcels.'

'Did you get my top?' asked Imogen.

Louise thrust the bag at her. 'Black, right? Just to make a change.' She took the drink from her husband. 'These horrible money men have taken it over.'

Jamie rummaged in the bags. 'Did you get my CD?'

'Vultures!' She gave her son the CD. 'And don't play it so we can hear.' She sat down at the table. 'They're absorbing everybody, or rationalising them, or whatever inhuman words you use –'

'*I* didn't do it,' said Robert.

'This nice, fusty old family firm that actually cared about books –'

'Darling, you only read *Hello!* –'

'And people like Stephen, who looks really nice, who's devoted his life to literature, they're just like old Kleenexes, just thrown away –'

'Why do you care so much?' asked Robert. 'Just because he's boffing your sister –'

She glanced at the children. 'Robert!'

'They're not listening. They're far too egocentric.'

'It's just such a vulgar way of putting it.'

'Sorry, oh builder's daughter,' he said. 'Thou hast never heard coarse language?'

'Yes, but *you* went to Charterhouse.'

Imogen said: 'I know about Stephen. He's got two boys. One of them broke his arm playing football. They live in Dulwich.'

Louise stared at her daughter. 'How do you know?'

'I heard Aunty Pru talking to him on the phone. Last Easter.'

Robert laughed. 'So let's throw it open. Jamie, Imogen, some input here. Would you like to share your thoughts on modern management methods and their effect upon legover situations?'

The teenagers shrugged. Louise got up. 'I'm going to make some supper.' She turned to her children. 'Did either of you dig up the leeks?' There was no response. 'I phoned!'

'Yeah,' said Jamie. 'In the middle of *Neighbours*.'

Louise sighed. She went to the back door, pulled her old gardening coat off the peg, and stomped out into the dark.

Maddy's love life had always been unsatisfactory. Her first lover was a man called Jake. He was a decent, bearded man who had run the adventure playground in Stockwell where

80

she had worked. He had relieved her of her virginity so gently that she had hardly noticed it was happening. For two years they had worked together, building walkways in the sky and painting them primary colours, constructing a club house and a ping-pong room. They had toiled against the odds – gangs of youths from the nearby housing estate vandalising the place, the local authority threatening to close it down and build flats on the site. Jake was a saintly man. Doggedly he reglazed broken windows and cleared up the mess. Like all good people he never hated a person, only the actions of which the person seemed so unaccountably capable. At the beginning Maddy admired this but as time went by she found it frustrating. Why couldn't he stand up and fight? Their relationship, never vigorous, petered out. His lovemaking no longer seemed gentle, just tepid. Perhaps it had always been tepid, she just hadn't used that word for it. She wasn't good with words. They had drifted into friendship, both secretly relieved that there had been no emotional showdown. Later, Jake found God and became a born-again Christian. It suited him. With his beard, his carpentry skills and his limitless compassion he had always resembled Jesus.

Her later affairs had followed the same pattern. She met a man. They became friends and eventually drifted into bed. She enjoyed the sex but in a companionable way. Two bodies rubbed together in a vaguely comical manner; there was a spasm of pleasure and then both parties got a good night's sleep. She didn't see what all the fuss was about. Oh, it was pleasant enough but it didn't touch her to the core, she could live without it. And for years, off and on, she did.

It took Maddy four days to pick up the phone. Finally, she did it. Erin said that she would come round that afternoon. She sounded brisk and businesslike. After all, it was a business transaction.

Maddy sat on the rim of the bath. She looked at herself in the mirror. The bathroom was lit by a frosted lozenge on the ceiling. Dead flies had collected in it; she could see their smudged shapes through the glass. She suddenly saw her surroundings clearly. What had she been doing all her life?

She looked at her face – properly, for the first time in years. Her tan had faded; in the harsh light she looked sallow. Her fringe was a straight line across her eyebrows; she had always cut it this way, it was the simplest. Under it, her face looked heavy. Square jaw, stubborn lower lip. She had always felt the odd one out; her parents had found her in a doorway and taken her home. That was why she had failed them and they had failed her.

Later, she remembered that moment when she sat in the bathroom, leaning against the blistered wall. She closed her eyes. She felt as if she stood at the edge of her old life, teetering on the rim. Ahead of her stretched an abyss. Did she dare to step out into the unknown? Upstairs, a woman shouted 'Damon!' She heard the clatter of pans. Upstairs, people's lives were carrying on as usual. Wasn't that strange?

The bell rang. Erin stood in the doorway. Maddy nodded hello and ushered her in. She opened the back door and stepped out onto the patio. She could feel Erin beside her. Kicking aside a bottle, she gestured around.

'You see, I'd like to clear it up a bit, to thank the woman who's lent me the flat. Maybe returf the lawn, it's got all mossy, what do you think?' She was gabbling. 'I don't know how much it would cost . . .'

The sun was sinking. It bathed the derelict garden in golden light. A blackbird sang, startlingly close.

Erin turned to her. 'You didn't ask me here to look at your garden.'

Erin unbuttoned Maddy's shirt. She ran her finger down Maddy's throat; she felt the hollow with her fingertip, the pulse beneath the skin. She kissed it, kissing her own finger there, including herself in Maddy's bumping blood. She reached into her bag and took out a phial of oil. Tapping some drops onto her finger she touched Maddy's throat, she anointed her temples. The scent made Maddy swoon. Erin ran her fingers over Maddy's breast. Such sensitive fingers she had, as if she were reading the Braille of Maddy's body.

'Your skin, it's wonderful,' murmured Erin.

'Is it?'

'Has nobody told you you're beautiful?'

Maddy shook her head.

'You've been touched . . . but nobody's really touched you, have they . . . ?' She moved her hands. 'Here . . . and here . . . like this . . .'

Maddy shook her head. She sat on the bed, her shoulders and breasts naked, her shirt bunched around her waist. She felt like a fruit that had just been peeled.

'Can you feel how lovely you are?' Erin murmured. She bent her head and licked Maddy's nipple.

A jolt shot through her. 'I've never –' she stopped.

'I know,' said Erin.

'Kiss me.'

Erin kissed her – a slow, deep kiss. Maddy's heart opened. Shyly, she stroked Erin's face. She slid her hand beneath Erin's embroidered jacket, beneath her satin blouse, and touched her shoulder. How smooth her skin was! How strange to feel skin that was as smooth as her own! Tentatively, she stroked her.

'Do you have a candle?' asked Erin.

Maddy stiffened. What was she going to do with it? She withdrew her hand.

'It's just this room's so sad.' Erin pulled a shawl out of her bag, like a magician, and draped it over the lamp. The dingy room was transformed; it was bathed in a rosy glow. 'You must learn to love yourself, my darling.'

She removed Maddy's shirt from around her waist. She took off her own jacket and blouse. Beneath it she was naked. She had large, heavy breasts and dark nipples. Maddy turned to her and buried her face in her, smelling the scent of her hair, the scent of oil on her throat. She moved her face down and smelt the sharp, animal scent of Erin's armpit. She shuddered.

Erin laid her on the bed. She lay down beside her and pushed the hair from her face. 'You're here at last,' she murmured. 'Isn't it lovely that you never knew what you were waiting for?' Maddy thrilled to her voice. Erin kissed her skin with feathery kisses, light as butterflies. She ran her finger over Maddy's mouth. 'All your loveliness . . . it's been waiting for me . . .'

Maddy lay there, trembling, while Erin unzipped her jeans. She pulled them down, with her knickers, and threw them on the floor. Erin took off her own clothes. The two women lay there, skin against skin. Erin stroked Maddy's belly; she stroked her thighs. She stroked her alive. Erin's hands knew her body, they were her own self caressing it, inflaming it.

Outside, darkness had fallen. Maddy lay still. Erin moved over her body, lighting each place upon which she landed. Maddy surrendered herself to Erin's hands and to her mouth, her fingers and tongue. Her breathing quickened as Erin's head moved down, between her legs.

Afterwards, Maddy sobbed. Erin gazed at her tenderly, and wiped her eyes with the edge of the duvet.

'I'm sorry,' muttered Maddy.

'Why?'

'I haven't cried since I was a child.' She laced her fingers through Erin's. 'I feel . . .'

'What do you feel, my darling?'

'I feel I've come home.'

Erin put her arms around her. Their skin was slippery with sweat. She enfolded Maddy, who buried her face in her shoulder.

'I never thought it would happen to me.' Stephen drained his gin and tonic. 'I read all these articles about it in the

Independent but it was like reading about an earthquake in Korea or something.'

'Who've you tried?' asked Prudence. They were sitting in a pub in Goodge Street. It was lunchtime; a week since he had left the office. 'Have you made a list?'

He nodded. He longed for another drink but he felt Prudence's eyes on him, monitoring him. 'Random House, Reed . . .' He knew people in most of the publishing houses, many of them he considered his friends, but suddenly a barrier had come down between them. Oh, they were sympathetic all right, they had read about his redundancy in the *Bookseller*, but they couldn't help and then their other phone started ringing. 'People are always in meetings, all the people I want to talk to. It's most peculiar. I feel I've got an infectious illness. I feel ill, actually.' He silently urged Prudence to finish her glass of wine so he could get them both another.

'Oh Steve . . .' She stroked his fingers. She gazed at him with her frank, clever face. Prudence was his sorrowful and sympathetic friend – far more of a friend than his wife – but even she couldn't understand. She was safe. Her brown hair was pushed back with a velvet snood-thing – her office hairstyle; she wore her businesslike blue blouse and jacket, unembellished by fripperies. She was a working person. He was out in the wilderness. He had been thrust into a cold, windy place that was in the outside world but not part of it. Of course, other people were out there, too – the unemployed, all those statistics. He knew many people who had lost their jobs. Strangely enough, this didn't help. He still felt utterly alone. It was terrifying.

'Where's that food?' He glared at the counter. 'They only have to bung it in a microwave.' He picked up her glass. 'Let me get you another while we're waiting.'

He went up to the bar. Prudence watched him. From the back he seemed to have shrunk. His shoulders drooped. Maybe it was because he wasn't wearing a jacket, just a sweater. He looked, literally, as if the stuffing had been taken out of him. Poor Stephen. What on earth was he going to do? He would be paid some redundancy money but it wouldn't amount to much, he had only been working at Beveridge and Bunyan for three years.

The question was: would he get another job? Only that week, Viking Penguin had announced that another thirty staff were to go. She looked at Stephen; he stood at the bar, scratching the back of his neck. She suddenly saw him clearly, as others might see him – a man whose chief asset was his charm, but where did that get anyone nowadays? A man with an only-average track record, who had never stayed anywhere long and who had muddled along with the help of efficient assistants and his old boy connections. A man who was good at lunch.

Stephen ordered the drinks. He looked at the other men standing at the bar. Were any of them in his position? Could they tell, just by looking at him, that he had lost his job? It showed; he was sure of it. Prudence would soon have to go back to work but he could stay here all afternoon. There was no shape to the day any more; it was as if the elastic that had held his life together had been snapped. It took him a moment to remember what day of the week it was.

He tried to rally himself. After all, he had only been out of work for a week; he had hardly started looking yet. But already he felt demoralised. How did other people stand it month after month, year after year, filling in application forms that asked them how many O levels they had got, for God's sake, and then getting the polite rejections. *'Unfortunately other candidates more closely matched our requirements . . . but we wish you good luck for the future . . .'* He knew what those letters were like because he had written them himself.

Stephen paid for the drinks. He counted the change and put it in his pocket. His attitude to money was already changing. Instead of flooding into his life on a regular basis like the tide flooding into a harbour, replenishing then ebbing, money was now a finite substance whose level sank with each transaction, as if run by a newly privatised waterboard which never repaired the cracks in the pipes. He thought: don't panic. Don't think about school fees. Don't think.

He carried the drinks over to Prudence. She told him about some crisis at work – a Cabinet minister was making a fuss about his book jacket. Stephen's attention wandered. Strange how involving all those books had once been – the biographies, the novels, even the celebrity cookery series. Now that they were somebody else's responsibility they were utterly irrelevant. All those books being published, week after week; the world could exist quite happily without them. He had suspected this in the past, and now he was certain of it. In fact he had forgotten about them already.

'Has anybody been offered my job yet?' he asked.

She shook her head. 'I think they'll get someone from outside.' She stroked his cheek. Now that they were no longer working together she had grown bolder in public. Maybe she was just sorry for him.

'What's it like at home?' she asked.

'She tries to be nice but I feel I'm getting in the way. I *am* getting in the way.' He pushed the lemon about in his gin and tonic. 'She's used to being alone during the day. She's doing these huge messy collages, she needs the space. I think she wants to hoover me up. High spot of my day is getting the boys from school.' He looked at her. 'I miss you so much.'

She said: 'I wake up with all these things I want to tell you, things in my head. Only an hour, I think, and I'll be in the office. Then I realise.'

He took one of her cigarettes and lit it. After twenty years, he had taken up smoking again. 'Look, on Friday we're taking the boys to my mother's for the weekend. I'll make an excuse for the Friday night and meet them on Saturday.'

'What are you going to tell her?'

He gazed at her tenderly through the smoke. 'I love you so much.'

She laughed shakily. 'You're going to tell her that?'

He shook his head. 'I'll tell her I'm going to Nuneaton for the night.'

'Nuneaton? Nobody goes to Nuneaton.'

'I do. This chap I know, Edmond, he runs a desktop publishing company there. I'll say I'm going there to ask his advice.'

'You mean – we can have a whole night together?'

He nodded.

She stubbed out her cigarette. 'Suddenly I'm ravenous.'

Stephen went to the bar to chase up the food. Prudence was letting him do everything that day. She wanted him to feel manly – in charge of something, even if it was only lunch.

He waved his ticket at the man behind the counter. 'Any chance of number twenty-four? A lasagne and a chicken tikka?'

The man went away. He returned a moment later. 'Sorry, mate. The cook says he never got the order. Bit of a backlog now. You'll have to wait.'

The man turned away to serve somebody else. Stephen stood there. His brief moment of optimism drained away. The man knew. He could sense that Stephen had all the time in the world, that other customers should be served their lunch first. Stephen was a non-person now, and he had better get used to it.

He went across to Prudence and told her. She looked at her watch. 'Hell! I've got a meeting at two-thirty.'

'Go to it then.' His voice rose with self-pity. 'Don't mind me.'

She put her hand on his arm. 'Don't be silly. Of course I'll stay.' She smiled at him. 'Let's talk about Friday.'

'I always thought it was my fault,' said Maddy. 'With men.'

Erin shook her head. 'It was theirs.' She stroked Maddy's breasts. 'Ah, what they're missing. You're as sexed as a panther . . . you're wonderful.'

'I've never felt like this before.'

88

'Know why?' She took Maddy's hand. She breathed in the scent of her fingers and kissed them one by one. 'Because your fingers are my fingers . . . and mine are yours . . . my honey.'

They were lying on the bed. Around them, candles flickered in saucers. Maddy rested her head on Erin's belly. She stroked the damp, wiry bush of her pubic hair; she ran her finger over the tattoo on Erin's thigh. It was a small blue dolphin, leaping upwards.

She marvelled at Erin's body. Through it, she marvelled at all women's bodies. These past two weeks had changed her profoundly. She gazed at women in the street through different eyes. She noticed their breasts, their hair, the way they moved. She felt as if she had had a blood transfusion. Until this moment, however, she had been living on borrowed blood; now she was filled with her own, down to her fingertips – how sensitive they were, how sweet their explorations! Anything was possible now, for Erin had set her free. Men suddenly seemed so limited, their lovemaking poky and focused. She pitied women who had only experienced that. 'Lying there like squashed beetles,' said Erin, 'being drilled. Being pumped full of something so dangerous they have to protect themselves against it. Sad, isn't it? They don't know what they're missing.'

Erin talked a lot about power – men's power over women. She talked about true sisterhood, where women liberated themselves through their own bodies. For Erin, no doubt, Maddy's two sisters were sexual slaves. Prudence was in thrall to her boss. Louise traded sexual favours for a home and security. It was strange to think of them like that, but Maddy saw everything anew now that she had been awoken from her long slumber.

Erin stroked Maddy's eyebrows. She licked them like a cat licking her kitten. 'Can you feel the blood-beat of yourself?' she murmured. 'Aren't we lucky? We're controlled by the moon. Each phase, new moon, full moon, there's a part to be awakened . . . here . . . or here . . .' She kissed Maddy's fore-

89

head, the lobe of her ear. 'We'll discover them together . . . Our own moonwalk across your lovely skin . . .'

Erin's words, like her fingers, thrilled Maddy. She used scents too. She rubbed oil into Maddy's toes; she lit joss-sticks and stuck them around the room. Her lovemaking opened up Maddy's senses; there was no time when it began or ended, it seemed to exist in all dimensions. Maddy was learning, too. She had bought and lit the candles; she had scrubbed out the bathroom and bought bottles of oils for when they bathed together. She had converted this place into a temple of love for Erin's visits. She hadn't been to Erin's flat yet; the daughter was there, Erin had so far kept that part of her life separate. Because of this Erin seemed mysterious, arriving for a few intoxicating hours and then disappearing into the night.

Erin rolled over. 'Shall we have a bath before I go, my sweetheart?'

Maddy nodded. She went into the bathroom and turned on the taps. She poured dewberry oil into the water and straightened up, looking at herself in the mirror. Surely it must be obvious? People in the street must know what had been happening to her.

Erin came up behind her, pressing her breasts against Maddy's back. The room filled with steam. Erin rubbed the mirror, revealing their faces. 'Am I making you happy, my darling?'

Maddy nodded. 'Nothing in my life had ever worked out.' She paused, wondering whether to tell her about Nigeria.

'That's because you didn't know what you were looking for.' Erin turned her around and kissed her. Maddy clung to her in the steam.

It rained heavily overnight. It seemed that autumn would never burst into glory but slide sullenly into winter. Dorothy's hip-bones ached; they did so, increasingly, in wet weather. The joints in her hands ached. She was getting old. She pictured herself confined to a wheelchair, waving weakly at her husband to get his attention. He was too impatient for illness. He boasted that he had hardly had a day off work all his life. Infirmity was something that people should snap out of; but one couldn't snap out of old age.

It was Friday morning. Irritably she watched him swabbing a piece of sausage in his tomato ketchup. Gordon always had a fry-up for breakfast and he always poured out too much ketchup. Over the years she must have scraped gallons down the sink.

She said: 'I'm doing the wages, Gordon. Then I'm going round to Forsythe's.'

'You're what?' He looked up from his *Daily Telegraph*.

'I'm going to get them to finish my kitchen.'

'Don't be soft!'

'And they can paint the bathroom while they're about it.'

'That's daft. Look, I'll get cracking over the weekend.'

'Six months, you've been saying that.' She pointed to her *Daily Mail*. 'Know what it says in my horoscope? *The choice to assert yourself is your own prerogative.*'

'Look, love. I promise.' He swallowed his tea and stood up. As he did so, he winced.

'What's the matter?'

He rubbed his arm. 'Just an itch.' He picked up his mobile phone, kissed her on the forehead and left.

'They're coming to stay?' Louise stared at him. 'This week-end?'

'Didn't I tell you?' Robert swallowed his coffee and got up.

Imogen rushed into the kitchen. 'Mum, come on!' It was time to go to school.

'But I'm working today.' Louise glared at her husband. 'The house is a pit, I haven't done any shopping, I haven't got the time –'

'They'll help,' he said.

'What, Henry and Sophie? They'll sit around drinking wine, sitting on the kitchen units so I can't get at anything,

91

and they'll say *what shall we do?* but everything takes far too long to explain, it's much quicker doing it myself, and anyway they're *guests*. The only thing guests like doing is shelling peas. And I haven't got any.'

Robert slipped out of the door. He was off to work.

'Come *on*!' said Imogen.

Louise grabbed her car keys.

Gordon was stuck in a traffic jam halfway down the Old Kent Road. He tapped his fingers on the wheel. 'Get a move on, you dozy buggers!' Gordon was the sort of man who carried on a one-way conversation with other drivers, admonishing them, chivvying them. His whole life seemed to be spent in traffic jams, stuck behind driver-only buses whose passengers spent ten minutes rummaging for the right change.

He had to get to the Elephant and Castle site; at nine sharp he had a meeting with the district surveyor. Then he had to check up on the Farleigh Road conversion, where items were missing from a delivery of sanitary fitments. His phone rang. It was Nobby, one of his plumbers. They were over in Lewisham, having problems with a catering oven. They couldn't get it through the hallway.

'. . . why didn't you measure the bugger first?' yelled Gordon. 'Is Frank there? . . . Well, where the hell is he?'

Louise was in Tesco. She was stuck in a trolley jam. Two shoppers were trying to pass in opposite directions. A temporarily abandoned trolley blocked the middle route. Why did people leave their trolleys in the middle of the aisle? They had only started to do this over the past few years; it was a new phenomenon, like the anarchy of the bus queues that she had observed when she went to London. A symptom of the fuck-the-rest-of-you malaise that seemed to be gripping the country as it slunk towards the millennium.

Irritably she pushed her trolley through. She felt guilty that she wasn't shopping in the village but she was in a hurry and she needed to get everything at once. Why hadn't Robert told her the Warshaws were coming? She flung in a packet of pasta. She flung in a bottle of sun-dried tomatoes – Robert called them 'dead men's ears'. When people came to stay they suddenly discovered they had enormous appetites. It must be the fresh air. They ate huge breakfasts. *We never have cooked breakfasts usually, do we darling?* They ate vast lunches. *I don't know how you do it, Lou, I wish I had time to cook like this.* They especially looked forward to her home-made bread. *Why don't you make bread, darling? Because I've been in Milan all bloody week, that's why.*

Louise saw a thin, fair-haired youth. Dressed in overalls, he was loading tins of cat food onto the shelves. It took her a moment to recognise her own son.

'God, you look quite grown-up!' she said, coming up to him.

'Mum!' Jamie frowned at her, indicating the other shoppers.

'Sorry. Get me some Whiskas, would you?' She pointed. 'Those ones.'

He passed down some tins. Their cat was finicky. At the moment he would eat only Salmon'n'Tuna Select Cuts. The trouble was he was also unpredictably fickle. He seemed to know, by radar, the moment when she had stocked up on his latest favourite. Then he would refuse to touch it. He would sniff the bowl, a look of pained revulsion on his face as if she had offered him a bowl of vomit. Then he would wander around the kitchen, stiff-legged, miaowing. Monty, who would have been waiting, saliva hanging from his jowls, would lumber forward and eat it up.

Louise left her son and pushed her trolley towards the meat counter. The trouble was that despite their enormous appetites her weekend guests were frequently faddy too. Was Henry or Sophie a vegetarian? Was Sophie on anti-depressants so she couldn't eat cheese? Last time she had talked about Prozac, how Henry's ex-wife was on it and how she was thinking of taking it too because she was so depressed at not conceiving a child. Oh, it was so complicated.

As she stood at the checkout Louise thought of her parents. They had been brought up in a world that was unrecognisable to her, let alone her children. Their class – the respectable working class – was more or less extinct. Besides, her parents had long ago struggled out of it. They had scrimped and saved – how quaint those words sounded now! – they had eaten tinned luncheon meat and mashed potatoes. The salmon her own cat sneered at would have been the height of luxury to them.

Louise carried her bags out to the car-park. She didn't know where this got her. Should she feel guilty for her petty preoccupations, for taking so much for granted? Should she feel guilty if, after all they had done for her, she wasn't happy?

Gordon was late for his next appointment. Where the hell was Frank, his foreman? He couldn't get him on his mobile phone. Frank had a drink problem. Every month or so he disappeared on a binge. God forbid that he should be off on one now.

Gordon hurried across to his car. A traffic warden was sticking a ticket to his windscreen. 'Hoi!' shouted Gordon. 'Hoi, mate! I'm just coming!'

But the warden carried on, deaf. Gordon bellowed in frustration.

Two mornings a week Louise worked. She was one of the Volunteer Reading Help team at the village school. Tim knew her exact times of arrival and departure. The school was situated across the green from his shop. On that Friday he was unblocking the gutter beside the front step; last night's downpour had clogged it up with some foul-smelling overflow from the drains.

At ten o'clock her Space Cruiser hove into view. His heart jumped. She was late; she usually walked. He straightened up and watched her park outside the school. She got out and hurried through the gates.

Even from this distance her Toyota looked as huge as a tank. It towered above the other cars; if it hadn't been Louise's he would have called it a monstrosity. It resembled a jeep pumped with steroids – bulging, silver, barricaded with cattle prods. Her husband had sealed her off from the world; he had reinforced the walls around her so that nobody could get in. Louise was a princess in a tower of her husband's making; she wasn't happy. Tim knew that; he, and only he, could see through the veneer. She was waiting to be rescued; it was only a matter of time.

'I'll be home by six,' whispered Prudence. 'Come as soon as you can.'

She replaced the receiver, picked up her papers and went upstairs to the editorial meeting.

Alan, the managing director, squinted at her through his cigarette smoke. 'Hey, Pru, you're looking bright and bushy-tailed this morning.'

It was lunchtime. The sun had come out. Maddy and Erin sat on a pile of rolled-up turf in a garden off Kensington High Street. The place belonged to an Arab who was never there. They sat side by side, eating mozzarella sandwiches. Maddy had become a vegetarian. She didn't miss eating meat. It was like men; she couldn't understand what she'd seen in it. The rolls of turf resembled fur, skinned from defenceless mammals.

'Look,' said Maddy, 'we've got the same sized feet.'

Erin rubbed her boot against Maddy's foot. 'I want you to come home with me tonight. I want you to meet my daughter.'

95

The sun had come out. Prudence sauntered down the street, swinging a Fenwick carrier bag.

From a doorway a voice called: 'Spare us some change?' A head emerged from a sleeping bag. He was a young boy, her nephew's age.

She bent down and gave him a pound coin. She smiled blithely and walked on. She thought how happiness makes us both blind and generous. We glide along so well armoured that nothing can dent us. She knew she should feel guilty for buying a silk slip that cost fifty times the amount she had given the boy. But then again, didn't she deserve to be happy, just for once?

She stopped. She must have passed this place countless times. In the window a sign said *Leg Waxing*.

Prudence smiled to herself. She pushed open the door of the beauty salon and went in.

What a day! Parking ticket, gas leak. The traffic was diabolical, the Friday afternoon scrum, drivers behaving like madmen and now Gordon's phone rang again as he drove across Waterloo Bridge.

'Thank goodness I've got you!' Mrs Malik's voice was hysterical. 'I'm in the bathroom, it's flooded. Oh, come quickly, please!'

'Don't panic, love,' said Gordon. 'Where's your mains stopcock?'

'I don't know!'

He changed direction and headed for Victoria. 'I'm on my way.' He blared his horn at an *Evening Standard* van that slewed around in front of him, making a u-turn. Drivers of *Evening Standard* vans were the biggest maniacs of the lot, they drove as if they were telling the world about the outbreak of war.

Gordon braked. Blast! Westminster Bridge was closed off with traffic cones.

Louise yanked the bottom sheet over the spare bed. She knocked over the carafe of water on the bedside table. Shit! *London's such a madhouse,* they said. *Bombs, car clampers, muggers . . . It's so peaceful here, we always sleep like a log, don't we, darling?*

She swabbed the water with Kleenex. She didn't even like Henry and Sophie much. Henry worked with Robert. They would spend the whole weekend talking about management buy-outs. Sophie worked as a PR in the fashion business and made it smilingly obvious that she considered Louise an empty-headed housewife.

Louise lifted up the duvet and tried to stuff it into its cover.

Gordon drove round the block twice. No bloody meters. He double-parked and hurried across to the house. He rang the bell. A small girl opened the door.

'Is your mum upstairs?' he asked.

She nodded. In the lounge, a crack had appeared across the ceiling. Water was already seeping through it.

Gordon pounded up the stairs.

Trish was putting on her coat. 'Sure you don't mind me going early?'

Prudence shook her head. 'Gather ye rosebuds while ye may.'

'You're very cheerful. Doing anything exciting tonight?'

Prudence smiled. 'Just staying in.'

'Oh, well. Never mind.'

Under the desk, Prudence stroked her shin. Even through her tights she felt it, smooth as glass.

Water shot out of the disconnected tap. The floor was awash.

Mrs Malik, a vague, frightened woman, was trying ineffectually to staunch the flow with a towel.

'The tank's on the roof?' asked Gordon, trying to remember the layout of the house.

'I don't know!'

'The stopcock?'

'My husband would know!'

He pointed to a trap-door in the ceiling. 'Got a ladder?'

'I don't know!'

'There's a stepladder under the stairs,' said the little girl.

Gordon raced downstairs. As he passed the lounge he heard a thud. He looked in. Plaster dust billowed out; a section of ceiling had collapsed.

He opened the cupboard and pulled out the stepladder. It was a heavy wooden ladder encrusted with paint. He struggled with it upstairs. In the bathroom he waded through the water, set up the ladder and started climbing. He pushed at the trap-door. It was stuck.

As he pushed, two things happened. His phone rang. Then a thick, elastic band tightened around his chest. It stopped his breath.

Gordon grunted. Mrs Malik stared as he fell. A bulky man, he grabbed at the ladder beneath him as it toppled over.

He landed with a splash. His leg was still hooked around the ladder. He lay in the water. His breath came in rasping, hoarse gasps. Mrs Malik screamed.

In the office, Dorothy was giving the lads their wages. It was five-thirty. Lloyd took his envelope. He was from Jamaica – the only black man on their payroll. *'First-class chippie, very sunny disposition.'* She blushed at her husband's clumsiness; why did he always put his foot in it? Something drove him, some perverse urge to say exactly the wrong thing. He was teasing his daughters but that didn't make it better. The trouble with Gordon was that he was exactly himself. He altered for nobody. *'They take me as they find me.'* How many times had he said that with bulldog pride? Some people, Gordon included, made a virtue of their own inflexibility. Nothing would ever change him.

'Have you seen my husband?' she asked.

Lloyd shook his head.

'I thought he was going to Farleigh Road,' she said.

'Haven't seen him all day.' Lloyd turned to go. 'Take care, Mrs Hammond. And you have a good weekend, right?'

She suddenly longed to touch Lloyd's hair, to feel how springy it was. She blushed.

Gordon was probably having a drink with their foreman, Frank. After all, it was Friday. And tomorrow she would tackle him about the kitchen.

Prudence had laid the table for two. Dinner simmered in the oven. She had changed the sheets. She had removed a half-corrected manuscript from the bedside table and replaced it with a vase of anemones. She had felt like the most tender of stage managers.

The bell rang. She ran downstairs. Stephen stood in the doorway. The sodium street light bathed him in its unearthly glow; shadowless, he looked like the hologram of all her desires.

She flung her arms around him. Ah, but he was real!

Some evenings it was worse than others, the longing that squeezed Tim's heart so tightly he could scarcely breathe. Some evenings he could battle against it.

Not tonight. She had cheated him of her walk across the green. He hadn't even seen her leaving at lunchtime, he had been busy with a customer. When he had looked outside, her Space Cruiser had gone.

Margot stood at the oven, mashing potatoes.

'Just going out for some fresh air,' he said.

'Don't be long,' she replied. 'It'll be ready at eight.'

He looked at her back. How vulnerable she seemed, his big wife whom he had once loved! Within that bulk there was still the woman who had once laughed her loud, fruity laugh, who had once been happy. In front of her the window was curtained with the poppy material from their old flat. They had chosen it together, soon after they'd married.

His eyes stung. He turned away. He put on his anorak and went downstairs. The shop was illuminated by the chill cabinet; the milk cartons stood there, mute witnesses in the bluish glow.

Prudence poured Stephen a gin and tonic. 'Just for once, I want us to be like everybody else,' she said. 'I want us to have supper, and watch TV, and go to bed.'

'How about doing it the other way around?' He grinned, taking his glass. 'What're we eating?'

'Guinea fowl braised in oranges and wine.'

'Mmm . . . I've cooked guinea fowl. It needs to be done for hours, so it falls off the bone . . .' He took her hand and stood up. He indicated the drinks. 'Let's take these into the bedroom.'

It was a cold, windy evening. Clouds chased across the moon. The church tower reared up.

Tim stood on tiptoe and peered over the wall. There was another, unfamiliar car parked in the driveway – a TVR. In the rectory, the downstairs windows were lit. He looked at the kitchen; he always looked there first. She was there, bending at the stove.

He slipped through the gateway. He moved across the spongy, damp grass and slipped behind the bushes.

Stephen unbuttoned her blouse. He stroked the silk slip – black silk, edged with lace. 'Mmm . . . very nice.'

100

'This is what we wear in Nuneaton,' said Prudence.

'Mmm, let's talk desktop publishing . . .'

'Let's talk Microsoft . . .'

'Mmm, so soft . . .' He led her to the bed and laid her down. 'Let's talk about layouts.'

'Mmm, lay me out . . . that's nice . . . Do you want to touch my spreadsheets?'

'Like this?'

'Mmm, like that . . .'

'Let's feel your disk-drives . . .'

'Hard or soft?'

'Can't you guess?'

'Oh! Mmm . . . I can guess . . .'

'Shall we start formating now?'

'First, you press here . . .'

'And here?'

'Mmm . . .'

The phone rang. They froze.

'It's on the machine,' she whispered.

She put her arms around him. They paused, waiting.

In the living room the machine beeped. They could hear a faint sound. It was her mother's voice.

'Prudence, are you there? Your dad's in hospital! St Mary's. . . . Are you there? Oh, where are you?'

Tim crouched in the bushes next to the lounge window. It was his usual place. Through the window he could hear the faint sound of laughter. Louise was passing glasses of champagne to her guests. She wore a loose blue dress he had never seen before. Her hair was loose, too; it glowed in the firelight. The horse whinnied. He jumped. Louise turned and said something to the woman.

The phone rang. Tim jumped. Louise walked over to the phone. It was near the window; she came so close he could almost touch her.

She picked up the phone. She listened for a moment.

101

She turned away from the window, her hand pressed against her mouth.

Maddy's bedroom was dark. The digital clock pulsed from 8.03 p.m. to 8.04.

Candlewax puddled the saucers that sat about on the carpet. There were two mugs on the bedside table, half-filled with cold tea. The bed lay there like a ship, berthed on its voyage of discovery. *My America, my new-found land.* Tonight the bed was empty. Maddy was at Erin's flat, two miles away.

The phone rang . . . and rang . . . There was nobody to pick up the receiver.

It rang and rang. And finally it stopped.

PART TWO

One

After sixty-five years Gordon's body had been taken away from him. It had been prodded, inspected and penetrated by lasers. It had been wheeled from one department to another; needles and tubes had been inserted into it, sucking out blood and pumping in fluids. Its life had been spirited along wires and reproduced on a monitor whose erratic zigzags danced beside him as he lay in bed, an oxygen mask clamped to his face like the sucker of an octopus. Only the pain belonged to him but even that seemed like an unwelcome visitor, an intruder that had lodged in his chest and stolen his normal sensations. It dared him to shift his position. It lurked, heavy and serious, beneath his ribcage and lingered in his leg where the angioplasty had been pushed into his vein. Over the past two days alien instruments had intimately explored his body; they were accompanied by a technical vocabulary with which he was now becoming familiar, though it still gave him a jolt when he realised that it was applied to himself.

Gordon was a man who had seldom known fear. He had rushed through the decades with little pause for thought. Now he lay immobilised by his own faltering mortality. On one side of him a man lay slumped in bed, wired up like a puppet and shaken by a cough that already resembled a death-rattle. Even Gordon's get-well flowers were expiring in the heat; their heads drooped as if bowing to a stronger will than their own. On his second night a screen had been hastily erected at the end of the ward; in the morning it was removed

103

to reveal an empty mattress. Gordon was gripped by panic. He clamped the hospital headphones to his ears and listened to radio phone-ins, whiny voices complaining about pavement potholes. He told himself that he was recovering and in a week he would be home, everything would be back to normal.

He dreaded Dorothy's visits because he saw his own alarm reflected on her face. On Sunday evening she arrived with a walkman.

'I borrowed it from Jamie,' she said. 'And here's some talking books I got from the library. That actor's doing it, the one who plays the vet on TV, remember?' She rummaged in her bag. 'I've got your pyjamas and some apple juice.' She wanted to surround him with familiar things. Clamped in his mask he felt like a deep-sea diver, nothing was familiar out there but he didn't let on. 'How are you feeling?'

'Fine,' he lied into the plastic. 'Right as rain.'

She talked about the girls, how they would come to see him the next day. She showed him some get-well cards and tried to prop them up on his bedside locker. She asked him what they had done to him that day, if they had got the results of the test, and then she fell silent.

He looked at her and thought: I nearly died. He saw the bathroom trap-door above him; he lifted it and a white light shone down, blinding him, dispersing him into atoms. He looked at his wife: wavy auburn hair, cream blouse and cardigan. To those who have glimpsed death, people once familiar to them are set apart, as if mouthing at them through glass. He was a deep-sea diver, clamped in his mask. Dorothy seemed to be talking again. He thought how brave she was, to tint her hair with such dogged regularity, trying to stop the greyness creeping through. Who was she fooling?

On Monday the consultant came round. His name was Mr Jarvis-Jones. He reminded Gordon of the fathers who had sat in front of him during Founder's Day at his daughters' school, blocking his view as if their backs declared: what right has this man to be here at all, who does he think he is?

'I see you're a builder, Mr Hammond,' he said, looking at his notes. 'Let's think of your body as a central heating system. Now, what happens when the boiler breaks down?' The ward sister gazed at him moistly. 'Now, you've had a small heart attack – I'd prefer to call it an episode. We should take it as a warning signal. Two of your main arteries are significantly narrowed. However, there is no reason for you not to lead a perfectly normal life for a man of your age, so long as you follow certain rules. Cut out the stress – probably plenty of it in your job, eh? Certainly plenty of it when *we* have the builders in!' He laughed. The ward sister laughed. 'Switch to a low-cholesterol diet, no more fry-ups I'm afraid.' He looked at the notes. 'And you're a smoker too. Dear oh dear. Give up the weed, there's a good chap. I'll see you again before you leave us.'

He left, accompanied by the sister. April came up to Gordon's bedside. She was a nurse – his named nurse, her name was on her badge.

'What a creep.' April jerked her head. 'Know something? He preens himself before he comes in. I've seen him in the car-park.' She gave Gordon his pills. 'Reminds me of my boyfriend. When I get home he's arranged the wardrobe mirror and the other one so he can see himself from the side. Pathetic, isn't it?'

'Pathetic.' Within his mask, Gordon smiled at her. April was a young black woman, bouncy and full of life. He liked watching her in the ward; she was like a cork, popping up, refusing to let the current pull her down.

'Men are much vainer than women, don't you think?' she said. 'My bloke, Dennis, he's into body-building. How're you feeling today?'

'It's odd,' said Gordon. 'There were all these jobs that needed doing on Friday, crises and such. Now it's like – it happened to somebody else. Know what I mean?'

'I suppose it doesn't matter any more, does it?'

'Other people feel this way, do they?'

She nodded. 'Some of the heart cases. They go home and their whole life's changed. One bloke, I bumped into him the other day. He'd left his wife and started a watercress farm.'

'Watercress?'

'Sort of soothing, I suppose. Like, watercress can't nag you, can it?'

'Poor Dad,' said Prudence. 'He's frightened. Nothing's supposed to frighten one's father.'

'Because he's supposed to last for ever?' replied Maddy.

'He's frightened of dying.'

'Oh, he'll be all right,' said Maddy. 'He'll just go on as if nothing's happened.'

'Will he?'

'Nothing can change our father.'

'You used to call him Dad,' said Prudence.

'Well, *I've* changed.'

They walked towards the car. The hospital loomed up behind them, its chimney belching black smoke. Prudence had been shaken by the sight of their father. She hadn't seen him in pyjamas for years; it seemed shockingly intimate. His chest hairs were grey, now, and thicker than she had remembered. Quite apart from the tubes, the act of wearing pyjamas had transformed their father into an old man. And she hadn't been prepared for the oxygen mask.

'Do I seem different?' Maddy asked.

'What do you mean?'

'Something's happened, you see.'

An ambulance passed, its siren wailing. It disappeared round the side of the building.

'Thing is,' said Maddy, 'I've fallen in love.'

Prudence stopped beside the car. 'Maddy! How wonderful.'

'It is, rather.'

'Who is he? Have you just met him? It's not that person in

106

Africa, is it, what's his name, the Swede?'

Maddy shook her head.

'Go on,' said Prudence. 'Do I know him?'

'It's Erin.'

Prudence stared at her sister. She felt her face heating up. 'Erin?'

'Are you surprised?'

'Yes – no – what do you want me to say?'

'I'm not,' said Maddy. 'That's the funny thing. It's the least surprising thing that's ever happened to me.' Maddy leaned against the car and gazed down at her trainers. 'It makes sense of everything. I had to tell somebody.'

'When did this happen? After you came to dinner?'

Maddy pulled at a thread on her sweater. 'She kissed me. It was like – all my life I'd been asleep and she woke me up.'

'Have you – er, been attracted to women before? God, I sound like someone on Channel 4.'

'You mean, am I a lesbian or have I just fallen in love with Erin?' Maddy raised her face – her square, honest face. Her cheeks were flushed. 'I don't know. I don't know anything. I'm just so happy.'

Prudence put her arm around her sister. Maddy stood there, stiffly. She wasn't a demonstrative person.

'Don't tell – you know,' she said.

'Poor Dad,' said Prudence. 'It'd give him another heart attack.'

'. . . our own sister! Does she look different? What did she say?' Louise picked up an empty yoghurt pot and flung it into the bin. With her free hand she was tidying up her daughter's room. 'Do we call her a lesbian or gay? We're out of touch here and I don't want to get it wrong. Trouble is they're always changing the word, aren't they, like the blacks, and it's bound to be the wrong one.' She clenched the phone against her shoulder, bent down, and sorted through a heap of dirty tights. Down the line Prudence's voice faded, either

107

through distance or excitement. 'Wish I was a lesbian.' Louise carried the underwear into the bathroom. 'No horrible children with their horrible horrible mess.' She dumped the clothes into the laundry basket and glared at the bath. 'Why don't they ever clean the bath? It looks like someone's washed a warthog in there. *And* she's used my body rub.' Dreamily, she said: 'No more adolescent daughters with their bloody hormones . . .'

When she put down the phone she wondered if she had been tactless to complain about her children to Pru. Pru's childlessness was something that was no longer mentioned between them, and though Louise presumed that by now her sister had come to terms with it – indeed, she suspected that Prudence never really wanted children in the first place – she also knew that, to the childless, a complaining parent is more hurtful than a boasting one, just as millionaires' complaints grate more harshly than their self-satisfaction.

Louise, like her father, was not by and large a reflective person. She lived instinctively, through her senses. She cooked, she mothered, she was stroked and loved. She heaved shopping bags and pulled up leeks, smelling the earth on her fingers. It was her surface that dazzled the world. Beneath it, her mind was unexercised. She felt the rusty cogs turning as she tried to reorganise her thoughts about her younger sister. Had Maddy always been a lesbian, was this the clue to her? Since childhood Maddy had been obstreperous and difficult, at odds with their father and, now Louise thought about it, men in general: their maths teacher at school; an apparent sadist called Barney who ran the project in Canada, and several others besides. Did lesbianism make sense of this, combing out the tangles of Maddy's psyche like cream conditioner, leaving her sister silky and manageable? Or was life more complicated than that? The whole thing was such a shock – deeply fascinating, but a shock. Louise had never met this Erin woman but by all accounts she was a powerful, charismatic creature. Had she corrupted Maddy or liberated her? For all her truculence,

Maddy was a vulnerable person who had always felt inadequate. Maybe this woman was just what she needed. Despite this, Louise felt lonely. Her sister was a lesbian. Applying this unfamiliar word made Maddy lost to her.

Meanwhile, their father lay in hospital, himself transformed into a statistic – a Heart-attack Victim. Though there was every hope of a recovery he too had been jolted away from her: in this case, towards death. Of the three sisters Louise had the closest bond with their father. All her life she had pleased him by her beauty and compliance. Her life was understandable to him – motherhood, home, the upholstery of wealth. His pride in her, though embarrassing at times, was something she had long taken for granted. She was a simpler person than her two sisters, and her anxiety about him was unmuddied by the currents that his brush with death had stirred up in the hearts of the other two.

Adolescents, on the other hand, are blessedly self-absorbed. Imogen was out riding. When she galloped the wind blew away her preoccupations but when she reined in Skylark they settled on her again like flies, briefly disturbed but returning buzzingly to crowd her. Was her chin too big? Were her breasts too flat? *Yes.* What did Karl really think of her, did he really want to show her the badger's sett? '*You're just a kid,*' he had said. What did he mean by that? She had replayed the scene so many times that it had lost all meaning, like her *Blackadder* videos. Oh his curly hair, dampened with sweat! The ruddiness of his neck . . . the battered leather apron slung around his hips . . .

It was a clear November morning. She rode along Westcott Ridge, following the bridle path. A chain-saw whined in the woods. She smelled her horse's sweat and the corrupt scent of silage. Down below lay a secret valley. A farmhouse nestled there, snug between the thighs of the hills. She lived there with Karl. In the mornings she flung open the door and threw grain to her chickens. Chunk, chunk . . . Karl was chopping wood. At night they climbed into bed, a brass bed with a featherdown duvet, and the moonlight shone through the window and silvered their faces. How immature Jamie's friends seemed, how giggly the girls at school! Imogen rode down the track, between the sighing pines. She rode along the main road into the village, past the council houses, past the cottages. She rounded the bend. There, in front of her, lay the village green. The church clock struck one. Outside the pub, Karl's van was parked.

Imogen's heart lurched. She reined in Skylark and dismounted. Her legs filled with liquid. She fiddled with Skylark's bridle. She adjusted the girths, glancing under the horse's neck at the door of the pub. She willed Karl to come out. She willed him with the muscle in her brain she had used since she was a child . . . If I count to ten . . . if I squeeze tight . . .

The door opened. Karl came out. She mounted her horse and rode over.

'Hi,' he said. 'Shouldn't you be at school?'

'I don't go in all the time now. I'm doing my A levels.'

He grinned. 'And studying hard, I see.' He wore a donkey jacket; a spotted scarf was knotted round his neck.

'I think better when I ride.'

He looked at her horse. 'Shoes okay?'

'Fine.'

'Be seeing you then. Cheers.' He climbed into his van and drove off.

She drank in the scent of his exhaust smoke. Thoughtfully, she rode home. She dismounted and led Skylark into the stable. Thoughtfully, she gazed at Skylark's hooves.

Then she went to her father's toolbox and took out a pair of pliers.

April was thirty – older than he had thought at first. She had such smooth skin, shiny as a plum. She was as ripe as a fruit. When she laughed, which was often, Gordon was startled by

110

the whiteness of her teeth. She was the only nurse who bothered to sit and talk to him. As the days passed he became entranced with the soap opera of her life, whose cast of characters was becoming as familiar to him as members of his own family.

On Wednesday she brought him in some cassettes. She put them on his bed, one by one. 'Alanis Morisette . . . Nina Simone . . . ,' she said. 'I like women singing about what a mess their lives are.'

He smiled. 'Because yours is so sorted out, right?' He settled down with relish. 'So go on, what happened yesterday, with the boxing promoter?'

'Well, he signed Dennis up and they both came home totally legless, with these other blokes, and they started singing and the people upstairs kept banging on the ceiling, and I'm trying to get some sleep. Then my aunty phoned up –'

'The one whose car burst into flames?'

She nodded. 'This is three in the morning, mind, and she says she thinks she's got Parkinson's and could I describe the symptoms. And meanwhile there's this crash comes from the lounge. The stupid buggers had been dancing on my glass table –'

She stopped. Dorothy had arrived.

Gordon introduced them. 'This is April. She's been looking after me.'

'So pleased to meet you,' said Dorothy, 'I've heard so much about you. He's doing very well, isn't he?'

'He's great. He's started reorganising the ward.'

'Gordon!'

'Give him a couple more days,' said April, 'he'll be reorganising the NHS. Probably do a better job than they are.'

She left. Dorothy said: 'What a nice girl.'

'Never guess what happened to her last week,' said Gordon. 'See, she's got this boyfriend, Dennis, sounds a right case to me, always getting into fights and she has to bail him out – well, they live above this optician's place in Brixton –'

Dorothy laid a hand on his arm. 'Gordon – take it slowly.'

111

He paused. 'Forget it.'

She took out some books. 'Got these out of the library . . .' She put them on his locker. 'Now, you don't have to worry about a thing. Frank's sorted out that business at Lavender Hill, and they've got the structural report on the Duke's Avenue site, Len's faxed it through, so they can go ahead there. I did the VAT last night.' She paused. 'Gordon?'

'What?'

'Are you all right?'

He said: 'I nearly died.'

She put her hand on his. 'No you didn't, love. You're going to be fine. But when you come home you're not to do a thing. No worries, no stress.'

'But lots of watercress.'

'What?'

'Bloke I heard about.'

She nodded. 'Plenty of healthy food, I'll see to that. And no cheating!' She smiled. 'Because I can always tell when you've been doing something you shouldn't.'

Night, and the library books lay unread beside him. He half-slumbered in bed, the walkman plugged to his ears. Nina Simone sang 'In the dark', her voice spread through his veins like black treacle, pulsing.

Gordon lay, surrounded by the ill and the dying. In his bones he felt the thump of the music, the heartbeat of it.

Two

On Wednesday Prudence was summoned to the Unimedia chairman's office where she was given a glass of chardonnay and offered Stephen's old job. Though disguised by a new title, editor-in-chief, and a rejigging of the departments, there was no doubt that this was basically the editorial director's position from which Stephen had been so ruthlessly removed. This fact somewhat tempered her pleasure at her promotion, but there was little time to dwell on this because Beveridge and Bunyan was in the throes of packing up in readiness for the move to the new Unimedia headquarters building in Docklands.

The musty old building in Bloomsbury had been sold, the office cat taken home by Muriel, the receptionist, who had been given early retirement. It was the end of the end of an era in British publishing and this, too, contributed to the mixture of emotions Prudence was feeling. Though she despised the old boy network she still felt a certain sentimental attachment to the past, much as those who are not religious feel an affection for churches and would be saddened to see them demolished. Besides, Stephen himself, with his bow ties and Oxford cronies, was part of such a tradition and on the Friday when she left Museum Street for the last time she felt an ache in her ribcage. Unlike her sister Louise, however – softhearted Louise – Prudence kept her emotions under control. She was the sensible one, the one upon whom others relied, and when she took her new department out for a lunchtime drink she radiated optimism for the future.

Unimedia House, headquarters of the communications empire, is a vast glass building complete with the regulation atrium and post-modern flourishes. Topped by satellite dishes it is situated in a no man's land of flyovers and building sites between Wapping and the Isle of Dogs. The penthouse boardroom commands a panorama of the River Thames and the smog-blurred skyscrapers of the City. The lobby, a vast expanse of tawny marble, displays clocks which show the time in Tokyo and New York. It is patrolled by security guards whose chests crackle with static. Outside, beyond the slip road and the car-park, the next building is sheathed in mirror-glass; it reflects Unimedia back on itself, a narcissistic contemplation of its own image.

Beveridge and Bunyan had been dusted off and installed on the eleventh floor. On Friday afternoon Prudence and Trish moved into their new office. It was an acreage of mushroom carpeting and white walls. They hesitated, clutching their potted plants; they felt dwindled and amateurish.

The phone rang. Trish grabbed it and said, in a silly voice: 'Editor-in-chief's office, Trish speaking, how may I help you?' She passed the receiver to Prudence. 'It's Stephen.'

Prudence grabbed the phone. His voice said: 'I wanted to be the first to call you. What does it feel like?'

'Strange. Big. Bare.'

'Why didn't you tell me they'd given you my job?'

'It only happened on Wednesday. Where are you?'

'Outside.'

Prudence moved to the window. Down in the road she glimpsed a figure, standing in a phone booth. With one hand she struggled with the window catch.

'We're air-conditioned,' said Trish.

Prudence banged on the glass. She beckoned. 'Come up!' she yelled down the phone.

'It's okay,' he said.

'I'm coming down!'

She hurried out. She pressed the button for the lift. There were three of them – glass capsules which crawled up and down the walls of the atrium. She jumped in one and descended to the ground floor. She clattered across the marble and rushed out into the street.

The phone booth was empty. Stephen had gone.

That week in early November Maddy also moved. She moved in with Erin. It was Erin's suggestion that Maddy live with her and help her with the gardening business. 'We'll work together, my darling.' She laced her strong chapped fingers through Maddy's. 'Would you like that?'

Maddy packed her belongings into plastic bags and Erin drove her to Hackney, to her house. Romilly Street was a decaying terrace that backed onto a school. When Maddy arrived it was the lunch-break. The children's shouts echoed from her own past in Purley, from the school veiled by birches at the end of the garden. Stirred by her memories, she stood in the bedroom with Erin.

There was a step on the stairs. They turned. Allegra stood in the doorway.

'What are you doing here?' asked Erin. 'Why aren't you at school?'

'Had to get my clarinet.' Allegra was nine years old, a wiry girl with dusky skin – her father was Indian.

'Are you really sure you don't mind me coming here, Allegra?' Maddy asked.

She shook her head. 'No. And you can call me Ally if you like.' She turned and went downstairs, idly scratching her bottom. 'Hope you stay longer than the last one,' she called over her shoulder.

On the Saturday Gordon was dressed and ready. The sister passed his bed.

'Excuse me, love,' he said. 'Where's April?'

'She's off today.'

'But I haven't said goodbye.'

115

'Shall I give her a message?'

He shook his head. He looked at the cassettes, stacked on his locker.

Dorothy arrived, and drove him home. Back in The Birches she settled him in the lounge. She tucked their picnic blanket around his knees. He felt pettish and restless; he longed for a cigarette.

'It's stifling in here.'

'I put up the heating.' She put down his bag and sat beside him on the settee. 'Gordon, I've been thinking a lot this past week. Since all this happened.'

'And what's that?'

'I think you should retire.'

He stared at her. 'Retire?'

'Frank'll look after things, at least for the time being.'

'Frank's an alcoholic.'

'We'll sell up,' she said. 'None of the girls are going to take over the business. It doesn't matter. None of it matters. I think we ought to move somewhere smaller, have some fun. Have time to ourselves, just you and me. Don't you?'

The cat had had an accident in the kitchen. Not an accident, actually – it was cold outside and he had simply not bothered to go out. Louise swept the result into the dustpan, walked out behind the stable and flung it onto the grass. As she did so she caught sight of a horseshoe, lying amongst the nettles.

She picked it up, fetched a hammer and some nails and attempted to hang it over the back door. Robert, who had a splitting headache – he had been to a company dinner the night before – came out in his dressing-gown.

'You sound like the porter at the Gates of Hell.'

She pointed with her hammer at the horseshoe. 'It'll bring us good luck.'

'With your family you need it. Father has a heart attack, sister becomes a lesbian. What else does fate have in store?'

'Nothing wrong with being a lesbian.'

116

'I know,' he said. 'I like having sex with women too.'

He took the hammer and banged in a nail. The horseshoe swung round, upside down.

'Don't,' she said. 'Something awful's going to happen.'

November is a melancholy month. The wind whips the leaves into the gutter; in gardens, small, silent deaths take place. Bones are chilled as winter approaches and summer's screen is blown away to reveal the ugliness that lies beyond. It is a time for facing the truth, even for a man such as Gordon, who was unsure what truth was being revealed to him or why he was being bowled along, as helpless as litter, by the unseen currents of his need. For he found himself driving towards Brixton, and as he drove he thought how some day he must die and the shops he was passing would carry on trading without him: Radio Rentals would never know that he had arrived on this earth and would some day leave it; he had lived his life never having sat on a number 3 bus, which he was stuck behind now. For once he didn't fidget; he didn't pull out and overtake. A troubled fatalism had settled upon him but he had no words to understand it; all he told himself was that he had cassettes in his pocket and an errand that he could put off no longer.

I live above Betterspecs. He knew that from their conversations; also that there was a Burger King opposite. At this stage, before it all happened, these clues gave him a prickle of childish excitement. He found the place and parked. He stepped out of his car and into another world. It was a windy, bracing day; he felt like his granddaughter's horse, when it was led out of the kitchen – its ears pricked, its nostrils flexing.

Next to the optician's there was a doorway. There were two bells; he pressed the lower one. An age passed. A man walked by, arguing into a mobile phone; a car drove past, thudding with music. He was about to try the upper bell when he heard footsteps descending the stairs. The door opened; April stood there.

117

He held out the cassettes. 'Just passing by,' he said. 'Thought I'd drop these in.'

'Come in.'

He looked at her. 'You all right?'

He followed her upstairs. She let him into her flat. A chair lay smashed on the floor. A mirror was broken and something – it looked like coffee – had been flung against the wall. April sat down on the arm of a settee.

'We had this row last night. He started hitting me. I thought he was going to kill me! So I got out and went to stay with my friend Beverley, and when I got back he'd gone.' She burst into tears. 'I don't know what to do.'

He stroked her hair – how wiry it was! It was pulled back with gold plastic clips. He thought how odd it was to see her in normal clothes – a red sweater and jeans. She was transformed from an angel of mercy, ministering to him. She was now a distraught young woman in need of his help. He felt a shameful jolt of pleasure.

'Don't worry, love. I'm here.' He removed his hand. 'You think he'll come back?'

She shook her head. 'That's what the row was about. I saw him coming out of the gym with this girl . . . you can tell, can't you, just by looking . . . body language.' She caught her breath. 'He's always been really jealous of me, and all the time he'd been – oh, I hate him!' She slumped into the settee. 'No, he's gone. He's taken his stuff.'

'You sit there. I'll make us a cup of tea.'

'It's you who should be resting,' she said.

'You looked after me. Well, it's my turn now to look after you.'

'Shouldn't you be at home?'

'To be frank, I was going barmy at home.' He looked around the room. Its big, grimy window faced the high street; a bus passed, startlingly near. People sat on the top deck. 'I'll have this place sorted out in no time.' Apart from the mess, the room was in need of a good lick of paint. 'You own the flat or rent it?'

'It's mine, I bought it.'

He went into the kitchen. He filled the kettle as if he lived there. It was the first practical task he had done for nearly two weeks; it felt exhilarating. She came in and opened the cupboard. That door needed fixing too; one of the hinges was broken. She took out a packet of tea-bags. It felt domestic to have her beside him, as if they had been doing this for years.

She fetched the milk. 'I'm glad you came.'

'I'll tidy up now, and I'll come back on Sunday with my tools,' he said. 'You working Sunday?'

She shook her head.

'That's all right then.' He tore off a piece of kitchen roll and gave it to her. 'Now, blow your nose like a good girl.'

Maddy and Erin were in Cheyne Walk. They were planting winter-flowering primulas in the garden of a Lebanese banker. Maddy was discovering that she loved the job. She loved driving around London in the van, part of the working current of the city and then for long periods separate from it, sealed off into the birdsong of hidden gardens. Maddy was tough; she didn't mind rain and cold. This gave her a rare sense of superiority over Erin, who suffered from poor circulation. Otherwise, Erin was the boss. A natural teacher, she was in her element instructing Maddy on soil composts. Like many bossy people she was gratified by someone else's ignorance and her pleasure in imparting information made her kind, even gentle. She had seven regular clients – both private gardens and business premises. Her jobs ranged from weekly maintenance – lawns, window-boxes – to landscape design and larger replantings. For Maddy, whose life had been rootless for so many years, the simple act of handling plants was soothing. Even in this dying season she felt invigorated, digging in the soil, lowering her leafy children into their beds and pressing down the earth around their stems. She was starting to feel healed, even safe. But could she trust in this?

119

'Has nobody lasted long with you?' she asked.

'We're here, now,' said Erin. 'Isn't that all that matters?' She straightened up and looked at her watch.

'So that's why you're checking on the time?'

Erin shook her head. 'I've got a meeting at five. About the book.' She wiped her nose, leaving a smear of earth across her cheek.

'Will you be seeing my sister?'

Erin nodded.

'I told her about us a couple of weeks ago,' said Maddy. 'In a funny way, she didn't seem surprised. Sometimes I think my sisters know me better than I know myself.'

'Maybe they do.' She scraped the earth off her trowel. 'Darling, could you pick up Allegra from school and take her to her dance class?'

Maddy nodded. 'Do you think she minds me living with you?'

Erin shook her head. 'She likes you.'

'Did she like the others?'

Erin straightened up and looked at her.

'Sorry,' Maddy said.

Maddy shook a primula out of its pot. As she did so, she thought about Erin's novel. Reading it had been a painful experience. The graphic sexual passages had shocked her, for though no prude she was unused to reading novels of this nature – in fact, she seldom read novels at all. She had been startled by her feelings of jealousy – gut-scouring, cheek-reddening jealousy, waves of it – for the heroine of the book was recognisably Erin and even now, bundled up in her old gardening coat and wrenching open a sack of peat, it was all too easy to picture Erin lying on a beach in Goa, annointing the nipples of her girlfriend with honey – a scene from the early pages of the novel, and one which culminated in passionate underwater lovemaking. Maddy was unused to such fierce feelings, her love affairs with men having been somewhat tepid, and though she was grateful to find herself capable of such ardour she was unprepared for its dark underbelly – jealousy.

Erin left as dusk was falling. Maddy rescued a worm and flung it out of the way. Five minutes after Erin had gone it started to rain. Maddy felt resentful. It was as if Erin controlled not only her, but nature, which didn't dare to send down the rain until she was out of the way.

Maddy sat in the van. In the mud outside, a footprint filled up with water. Erin's boot had made the print. Gazing at the pitted surface she suddenly felt dizzied with love. How lucky that water was to collect in the space where Erin's foot had been!

The rain ceased as abruptly as it had begun. Maddy started packing up. How simple her former life had been; how confusing it was, when one finally opened one's heart!

In the conference room Brian, the art director, was showing Erin the mock-up of her book jacket. Prudence hovered anxiously. She found Erin intimidating. Even the woman's dirty fingernails seemed a statement of superiority, as if Erin were engaged in more honest toil than these media types.

'It's a great read,' said Brian. 'Your name goes here, thirty-four-point.' He was a sixties whiz-kid, one of those Cockney lads who had made good. Though wizened now, he had a certain twinkly charm to which Prudence presumed that Erin was immune. 'No, seriously, my girlfriend couldn't put it down. She missed her stop and ended up in Hounslow East.'

'That's the reaction we're getting from everyone,' said Prudence.

Brian pointed. 'The title goes here, *Playing with Fire.*'

'Are these supposed to be women's bodies?' asked Erin.

Brian nodded. 'People'll spend so long working out who's doing what to who they'll end up buying the book.' He laughed. 'No, seriously, we're dead pleased with it.'

Prudence asked Erin: 'What do you think?'

'My novel's about language,' said Erin. 'It's about a woman's search for freedom.'

'Yeah, but there's a lot of bonking too,' said Brian.

121

Prudence froze, but Erin smiled. 'Why do you think I put it in?' she said. 'We want this book to sell, don't we?'

Prudence smiled. 'So let's go for it!'

Her relief, however, was short-lived. Walking to the lift with Erin she asked: 'How's Maddy?'

'Fine,' said Erin. 'She's working with me now. She's very good with plants.'

'You must come round to dinner soon. It's all been a bit chaotic this past month, what with Dad, and the move to this place. Maddy seems very happy – you know, with you.'

Erin nodded. 'She's finally stopped running.'

'Running? What's she been trying to get away from?'

'You, of course,' said Erin.

They had arrived at the lift. Two secretaries from Prudence's department, dressed to go home, stood there.

'Me?' asked Prudence.

'You and your sister.'

'What do you mean?' Prudence stared at her. The two secretaries listened with interest.

'She always felt inadequate compared to you two,' said Erin. 'Didn't you realise? Louise so beautiful ... you so clever. And your father didn't help. She's a very damaged person.'

Prudence stood there, numb. The lift doors opened. Erin and the two girls stepped in, and the doors closed behind them.

At six-thirty Prudence left the office. It had stopped raining. Stephen sat on a wall. He was illuminated by the arc-lights of the car-park. Unshaven and raincoated, he looked as if he were waiting for Godot.

'Why didn't you come in?' she asked, and instantly re-gretted it. Of course he wouldn't come in. She took his arm. 'Let's have a drink.'

They drove off. Ten minutes later they found themselves in a Bovis estate of half-built maisonettes. Prudence backed the car out and turned it round. A one-way system swept them up onto a flyover, past Canary Wharf, down through an underpass and out onto a roundabout.

'Where's a bloody pub?' muttered Prudence.

He looked out of the window. 'Weren't we here five minutes ago?'

'Bloody one-way system,' she said. 'We're caught in some awful loop.'

He pointed to a slip road. 'Try that.'

'Shit.' She had missed it. She drove on, gesturing around at the no man's land. 'Welcome to the brave new world of publishing. Aren't you glad you're out of it?'

'No, actually.'

'Sorry. It's been an awful day, and then Erin Fox came in and told me I'd damaged my sister by being too clever.'

'I disliked that woman on sight. Bossy, humourless, fancying herself.'

'She seems to have Maddy in her thrall,' said Prudence. 'I've never seen my sister so radiant.'

'Maybe it's better with a woman.'

'I can't remember what it was like with a man.'

'Stop the car,' he said.

'I can't!'

'Just stop.'

Prudence slewed the car onto the pavement. Traffic thundered past them. She switched off the engine.

Stephen said: 'Prudence, I've lost my job. I've seen you get it, which is fine, I'm delighted for you, but it's hardly the most tumescing of circumstances. I've spent the last month hawking myself around every publishing house in London. I've even started filling in applications for selling insurance. How low can you get?' He gazed out at a crane, poised over a warehouse. 'My marriage is strained to breaking point. I'm in no state for anything. I can hardly manage to get my clothes on in the morning.'

'I'm sorry.'

'No, *I'm* sorry.'

123

She paused. 'It's just – I can't stand this any more. My father nearly died. You and me, we'll both be dead one day –'

'This *is* a cheerful conversation –'

'What's the point of it?' She turned to look at him. 'We're living this half-life, not really living at all, just causing each other pain, a sort of non-everything. Only the pain is real.' She looked out of the window. 'And we can't even find a fucking drink.'

'Funny to hear you swear.'

'Well, I do now.'

'It's rather nice,' he said.

She gazed at the overflowing glove compartment. A lorry thundered past, shaking the car. She felt they were in the frailest of vessels, flotsam in the windy world.

'Steve, we've got to stop. You know that, don't you?'

They sat there, tears sliding down their cheeks. She didn't turn, but she could feel him nodding.

'Dot? Just going out. Be back later.'

'Out where? You shouldn't be driving.'

'I'm fine. Just going into town.'

'Why?'

'Drop off some paint at Lavender Hill.'

'But it's Sunday.'

'Yes – but then it'll be ready for tomorrow, won't it?'

'Honestly, Gordon. Still, I'm glad you're feeling better.'

'See you later.'

'Well, take care. Don't start shouting at other drivers.'

'Bye.'

Imogen heard the sound of an engine. Tripping over Monty, she darted to the kitchen window. It was his van. She hurried out of the side door and, when she turned the corner, sauntered casually across the gravel.

'Hi,' she said. It must show on her face. She felt transparent, like one of those grubs whose skin reveals the pumping organs within, the pulsing hopes and fears.

Karl picked up his bag of tools. Today he wore a peacock-blue shirt and spotted scarf. He had had a haircut; the curls on his neck had been shorn off. It made him slightly less attractive. As she followed him into the stable she felt grateful for this; it made it more possible that nobody else would want him.

'Nice of you to come on a Sunday,' she said.

'It's an emergency, isn't it? And I'm booked up all next week.' He lifted Skylark's hoof. How glad she was that a horse couldn't speak! 'Must've been one hell of a wrench.'

'She tripped on something and then I heard this clanking noise.'

'When did I shoe her?'

'Five weeks ago,' she said promptly. 'But I've been doing lots of riding.' She stroked Skylark's neck. 'In fact, I've been trying to find that badger's sett.'

'Badger's sett?'

'You know, that you were telling me about. In Blackthorn Wood.'

Karl held the new shoe against the hoof. 'I know the one.'

'You said you'd show it to me.'

'Did I now?'

'I love badgers,' she said.

He started hammering. 'We'll see about it then.'

'I'm free most evenings.' She added hastily: 'I mean, I'm out quite a lot, but if I knew in time –'

He looked up at her. 'How old are you?'

'Sixteen. I told you before.'

'Well, sixteen-year-old, you should be staying home doing your homework.'

'I bet you never did.'

'Now how did you guess?' He grinned at her, and rubbed his shorn neck. Who had cut his hair, a hairdresser? He didn't look like the sort of person who went to a hairdresser. He said: 'Okay. How about tonight, then? At dusk.'

She nodded. She felt the heat spreading over her cheeks.

125

It was Gordon who wore the uniform now – his overalls. There was a pencil slotted behind his ear. He lowered his Hitachi drill and pointed.

'I been thinking. See, if we moved that over there . . . you could put your table that side, gives you more space. The door won't keep banging into it . . . Build a little cupboard there, for your videos . . . sort out that damp over there. My guess is that it's a cracked downpipe. Have to talk to the free-holder about that.'

April smiled. 'You're always like this, aren't you?'

'Like what?'

'Sorting things out.' She pushed a cushion back into its cover; she had been washing the covers in her machine. 'You're wasted in your job. Should be running an army.'

'I do. Except they're all deserters. Specially on Monday mornings.'

She laughed and zipped up the cover.

'Used to make my daughters laugh.'

'Don't they any more?' she asked.

'Not at my jokes. I'm a bit of a liability, as far as they're concerned.'

'Why?'

'Because I'm their dad. A dad's always in the wrong, isn't he?'

She plumped up the cushion and put it on the settee. 'Wish I'd known mine. When I was six he sent me this pair of boots, red suede, really pretty, but I couldn't get them on. I suppose I'd grown up faster than he'd realised.'

'How could he leave somebody like you?'

She stuffed the next cushion into its cover. 'He didn't feel like that, did he.' She paused. 'Last thing I heard he'd gone back to Jamaica.' She dropped the cushion onto the settee. 'Sometimes I think about him. When I'm on nights. You have time, then. It's like the whole world's asleep. It's just you and these, like, these souls in your care. Just their heartbeats jumping in the monitors. They're, like, all your children and you've got them safe. Just for the night.' She shrugged. 'I think about him then. And I don't even know what he looks like.' She jerked her head at the room. 'Easier to sort this out.'

Gordon gazed at her. He felt the room ebb away, like a wave hissingly pulling away from a beach. He and she were left there alone, high and dry.

It had been one of those dirty November days, grey and smeary, a day that held the dusk within it throughout the hours of daylight. Imogen, in her room, put on her star-shaped earrings. She looked at herself in the mirror. Earrings for badger-watching? She pulled them out.

She went downstairs and unhooked her coat. Her mother appeared in the kitchen doorway.

'Where're you going?'

'To Sandra's,' said Imogen.

'Why?'

'To watch a video.'

'You said you'd never talk to her again after she taped over your *Withnail and I*. Anyway, you're not going out till you've tidied your room.'

'Mum –'

'It'll only take half an hour.'

'I can't!'

'The video can wait. That's the point of videos. Phone her up.'

'I can't!'

Imogen rushed out.

Jamie sauntered out of the kitchen, eating taramasalata from a tub. Louise turned to him.

'What have I done wrong?' she asked. 'I was never like that with my parents. I was nice and neat and tidy.'

'Oh yeah?'

'I helped my mother. I laughed at my dad's jokes.'

'Bollocks.'

'It's true!'

'Bet you were just like us,' he said, and went back into the kitchen.

She followed him. Bags were heaped on the table; she had just returned from Sunday worship at the cathedral of Tesco. The bags were riffled, as if a rat had been at them; her children were experts at filleting out what they wanted to eat – Fruit Corners, taramasalata – and bundling the rest of the stuff back into the bags.

'Maybe I should phone your granny,' she said. 'See how Grandad is. Haven't spoken to them for a week.'

'Such a good daughter,' said Jamie.

Ignoring this, she punched in the phone number. As it rang, she pointed to the shopping. 'Put that away, will you?'

'Mum! I spend the whole week stacking shelves. Probably stacked *these*.'

Dorothy answered the phone. They were fine, she said, but she was worried about Gordon. He was restless and fidgety; he was finding it a torture to give up smoking. Over the past decades he had tried, several times, and failed. 'I think he slips out of the house so he can have one on the sly, without me seeing.'

'Put him on. I'll read him the riot act.'

'He's not here. He went out this morning and he hasn't come back yet. In fact I'm starting to feel worried.'

'I don't want a cigarette . . . I don't want a cigarette . . .' chanted April. 'All nurses smoke. Funny, isn't it, seeing as we know what it does to people.'

Gordon said: 'You don't have to do this, just to keep me company.'

'I'm starting a new life. I've decided. Who needs blokes? I even ironed his shirts. Nobody irons blokes' shirts any more.' They were sitting in the kitchen, drinking tea. She squeezed her earlobe. 'Do this, when you feel the urge coming on.'

He held his earlobe. 'Like this?'

She leaned over the table and squeezed his earlobe. 'Like

128

this. My friend Beverley showed me. There's these pulse-points, see, and this is the nicotine one. She learned it from her swimming instructor.'

It was strangely comforting, having his ear held. As she leaned towards him her breasts, in their paint-spattered T-shirt, pressed against the table. 'How long do we do it for?' he asked.

'Till the urge goes.'

A minute passed. The fridge rumbled into life. Out in the back yard below her flat somebody was whistling. It was the opening number from *Guys and Dolls* – *I Got The Horse Right Here* . . . He knew the words by heart. He tried to concentrate on them, rather than his overpowering need to draw tobacco into his lungs. 'It's getting worse,' he said.

'You're not trying.' She took her hand away. She had strong, nurse's hands, chocolate-coloured skin, pale palms and startling, milky nails. She placed his thumb and forefinger around his earlobe. 'There. You don't want one, do you?'

He shook his head. 'It's no good.'

She laughed, and held his earlobe again. Her hand was warm. 'I can't do this for ever.'

'Why not? I'm growing attached to you. I think I'll take you around with me everywhere.'

'We might get some funny looks. Where will you take me, then? Somewhere exciting?'

He nodded. 'How does Neasden grab you?'

'Mmm, lovely.'

'Ponders End . . . you name it, sky's the limit.'

'How about somewhere really thrilling, like East Bromley?'

'Oh, I don't know about that. They've got tigers there, I've heard. They come out at night, in the Bejam car-park.'

She laughed, and let go of his ear. He looked out of the window. Lights shone from the back windows of the flats opposite. Darkness seemed to have fallen.

'Heck. I got to go.' He looked at his watch. It was five o'clock.

He packed up his things. They went downstairs. She

opened the door for him.

'Thanks for everything,' she said.

He said goodbye and walked round the corner, into the side street where he had parked his car. The Mercedes sat there in the lamplight. It looked strangely low, as if it had sunk into the road.

Then he looked again. The tyres had been removed.

She followed Karl down a muddy path. Branches brushed her shoulders. It was so dark that she couldn't see where she was going. She stepped into a rut and stumbled.

He took her hand. How large and dry his hand was! Was he just holding hers to steady her?

He whispered. 'No chattering when we get there. Right?'

'I'm not going to chatter!'

They stumbled on.

Gordon gave her back the Yellow Pages. He had phoned three tyre suppliers; as he had suspected, they were all closed.

'Won't be open till tomorrow,' he said. 'Monday.'

'Don't you want to phone the police?' April asked.

He shook his head.

'Phone your wife,' she said. 'Tell her what's happened.'

He went to the front window. The Burger King opposite blazed with light. 'What a disaster,' he said.

'What's the matter?'

Down in the street a woman ushered children through the door; silver balloons bobbed above their heads as they went into the Burger King. 'See, I didn't tell her I was going to be here.'

There was a silence behind him. 'Oh.'

He addressed the street. 'Don't know why.'

'No.'

He moved away from the window. 'Better phone her.'

Turning his back on April, he dialled his number. When Dorothy answered he found himself stumbling over his words. '. . . it's the blooming gearbox again, been trying to fix it. Didn't see the time . . . no, it's okay, I'll get the train. Be with you in an hour.'

He put down the phone. For some reason he felt short of breath.

April fingered the gold chain around her neck. 'Why didn't you tell her the tyres've been stolen?' she asked.

'Search me.' He picked up his things again. 'Better go.'

The phone rang. He froze. How had Dorothy got the number?

Finally, after several rings, April picked up the receiver. Gordon could hear a man's voice on the line. It seemed to be shouting. April gripped the receiver. 'Don't you dare!' she said. 'I'm going out! I've changed the locks!' She stopped and listened. 'Dennis?' A buzzing sound came from the phone. She replaced the receiver. 'It's Dennis,' she said. Her face looked drained. 'He's coming round.'

She burst into tears. Gordon put his arms around her. She felt familiar to him now – her large, beefy shoulders – she was a big girl – her firm breasts. She smelt of turps, and musky perfume.

'I'm staying,' he said.

'You can't.'

'Ssh. I'm not leaving you now.'

Imogen's eyes were getting used to the dark. Above her the black, clotted pines reared up. In the silence she could almost hear them breathing. A few yards in front of her was the paler glimmer of a bank. Within it was the dark mouth of the sett. Hunched in her overcoat, she sat next to Karl. He had laid an old jacket on the ground; this meant that she had to sit close to him, their shoulders touching. He pointed. 'They'll be coming out to go hunting. A sow and a boar.'

'Do they mate for life?' she whispered.

He shook his head. 'They're not that stupid.'

She smiled. She couldn't see if he was smiling too. She shifted slightly, to pull out the camera. As she did so, her thigh rested against his.

'Hey, you can't use that,' he whispered, his breath warm on her face. 'It'll scare them off.'

'It's infra-red. It's my dad's. Look.' She turned the camera on him and clicked the shutter. 'No flash, see?'

He took the camera. 'Wow.' He held it close to his face, looking at it. 'Loaded, isn't he. Your dad. What's he do, then? Work in the City?'

'Ssh,' she hissed. 'We're not supposed to chatter.'

He fell silent. The balance between them shifted. Just for a moment, despite the frisson of sitting next to Karl, she thought about Jamie and their childish battles for supremacy. Her brother usually won, of course – he was older, he was a boy – but on the few occasions when she did, how sweet was her victory!

Besides, she didn't want to talk about her father. She didn't want to tell Karl that he was a venture capitalist. For one thing, she didn't know what it meant. For another, it sounded so boring. Besides, she didn't want to think about her parents. Karl was sitting beside her. What a miracle! The trouble was, she had dreamed about it for so many weeks that now it was finally happening she could hardly take it in. She felt numb. She wanted it to be over so that she could sit in her room and luxuriously relive every moment.

It was damp; she felt the chill seeping into her bones. Karl's breath, a grey cloud, mingled with hers. How close! As if their spirits were fusing. How she envied his lungs, snug in his body, pumping away. What a miracle that he was alive, and wanted to be sitting next to her in this wood. For the hundredth time she wondered whether he was really inter-ested in badgers or just wanted an excuse to bring her here in the dark. He had long ago let go of her hand. Did he want to take it again? Did he, oh bliss, want to kiss her? She, of course, couldn't care less about the badgers. She had seen one once, lying dead on the road to Beaconsfield; she had seen them alive on TV.

She gazed at the mouth of the hole; it was so black that it looked solid. The only point of the badgers was to show Karl how patient she was, sitting here minute after minute, how unlike other girls her age; how in tune with nature. And if one emerged from the hole, it would give her an excuse thrillingly to grab his arm.

Time passed. She could smell his aftershave. Had he washed and groomed himself especially for her, or – horrible thought – was he going on somewhere afterwards? She knew nothing about him, nothing about his life except his address, which she had found in the Yellow Pages under *Farriers* when she and her mother had looked for a blacksmith. *14, Riverview Close, Tetbury Magna* – a village ten miles away, out near High Wycombe. She knew the address by heart, of course, it was engraved in her soul. Apart from this, she knew nothing – just that he was a man, a real one, muscular and ruddy as a gypsy, not one of Jamie's weedy friends. A man who, it seemed, actually wanted to be sitting next to her.

Had the badgers already gone? She gazed at the black hole. If she kept her eyes on it, it seemed to expand and contract like a living thing. She stiffened – was that a movement in it, or just a trick of the dark? She wanted to ask Karl but she didn't want to break the trance in which they sat, their twin hearts pumping.

Gordon was unused to lying. Like many honest people, once he had to lie he built such an elaborate edifice, so cumbersome and over-embellished, that only those who, like his wife, had had years of trusting him could possibly believe in it. Over the phone he laboriously explained to Dorothy that the car had happened to break down in Herne Hill, near Frank's place; that he had gone to see his foreman and found him in a terrible state, halfway through a bottle of scotch and heading for one of his binges, so he had decided to get some food in – Frank's place was a tip – and stay there to sort him out.

'He's a grown man, Gordon.' Dorothy's voice crackled down the line. 'He can look after himself.'

Gordon paused. 'To tell the truth, I don't feel so hot.'

'Oh, you poor love, why didn't you say? Shall I come over? What do you feel?'

'Just knackered.'

'I told you not to go out –'

'I'll be fine,' he said. 'I'll take a pill and kip down on his sofabed.'

He put down the phone. April had removed herself to the bedroom but she had probably heard every word. He felt intimate with her, she was sharing in his lies. He felt sick.

He dialled Frank's number. 'Look, if Dorothy calls, do me a favour. I'm staying at your place, don't ask me why . . . no, it's not like that! I'll explain tomorrow. Thanks, mate.'

He felt the corruption spread, like dry rot. It pushed its poisonous fingers everywhere. April came in.

'You look terrible,' she said.

'I'm not in the habit of this.'

She picked up the mugs. 'You've not done anything wrong.'

'No.'

'You can go home. Honest. He probably won't come.'

Gordon looked at her. At last he spoke the truth. 'I want to be here,' he said.

Imogen wasn't prepared for the effect they would have on her when they appeared. A striped face, black and white; first one and then another – friendly triangles. Then she heard them – a snuffling, busy sound, a companionable badger conversation that sounded married. She thought they would lumber around but Karl was right; they were surprisingly light on their feet. She gripped his arm without even noticing she was doing so.

The two badgers sniffled round. When they turned, their bold faces disappeared and they were just a grey bulk in the darkness. She felt deeply moved to be eavesdropping on their emergence into a night which, for them, must be like any other. They turned back, and seemed to inspect her and Karl with benign tolerance. *So you're watching us? Well, you're welcome to it.* They scratched about for a few minutes. She could hear them breathing. It made them seem human – an elderly couple, wheezing. Then they trotted off.

Up in the trees a bird shrieked. It was an alarm call – a screeching sound like a carving knife being sharpened. Something barked – could it be a fox? Karl's arm tightened, wedging hers against his side. She thought: I shall remember this night, all my life.

Down in the street somebody shrieked with laughter. Gordon stiffened. He heard the sound of breaking glass. Was it his car, were they finishing it off? He lay there, tucked up on April's settee. The pillow had flattened beneath his head, which was wedged against the armrest.

Through the curtains, the street light glowed. A lorry thundered past, rattling the window-panes. It was well past midnight but outside the place still seethed with life. In fact, it was bloody noisy. How loud it was, compared to the hush of Purley. How strange, not to be sleeping in his own bed. He was lying on the settee of a young black woman whose surname he didn't even know. He had eaten a takeaway pizza with her. He had sat next to her on this settee, watching episode three of some TV drama she was hooked on. In fact, now he thought of it, Dorothy liked it too but he had never seen an episode – well, one week he'd been in hospital, hadn't he?

He had used April's toothbrush. He had showered under the shower attachment in her bath, gazing at her shelf of intimate items – body gel, shampoo, a tube of something called Black Beauty Hair Relaxer. The strangeness of all this obliterated the guilt. After all, he had done nothing wrong except lie to his wife. Apart from this, he had simply helped April sort out her flat and comforted her when she'd cried. That was all. Today was just a bizarre adventure, the sort nobody believed he was capable of. *He* hadn't believed he was capable of it. He felt a tweak of pride that he was behaving like a student – like one of his own grandchildren.

Down in the street a man started shouting. Gordon stiffened. Maybe it was the boyfriend. Maybe he would start battering at the door downstairs. Somewhere in the high street a shop alarm wailed.

The bedroom door opened. Light shone into the room. April appeared. She wore pyjamas; they made her look like a child. Wordlessly she came over to the settee.

Gordon said nothing. He lifted the duvet; she slid in beside him – it was a tight fit, with the two of them. Awkwardly he put his arm around her. She grunted. For a moment he thought she was sleepwalking but then he smelt the sharp, animal sweat of fear. She lay there in his arms, her chin resting on his chest. And soon her breathing deepened and she slept.

In the silence of Purley, in the floral-papered bedroom, Dorothy slept. Outside it had started to rain. A car swished by, and then all was quiet. Dorothy was dreaming. The white Mercedes estate, smeared with mud, was driving the wrong way down an underpass. It was loaded with bodies, wrapped in heavy-duty builders' bags. She could see Gordon in the driving seat. She ran along the tunnel, shouting to stop him, but no sound came from her mouth. The car, disappearing round a corner, was weighed down so heavily that its undercarriage scraped along the road. Dorothy slept, and the next morning all that remained was a feeling of unease.

In the Old Vicarage, in the big brass bed, Louise lay alone.

136

Robert was downstairs, drinking whisky and watching an old video of *Die Hard* with Jamie. She was glad, of course, that he was bonding with his son. For two people who lived in the same house they managed to have minimal contact with each other, a fact she put down to Jamie's age and their mutual contempt for each other's lifestyles. More and more often, however, Robert seemed to stay downstairs until late, only coming to bed when Louise was asleep. He shut himself in his study and worked; he fell asleep in front of the TV. For many years they had gone to bed at more or less the same time, an unspoken erotic synchronisation. They had withdrawn from the family spaces downstairs, the dog hairs and domestic tasks, and had retreated into the intimacy of their preparations for bed.

Why was he avoiding her? They hadn't made love for ten days, not since they had returned home, flushed and giggling, from dinner with the only other villagers that Robert found marginally amusing, a sozzled old journalist and his boyfriend. And yet this neglect alternated with periods of fierce lovemaking – no, not lovemaking: sex. There was something impersonal in Robert's passion. Gripping her in his hairy arms he seemed to be penetrating her body without somehow acknowledging it, as if she were irrelevant to some angry dialogue between himself and his penis. Afterwards, he kissed her abstractedly and fell asleep. Throughout their marriage she had felt that her body had a separate sensual existence for her husband but there was something different in his split impulses now. It was as if he had split off altogether from her.

Louise turned off the light. Despite her beauty she had had a limited experience of sex; Robert had snapped her up too fast. Since then she had remained faithful to him, and now she had been married for so long she had no comparisons to make with him and his behaviour. As she curled up, phrases from her magazines rolled around her head: '*male menopause, mid-life crisis* . . .' Finally, she fell asleep.

Imogen lay in bed. Below her, machine-guns rat-a-tatted; plate-glass windows were blown to smithereens and Bruce Willis leaped across the TV screen. Imogen lay there, her eyes open. On the floor her damp clothes lay in a heap. Far away, a dog barked.

It had been a magical evening. When the badgers had gone she and Karl had walked back through the wood. It started to rain, but that only intensified their separateness from the rest of the world, boringly tucked up in front of their TVs. They drove to Beaconsfield. Sitting in the van as the houses slid past she felt like an outlaw; she felt as raffish as a gypsy, her hair plastered to her forehead. Karl bought her some chips. The man behind the counter knew her, she bought chips there after school, but she was a different person now and she smiled at him condescendingly from her adult status.

Karl drove her back to Wingham Wallace. He fiddled with the knobs on the radio – lucky knobs! – and found The Doors singing *Come on baby light my fire*. She liked it because the guitar solo went on for ever, not breaking the spell. The chip bag lay in her lap. Karl reached into it, took chips out one by one and put them into his mouth. This seemed more thrillingly personal than any amount of kissing. At the church he dropped her off. No kiss, he just ruffled her hair and said, 'Be seeing you then. Take care.'

Twenty miles away, in Clapham, Prudence lay awake. She had consumed a whole bottle of Bulgarian cabernet sauvignon but it hadn't put her to sleep. She hadn't heard from Stephen since their break-up the week before. No phone call, nothing.

Her cat, Cedric, lay on her stomach. Even at this hour, cars still swished past on the one-way system; Titchmere Road was always busy. If all the parking spaces were full, which was usually the case, anyone who wanted to stop had to double-park, forcing the traffic to slow down and squeeze past. Only the fearless dared stay parked there for long.

Stephen was not of their number. He had only visited her life, his indicators winking. For a year he had been poised, his hand on the gear-stick, ready to drive off. He hadn't wanted commitment – a ghastly but appropriate word. He hadn't bothered to search for a parking meter, let alone apply for a resident's permit.

Prudence was laughing – hard, dry hiccups. The cat rocked up and down on her stomach. She thought: all this time he's kept his engine running, the bastard. And now he's safely back in his fucking garage in Dulwich.

She wasn't laughing, she was crying. Dry, wrenching sobs. Finally, the cat could stand it no longer and jumped off the bed.

Maddy spoke into the darkness. 'My father hated me because I was different. I didn't do the things normal little girls did. I didn't try to please him.'

'He sounds a deeply conventional man,' said Erin, lying beside her. 'Nothing's going to shake him up. He lives an un-examined life and your mother colludes in that, she's got the role down to a T. Good little wifey making his dinner, help-ing him with his work.' She yawned, and nuzzled Maddy's neck. 'He'll never break out. Sad, isn't it?'

Maddy suspected she was too old to moan about her parents; it was an adolescent thing to do. But Erin encour-aged it. Besides, it drew her and Erin closer, it was a mild kind of aphrodisiac. She twined her feet around Erin's. Down in the street a car alarm wailed; in Erin's neighbourhood cars were regularly vandalised.

'I always seem to rub men up the wrong way. That's why I left Nigeria.' Maddy paused. She had told nobody, not even her sisters, what had happened. 'This man, Pierre, who ran our project, he was a pig. God, he fancied himself. He hated me because his charm didn't work on me. He was a crook. He was screwing this Ibo woman, she was the daughter of some

139

general or something, and he used to get Ibrahim, that was our driver, to take him to the local hotel to have it off with her. And some money we'd been given, for a consignment of powdered milk, he bought her an air-conditioner with it.' She paused. 'Then one day I discovered that he'd been using the workmen, who were supposed to be building our baby clinic, he'd got them to build him and his wife this veranda on the back of their house. I told my colleagues but they didn't believe me, they thought I just didn't like him. They all ganged up on me. Pierre got me sacked. I could have fought it, I suppose, but suddenly I felt too bloody exhausted.' She lay there, gazing into the blackness. Something in Africa, in the very air, had seeped into her bones. The inertia, the corruption. After a lifetime of speaking up and battling against the odds she had given up – brave, fearless Maddy. 'So I packed up and left. He's still there. Oh, I despised him all right, but I despised myself more for doing bugger all. Do you understand?'

The body in her arms had grown heavy. Erin had fallen asleep.

Three

Some things are easily sorted out. Tyres, for instance. They were sorted out by ten-thirty Monday morning and paid for in cash. A transaction was completed and Gordon – showered, though still wearing Sunday's clothes – drove along to the Dawlish Road site where Frank stood stony-faced beside a skip.

'We should've been out of here by the end of the week,' Frank said. 'More like the end of the bloody year. Bob's not here, Len's taken it into his mind not to turn up, I've got no-body to do the plastering. And what were you supposed to be doing at my place last night?'

'Look Frank, I'm sorry –'

Suddenly, Frank grinned. He was a volatile man, his moods changed at the throw of a switch. 'Just hope she was worth it.'

'It's not like that –'

'It's okay. Your secret's safe with me.' Frank turned and went into the house.

'It's not –'

'You old devil. Who'd have believed it?'

It's stupendous, the effort we make when we are trying to avoid the truth. There is something heroic about it. All that energy we expend, the excuses we create for ourselves, if we plugged them into the national grid we could light up a city with our self-delusion. What did Gordon persuade himself?

141

That April needed help of the practical nature that only he could supply. That he was only doing a job – unpaid, of course, but if you cannot bring yourself to help out a nurse what sort of human being are you? That it wouldn't take long anyway, five days maximum. That if the jobs weren't done now conditions would only get worse – that leaking connection under the sink, for instance, the water was seeping under the lino, if they waited any longer April would have wet rot to contend with. He told himself that he needed to use up some half-finished buckets of trade emulsion – yes, he even told himself that. He told himself he was doing nothing wrong.

He also told himself, edging nearer danger, that April had been treated so badly by her brute of a boyfriend – and indeed by the boyfriend who had preceded him – that she deserved a little kindness to restore her faith in the male sex. Her father had deserted her; Gordon himself had been deserted by his daughters through the natural process of their growing-up. The lives of two of them were virtually incomprehensible to him and even Louise, the closest to him emotionally, was geographically distant and was sealed into a lifestyle that made him feel clumsy and inadequate. After his visits to her he felt exhausted, as if he had had to spend a day in the wrong, tightly fitting clothes.

Edging into even more dangerous territory, he told himself that it was invigorating to develop a friendship with somebody who liked him for himself, or who seemed to; someone in whose company he felt utterly himself, yet somehow renewed – a better Gordon, whom he himself recognised but nobody else seemed to. What an adventure: to be admitted into somebody else's life, to start afresh with somebody who laughed at his jokes, even for the limited period – five days, a week, maximum – that he told himself it would take.

He told himself this, not at home – for some reason he didn't want to think about April when Dorothy was in the room – but when he was in the car, driving from one job to another. He was supposed to be taking it easy, he was for-

142

bidden to lift any heavy weights, and this gave him the excuse never to stay anywhere long. Besides, he was restless and could only feel at ease when he was alone in the traffic.

And, of course, when he switched off his phone nobody knew where he was. The boss of a building firm is always somewhere else. On the road, out and about. That is what they're like, isn't it?

'Where is he?' Dorothy asked Frank on the phone. It was Wednesday.

'He's with Jeremy Dawson, I reckon.' Dawson and Associates were the architects at Elephant and Castle.

'I've rung them. I've been trying to get hold of him all day.'

'Said he had some errands to run. You know Gordon.'

'I've got to talk to him about the planning permission refusal. I've had the Simmondses on the phone all morning.'

'Haven't seen him all day. Maybe he's gone to Sidcup.' There was a timber yard there.

'I spoke to Mavis. He hasn't been.'

'I'm sure he's fine.'

Later, when he looked back on it, that week had the weightlessness of a spell. Someone else had set it in motion; he floated helplessly, blown like thistle-down by a powerful force. He felt disconnected from the outside world, from the clamouring tasks and responsibilities, as if he were sealed away in hospital, but this time without the pain.

The sun shone, warm for November. It glowed above the turreted roof-tops of the shops opposite; it blessed him as he stroked the creamy-yellow paint onto April's walls. There was a fairy-tale innocence about those days. In the next room April lay sleeping. She was working nights, that week, and had given him the key. He unlocked the door to find her tucked up in bed, her uniform hung over the chair like the empty skin of a chrysalis. During the hours of darkness,

143

when he had slept, she had guarded a wardful of souls and dreamed about her father. She was Gordon's own daughter, polished brown, made strange and strangely familiar, returned to him.

That was how he felt about her; that was allowed, wasn't it? That was why he had tiptoed into her bedroom to check if she was still breathing, to see the miracle of her, as he had tiptoed into his daughters' rooms when they were little. April's possessions, as she lay there unconscious of them, grew dear to him – her Van Gogh poster, her fluffy toys, the blue-glass bottles she had brought back from a holiday in Venice. (She had gone there on a weekend package with a group of Geordies who had drunk themselves into a stupor. She said, '*I wish I'd been in love.*') In the bathroom her tights lay over the towel-rail; in the kitchen her jars, filled with tea-bags and sugar, each according to its label, brought tears to his eyes.

The lounge, on the other hand, was stripped of her personality. He had moved the furniture into the middle of the room and covered it with dust-sheets. It smelled of paint, the aroma of his working life, and of renewal. Her past had been stripped away like the blistered gloss on the window-frames. He had filled the cracks; he was painting her a bright new future where anything was possible, creamy-yellow emulsion (Hint of Buttercup) over the terracotta of her former life.

It was Thursday morning. There was only one wall left to paint. Gordon dipped his brush into the pot. His hand moved, it had a life of its own. It wrote I LOVE YOU.

Gordon gazed at the letters. They were large and lopsided, trailing off at the end. A drop slid down from the O, down the wall to the skirting-board. Outside, a bus passed. The sounds in the street were suddenly distinct – a shout of laughter, the rattle of a delivery to the off-licence nearby. He stood there weightlessly, hearing the life of the city beyond the street, beyond the streets beyond. In the room he heard the floorboards sighing, or maybe the sound came from within his own body.

Gordon plunged his brush into the paint-pot. When April

woke up – the creak of the bedroom door, the flush of the toilet – when she came into the room the words had long since
been obliterated.

'Where have you been all day?'

'Just out and about.'

'There're about ten messages here. If you'd phoned in I
could have dealt with them.'

'I'm sorry, love. The traffic was terrible.'

'Frank's livid. You were supposed to meet the surveyor at
three.'

'I was?'

'Where *were* you?'

'Went down the Tottenham Court Road. Looked at some
office systems. You said that printer's driving you round the
bend.'

'Are you all right, Gordon? Is anything the matter?'

'I'm fine.'

On Friday afternoon Gordon had finished. The room looked
larger and more gracious. Classy, they agreed. April helped
him rearrange the furniture.

'It looks great,' she said. 'Ever thought of taking it up
professionally?'

He wiped his hands on his overalls. 'Someone did suggest
it once. I said I'd stick with the brain surgery.'

She laughed, and pointed to the window. 'You've showed
me up. Have to get new curtains now. Don't those look
grungy?'

'There's this bloke I know, can get them for you at cost –'

'Gordon! You've done enough. Aren't they saying things at
work?'

He looked up at the ceiling. 'There's a bit there I've
missed –'

'Stop it!' She took his arm. 'Sit down.'

145

She went into the kitchen and came back with a bottle and two glasses.

'It's only sparkling Australian,' she said.

'They're the worst, the sparkling ones. You stay away from them.'

She chuckled. He loved her chuckle, it was deep and surprisingly rude. He untwisted the wire and pushed out the cork with his thumbs.

They drank. The sun, a red disk, slid below the buildings opposite. Down in the street the rush-hour traffic swelled murmurously. Over decades of Friday afternoons he had fought his way through it, alternately blaring his horn or lavishly beckoning out cars from the side streets – as a driver he had always had an emotional relationship with the other vehicles on the road. He had struggled home to Purley, exhausted, only to gather himself together at seven a.m. on Monday morning to start the whole thing again.

'I'm dying for a cigarette,' she said.

'Ssh.'

'How long's it going to last?' she asked.

He looked at her. She wore a navy-blue tracksuit. In the past, he hadn't found tracksuits appealing. 'That's up to you,' he replied.

'It's up to both of us.'

Did she mean the smoking? She drained her glass, got up and went to the window. 'I look at people sometimes,' she said. 'Out there, I look at them and think – don't they know what's going on inside them, what a miracle it is? It doesn't matter what an idiot someone is, how stupid or selfish, still their bodies go on digesting, pumping . . . the aortic valves, the gut, the lungs, working like the clappers. However wicked we are, our bodies still go on sterilising and cleaning, balancing fluids and electrolytes, defending us from infection . . . however bad we've been our bodies will always forgive us . . . Heart-breaking, isn't it?' She turned round. 'You look after yourself, see?'

He picked up his jacket. She put her arms around him and

hugged him, her cheek pressed against his. And then somehow their heads turned and they were kissing. How soft her lips were, how sweet the taste of her tongue! He felt a dam unblocking. The water gushed through, flooding him.

They disentangled themselves. He was trembling.

'Think I'd better go,' he said. He picked up his things and left.

That weekend the weather changed. The wind swung to the north, the temperature plummeted. Sleet blew across the streets, sending people scuttling for shelter. Trains were delayed, leaving passengers stamping their feet on station platforms. Freezing fog brought the M1 to a standstill. Torrential rain caused chaos in Southern Europe, and out in the Gulf of Mexico a hurricane tore across the Windward Isles, leaving behind a trail of wreckage. Yet New York was enjoying its warmest November since records began. The experts were baffled. As the century drew to its close, nature flexed herself and made the earth tremble.

Outside The Birches, the garden was frozen as if the gear of the past had locked and life would never get started again. Gordon moved slowly around the house. It was Saturday. Dorothy was away, visiting an aged aunt who had broken her hip. Gordon gazed at the dishwasher but he hadn't the energy to open it and put in his dirty plates. The paper lay unread, its Saturday supplements still folded within it. The house felt chilly. He wandered around, putting his hand on the radiators. Was April's central heating working all right? He had forgotten to bleed her rads.

He gazed out at the houses opposite – detached, half-timbered. Their inhabitants were supposed to be familiar to him – they were his neighbours, for God's sake. The Bosworths, who had lived there as long as he had; the Dorrells, whose son used to borrow his jump-leads to start his car. For over twenty years Gordon had lived there and yet time seemed to have telescoped; his street was as alien as

147

when he had first arrived.

He stood on the upstairs landing, looking into the girls' bedrooms. His wife had long ago taken over Prudence's, which faced south, and had installed her sewing machine there. Heaps of washing were stacked on the ironing board; Dorothy always put off the ironing until there was something good on the radio. The other two rooms had long ago lost all traces of their occupants. It was as if his daughters had never existed. Their childhood seemed to have passed in a flash; they had simply perched in this house like migrating birds.

He went downstairs. He thought: it happens all the time. Married man falls for younger woman. The papers are full of it. However, this description didn't fit him. What he felt was more complicated than that, more profound. It was as if he had lived his life in monochrome and now, suddenly, he was experiencing colour. Had he felt like this long ago, when he had first met Dorothy? He couldn't remember it. His body ached with desire – yes, he could admit it. But it was more than lust. It was as if a door had opened and out there, beyond it, the world was sunnier and more intense. If he surrendered himself up and stepped through the door, then anything was possible.

Oh, it was more than that, he hadn't the words for it. He was unused to thinking like this; by the evening he felt as if he had been heaving sacks of cement all day. Dorothy was staying away overnight. He was alone. He didn't put on the TV; it seemed too brash an intrusion, Anthea Turner yacking at him. He chewed some spearmint gum. April had given him a packet to help him stop smoking. He felt like a gum-chewing imposter in his own home. He put on a CD – a Mozart piano concerto that Prudence had given him. Most of his collection consisted of Broadway hits. Nowadays it was Mozart, however, who spoke to his heart.

Rubbing his neck – it ached from painting April's ceiling – Gordon pulled open a cupboard and took out the photo albums. He opened one. Dorothy stood on the steps of their first flat – how many years ago? Nearly half a century. She

148

held the baby Louise in her arms. He closed the album and opened another. He looked at a holiday snapshot of his three daughters. Wearing their swimsuits, they sat around the table outside the caravan. They gazed at the camera warily as if, all those years ago, they already suspected him of one day betraying them.

He closed the book. He had done nothing yet – just told some harmless lies and concocted some small alibis. Already, however, his soul had left this house. Closed in their plastic albums, his children could sense that. Even the furniture looked accusing. The street lamp shone into the room – he hadn't drawn the curtains and made the room cosy, he hadn't Dorothy's home-making instincts. The place felt unlived-in. He was a lone man, roaming through rooms that no longer belonged to him. Every bone in his body ached for April; he longed to pick up the phone and speak to her. He knew he must resist the temptation. He must forget about her and remove her from his life.

Outside, the land was locked into its own paralysis. Indoors, Gordon, who didn't know how to get through the evening, sat at his desk and toyed with his paperwork. He had some inner prompting to put his things in order, as a man does when he has been told he is going to die.

Out beyond Beaconsfield the hills were dusted with white. Robert, driving in his BMW, skidded on some ice and nearly ended up in a ditch, like the badger. Imogen stayed in her bedroom copying out her friend Sandra's notes on *Cold Comfort Farm*. It was the only set book she liked; in general she found her A levels a struggle. Jamie had sailed through his, which of course only made it worse. It wasn't fair, him being tall and blond whilst she was stunted and dark. If she didn't shave them, her legs would be practically as hairy as her father's. Could Karl really find her attractive? For the twentieth time she opened her *Student's Guide to the Ancient World* and took out the photo. Karl, his eyebrows raised, stared at her. Depending on her mood, his expression changed. Sometimes he looked at her with such ardency that her bowels melted. Sometimes he looked as if he had seen a ghost.

She drew the photo to her and kissed it. His mouth opened against hers, his breathing quickened. She ran her finger along his stubbly cheek. She replayed the moment when his hand had reached into her lap for a chip. At the time she had sat there rigidly, waiting for something else to happen. Now, faint with desire, she could make him do exactly what she wanted.

On Monday it was still bitterly cold. Gordon got up at seven, as usual. He ate breakfast with his wife – cornflakes and toast, no more fry-ups. He went to work. He drove a new plasterer over to Orpington to put in a day on a flat conversion. He picked up some brochures for fitted kitchens and delivered them to Frank, who made some suggestive remarks at his expense. He dropped in on Farleigh Road, where a lone chippie worked on a job that should have been finished weeks before.

His phone rang. It was Mrs Malik. She asked after his health and then said that she was worried about her pipes bursting. It gave him a jolt to hear her voice – the last voice he had heard before the trap-door had opened and he had been flooded with light. As she twittered down the phone – she was one of his more anxious customers – he felt a wave of fondness for her.

The afternoon dragged by. Gordon willed it to end. On the other hand, playing for time, he urged it to go on for ever. He told himself that it was a normal Monday. After work he would go home to his wife, eat a meal, put his feet up. Those who worked with him noticed no difference. He was the same old Gordon – brisk, fidgety, jokey. None of them noticed – why should they? – when at four-thirty he made his decision.

He was standing on a landing, halfway up the stairs in the house they were renovating in Dawlish Road. Down in the basement there was the sound of hammering. Gordon took out his phone and pressed his home number.

Dorothy answered. 'Hello?'

Gordon stood there, poised. He could climb the stairs or descend them. Now or never; he had the choice. Behind him, plastic sheeting flapped in the empty window-frame.

He said: 'Never guess who I bumped into. This bloke Graham, same regiment as me – you know, up at Nottingham.' Behind him the plastic slapped as if it were trying to attract his attention. 'So he's in London for the night and he said why don't him and me go out for a drink, maybe a bite to eat. That okay?'

Dorothy said that was fine. He switched off the phone and went downstairs to his car.

April was working the day shift that week. At six-thirty she left the Cardiac Unit, buttoning up her coat. She stepped out of the hospital lobby and paused, looking up at the sky. She wound a red scarf around her neck.

Gordon drove up to her, stopped the car and opened the door. She looked at him. Wordlessly she climbed in. He drove her home to Brixton. Still they didn't speak. They climbed the stairs to her flat – she picked up her mail on the way – and went into the bedroom. She switched on the light and sat on the bed.

'You shouldn't be here,' she said.

He nodded. She sloughed off her coat. She raised her arms like a child and he pulled off her sweater. Beneath it she wore her uniform. He undid the buttons at her neck. She unbuckled her belt. One by one the letters slid off the bed. She sat there, gazing at them scattered on the carpet.

She raised her head and frowned, searching his face. He put his arms around her and pulled her to him.

151

Four

It was mid-December, four weeks since Prudence had seen Stephen or heard his voice. Her weak, vacillating lover had finally taken a decision and stuck with it. At times she could admire him for this. If his pain at their separation – amputation seemed a better description – were anything like hers, then he was demonstrating a remarkable strength of character. On the other hand, she presumed that it was easier for him: he had returned to a wife and children whom he loved, and whom he had never left in the first place. Maybe – horrible thought – he was forgetting her. The water of his family life had risen up and closed over the past. She was starting to realise that she, too, must get on with her life without him. She must stop these one-way conversations with him that still carried on in her head. *Can you believe what Alan said to me in the marketing meeting? What do you think about this Princess Di business?* She longed to know if he had found another job but there was nobody she could ask. His removal, not only from her life but from Beveridge and Bunyan, meant that he had disappeared from the lives of the few remaining colleagues at the office with whom he had been close. She hadn't met any of his other friends, she had been kept secret, so she couldn't keep track of him through them. She had been cut off from him as if he had died.

She had told her sisters what had happened – reluctantly, in the case of Maddy, because she knew that Maddy had never liked Stephen and though her sister wasn't the type to say *I told you so*, she wasn't a crowing sort of person, the

152

confirmation of her suspicions about Stephen, that he was simply a philanderer, seemed crudely simplistic and caused Prudence to rush to his defence and say that it was she herself who had broken it off. 'He only honoured my decision,' she had said. Maddy sometimes made her talk pompously.

She tried to get on with her life. Britain was full of women like herself, tender episodes in the lives of men who had returned to their families. Oh, but she missed him! The day of the party she put on the black slip she had bought for their night of pleasure. She stood in the bedroom, stroking her silky flanks. She remembered how that night had ended: not with love, but with a dash to hospital to sit beside her father's bed in Intensive Care. Later, this had struck her as a premonition.

Maddy didn't like parties. *Who are all these people?* she would think. *What are they doing here?* What was she doing here? What was the point of standing there, wearing shoes that hurt, being shouted at by somebody who didn't have the slightest interest in her and whom she couldn't hear anyway? They laughed uproariously at jokes whose punchline she couldn't catch. They looked over her shoulder. Years of living abroad had set her apart from English people, whose preoccupations seemed parochial. Sometimes they politely asked her about herself but they had never heard of the places she had been, and even if they had they soon got bored anyway. She felt inadequate and yet prickly. She wanted to go home. She never felt that she was wearing the right clothes and the cigarette smoke made her eyes water. Besides, there was only so much orange juice she could get down before she started to feel sick.

So it was with some reluctance that she accompanied Erin to the editorial department party at Unimedia House. She went simply because Erin suggested it and she was so pleased to be asked that she agreed. She was also mildly curious to see where her sister worked. Maddy was no bookreader, she had little knowledge of Prudence's job. In fact, she realised with shame, she had only once visited the old premises in Bloomsbury. But now she was in love with a novelist she found herself drawn to the place, as a woman who has fallen in love with an Arsenal supporter suddenly wants to go to a football match. However, when she arrived at the building – a huge, modern place – she felt chastened that it was her love for Erin rather than for her sister which had prompted her to come.

How impressive Prudence was! She wore an unfamiliar black dress – almost slinky, in fact – with gold stuff around the neck. She was the hostess, smiling and confident, a Prudence that Maddy had never seen. Maddy's heart swelled with pride. Her sister, in charge of all these people! Fifty of them, at least. They looked intimidating. Prudence climbed onto a platform and tapped her glass for silence. Maddy, just for a moment, wished that her parents were here. In some sense Erin had been right: she had always felt intellectually inferior to her sister. But Erin was an only child; she had no understanding of sisterly love, the thickness of its brew and the complex feelings that rose to the surface when it was stirred.

'Welcome, everybody, to our Christmas party!' Prudence's voice rang out, clear and confident. Like all good professionals, she looked as if she were enjoying herself. 'It's been a year of upheaval and change – new premises, new owners. B&B has been dragged, somewhat protestingly, into the brave new world of publishing but I'm thrilled to be leading our editorial team and, with Unimedia back-up, we've had our most successful Frankfurt ever . . .'

Next to Maddy, people stirred. She turned. A bearded man stood at the back of the room, swaying. He wore a raincoat; he must have just come through the door. Even at this distance Maddy could see that he was drunk.

'And we have a marvellous spring list,' said Prudence. 'Some of our favourite writers are here tonight – Corey Deacon, author of *I Can't Get Enough – Feminism and Pasta in the Millennium . . .'*

It was Stephen. Maddy recognised him now.

'. . . Stanley Dibbs, author of the wildly successful Detective Patel series . . . Erin Fox, whose first novel *Playing with Fire* is one of our leading fiction titles –' She saw Stephen. 'So fill up your glasses and have a wonderful evening –'

'And don't let anything spoil your fun!' Stephen bellowed.

Maddy pushed her way through the crowd and grabbed his arm. 'Stephen, shut up!'

He pulled away. 'After all, what do thirty redundancies matter? We're only people!'

'Let's go,' muttered Maddy.

'Our children asking us *Daddy, why aren't you going to work today?*' he shouted. 'What's a bit of human misery when it comes to the bottom line?'

Someone tittered. Prudence hurried over. Together with Maddy she half-pushed Stephen out of the room and down the corridor. He stumbled ahead, like a clockwork toy. Prudence opened her office and pulled him in.

On the carpet was heaped a pile of belongings – a suitcase, a hold-all, some bulging carrier bags.

Prudence stared. 'What's happened?'

'I've left her,' he said.

'What?'

'I did it. I left Kaatya.'

'What about your kids?' demanded Maddy.

He sank to the floor as if his strings had snapped. He started shuddering. Prudence knelt beside him.

'Can I get you anything?' she asked. 'Coffee? Water?'

'I feel like a murderer,' he said. 'Their faces, Pru . . . when I was leaving . . . Pieter turned away and went up to his room . . . Dirk just stood there looking at me, tears running down his face . . .'

'You're making her feel really great,' said Maddy.

He raised his head and looked at Prudence. His hair was sandy but his beard was a startling ginger colour; it looked as

155

if he had dipped his chin in blood. 'Have you got room for me?'

'Of course,' said Prudence, stroking his head.

'A drunk, a murderer . . . Christ, I really put the kibosh on your party, didn't I . . . Are you sure you want me?'

'Of course I want you,' she said. 'Isn't that the point of all this?'

She leaned down and kissed him. Maddy got up and left them to it. She closed the door behind her. Erin was waiting in the corridor.

Maddy said: 'And I used to think my sister was intelligent.'

'Sorry,' said Stephen. 'I seem to have spread.' He gathered together the newspapers.

Prudence had come in from work. It was two days later. Stephen, lulled by the inertia of the unemployed and the fumes of her gas-effect fire, had been dozing in the armchair.

She picked up the Appointments page and looked at it. 'Why do all the jobs seem to be for commis chefs?'

'And typists with Windows.'

'As opposed to doors. You don't have computer skills, do you?'

He shook his head. 'My secretaries did all that stuff.'

She sat down. 'There must be something.'

'Are you glad I barged into your lovely ordered life?'

'It wasn't lovely,' she said, 'without you in it.'

'Leaving the loo seat up and getting in your way?'

She stroked his leg. Of course she was glad – the word was pitifully inadequate. All day she felt ill with happiness. So far, however, there was a feeling of unreality about it. Despite the physical evidence of his occupation – his hold-all stuffed into her wardrobe, his boxer shorts stuffed into her dirty-linen basket – despite the invigorating air of masculine occupation, she couldn't believe he was really staying. When she opened her door she expected to find the flat empty and a '1' on her answerphone.

'I want you to be here,' she said. 'I want us to be a real couple, like other people.' She rubbed her cheek against his – he had shaved off his beard, thank God, and his skin felt familiar again. 'Listen, I'm going to my parents this Sunday. Come with me. That's real enough for anybody.'

If it was strange, having Stephen living in her flat, it was even stranger taking him home. So accustomed was she to keeping him secret that she couldn't slot the two sides of her life together. How would he behave? She had so seldom been with him on any social occasion that she felt they were starting from scratch – the most treacherous of beginnings, under the beady eyes of her family.

Even Maddy was there – she had dropped by to borrow the lawn-mower and had been persuaded to stay to lunch. Maddy was a stranger to discretion. Would she blurt out about his drunken behaviour during the week? It took Prudence by surprise, how much she wanted her parents to like him.

They were in the hallway. Louise's family was already there. She introduced Stephen to them. Stephen looked around. 'So this is where you grew up.'

'The Purley Queens,' said Robert. 'No man was safe.'

Prudence pointed out of the back window. 'That's our caravan. We used to play in there. Till Lou started to take her boyfriends into it and bribed us to stay away.'

'She never took *me* in,' said Robert.

'You wouldn't have liked it,' Louise replied. 'There were spiders.'

As they stood there, the door of the caravan opened. Gordon stepped out. He made his way across the garden, towards the house.

'What on earth's he doing in there?' asked Louise.

They went into the lounge. Dorothy went into the kitchen. Gordon came in.

'What were you doing?' she hissed. 'I've been looking for

157

you everywhere.'

'Just tidying up,' he said.

'Tidying up? They're here.'

Gordon, who had simply been sitting in the caravan staring at its walls, who had been doing nothing, picked up the tray of drinks. 'These going in?'

Meanwhile, in the lounge, Prudence whispered to the others: 'Don't let on that, well, Stephen's married.'

'Course not,' said Louise.

'They'll disapprove. *I* disapproved. Until it happened to me.'

Jamie said: 'Everyone's doing it anyway.'

'Jamie!' said Louise. 'Don't be so cynical.'

Gordon came in and put down the tray. He shook Stephen's hand.

'Gosh, Grandad,' said Imogen. 'You've got so thin!'

Dorothy said: 'He's not been looking after himself. The doctor warned us. I'm worried about him.'

'How do you feel?' Louise asked her father.

'I'm fine,' he said.

'He's never here,' said Dorothy. 'He promised he wouldn't, but he's worse than ever.'

Robert grinned. 'Up to your old tricks, Gordon?'

'I never see him from morning to night,' said Dorothy.

Gordon uncorked the wine bottle. 'I've told her – we're short-staffed at present. I'm three labourers short, my best chippie's off sick –'

'Leave it to Frank,' said Dorothy. 'He'll sort it out.'

'And my chief plasterer seems to have buggered off completely.' He turned to the teenagers. 'Excuse my language.'

'He the one with the love nest?' asked Robert.

Dorothy turned to Stephen. 'He's got these two families who don't know about each other. One in Tufnell Park and the other in Crouch End.'

'The energy of the man!' said Robert. 'One has to admire it.'

Prudence said: 'Dad's lads have very complicated love

158

lives. Mum's their mother confessor.'

Gordon passed Robert a glass of wine. 'Hope it meets with your approval,' he said. 'New Zealand, on your recommendation.'

'Anyway,' said Dorothy, 'I've decided that he needs a proper holiday, so I've got these brochures.' She picked them up from the side table. 'We thought we'd go away for Christmas. It's not too late for some of them.'

Prudence took the brochures. 'Where're you going to go? Somewhere hot?'

'We thought Bermuda,' said Dorothy.

'How lovely!' said Louise.

'But Dad,' said Maddy, 'it's full of blacks.'

'Maddy!' said Dorothy.

Maddy turned to Stephen. 'Our father calls Africa *Wogland*.'

'He's only winding you up,' said Prudence.

Imogen put her arm round her grandfather. 'I think you're lovely. It's just that you probably don't know any. I don't either, there's none at my school.'

Robert laughed. 'Beaconsfield's not known for its ethnic diversity.'

Louise took the brochure. 'It looks wonderful.'

'We've booked this one.' Dorothy pointed. 'Look, you have your own little hut.'

'Thatched and everything,' said Louise. 'How romantic! Like a second honeymoon.'

Gordon remained silent. Prudence looked at him. How pale he looked, pale and shrunken, in the large armchair. 'It looks wonderful, Dad. Just what you need.'

'We're flying out on Christmas Eve,' said Dorothy.

'So you won't be having Christmas with us,' said Louise.

'Lucky sods!'

'Jamie!'

Gordon fingered his earlobe. His silence was like a black hole, a vacuum sucking them in. Prudence thought: he's more ill than he admits, but then he never admits anything.

159

Gordon rallied. He patted Imogen's knee as she sat beside him. 'You're looking very pretty, Immy.'

'She's madly in love,' said Louise.

Imogen stiffened.

'How lovely!' said Dorothy. 'Who is he?'

'Her horse,' Louise answered.

Imogen relaxed.

Maddy, who was not attending, gazed around the lounge. She hadn't set foot in The Birches for a long time. The old claustrophobia gripped her. Purley wasn't just a suburb, it was a state of mind. There was no beginning to it and no end. One street led to another, houses and houses and more houses, big houses with their big gardens. What could people possibly do in all those rooms? Didn't they ever want to break out into the world?

She looked at her father. She thought: when he dies, what can he boast? I lived in Purley.

She longed to be home with Erin. She longed to be in their bed, the most adventurous place on earth.

Lunch was over. Jamie had escaped to the caravan. He sat there, eyes closed, inhaling on a joint.

Back in the lounge they were drinking coffee. 'That was delicious, Dorothy,' said Stephen.

'Lou thinks I married her for her gorgeous legs,' joked Robert. 'In fact it was for her mother's roast potatoes.'

Dorothy smiled. She thought how rare it was for them all to be gathered together like this in the companionable inertia of a Sunday afternoon. The presence of an outsider, Stephen, gave her family a solidity that it hadn't possessed for years. She looked at Prudence, who was telling him about the time when they had all had a craze for Cluedo. Prudence's cheeks were flushed; her brown hair, loose around her shoulders, shone. Today she looked the most beautiful of them all. Dorothy thought: how invigorating it must be to have plenty of sex. She blushed. Stephen stood up.

160

'Would you mind if I used your phone?'

Dorothy told him there was one upstairs. Prudence watched him leave.

Dorothy refilled her daughter's cup. 'He's very nice. You've kept him very quiet.'

'He was my boss,' said Prudence. 'It was kind of awkward.'

'Then she got his job,' said Louise.

'I think it's amazing he's even speaking to you,' said Robert. 'I wouldn't.'

It would suddenly hit Stephen, the need to speak to his sons. His insides would buckle as if he had been punched in the gut. He remembered when he was a new boy at Bryanston being suddenly winded by homesickness. It was like that but worse, much worse.

He had to check that Dirk and Pieter were still speaking to him, that they were still alive. He had to hear their voices. He kept picturing the house falling down or going up in flames. Had Kaatya bolted the back door and screwed the security locks right in? What if the pilot light went out in the boiler: would she remember to push down that lever thing that stopped the whole thing blowing up when she relit it? And what about all those bloody candles she put everywhere? He pictured his sons – pale, solemn, alone in a world that throbbed with danger. He should be there protecting them. He should be keeping them safe. It was so unnatural to be wrenched away from them; it felt as if nature had been pulled inside out.

He couldn't tell Prudence, of course. It would upset her and make her think he was unhappy. He wasn't unhappy, he was just pining for his sons. Usually he phoned when they got home from school and Prudence was still at work. He needed to be reassured by their voices, however wary – cool, even – they had been during this past week. He needed to re-assure them that he was still there, he hadn't gone far. That he loved them. That none of this was due to them, it was

161

between himself and their mother. Grown-ups changed; sometimes they couldn't live together any more – all that.

He never got this far. He had tried to explain on that nightmarish evening when he'd left home, but they had refused to listen. Now, when he phoned, he just talked about safe, normal things – how was their day? How was Dirk's project going? He felt that he was dabbing ointment, diffidently, on their flinching skin.

Kaatya, to do her justice, always put them on the phone. *'Oh, it's you,'* she said, sounding somehow more foreign. He had always noticed her accent on the phone but now it seemed more pronounced, as if they were separated by national as well as emotional barriers. Then she would yell for the boys. *'It's your father!'* she said, as if she had found some cat sick on the carpet.

Stephen sat on the bed upstairs. He was in Prudence's parents' room. How large and smug the bed was! They had been married for over forty years; they had managed it.

'Hi, Dirk, how are you? How was football yesterday? – What? Which one? Ah, *Goldfinger*, that's a good one, isn't it ... No, you'd better get back to it – Is Pieter watching it too? ... Ah ... Give him my love, then – I'll talk to you tomorrow.'

Down in the lounge Prudence said: 'Nearly two months. It's terrible to see that happening to a man. He's desperate for anything, anything at all. He'll take any sort of job. Boring, dirty, mindless.'

'Why doesn't he work for Grandad?' said Imogen.

There was a silence. They stared at her.

She turned to Gordon. 'You said you were short of people. Stephen could work for you.'

Footsteps descended the stairs. Stephen came into the room. They gazed at him.

Prudence, yawning, stood in her dressing-gown buttering

slices of bread. It was seven o'clock. She laid slabs of cheese on the bread and pressed down the top slice. Stephen came into the kitchen. He was dressed in his jeans and a sweater.

'I haven't got up this early since rugby practice,' he said.

She took out a Thermos. 'Look what I've got. Belonged to my parents.'

'Ah, for me tea,' he said in a Yorkshire accent.

'After your manly toil.'

'Come here, woman.' He slid his hand under her dressing-gown. 'Feel these horny hands.'

'They're not horny yet.'

'Ah, but they will be,' he leered.

She wrapped up his sandwiches. 'Thou'll be late for thy bus.'

Stephen's experience of builders was limited to those he had employed in the past. In his memory, that meant men whose unexplained absences alternated with long periods spent drinking tea and explaining the situation in Northern Ireland to his flatmates or, in the case of Kaatya, telling her about their aches and pains and sampling her homeopathic remedies. Builders hung around. That was their job. Wolf-whistling at passing girls, they waited for hours for their boss to deliver a length of coving. An hour after they arrived they knocked off for lunch, and on Friday afternoons they disappeared altogether to the pub.

In his experience it was he himself who did all the work. Clearing up the place before they arrived, rushing to the shops to buy them sugar for their tea and queuing in the bank to get them out cash so they could swindle the Inland Revenue. Their tools broke; he would spend hours searching the house for masonry drill attachments and extension leads. He would field phone calls from their girlfriends when they were up ladders and finally rick his back by trying to push-start their hopeless, untaxed vans.

How wrong he was. My God, how wrong. That first morn-

163

ing he was sent to a house in Kennington which was being renovated. He met Frank, a quick-tempered man with a high complexion, who soon left him alone with a young Ulsterman called Eamonn, who was built like a bull and who lifted sacks of cement with humiliating ease. Though it was bitterly cold Eamonn wore a singlet. Shiny with sweat, he heaved sacks of rubble down the stairs and loaded them onto a wheelbarrow. Outside, a plank was propped against a skip. Eamonn took this at a run, tipping the sacks in and backing off in a cloud of dust.

He treated Stephen with benign contempt, as if he were re-tarded. 'Not done this before, have you?' he said, taking the shovel from him and demonstrating how to mix sand and ce-ment, folding them into the puddle of water like a chef fold-ing a sauce. Stephen had never worked so hard in his life. As the hours dragged on he felt like a beast of burden. His mind, far from being freed by such toil, went leaden. All he registered were the jolting stairs as he trudged up and down, bent double. Eamonn spoke little too. He seemed incurious that this middle-aged man, so obviously unfit, should have joined him as an apprentice.

By mid-morning Stephen was exhausted. His back ached; his hands were blistered. When he straightened up, pain shot down unfamiliar muscles at the back of his calves. He sat down heavily on the stairs, wiping his nose.

Stephen took out a pack of cigarettes. 'Fancy a gasper?'

Eamonn shook his head. 'Know what that does to your lungs?'

Stephen put the packet back in his pocket and unstoppered his Thermos. Eamonn took out a plastic bottle.

'What's that?' asked Stephen.

Eamonn showed him the label. 'Sparkling water with a hint of mango.'

'Goodness.'

'Personally, I prefer the pomegranate,' said Eamonn.

In the following silence Frank returned.

'Gordon been in?' he asked.

164

They shook their heads.

'If he comes, tell him I've gone to Sutton.'

Stephen had been dreading meeting Gordon. It embarrassed him to be working for his girlfriend's father, particularly as he was proving so incompetent. He was too inept, too unfit. He was determined to make a go of it, for Prudence's sake as well as his own, but he wanted to avoid his boss until he had more fully mastered his craft. For this reason he was relieved that Gordon didn't show up that Monday. Or, indeed, the next day. In fact, during that week Gordon hardly showed up at all.

It was April's day off. Outside it was already dusk. In the fog, the street lamps glowed smudgily. Christmas lights chased themselves around the shop windows.

Gordon and April lay in each other's arms, naked under her duvet. 'It's all wham-bam-look-at-me, aren't I a stud, where's my medal?' April said.

'Would I get a consolation prize?' asked Gordon.

'You're lovely . . .' She stroked him. 'You're kind and caring, you're not trying to prove anything.'

'If I did, I'd probably have another heart attack.'

She chuckled. 'And you're cuddly . . .'

'And I've got a lovely bald patch . . .'

'And sweet little hairs coming out of your ears.'

'All the better to hear you with. Any more?'

'No, I've finished now.'

He kissed her broad forehead. 'You're a miracle to me, know that? My April, my spring blossom . . . I want to take you places and teach you things, I want to take you to Paris.'

'That's an improvement on Neasden.'

He whistled 'April in Paris'.

'What's that?' she asked.

'I'll teach you . . . oh, my love, what do you see in me, apart from my sophisticated and experienced lovemaking . . .'

'Your extensive repertoire of old songs . . .'

165

'My plumbing skills?'

'Search me.' She took his hand and moved it down her belly. Her pubic hair was enchantingly neat, as if she kept it clipped. Wiry little whorls of hair that just covered the mound. His fingers smelled of her – a moist, musky smell that made him dizzy. Sometimes, back home, he pressed his fingertips against his nostrils, breathing her in. He inhaled her until he felt faint.

She rolled on top of him and sat up, straddling him. He touched her nipples; they were small and dark, puckered like currants. She liked manhandling him in bed, pulling him this way and that, telling him with her body what she wanted. He was unused to this – he was unused to any of this. He'd been young when he had met his wife and had had little experience of women.

She gazed down, seriously, into his face. 'I love you because you're a decent, kind man and you make me laugh.' She traced his nose with her finger. 'Because I trust you and you make me feel safe. And you stayed with me when I needed you. No bloke's ever done that.'

'Doesn't sound too exciting.'

'Oh, it's exciting all right. Believe me.'

They got up and had a bath together. This was something else he had never done before. April was voluptuous; it was a tight fit. He slotted his legs around hers. He never ceased to marvel at the beauty of her skin, the darkness of it pressed against his pallid flesh. She soaped him tenderly. Her expression was intent – impersonal, even; it reminded him of Louise when she had been playing with her dolls.

Dizzied with love, he gazed at April. The light shone on her hair. Oiled and wiry, it was scraped off her face and tied with an elastic band threaded with plastic daisies. He had never seen it loose. Even in her most abandoned moments it stayed fixed, like sculpture. He gazed at her lips, beaded with moisture. He thought: in five minutes I'm going to have to get up and go home. He felt ill – the familiar, sour guilt, scouring out his stomach.

166

He climbed out of the bath. She climbed out. They rubbed each other dry.

'What's she like, Gordon?'

He paused. 'All my life, she's been a part of it. We're friends, old friends. She's my *wife*.'

'But what's she like? I've only seen her once. I want to know about her.'

Gordon went into the bedroom. 'I don't want to think about that.'

'Please.' She followed him in.

He sat down heavily on the bed. 'It's like I'm in this boat, and I've pushed off from the shore . . . And there's this person there, waving and shouting but I can't hear the words . . . That's her. That's the truth of it.' He pulled on his socks. 'I can't help it, April. I've gone from there. I'm here with you. I felt – my life was ending. But it's only just started.' He stood up and pulled on his shorts. 'All the clichés – moon in June – all the songs – they're true, aren't they? All those songs I've been whistling and I never knew why.' He looked at her. 'You feel that, too?'

She nodded.

It was Friday. Tesco was jammed with shoppers stocking up for Christmas. There was that seasonal panic in the air, as if nuclear war had been announced. Louise pushed a trolley so overloaded that she had to support one side with her hand. She bumped into her son, who was stocking shelves as fast as they were emptied. She liked these occasions; there was an intimacy about meeting Jamie outside the home.

He gazed at her shopping. 'Blimey, Ma.'

'Cranberry sauce,' she muttered. 'Double cream. Forgot to ask if Erin's a vegetarian. I bet she is.'

'Because she's a lesbian?'

'Ssh!' Louise looked around. 'She just looks like one.'

'A lesbian?'

'A vegetarian!'

Jamie pushed the jars of gherkins to the back of the shelf. 'What do lesbians do?'

Louise lowered her voice. 'I don't know. Same as everybody else, I suppose.'

'But isn't there an item missing somewhere?'

'They seem to manage. Pass me one of those, will you?'

He handed her a jar of olives. 'Do Granny and Grandad know?'

She shook her head. 'They'd have a fit. She's just Maddy's flatmate. Anyway, they won't be here. They're leaving tomorrow.'

'Lucky sods.'

She trundled her trolley away down the aisle.

In the office, the lads were queuing for their wages. There was a pre-Christmas buzz in the air. Dorothy gave out the envelopes.

'Happy Christmas, Kevin. So who're you having it with this year?'

'Charlene and the kids.'

'Is it their turn?'

He nodded. 'Twins on Boxing Day.'

Stephen stepped up, the next in the line. She gave him his envelope. 'So how did you enjoy your first week?' She stopped. 'Your poor hands!'

'They're fine,' said Stephen.

She took his hand and inspected it. 'I've got some TCP in the house. I'll get it for you.'

'No, honestly –'

They looked up. Prudence had arrived. 'I got off early,' she said, turning to Stephen. 'I'll give you a lift home.'

Dorothy reached down and gave her two carrier bags. They were filled with Christmas presents for the family. 'They're all labelled. Thanks for taking them down.'

'No problem,' said Stephen.

Prudence stared at him.

'What's the matter?' he asked.

'You've never said *no problem* before. Where's Dad?'

'I don't know,' said Dorothy. 'He's supposed to be taking the lads out for a drink.'

'Oh well, give him my love.' Prudence kissed her mother. 'Have a wonderful time.' She turned to the men. 'Happy Christmas!'

Stephen picked up the carrier bags and they left.

In the General Stores Mrs Malcolm, an elderly widow, put a tin of cat food into her basket. The only other customer was Imogen, who was inspecting the rack of Christmas cards. They were of the spangled, coach-and-horses variety.

Outside, Louise parked her Space Cruiser. It was loaded with her carrier bags. She came into the shop and greeted her daughter. 'Forgot the sugar lumps.'

'For Skylark?'

She shook her head. 'For your dad's champagne cocktails.' Picking up a packet, she called out to Tim, 'So what're you doing for Christmas?'

'Quiet,' said Tim. 'Just myself and Margot. Actually it may be our last.'

'You can't close! I'm going to organise a campaign in the New Year. *Support Our Village Shop.*'

Imogen whispered, 'Hypocrite! You did all your shopping at Tesco.'

Louise ignored her. She went up to the counter. 'Can't you have, well, more fresh stuff? The shop at Hadleigh has organic vegetables and home-made cakes and things.'

'It's a question of turnover,' he said. 'Last week Margot and I had to eat up all the pork pies ourselves.'

'Why?'

'They were past their sell-by date.'

Louise sighed. 'I know the feeling.'

'Don't say that!' he said abruptly.

Louise smiled at him and went to the door. 'Want a lift

169

home, Immy?'

Imogen shook her head. 'I'll walk.'

Louise left. Imogen waited until her mother had driven away. Then she selected the least embarrassing Christmas card – a robin surrounded by holly – and took it to the counter. 'Can I borrow a pen?'

A few moments later she emerged into the dark. It was six o'clock; behind her, Tim turned the sign to SORRY, WE'RE CLOSED.

Karl's van was still parked outside the pub. Imogen looked around. There was nobody in sight; just parked cars, already matt with dew beneath the Christmas lights.

She hurried up to his van, slotted the card beneath one of the windscreen wipers and hurried away.

Gordon parked his car in the garage. Its headlamps illumin- ated the stacked lumber of family life – the old dart-board, the pairs of skates. On the dashboard, the clock displayed 6.34. He switched off the headlights and sat there.

After a while he got out of the car. He let himself into the house. The lounge was in darkness.

Dorothy had found out. She had left him. She had left no note, nothing; he would never see her again. He felt such airy gratefulness that he suddenly loved her again.

He sat down in the gloom, took out a pack of cigarettes and lit one. Upstairs, he heard her moving about. He inhaled deeply.

'Gordon, is that you?'

He stubbed out his cigarette and climbed to his feet. He went upstairs.

'Gordon? Come in here!'

He opened the bedroom door. The room blazed with light. Dorothy had been packing; her suitcase lay on the bed. She stood in the middle of the room. She wore a flowery dress, big red roses. It was too short for her.

'Do you like it? I got it at Fowler's.' She pirouetted around.

170

'You don't think it's too young for me, do you?' She grabbed a piece of cloth and held it against herself. 'Look at this! It's a sort of sarong thing. The girl said everybody's wearing them now.' She wrapped it around her waist. 'When you come from the beach you just do this . . . what do you think?' She turned around. 'Does my bottom look too big?'

She turned back to face him. She stared.

Gordon was crying.

It was Christmas Eve, a clear, starry night. All over Britain the mad scramble to buy had ceased. The supermarkets had emptied; peace had descended on earth. In Wingham Wallace the curtains were drawn, the fireplaces blazed, the Range Rovers were locked away in their garages. Its inhabitants hunkered down for an orgy of consumption. The lanes were silent. In the fields, lone trees raised their arms to heaven. The church interior was lit, illuminating the Burne-Jones stained-glass window.

The windows of the Old Vicarage, too, blazed with light; a Christmas tree glittered in the living-room window. Robert and Louise opened the door and greeted the arrivals – Erin, Maddy and Allegra . . . Prudence and Stephen. Their glamour bathed their guests like the light flooding from the hallway. It blessed those less fortunate than themselves.

The living room was festooned with cards – what a large number of friends they had, and possessed of such taste! Upstairs, in the two spare bedrooms, fresh sheets awaited the visiting pairs of lovers – heterosexual or homosexual, both were welcome.

In the stable Imogen and Allegra threaded tinsel into Skylark's mane.

'Do you believe in Father Christmas?' Imogen asked.

Allegra shook her head. 'Mum says he's a patriarchal child-abuser.'

171

This struck Imogen as sad. 'What happens when you want to make a wish?'

'I do it anyway.'

'What do you want for Christmas?'

'I want my dad.'

'Don't you see him?'

'Not really. Mum just used him for his sperm.'

Imogen laughed. 'Very romantic.'

'Mum doesn't like men.'

'No, I gathered that.' Imogen leaned against Skylark's neck; she breathed in her scent. 'Well, *I* like men. Nice and big and strong, with lovely strong hands, and we'll gallop off into the sunset –'

'*Imogen!*' Her mother's voice called from the house. 'Come and lay the table!'

In the living room Robert was teaching Allegra how to make champagne cocktails. The fire crackled and spat. The guests' faces were rosy in the leaping light.

'Lump of sugar . . .' He popped it into a glass. 'Bit of brandy, slosh of Bolly . . . When you grow into a gorgeous young woman, Allegra, and chaps ask you out, insist on Bollinger.'

'Dad, you're so un-p.c.,' said Imogen. 'Women buy their own drinks now.'

'Not if they've got any sense.' Ignoring Erin's glance he passed around the glasses. 'You're in Buckinghamshire now, not the People's Republic of Hackney. The only p.c. we know stands for the Pony Club.' He raised his glass. 'Welcome to the Old Vicarage, let the festive season begin. Here's to us.'

Louise turned to Prudence and Stephen. She raised her glass. 'Here's to you two. It's lovely to have you here.' She turned to Erin and Maddy. 'And here's to you.' She smiled at Allegra. 'And you.'

'I like this house,' said Allegra.

Louise turned to Erin. 'And here's to your book. Prudence

lent it to me. I loved it.'

'Thank you,' said Erin.

Robert looked at his wife. 'You don't read books. Not unless they're heavily disguised as a copy of *Options*.'

'Shut up,' said Louise. 'I read hers.'

Prudence raised her glass. 'And here's to Mum and Dad. At this very moment, thirty thousand feet above Newfoundland . . .'

'Trying to open their packet of dry roasted peanuts,' said Robert.

'Listening to the distant rattle of the drinks trolley,' Stephen added. 'Will it ever arrive?'

'Maybe they're toasting us at this very moment,' said Prudence. 'They said they would.'

'Here's to Mum and Dad, and their second honeymoon.' Louise raised her glass.

The doorbell rang. They looked at each other.

'Who could that be?' asked Louise.

Robert grinned at Allegra. 'It's Father Christmas.'

Imogen was about to say that she didn't believe in him. She stopped. They heard footsteps in the hallway. Jamie came back into the room. He was accompanied by Dorothy. Her face was ashen. She carried a suitcase.

'Mum!' said Louise.

'What's happened?' asked Prudence.

Dorothy said: 'He's left me.'

PART THREE

One

It was Friday, the middle of the dead week between Christmas and the New Year. London lay under a spell. Its streets were empty, its offices silent except for the chatter of answerphones. Even Brixton seemed half-asleep. Dorothy, accompanied by two of her daughters, stood outside Betterspecs. The video shop next door was doing a brisk trade for it was a cold, sullen afternoon. A large Rastafarian came out, carrying a pile of videos, and grinned at them.

There were two bells. Maddy pressed the top one. They waited, looking up at the windows. On the top floor the curtains were closed. They all pictured the same thing – Gordon and this April woman were in bed. They had been in bed since Christmas.

There was no reply. Maddy pressed the lower bell. The curtains on this floor, the floor above the shop, were open. After a moment they heard footsteps descending stairs. The door opened and Gordon stood there. He wore an unfamiliar blue sweater. He stared at them.

'Hello, Gordon,' said Dorothy. She indicated her two daughters. 'They wouldn't let me come alone.'

Gordon gestured at the street. 'It's perfectly safe.'

'She doesn't mean that,' said Prudence.

There was a pause. Dorothy asked: 'She at work?'

He shook his head. 'No, but she's out.'

He let them in. Narrow hallway, woodchip wallpaper. They climbed the stairs behind him. He opened the door and they followed him into April's flat, into a large living room –

yellow walls, potted plants. The only sign of Gordon's residence was a pair of his shoes on the floor. The three women went into the middle of the room and stood there. For a moment nobody knew what to do.

'Can I make anyone a cup of tea?' he asked.

Nobody replied. Maddy sat down. The others remained standing.

'Mum's had a pretty awful Christmas,' said Prudence. 'As you might expect.'

'I'm sorry,' he said. 'I didn't mean it to happen like this.'

'How did you mean it to happen?' asked Prudence.

'I didn't,' he said. 'I'm sorry, Dot.'

'Come home,' said Dorothy. 'We've got the car.'

Gordon reached in his pocket and took out a packet of cigarettes. Dorothy opened her mouth, but said nothing. He lit one.

'Dad, please . . .' said Prudence. 'You know this is completely mad.'

'Come home and we'll sort it out,' said Dorothy. 'We must talk.'

'She's half your age,' said Prudence. 'You've got nothing in common.'

'How do you know?' he asked.

'You're so – well, different.'

'Why?'

'Maybe she's after your money,' said Prudence. 'Have you thought about that?'

'Come on!' he said.

She gazed around the room. 'What do you *do* all day?'

There was a silence. They could all guess.

'Please, love,' said Dorothy. 'Pack up and come home.'

'This is my home,' he replied. He stood there, his stubborn lower lip thrust out.

Dorothy looked around. 'You've done it up,' she suddenly said.

'What?' he asked.

'You've done up this room, haven't you?' She looked at

him. 'You bastard!'

They all stared at her. 'Mum –' said Maddy.

'All these years and you've never even finished my kitchen.'

'Look, she'll be back any minute,' said Gordon. 'Can we talk about this another time?'

Maddy got up and looked out of the window. 'You, living here. I can't get over it.'

'Why don't you leave this to me and your mother,' he snapped.

'I didn't think you had it in you.' Maddy's voice was full of admiration. They looked at her in surprise. 'You've always been so conventional.'

Dorothy said: 'Whose side are you on?'

'I just think – it's amazing, that's all. I didn't know you had it in you.'

'That's a great help,' said Dorothy. 'Thank you, Maddy.'

Maddy said: 'Why don't *I* make us some tea.'

Gordon moved towards the kitchen. 'I'll help you.'

'Coward!' said Dorothy. She turned to Maddy. 'Traitor! For God's sake, what's the matter with everybody?'

'It's all right, Mum,' said Prudence.

'It'd be better if I spoke to her alone,' said Gordon.

'She wanted us to come,' said Prudence. She looked around at the room. 'Anyway, I was curious.'

Footsteps sounded on the stairs. The door opened. April came in and stopped dead. She put her shopping bags on the floor.

'Hi,' she said.

'I think you've met my daughters.'

April nodded. 'At the hospital.'

'Would you like some tea?' asked Maddy.

'Do shut up about tea!' Dorothy turned to April. 'We want him to come home.' She turned to Gordon. 'Come on, love.'

Prudence said to April: 'You don't really want him, do you?'

Gordon glanced at his daughter. He stubbed out his cigarette.

April sat down. 'Mrs Hammond, I'm ever so sorry. I tried

to stop him, I didn't mean him to do this, not like this, not so quickly.' She wore a puffy anorak and jeans. She was a big girl; healthy, sporty-looking. 'I don't want to break up a family, I've seen enough of what it can do. But he said his marriage was over, it had been over for years –'

'You said that?' Dorothy swung round and glared at her husband.

'Actually,' said Prudence, 'we thought they were perfectly happy.'

'Maybe they were,' said April. 'I don't know, it's not my business –'

'It is your business,' said Prudence.

'Maybe they were happy when they were with you.' April turned to Prudence. 'But you don't see that much of them anyway, do you? I'm not accusing you or anything, but you're all grown up, you've got your own lives.'

'Look, we don't want to blame you,' said Prudence. 'We just think he should come back to the house and talk things over, talk with Mum. He's always been a bit impulsive.'

Dorothy looked at April. 'I thought you were so nice. Looking after him. I said, "What a nice girl."' She started to cry. 'When I came to hospital, he seemed so ... well. I thought, what a good recovery he's making. I bought you a box of truffles, remember?' She pulled a Kleenex out of her bag and wiped her nose. She said, her voice oddly formal: 'I'd just like you to know one thing. The physical side ... we've always been perfectly happy with that ... whatever he's implied. I just want you to know. Though it's none of your business.'

They gazed at her, blushing for her. Suddenly she caught her breath. Her face looked startled, as if she had been stabbed in the back. She bent double and, with a small whimpering sound, crumpled onto the floor.

They stared at her. For a moment they thought she was pretending; it looked so artificial. April bent down, lifted her wrist and felt her pulse. She looked up. 'Call an ambulance.'

Gordon grabbed the phone. April laid Dorothy on the

carpet. She unbuttoned Dorothy's blouse at the neck. She leaned over and put her mouth over Dorothy's.

The two daughters gazed at the young black woman giving their mother the kiss of life. It was a disturbing, strangely erotic sight. They watched, transfixed.

A small crowd had gathered in the street. An ambulance waited, its light flashing. Paramedics carried out Dorothy on a stretcher. April – professional, efficient – said something to them. She jumped into the back of the ambulance. Gordon followed her. The two daughters watched as the ambulance sped off down the street.

It was called a transient ischaemic attack; a sort of spasm, apparently. They were only keeping Dorothy in for a couple of days, for tests. Thank God she was all right. Thank God, too, that she had been taken to a different hospital from the one which had treated their father. The image of April nursing their mother back to health, even working in the same building, was too bizarre to contemplate.

On the other hand, April had saved their mother's life. Maybe not saved – who knows? – but she had sprung up and helped her in a way that neither of her daughters could have managed. How confusing to be grateful to their father's mistress!

'I feel so awful because *I* upset Mum, too,' said Maddy. 'You see, for the first time in my life I sort of admired him.' It was midday on Sunday; Erin lay beside her in bed. 'It's as if he had sort of joined me. Us. Joined the club of people who've done something nobody had expected them to.'

'He can change too, I guess,' said Erin.

'It was the funniest feeling. All my life I've been the odd one out, he's been disappointed in me. And now, maybe, he'll understand. Oh, I don't know. It's such a mess. Because I should be feeling sorry for Mum. I *do* feel sorry for her. He's

179

been such a shit.'

She wanted Erin to rescue her with certainties. Erin was so strong. Many of Erin's friends regarded men with contempt, even hatred. Erin's attitude towards men was subtler and somehow more damning. She pitied them. She pitied their aggression, the way it sprang from fear. She pitied the linear way that, imprisoned by testosterone and centuries of conditioning, they pushed their way blindly through life. She pitied their pride in the thing between their legs, as if it were a lovingly polished trophy won in some boring and irrelevant tournament. Didn't they know what they had been missing?

She damned them by their irrelevance. Only women could feel the powerful pulls and eddies of nature. Only women, with other women, could truly be free – stirred by the same tides, by the beat of their blood. She washed Maddy's feet in glycerine and scented water; she murmured to her strange and wonderful words ... *nectar* ... *honey-basket* ... *finger-frolics* ... In the past, such words would have bemused Maddy. Embarrassed her, even. But now she was enraptured.

Maddy removed the tea mugs and buried her face in Erin's shoulder. Forgetting her parents, she kissed the sweet dip in Erin's throat. The doorbell rang.

'Don't go,' she whispered.

Erin opened the door. Aziz stood there. He was a delicate Indian man – small, with finely drawn features. Erin raised her eyebrows. Tall and tousled, wearing her satin bathrobe, she looked like a Valkyrie.

'Is Allegra ready?' he asked.

Erin shook her head. 'She's gone to a birthday party.'

'But it's Sunday,' he said. 'You knew I'd be coming.'

'Didn't I tell you?'

'Erin, I have one Sunday a fortnight to see my daughter. The past two times she's been out.'

'I'm sorry,' said Erin. 'She's been looking forward to it all week.'

180

'Well, *I'd* been looking forward to taking her roller-skating.'

Erin gazed at him – not coldly, that would have been bearable to him. She gazed at him with detachment, as if he were a milkman and had come to the wrong house. 'I'm sorry. Come back next week, I'll make sure she's here.'

'I've got to go to Glasgow on Thursday! You know that –'

She shrugged. 'Well, if your work's so important . . .'

'Erin! That's not fair! I need her.'

'I think that's nearer the point.'

He turned on his heel and left.

Dorothy sat in her dressing-gown. The watery sun shone through the hospital window. It shone onto the mismatched chairs and the milky cataract of the TV screen. Gordon sat opposite her.

'Strange to be kissed by your own husband's girlfriend,' she said. 'And to cap it all, I had to be grateful.'

Gordon nodded. 'She brought *me* back to life too.'

Dorothy raised her eyebrows. 'You've made many tactless remarks, Gordon, but that has to take the biscuit.'

'I'm sorry, love.' He gazed around the TV room, as if it might help. The empty chairs faced him. 'I've been home and paid the bills. Sorted out some paperwork. I've not taken anything, bar my clothes.'

'How nice of you.'

Down the corridor a Tannoy called, '*Doctor Mulbarek.*' The name sounded familiar. Wasn't he the President of Egypt?

'Our life here on earth, it only comes the once,' he said.

'I know that, Gordon.'

'When I had that heart attack – episode – can you understand, love? I'd been working myself to the bone, head down, year after year. I'd not started to live.'

'I'd been telling you that,' said Dorothy. 'I told you for years and you never listened. That's what really gets me. You never listened to *me*. I felt that too. I told you we should give

181

up the business, retire, have some fun. I told you that and you didn't take a blind bit of notice. Oh, but the moment *she* said it you listened.'

'She didn't say it. I did.'

'Oh, wipe that dopey look off your face, for God's sake.'

A nurse came into the room. She was black. Dorothy's heart jolted.

'Just want to take your blood pressure,' said the nurse.

Dorothy got to her feet and left the room.

Erin lounged on her sofa, her leg flung over the armrest. Today she wore a shirt, jeans and boots like a farmgirl. She was being interviewed by a journalist – one of the eager, young, female kind.

'My novel's about courage,' said Erin. 'It takes courage to fall in love, don't you think? Oh, people say they do, all the time, they say the words because everybody else says them. But very few people know how to truly love another person without the need to possess them. It takes enormous courage to give another person freedom.'

'Now, you make no secret of your own sexual orientation,' said the journalist. 'Could you tell me –'

She stopped. Maddy came in, carrying shopping bags.

'Oh. Sorry,' said Maddy.

The journalist switched off her tape recorder.

Erin said: 'Maddy, this is . . .'

'Alison.'

'Alison, from the *Independent on Sunday*.' She turned to the girl. 'Would you like some tea? Earl Grey, Rosehip, Lapsang?'

'Lapsang would be lovely.'

Erin smiled at Maddy. 'Lapsang for both of us, sweetheart. Thanks.'

Maddy left. Alison switched on her tape recorder. 'I believe you had your daughter Allegra by artificial insemination –'

'Oh no,' Erin replied. 'I fucked the guy.'

'Oh. Anyway, why did you decide to bring up a child

182

alone? Wasn't that a very brave decision?'

'I didn't want to miss out on motherhood.' Erin stopped. 'Hey, that's a great bracelet.'

Alison glowed. Erin smiled at her.

In the kitchen Maddy, filling the kettle, heard Erin's voice.

'. . . living with someone should be a celebration, not subjugation. With no man in the house all the power-games disappear – who's doing the chores, who's resenting having to take time off work. Have you noticed how we always thank a man when he makes a meal and never a woman?'

Maddy started to unpack the shopping.

Prudence drove her mother home. It was Saturday morning and the streets of Purley were empty. When she was young the streets had been full of children; now there were just parked cars. Since her childhood, car ownership had doubled and children had disappeared. They were sitting at home, watching the CD Roms her company was producing. Driving past the houses, she mourned her lost youth. The break-up of her parents' marriage had separated her from her past; it had broken away, like an ice-floe, and drifted into the distance.

Prudence looked at her mother. There had always been something blurred and undefined about Dorothy. She didn't even look her age. An unremarkable, pretty face if one tried to assess it. Maybe everybody felt that about their mother; they were too close to have a shape, too out-of-focus. But Louise was like that too. Like her flyaway hair there was something fuzzy about her. Perhaps it was because both women had spent the years servicing the needs of other people. Maddy was strong and square; like her father, there was a solidity to her. But Dorothy was a mother and a wife; her own identity had somehow been lost. Now, at the age of sixty-three, she was alone. Gordon wasn't coming home, Prudence knew it now. How was her mother going to cope? Her sudden flare-up in April's flat had startled Prudence. Already her mother was revealing a hidden part of herself. In

183

the coming months was she going to disintegrate or grow strong? Was she going to surprise her daughters and those who loved her? Prudence had no idea, and felt panic-struck on her mother's behalf.

They arrived at The Birches. Prudence unlocked the front door and picked up the letters that were spewed onto the doormat. 'I'll put the heating on.'

Dorothy went into the lounge. She had been away for a week – three days in hospital and four days of convalescence with her friend Connie in Harrow. Connie was a divorcée; until recently, such women had been a separate species. Sometimes Dorothy had pitied them; sometimes she had envied them their freedom. She thought: I've stepped across the threshold now.

Hunched in her overcoat, she sat down. Her absence had changed the house; it was no longer hers. When her grandmother had died she had sat with her; she had sat beside the bed for hours, unable to leave because she knew that when she returned her granny would be changed into a corpse.

Prudence came into the room. 'Let me help you unpack,' she said.

Dorothy looked at the framed photographs, at the forty-four years of married life. She sat, perched on the edge of her chair as if she were just visiting. She wondered whether Gordon would come into the office on Monday. She tried to picture him leafing through invoices and scattering cigarette ash. She tried to make him act as he had always done.

Prudence said: 'You're coming home with me.'

'I'm fine, really,' said Dorothy. 'I've got plenty to do here.'

'Come on.'

Prudence's hand slipped into hers. It was dry and cool. Dorothy stood up like a sleepwalker and let herself be led to the door.

Prudence managed to find a parking space only a few yards from her flat. This struck her – erroneously, as it turned out –

184

as a good omen.

'Can you wait here a sec?' she asked her mother. 'I'll just, er . . .'

She left her mother, ran to the door, let herself in and ran upstairs. She unlocked her front door and, hearing a whirring sound, went into the kitchen. Stephen stood at the blender.

'I asked my mum to stay, just for a night or so. Do you mind?' She kissed his cheek. 'I just couldn't leave her in that empty house all by herself.'

Prudence looked at the blender. It appeared to be full of milk shake. She turned. Dirk stood in the doorway.

There was a moment's silence. 'Hello, Dirk!' she said.

'Kaatya had to go on some course,' muttered Stephen. 'Some Saturday workshop or something. I've got them till six.'

Dirk poured the milk-shake mixture into a glass and took it into the living room. Prudence followed him. Pieter lay on the carpet, surrounded by sheets of paper.

'Hello, Pieter,' she said. 'How lovely to see you.'

'What do you know about Bismarck?' he asked. 'Dad's hopeless.'

Prudence hurried back into the kitchen and closed the door behind her. 'Take them out!' she hissed. 'Take them for a walk or something.'

'I can't!'

'She can't find out about them now. Not in the state she's in.'

'She's got to sooner or later,' he said.

'Not now! Put them in the bedroom, just for half an hour. Then I'll take her off shopping or something.'

She went back into the living room. 'Listen, chaps. Let's play hide-and-seek!'

'I'm thirteen,' said Pieter.

Stephen gathered up the papers. 'Please, Pieter. You can do your project in there.'

Dirk said: 'There's no TV in there.'

Stephen ushered him towards the bedroom door. 'And

185

keep really quiet, okay? Is that a deal?'

'How much will you pay us?' demanded Pieter.

Prudence stared at the boy. 'What?'

'How much, Dad?'

There was a pause. 'A quid each,' said Stephen.

'Stephen!' said Prudence.

Pieter shook his head. 'Five pounds.'

'What?' Prudence stared at him.

'Five pounds for the two of us,' said Dirk.

'Oh, all right,' said Stephen.

The two boys went into the bedroom and shut the door.

Dorothy sat beside the eternal flames of the fire. 'Honestly, I was perfectly all right,' she said.

'Don't be silly. That's a sofabed, remember?' said Prudence. 'You can stay as long as you like.'

Stephen carried in a tray of coffee. 'Of course you can,' he said.

Dorothy looked up at him. 'Forty-four years, Stephen. That's how long we've been married. How could he do it?'

'Would you like some sugar?' Stephen asked.

'You're a man,' said Dorothy. 'Tell me.'

'I can't imagine,' he said, passing her a cup. Prudence looked at him sharply.

Dorothy said: 'It's as if he's just screwed it up and thrown it away, all of it. As if our marriage never happened.'

'I'm sure he's feeling terrible,' said Stephen.

'You're so nice,' said Dorothy. 'You needn't defend him.' She sipped her coffee.

Prudence lifted her cup. Some of her coffee had spilled into the saucer. She watched Stephen's foot; it was stirring the fringe of the hearthrug.

'He's a foolish man,' said Dorothy. 'Innocent, really. He's brought up three daughters and he still doesn't know anything about women. First girl who sets her sights on him – God knows why, maybe she *is* after his money, I don't know.

Maybe she wants a father figure. She makes a play for him, he's putty in her hands. She's not even that attractive, compared to some of them.'

'I'm sure it won't last,' said Stephen.

'How do you know?' Prudence asked sharply.

'I don't know,' said Stephen. 'I'm just guessing. Maybe it's some sort of mid-life crisis.'

Dorothy nodded. 'He probably thinks – oh, everyone's doing it nowadays, why not him?'

'He'll come home with his tail between his legs,' said Stephen.

'You sure?' asked Prudence.

There was a thump in the bedroom.

'What's that?' asked Dorothy.

Prudence drained her cup. 'I'm taking you out,' she said to her mother. 'We'll go into town, we'll have lunch at Fortnum's and go to a matinée, that Gershwin thing.' She got to her feet. 'And we'll go to Selfridges and squirt ourselves with perfume. We'll forget about everything and just have fun.'

'Sure you've got the time?' asked her mother.

Prudence nodded. 'I've got all day.'

Gordon was cut adrift. It was true, what he had told April. His old life had receded, its shoreline barely recognisable. He was helpless – he, Gordon, who had once fancied himself in control, who had spent his life telling other people what to do. Once it had been simple: you laid the foundations, you placed one brick upon another. Who would have guessed how flimsy the structure was, once you shook it, how easily it crumbled?

He had caused terrible pain and was continuing to cause it. His wife had crumpled onto April's floor as if she had been shot. During those winter days even Gordon, not the most reflective of men, tried to find a reason for what had happened. He told himself that his marriage, though companionable, had quietly died. It had succumbed to decades of familiarity. He and Dorothy had little in common, they had just been cemented by child-rearing and the comforting, blinding routine of daily life. He told April this, trying to make sense of it. But hindsight simplifies the past; in the effort to justify what has happened, one coarsens the preceding events. No marriage can be reduced to clichés but clichés were what he needed to simplify the chaos.

The truth was: he had fallen in love. He had embarked on a great adventure, probably the last great adventure of his life. He and April were lost to the world, but who needed the world when they had each other? Since moving in, just before Christmas, he had met few of her friends. He himself had little contact with anyone for he was an outcast now. He sporadically went to work, driving to his various sites just to reassure his men that he existed. He was impervious to their innuendoes or their disapproval; he blanked himself off to anything but the tasks that demanded his attention. It all seemed irrelevant – had seemed so, in fact, since that day in October when he had had his heart attack.

He knew he had to sort out his life, for everybody's sake, but he felt paralysed. His brain was locked, for if he dared to think it was insupportable. Dorothy had gone home on Saturday; he should have been there to heat up the house and look after her, as she had looked after him. Instead, his daughters were doing his job and he was walking down Prowse Street, Walthamstow, showing April the place where he had grown up.

'The coalman lived there.' He pointed. 'He had one eye, scared the living daylights out of me.'

'Where did Kenny live?'

He pointed to a house. 'That's his bedroom window, where he used to dangle the messages.' The houses looked smaller than he remembered – shabbier too, most of the plasterwork was in a terrible state. 'They had the first TV.' He linked his arm with April's. 'It's another world, sweetheart, even to me. God knows what, to you.' He pointed to a used-car dealer's on the corner. 'That's where the air raid shelter was. I sat in there, counting my shrapnel collection. My mum thought we were going to die, but I didn't.'

'Why not?'

'Kids think they're the centre of the world, it's just there for them.'

'Egocentric little buggers, weren't we,' she said.

He nodded. 'I thought I'd live for ever, and here I am, with you at the end of it.' He squeezed her arm. 'So I was proved right, wasn't I?'

'Did you bring your daughters here?'

He nodded. 'Had to drag them. I was just boring old Dad, droning on about the war. When you're a dad, everything you do is boring.'

'Even this? What you've been doing with me?'

He didn't reply. He stopped and pointed. 'That's my house. Forty-six.'

She closed her eyes. 'I'm going to imagine you coming out.'

She opened her eyes. The front door of number forty-six opened. A family came out – mother, father, two little girls. They were black. April burst out laughing.

Gordon was a Londoner. He had loved his city for sixty-five years; he felt a Cockney's proprietorial pride in it. He had delved into its buildings. His work had made him intimate with its past – the craftsmanship of joiners and brickies long since dead. Like most men of his age he felt a nostalgia for what can never be recaptured. April led him into new places which until now he had only heard as a distant throb. Maybe his daughters were right, he had been prejudiced. He preferred not to think about that; he blocked it off, he was good at that. Willingly he was led by April into her world, just as he had led her into his. That afternoon they were shopping in Electric Avenue as if he had been doing it all his life. They walked through the covered market. She waved at her friend Carole who had a hair salon in Second Avenue, next to a spice

189

shop. Dazzling fabrics hung from stalls. Music blared from a shoe shop where an Indian boy kicked a football to and fro, rocking the shoe boxes. Two huge women passed, dressed in tribal robes of some sort, maybe from Nigeria, who knew? He knew little about the place where Maddy had lived. He knew nothing about anything.

'Don't get me wrong,' he said. 'I love them dearly. But they make me feel stupid. Stupid old Dad.'

April nodded. 'They are pretty intimidating.'

'Even when I've done nothing wrong. I've given them this education, see. Private schools, the works. I wanted them to do well for themselves, I worked hard for that. And now we've got bugger-all to say to each other.'

'You haven't lost them. Not for ever.'

They stopped at a vegetable stall. It was heaped with strangely shaped objects; they shone in the electric light. 'Go on, educate me.' He pointed. 'What're those?'

'They're yams. And they're plantains.'

'How do you cook them?' he asked.

She laughed. 'Search me. Fancy a McDonald's?'

They walked out into the street. 'Teenagers didn't exist, see,' he said. 'We were little old men wearing little old men's clothes.'

'Most of the blokes I know have never grown up.'

'Can I join them for a bit?'

She nodded, and rubbed her shoulder against him as they walked.

The house had been put on the market. Dorothy and Gordon stood in the lounge. There was a chill, uninhabited air about the place; they both wore their overcoats.

'You never did finish those shelves,' said Dorothy.

'Dorothy –'

She gestured around the room. 'Frankly, I'll be glad to get shot of it. It's far too big, been far too big for years. All that bloody cleaning. And the new people next door making a

190

fuss about the yard.'

'Aren't you being hasty?'

'Me? Hasty?' She looked at him. She wore the fawn coat he hadn't seen for years. Why was she wearing it now? He had no idea. Her face looked tighter somehow, there was a hardness about her that he hadn't known before. Already, she had changed. 'You can do what you like with the business, I don't give a damn.'

'But Dot –'

'You haven't even been in this week. It's finished, Gordon, the sooner we get shot of it the better. I'll do another month and that's it.' Her face softened. 'No more getting up at six in the morning,' she said dreamily. 'No more queuing in the bank, no more blasted VAT. Think I enjoyed all that? I did it for you, Gordon. For us. I've been fed up with it for years, not that you'd noticed. I've worn myself out and now I've had enough.'

'But what're you going to do?'

'It's none of your business.'

'But I'm worried about you,' he said.

'Oh yes?' She laughed mirthlessly. 'I'm going to buy a flat, just big enough for me. Half this house, I'll get somewhere really nice, with something over. You don't have to worry about me, I'll be fine.'

He pointed at the furniture. He couldn't think what else to do. 'But what about –'

'All this? Oh, we'll sort it out later. I only want that –' She pointed to the brass lamp '– and that, and the desk. You can have the rest for your love nest –'

'I don't mean that – I don't want –'

'Give it to Oxfam,' she said. 'Give it to the girls. I don't care. But I'm having the photo albums.' She looked at her watch. He had given it to her on her sixtieth birthday; it seemed the only familiar thing about her. 'Got to get back,' she said. 'I'm cooking Pru and Stephen dinner.'

*

191

It was Monday morning. Stephen was travelling to a roofing job somewhere in south-east London. He sat in the front of the van with Frank and a roofer called Phil – another mere boy who made Stephen feel inept. Kendal Contractors seemed to have an inexhaustible supply of these young men. Bounding over scaffolding like mountain goats, they shouted out orders to Stephen in their incomprehensible brogues – Geordie, Irish – and cracked jokes whose punchlines floated away in the wind. The stamina of them! The expertise! After three weeks Stephen had got the hang of the simpler tasks, he had done some of them at home, but the effort of learning new ones, and pretending he knew how to do them when he had been told several times, left him with the sort of headache he had had during Latin lessons at school. At the end of the day he fell into bed like a sack of cement, incapable of any movement, let alone making love to Prudence.

As they drove through the streets he counted backwards. Five consecutive nights, in fact. This was all right for an established couple – even the sexually voracious Kaatya had let him off the hook, sometimes for a week at a time, during the course of their marriage – but when a chap had broken up his home to live with his mistress he was duty-bound to perform frequently. Wasn't that the point?

Apart from sheer exhaustion, the other impediment was Dorothy. She had been staying with them for a week now; Prudence couldn't bear to let her go home to the empty house. In some respects Dorothy was a model guest. She shopped and cooked while they were at work, and frequently disappeared to Purley to look after the office. But her presence was a daily rebuke to him. Her pale, unhappy face was his own conscience. She was an abandoned wife, an older version of his own, left helpless to fend for herself.

Besides, with her there he couldn't tell Prudence about problems at work – after all, she was his employer. Muttered conversations took place in the bedroom, where he also phoned his sons – Dorothy's presence was inhibiting in this respect, too. And Prudence herself changed when her mother

192

was around. She became desexed; she reverted to being a dutiful daughter. All in all the place was too small for the three of them. No wonder he couldn't get it up any more.

Stephen, preoccupied, failed to notice where they were going. Looking out of the window, he recognised the houses. They were driving through Dulwich.

'I'll drop you off there and get the bitumen,' said Frank.

'The boss going to show up today?' asked Phil.

'None of your business, young Phillip,' replied Frank. 'You're getting paid, aren't you?'

'Lucky for some, eh?' muttered Phil.

Frank passed Stephen the *A–Z*. 'You're the intellectual. Find Agincourt Road.'

Stephen paused. 'It's third on the left.'

'Know this area, do you?' Frank hooted and overtook a learner driver.

Stephen nodded.

He sat, rigid, as the van drove along Abbey Way. He watched the familiar houses slide past. Then the shops – the off-licence, the delicatessen. The pet shop had a TO LET sign above it; Chattles had a CLOSING DOWN sale. Already things were changing; where was Dirk going to buy his gerbil food now?

Frank turned left and drove down Agincourt Road. He slowed down. 'Number thirty-six,' he said. 'Keep your eyes peeled.'

The van stopped outside Stephen's house.

'Keys under a plant pot, apparently,' said Frank.

Phil got out of the van. 'Bit foolish, isn't it? Anyone could get in.'

Stephen remained, frozen to his seat. Phil unloaded the gear from the back of the van and came round to the passenger side. 'Hoi, mate. You coming?'

Stephen climbed down. Frank drove off. It was nine-thirty; the boys must have left for school. The drive was empty; Kaatya's battered 2CV had gone.

Nothing had changed. The house gave no sign of the

traumas that had taken place within it. Kaatya's plants still pressed against the downstairs windows, seeking the sun – everybody in Amsterdam seemed to cram their windows with plants, it was one of the more charming Dutch habits. A games sock lay in the porch, and a Sainsbury bag of what looked like empty wine bottles lay slumped against the boot-scraper. With whom had Kaatya been drinking wine? Somebody he didn't know?

'Which bloody plant pot?'

Stephen jumped. Phil, gazing at the row of pots in the porch, was muttering to himself.

Stephen pointed. 'Try that one.'

Phil lifted the pot. He picked up the keys and raised his eyebrows at Stephen.

Phil unlocked the door – the Chubb lock was stiff, it needed a special jerk, but Stephen didn't come to his rescue. They went in. Stephen stood in his hallway.

He hadn't stepped inside his home for a month. The boys' bikes were propped against the wall. The pegboard was pinned with the cards for Dyno-Rod and minicabs that he and Kaatya had never used. Everything was the same. It was as if he had just popped out, five minutes ago, to get the paper. Maureen, the cat, came out of the living room and rubbed herself against his shin. Stephen felt a squeezed sensation within his chest.

It was stifling. Kaatya had a fine disregard for economies and had probably had the boiler on 'Continuous' since he had left in December. He was thinking this, and trying to work up the old irritation, when the phone rang.

He jumped, as if he had been stung.

'You coming?' Phil had come down the stairs. He pointed to the bag of tools. 'Want a hand with that?'

The phone went on ringing. Stephen picked up the bag and trudged upstairs. Down in the hallway the phone finally stopped. He passed the bedroom. The door was open. The bed was unmade; Kaatya's Chinese dragon dressing-gown lay in a heap on the floor. It was surrounded by scattered

194

sections of the *Sunday Times*. It was the only paper she read; it took her a week to get through it. He stepped in. The room smelt of sandalwood and stale smoke. Kaatya hand-rolled her cigarettes from Samson tobacco.

Stephen turned away and climbed the stairs to the top floor. The skylight was open. He heard Phil tramping around on the roof. He looked into Pieter's room. There was a stain on the ceiling – larger than before. They had always had trouble with the roof; occasionally he had tried to fix it. Pieter's room was a pigsty, as usual. Today, however, the mess no longer seemed the normal adolescent chaos; it looked like the bedroom of a boy who had been traumatised.

The ladder creaked as Phil came down. He came into the bedroom. Stephen was looking at a new poster on the wall – that model girl, whatever her name was, pouting and thrusting her thumbs down the front of her jeans.

'Somebody's done a right wally job up there,' said Phil, indicating the roof. 'Tried to patch it up, hadn't a clue. Just made it worse because the rain-water's penetrated behind the flashings.'

Stephen didn't reply.

Phil looked into the bedroom. 'Blimey. Some people. Live in a nice house like this . . . Would you believe it? My kid, I'd stop his pocket money for a month –'

The doorbell rang. Stephen stood rooted to the spot. Phil went downstairs and returned with Frank.

Frank dumped the pot of bitumen on the landing. Phil said to him: 'It's a major job, Frank. These people know that? Half the flashings've gone, there's damp in the roof joists, cracked tiles, at least two dozen got to be replaced.'

'The lady of the house'll be back soon.' Frank looked at his watch. 'Said she'd be back by ten.'

Stephen moved to the top of the stairs. 'I'm sorry,' he said. 'I've got to go.'

'What?' said Frank.

'Toilet's down there,' said Phil.

'I've got to go,' said Stephen. 'I'm sorry. Give me the sack if you like –'

'Hey, mate,' said Frank, 'you can't do this –'

'I'm not really cut out for it anyway, am I?'

'I need two men up there.' Frank's face reddened. 'If you're going to leave, you leave at the end of the week.'

'I'm sorry.' Stephen ran downstairs.

Frank thudded after him. 'You listen to me!' he yelled.

'I can't stay!'

Stephen reached the hallway. Frank grabbed his shoulder and tried to turn him round. Stephen grabbed the doorhandle, turned it and wrenched the door open.

He turned to face Frank. 'You don't understand,' he said. 'It's my house.'

Maddy was working at a Housing Association project, laying turfs. She liked this job. There was something magical about rolling out sections of carpet and effecting such an instant transformation. She was worried, however, that she hadn't raked the earth flat enough beforehand; the lawn looked bumpy. Compared to Erin, she was clumsy and amateurish. She wanted to please her. Erin seemed happy with her work but Maddy still felt intimidated, as if Erin were some charismatic schoolteacher, the sort girls had crushes on, and Maddy had to try harder than anyone to gain her favour.

A voice called out: 'Hoi, love. Green side up, remember!'

Maddy looked up. Two decorators were putting the finishing touches to the windows. Maddy picked up another roll. Though she had been brought up amongst builders she had never liked the badinage; she hadn't known how to respond. Since meeting Erin men had seemed coarser and more pitiful – builders, not suprisingly, even more so. She still felt inadequate, however. For a fleeting moment she wondered how Stephen was managing; he seemed far more unsuited to a labouring job than she was.

The van arrived. Erin climbed out. She was dressed up – velvet hunter's jacket, long skirt. She opened the back of the van and pointed to a sack of peat.

'Darling, could you take this?'

Maddy, wiping her hands on her jeans, walked over. Erin saw her expression and looked abashed – a rare sight.

'Sorry, sweetie. Got to meet the marketing people. Some do in an awful hotel. I'd much rather be here with you.'

'Would you?' asked Maddy.

'Of course.'

Erin kissed her lightly on the mouth. The workmen whistled. Ignoring them, Erin climbed into the van and drove off.

Dorothy was sitting in the office. In front of her the computer hummed unheeded.

'. . . it turns out his wife and kids live there,' said Frank.

She stared. 'What?'

'He was useless anyway.' Frank stubbed out his cigarette in her tea saucer. 'I only took him on as a favour to you. The bloke was a liability.'

'He's got a wife? And children?'

'Does everybody lie to me nowadays?' wailed Dorothy.

'I didn't lie,' said Prudence. 'I just didn't tell you.'

'I've been living here for a week. Two weeks, nearly. Why didn't you?'

Prudence stirred the sauce. 'There never was the right moment. I didn't want to put you against him. Or me.'

'Oh, I don't know anyone any more.' Dorothy glared at the saucepan, as if it were responsible.

Stephen came in. She didn't turn round.

'Look – this is what happened,' said Prudence. 'Stephen and I, well, we'd been seeing each other for a year –'

'A year? I thought it was two months!'

'One month ago, in December, he left his wife and came to live here, with me. The whole thing is awful, don't make it more difficult. God, *you* know what it's like.'

197

Dorothy swung round and spoke to Stephen. 'How could you do it?'

'Mum!' said Prudence.

'What about your children?'

'Look, it wasn't like Dad,' said Prudence. 'Stephen agonised about it for months and months.'

Dorothy walked to the door. 'Oh, why can't you men just keep it in your trousers?'

'Mum!'

'I'm fed up with the lot of you,' she said.

Stephen followed her into the living room. Prudence turned off the gas and went after them.

'You're right,' he said to Dorothy. 'All I've caused is harm. When I went to the house today – my son had this poster pinned up, that model girl . . . he's growing up without me. You really think I don't feel guilty? It's as if I don't exist any more.'

'Rubbish,' said Prudence. 'Every day you're on the phone to them. That's how they knew you were working for Dad. That's probably why she called them to come and fix the roof. So she could get her claws into you again.'

Stephen sat down. 'She doesn't want me. How could she?' He looked up at Dorothy. 'I'm a cheat and a failure –'

'Oh do shut up,' said Prudence.

'Can't even hold down a bloody labourer's job –'

'Nothing wrong with labourers!' said Prudence.

'I don't deserve your daughter,' he said. 'All she's got is a human wreck –'

'Do stop snivelling, Stephen!' Prudence glared at him. 'If you're so miserable, why don't you go back to her? I'm fed up with being so bloody understanding all the time, listening to you droning on about your marriage – when have you ever listened to me?' Her voice rose. 'You never ask *me* about any of the men *I've* known, you're not the slightest bit interested in what *I've* been through –'

'Look, I've brought some wine,' said Dorothy. 'Why don't I open it –'

198

'No, thanks, Dorothy.' Stephen got up. 'I'm going out.'

He stormed out of the room. They heard the pause as he grabbed his overcoat. Then the front door slammed.

'Oh shit,' said Prudence.

Two

Fiona's grave was in Potters Bar, where Tim and Margot had been living at the time. Over the past six years new graves had been dug nearby – yellow clay, horribly fresh, heaped with flowers. Sometimes when Margot visited there was a new arrival. She wondered who these people were, lying so near her daughter. It was a relief when headstones were erected; she didn't like her daughter being alone amongst the nameless. The older headstones were familiar to her – polished granite slabs with names cut into them: *William James, Beloved Father, Died aged 63 years* lay next to Fiona's rectangle of marble chippings. It struck Margot, today, that her daughter had spent longer in the company of someone else's father than her own.

Margot arranged the daffodils in the vase. She looked at the grave. For six years, inconceivably, life had gone on without Fiona. It still struck her with surprise. People had shopped and gone to work and driven their cars. They had grown older too, as if there was nothing to it.

Above, the wind blew the rooks around as if they were paper. They seemed to have no will of their own. Margot climbed to her feet. Fiona would be ten now. Putting daffodils into a vase would be one of the skills she would have mastered a long time ago. What would she think of the place in which she had spent so long? Creepy, probably: lots of dead people. A good place for hide-and-seek.

Margot stood there. Her daughter – tall and slender now – darted behind a gravestone. *'Come and find me!'* she called.

Margot picked up her bag. The wind blew across the graveyard, carrying the noise of traffic on the main road.

Tim was slotting magazines into the rack when Louise came in. She wore jeans and her blue fluffy jumper. She looked fragrant. Tim thought about his wife; he thought how depression makes a person smell. It's not just that they cannot be bothered to wash; they give off the odour of despair. He hated himself for thinking this.

Under her arm Louise carried something, rolled up. 'I'm not going to let you go,' she said.

He blushed. Though naturally a charming woman, and used to flirting with men, she had only the vaguest idea of the effect she had on him.

'What do you mean?' he asked.

'Now term's started I've got Mrs Monson to rally the kids. You can put it in your window.' She unfurled the banner. Embellished with childish paintings, it said SUPPORT OUR VILLAGE SHOP.

'That's very kind.'

'It's not kind,' she replied. 'I want you to stay. I'm sure we can get the local paper on the case. And Robert knows somebody on the *Financial Times*.'

He walked behind the counter. He felt less exposed there. 'You really want to do all this?'

'You and me, we'll make a great team.' She dumped the banner on the counter. 'Are you game? I've done some research already, stuff in the papers about post offices closing, statistics and things. Robert thinks I'm an airhead –'

'That's not true!'

'Well, we'll show him. He's hardly here anyway, he doesn't know anything about village life –'

'Too busy jet-setting about the country, I suppose,' he said.

She nodded. 'He only comes home to sleep.'

Tim took a breath. 'Maybe, after I close up one day, well, you and I could –'

He stopped. The bell tinkled and Margot came in. She had

201

been up in London, in Potters Bar. He looked at her face and he thought: what sort of man am I?

'Hello, Margot,' said Louise. 'Things are hotting up.'

'She means the campaign, dear,' he said.

'Oh. Good.' Margot, bundled up in her coat, opened the door to the flat. 'Just going to lie down.'

She closed the door. They heard the stairs creak. Tim fingered the banner. 'Today's a bad day,' he said. 'It's the anniversary.'

'Oh. I'm so sorry.' Louise knew about his daughter. He had told her years ago, when he had felt a sudden need to blurt it out. Louise had looked sympathetic; she had children of her own. He presumed the whole village knew, though it had never been mentioned.

'Can I do anything –' Louise stopped. Jamie came in. His bike lay outside, flung on the grass, its wheels spinning.

'Hi Ma!' he said. 'What a day! Battle of the Killer Trolleys!'

'Jamie . . .' She frowned at his tactlessness – either in butting in so cheerfully or mentioning that Tesco was crammed.

'Going up to London tomorrow,' said Jamie. 'Going clubbing with Trevor.'

'Who's Trevor?' she asked.

'Bloke I work with at Tesco. He's a nutter. Just telling you, so you can give us a lift to the station.'

'Might as well just live in the car.' Louise looked at her watch. 'Must rush. Got to fetch Immy from the dentist.' She put her hand on Tim's arm. 'Bye.'

Why had she touched him? Because of his dead daughter? Outside her engine revved up.

Jamie approached the counter. 'Twenty Bensons, please.'

Tim passed him the packet. 'You shouldn't smoke, young man. Do you want to die?'

Jamie laughed. 'Great sales patter.'

Tim gestured round the empty shop. 'Works a treat, doesn't it?' He heaved the banner over the counter and dumped it on the floor. 'It just seems such a waste, that's all.'

'Want to know my philosophy of life?' Jamie pocketed his change. 'Short and sweet, that's what life should be.'

Tim paused. 'You really believe that?' he asked.

Jamie nodded. He left the shop. Tim turned the sign to CLOSED and went upstairs.

'Margot?' he said.

On Saturday afternoon Robert arrived home in the Space Cruiser, towing the caravan. Louise came out of the house to look at it.

Robert climbed down. 'Hope nobody I know saw me.'

'Why?'

'So Bognor, darling.'

'You're such a snob.' She gazed into the dirty window of the caravan. 'Nothing wrong with Bognor. Just because you spent your holidays in the South of France, sipping champagne in the Sipriani.'

'Cipriani,' he said, correcting her pronunciation. 'And that's in Venice.'

'Well, there too.'

The dog greeted him, pushing his nose into his groin. Robert shoved him away. 'Think it was fun, trailing after my mother's latest bonk, being ignored by them or nauseatingly sucked up to, I never knew which was worse. Hanging around while they got pissed?' He pushed Monty away again. 'Think it was fun being baby-sat by the chauffeur?'

Louise ruffled his hair. 'Poor diddums.'

He pointed to the caravan. 'You lot were probably quite happy there. In your own little way.'

'Robert!'

'Still, it doesn't solve the problem of its incredible ugliness.' He looked around. 'Where shall we put it so it can't lower the tone? Behind the stable?'

'We *were* happy, actually,' she said. 'At least, I thought so. I mean – Maddy and Dad quarrelled, things like that. But I always thought my parents loved each other.'

203

'They probably did,' he said.

'In their own little way.'

He walked towards the front door. 'Seems a miracle a marriage can last twenty years. Let alone forty-four.'

She looked at him sharply. Just then Jamie and his friend Trevor came out of the house. They were dressed up for their night in London. Jamie's hair was sleeked back with gel; Trevor's stood up in spikes. They both wore black.

'Lo, the princes of darkness,' said Robert.

Jamie looked at the caravan. 'What's that doing here?'

'I told you,' said Louise. 'Now that Granny and Grandad are selling the house, they said we could keep it.'

'Wicked,' said Jamie. 'Can I have it?'

'You cannot,' replied Robert. 'Who's this?'

'Trevor,' said Jamie.

'Hello, Trevor,' said Robert, extending his hand. 'Love the nose-ring. Is your father a farmer?'

'Dad!' said Jamie.

Louise interrupted: 'They got an offer yesterday. On the house.'

Robert raised his thick black eyebrows. 'Somebody actually wants to live in Purley?'

'God, you're a snob,' she said.

'You, if I remember, couldn't wait to leave.'

Jamie shifted onto the other foot. 'Mum, we'll miss the train.'

Robert said suddenly: 'I'll take you.'

Louise stared at him. 'You?'

'Can we go in the BMW?' asked Jamie.

Louise gazed at her husband. 'Why are you being so nice?'

'I want to bond with my son,' said Robert. 'And his friend.'

Robert, accompanied by the two boys, walked to his car. Jamie said to Trevor: 'It's got a car phone in it. We can ring people up.'

'No you can't,' said Robert, unlocking the door.

Jamie peered into the car. 'Where's it gone?'

'It broke. It's being repaired.'

'We're not going then,' said Jamie flouncily. 'Are we Trev?'
They grinned and climbed into the car. It drove away.

Louise, who had been mildly surprised by this but who suspected nothing, gazed at the trail of horse droppings across the gravel. Couldn't Skylark wait until she got into the stable? It was impossible to dig them out without taking half the gravel with them. She thought of calling Imogen, but she was shut away in her bedroom doing her homework. Louise sighed, and went to fetch the trowel.

Robert dropped the boys off at Beaconsfield station. He hadn't managed to get a word out of Trevor, who seemed to be a deaf-mute. Still, that wasn't his problem. He had other things on his mind.

Driving home, he stopped at a phone box beside the road. He went in, inserted his phone card and punched a number. How generous he had been to give the boys a lift.

Meanwhile, in Hackney, four women lounged on cushions in Erin's living room. Mugs of tea and a half-eaten cake sat on the hearthrug. A woman called Lesley was talking.

'Last week, when we were talking about our fathers...' She laughed. 'Well, we're always talking about our fathers –'

'Question is,' said another woman, 'are our fathers talking about us?'

Erin smiled. 'If they were, we wouldn't need to sit around talking about *them*.'

Lesley yanked up her socks. 'Well, I've been working on my feelings of rejection. Did I tell you about when I was ten, and he bought my brother a Red Indian outfit?'

Erin nodded. 'He took his photo in it, for the Christmas card.'

Lesley nodded. 'I pretended I wasn't hurt, but the thing is, I'm still seeking his approval.'

The other woman nudged her, smiling. 'It's the little girl in you, Les.'

Lesley pointed at the plate. 'That piece of cake, for instance. He's telling me not to take it because I'll get fat.'

'Wish *I* looked like you in your swimsuit.'

'Yet this cake is calling *eat me!*'

They laughed. Erin gave her a slice.

Upstairs, Maddy was sitting on the floor in Allegra's bedroom. They were playing with the Barbie doll. Allegra held up a gold lamé evening dress. 'Should she wear this on a first date?'

'I don't know,' said Maddy. 'Maybe the trouser suit.'

'But she doesn't like purple.'

'Why's she got it then?'

'It came in the box.'

Maddy leaned back against the bed. 'I used to knock my sisters' dolls over with my bulldozer.'

'Why?'

'Because I didn't like them.'

Allegra sat the naked doll on her knee. 'Shall we wash her hair again?'

The doorbell rang. Maddy jumped up and ran down the stairs. 'Pru! Come in.' She put her finger to her lips. They walked past the living room.

'What's happening?' Prudence whispered.

'It's Erin's group. They come here after swimming.'

They walked upstairs. Prudence pointed to the doll. 'She looks pretty.'

'She looks stupid,' said Allegra.

The two women went into the other bedroom. Prudence sat down on the bed. 'Maddy, I'm desperate. I couldn't phone from home because they're both *there*. Anyway, I needed to get out.' The bedcover was embroidered with little mirrors. She picked at one. 'Please take Mum for a bit.'

'Pru –'

'It's been two weeks now. I'm going mad.'

'Why can't she go back home?'

'She can't. Anyway, it's being sold.'

'Why can't she stay with Louise?'

'She can't leave London,' said Prudence. 'She's trying to sort out the business – find somebody to take it over. Dad's useless. Half the time he's not there. Please, Maddy. It's messing things up with Steve.'

'Why?'

'Why do you think!'

Allegra came in, carrying the doll. It was dressed up in chiffon. 'Does this suit her?'

'Very nice,' said Maddy.

Prudence shook her head. 'Beige is awfully Rotary Club.'

Allegra went back into her bedroom. Maddy stood at the window, looking out. Prudence addressed her back – jeans, yellow T-shirt. Was Maddy putting on weight? She seemed squarer, somehow. Robert said that all lesbians were fat because then they could look as unattractive as each other, but Robert said things like that.

'Mum brings out the worst in him, I can't describe it, or he does in her, who knows – We're all on top of each other –'

'Why doesn't he get a job then?'

'Why are you so hostile towards him?'

Maddy picked at the wax in a candlestick. 'He's not good enough for you.'

'That's not true –'

She turned round. 'You never look happy. Even now he's living with you you don't look happy.'

'That's because Mum's there. Look – take her for tonight. Please! Steve and I want to have dinner together, just us two. He didn't leave home to live with our mother.'

'That's his fault.'

'God, this place is getting to you,' said Prudence. 'All that sisterhood stuff downstairs.'

'She can't come tonight,' said Maddy. 'The group always stays for supper.'

'They're pretend sisters. We're real ones.' Prudence urged her: 'Come on, be a real sister to me. Take her tomorrow then, have her for a few days. She's looking for a flat, she'll be off our hands soon.'

'I'll have to ask Erin. It's her house.'

'Tell her it's an emergency,' said Prudence.

'Mum's angry with me at the moment.'

'She's angry with everybody.'

Maddy ran her fingers through her hair. She had cropped it shorter; perhaps that was why she looked bigger. 'She'll find out.'

'What?' Prudence paused. 'Don't worry about that. She thinks you're just flatmates. Housemates.' She got to her feet and stood at the window, next to her sister. 'She's got to know sooner or later.' She looked at Maddy's profile. 'Come on, Maddy. You've always been brave. Much braver than me or Louise. You've stood up to Dad. You've worked in a bloody war zone in Africa.'

'This is different.'

'If I was starving and black you'd help me.'

Night had fallen. Jamie and Trevor sauntered along Brixton High Street, trying to look cool. The place was seething with people – mostly black, mostly kids – out for Saturday night. Trevor lit a cigarette and flicked the match into the air.

A man, leaning in a doorway, muttered something to them. They stopped and looked at each other. A bus rumbled past. It was Trevor who finally nodded. They rummaged for some money. The man slipped a small package into Trevor's hand.

Maddy was washing up. The front door slammed; the last of the women were leaving.

Erin came into the kitchen and put her arms around her. 'Stop that, Cinderella, I'll do it in the morning.' She kissed Maddy's earlobe. 'I thought they'd never leave.'

'But you like them.'

Erin's voice was low and thrilling. 'All I could think about was you . . . how I was going to touch you here . . .' She slid her hand under Maddy's T-shirt and fondled her breast. 'And here . . .' She touched her mouth. 'My darling, my honey . . .'

Maddy's throat closed up. She stood there, unable to move. Erin pulled the T-shirt over her head. Maddy shut her eyes. All she could hear was the dripping tap.

Erin dipped her finger into a pot of honey. She anointed Maddy's nipples, one and then the other. She bent her head and licked Maddy's honeyed breasts. Maddy, swooning with pleasure, stumbled against the sink.

Jamie was impressed by Trevor. Trevor came from the dodgiest estate in High Wycombe. His father had a prison record. Trevor nicked things from Tesco and had been banned from every pub in Beaconsfield. He had an encyclopaedic knowledge of drugs, which he mixed and matched with a connoisseur's precision. Jamie was deeply flattered to be his friend and longed to impress him.

They arrived at The Fridge and joined the queue. Suddenly, Jamie stared. Walking towards them was a man who looked like Grandad. It *was* Grandad. With him, arm-in-arm, was a black woman.

They drew nearer. Jamie knew, of course, that his grandfather had shacked up with this April person and come to live in Brixton. However, he wasn't prepared for the shock of seeing them together; he was so used to seeing his grandfather with Granny. Suddenly, he felt a surge of pride. He stepped out of the queue and greeted them.

They said they had been out for a meal. 'I've heard a lot about you,' said April, shaking his hand. She had a round, vibrant face – big features crowded together. 'Straight As and all.' She indicated Gordon. 'He's very proud of you. When are you going to York?'

'In October.'

She pointed to The Fridge. 'Who's playing?'

'Adrenalin Village.'

'Mmm. Just feel like a dance.'

Gordon squeezed her arm. 'Go on then, go and enjoy your-

209

self.' He grinned at them both. 'I'll just tuck myself up with a hottie.'

Maddy and Erin lay in bed, skin to skin. Maddy stroked the slippery channel of sweat between Erin's breasts.

'You've learned a lot, my little mouse,' murmured Erin. 'How shy you were once . . . shy and timid, afraid to come out . . .'

'It's you who taught me.' Beside them the candle guttered and expired.

'I want to tell the world, tell women, what they're missing.'

'Don't tell my mother.' Maddy spoke into the blackness. 'Are you sure you don't mind her coming?'

'Aren't you proud of us?'

'I'm still a mouse in that respect,' said Maddy. 'Give me time.'

Erin rolled over to face her. 'We've got all the time in the world, my love.'

'Can I sleep in your study? It'll only be for a couple of nights.'

'I'll creep in and ravish you on my fax machine.'

Maddy said: 'If you ravished me on your computer, I could be a computer mouse.'

Maddy had cracked a rare joke. Erin smiled, and held her in her arms.

There is always a moment of embarrassment when you first see somebody dance. It is like the first time you hear them speaking French. Jamie was gratified to see that Trevor, despite the dope he had smoked, was even more inept than he was. Trevor was weedily built and belonged to the limp puppet school of dancing. Scowling into the middle distance, he jerked around to his own private rhythm, just disconnected to the beat, as if pulled by invisible strings. April, however, was a terrific dancer. Jamie could hear his father say

210

natural sense of rhythm but his father was thankfully absent. Her joy was infectious, however, and Jamie felt himself loosening up. Trevor even smiled – a sight Jamie had only seen once before when, after work, he had pulled out a side of smoked salmon from his jacket.

Jamie was proud, too, to be dancing with a black woman and mouthed at her like a goldfish so that people could see she was with him. The place was crammed. April, perspiring in a short skirt and knitted vest, mouthed back. She was a well-built woman; Jamie tried not to stare at her breasts. They moved up and down within her vest as if they had a life of their own. How weird, to think that his own grandfather handled those each night! Grandad was an old age pensioner. Jamie squeezed his eyes shut and gave himself up to the music. It thrummed through his brain; it shook his bone-marrow to jelly.

Afterwards, they spilled out into the night. Trevor left; he was going to stay with his sister in Streatham. April had invited Jamie to stay the night at her flat.

They walked down the street. 'Does he ever talk?' she asked.

'No.'

April opened the front door. They climbed the stairs and she let him into her flat.

He looked around. 'Wicked place. Wish *I* lived here.'

'Don't you like living in the country?'

He shook his head. 'It's not even the real country, it's full of stockbrokers and people who've had golden handshakes. There's nobody like you there –' He stopped. 'If you see what I mean.'

She laughed. Now he could see her in normal light – not the strobes of The Fridge or the sodium orange of the street – he saw that April's skin was beautiful. It was the colour of the polished conkers with which he used to play. Her teeth were white as milk. Her broad lips were a colour for which he had no words. Blushing, he wondered what it would be like to kiss them.

211

April went into the other room and brought back an armful of bedding. She pushed the bedroom door shut with her bottom.

'He's sleeping like a baby,' she whispered.

Jamie took the duvet and put it on the sofa. 'It's weird,' he said.

'You mean, me and your grandad?'

'What do you see in him?' he asked.

'You been in love yet?'

He shook his head.

April sat down on the duvet. 'When it happens, it may not be the prettiest girl you know, or the cleverest. If it was like that, what would the rest of us do? Love doesn't work like that, thank God.' She plumped up the pillow. 'Nothing matters – their age, nothing. You just know, when you're with that person, you're utterly yourself. You're the Jamie you like the best.' She looked at him. Her face was open and frank. 'I don't care what other people think. Maybe he's looking for another daughter and he'll get it right this time. Fathers always think, if only they had done this, or that. Maybe I'm looking for a father. I don't know. I don't care.'

Jamie blushed. He spoke to the carpet. 'I think he's really lucky.'

'We both are,' she said. 'Believe me.'

It was the next day, Sunday. Imogen was riding her horse. They galloped along the edge of a ploughed field, up along Cobbett's Rise. Her village lay below her, shrouded in mist. Poor souls, she thought, living there so blindly in their fog. Up here it was sunny; she was free. Skylark's muscles moved beneath her; twin plumes of breath pumped from the mare's nostrils. Lapwings rose up, their wings flickering black and white, and skittered down in the next field like glitter shaken from a Christmas tree.

Skylark's neck was damp with sweat; her body heaved for breath between Imogen's thighs. Imogen reined her in and headed left, towards Blackthorn Wood. With her hand, she checked that the saddle-bag was still there. She had even brought some cans of lager.

Karl's van was parked in the clearing. Imogen's heart jolted. He leaned against a tree, smoking a cigarette. She rode up to him and dismounted.

'Hi,' she said.

Louise was cleaning out the rabbit hutch. She glared at Boyd. He sat, his ears flattened, in his sleeping quarters.

'Don't you growl at me,' she said. 'I don't want to be doing this either. Where's Imogen, you may ask? She's found a new object for her devotion.' She jabbed at the droppings with her trowel. 'Females are fickle creatures, aren't they, Boyd? You know that by now.'

The phone rang. She straightened up and called 'Robert!' but there was no reply. She shut the hutch door and ran into the house.

It was Jamie, calling from Beaconsfield station. Louise wiped her hands on a tea-towel. She picked up her car keys from the dresser. Today she felt as if she lived in a saucepan. The lid was squashed down on her; she bubbled up, trying to prise it open with the mere force of her frustration. Of course, it didn't budge. She blamed it on the fog outside, pressing down on her spirit.

Imogen tipped up the can and drained the lager down her throat. 'A lot of my friends, their parents have split up. But not their grandparents. I mean, grandparents are supposed to stay the same. That's the point of them.' She shivered.

'Here.' Karl took her hand and rubbed it.

'I mean, Grandad must be . . .'

'Doing it,' he said.

'Don't!'

'Nasty thought, eh?' he said. 'Probably give him a hernia.'

213

She laughed.

He looked at her. 'You look pretty when you laugh.'

'Isn't my nose blue?' she asked.

He nodded, and covered her nose with his hand. 'Your lips have gone kind of purple too.'

She covered her mouth. 'Don't!'

'Here. I'll help.'

He leaned over. His lips brushed hers.

'That better?' he asked.

Her voice shook. 'You're so warm,' she said.

Karl pointed to his chest. 'Got me own forge in here.'

She laughed. He tilted her head. Their noses bumped. He kissed her. It was a long, deep kiss. His tongue slid into her mouth. She put her arms around him, inside his jacket, and felt the muscles move in his back.

'He stayed with them!' Louise stood, with her son, in the kitchen.

'What?' Robert looked up from the paper.

'Dad and that girl. Jamie stayed the night with them!'

Robert looked at his son. 'Is she gorgeous? I don't trust your mum, she's biased.'

'She's really sorted,' said Jamie.

'Sorted!' Robert laughed. 'I can tell you stack shelves for a living.'

'She's great.' Jamie opened the fridge. 'She knew the bloke behind the bar.'

'He slept in the flat!' Louise hissed. 'Dad made him breakfast!'

'She's got this wicked coffee-maker.' Jamie pulled out a tub of guacamole. 'One of those espresso things.'

'What would Granny say if she knew?' asked Louise.

Robert tipped back his chair. 'I don't see what's wrong.'

'It's so disloyal,' said Louise. 'Whose side is he on?'

Jamie dipped his finger into the guacamole and licked it. 'Why do we have to take sides?'

214

The door opened. Imogen came in. She glowed from her ride. Louise said to her: 'Jamie stayed the night with Grandad and that girl.'

Robert turned the page of his paper. 'She's gorgeous, apparently. Really sorted.'

'It's not funny,' said Louise.

'– the lucky old tosser.'

'Robert!'

'Getting his leg over at his age.' Robert turned the next page. 'Gives hope to us all.'

Imogen flinched. 'Dad!'

'And with somebody in a *nurse's uniform*. Oh bliss!'

Monty clambered to his feet and barked. 'Shut up!' said Louise. He wagged his tail and sat down again.

'I always had a sneaking liking for the old sod,' said Robert, 'when he wasn't boring me to death. In fact, on many occasions I've offered him my moral support when you lot –' He indicated Louise '– were ganging up on him. Poor bugger was outnumbered. But he's certainly gone up in my estimation now.' He laughed. 'Good old Gordon, the Humbert Humbert of the building trade.'

'The what?' asked Louise.

'*Lolita*,' said Jamie.

'April's no Lolita,' said Louise. 'She's thirty.'

Robert leered. 'Still cradle-snatching, in my book.'

Imogen turned on her heel and left the room. Louise followed her daughter into the hall.

'Did you have a good ride?' she asked.

'It was okay,' said Imogen, and went upstairs.

Louise felt rebuffed. Just then Jamie shouted from the kitchen: 'Bloody rabbit's out. Who left the hutch open?'

It was five-thirty that afternoon. Maddy was making up the spare bed in Erin's study. She fixed her Amnesty poster on the wall so it covered up the gardening diary-planner. She had covered the computer with a Kashmiri shawl. It almost

215

looked like her bedroom.

She looked round. Allegra stood in the doorway. 'I won't tell if you give me a Barbie ballerina.'

'Ally! That's blackmail.'

'Please!'

'I haven't got any money,' Maddy said.

'Doesn't Mummy pay you for gardening?'

Maddy shook her head. 'It all goes back into the business.'

'But you do most of the work.'

'Only because your mum's busy with her book.' Maddy rolled the Blu-Tack into a ball. 'Please, Ally. It's not nice to blackmail me.'

'All right. Not the doll then. Just the ballet dress.'

Jamie and Imogen sat in the caravan. It seemed colder in here than outside but Jamie wanted to smoke a joint. He sat on the hard little bed and Imogen sat on the seat that turned into a bunk. They pictured their aunties sitting there, long ago, and telling each other secrets.

'Mum and Dad, they don't know what love is,' said Imogen. 'They're so crude.'

'So what happened?' Jamie offered her the joint.

Imogen shook her head. 'You wouldn't understand.'

'Immy!'

'I love him.'

Jamie took a drag and exhaled it slowly. 'This bloke, you don't know anything about him. Has he got a girlfriend?'

'He used to live with somebody but it's all over.'

'What did he do? Come on, sis.'

'He kissed me.'

'Where?' he asked.

'The normal place.'

'No – I mean, where were you?'

'In Blackthorn Wood.' She closed her eyes. 'It was so beautiful. The birds were singing and the sun came out –'

'Did he do anything else?'

'No! It's not like that. Oh, you wouldn't understand.'

He took another drag. 'Did you feel, like, your best self with him? Even though you haven't got anything in common?'

She stared at him. 'What?'

Maddy was cooking supper. Her mother leaned over and looked into the pot.

'That looks interesting. What is it?'

'Chick peas and okra,' said Maddy.

Allegra looked up from her homework. 'You know – ladies' fingers.'

Maddy stirred the mixture. 'I used to eat them in Nigeria.'

'They go all slimy when you cook them,' said Allegra.

Dorothy asked Allegra: 'Have you always been a vegetarian?'

Allegra shook her head. 'When my daddy takes me out we go to Burger King.'

'Who is your daddy?'

'He's called Aziz. Mum just used him for his sperm. He takes me roller-skating.'

'I see.' Dorothy cleared her throat.

'He doesn't come here much but he sends me faxes.'

'Faxes?' asked Dorothy.

'You know,' said Allegra patiently, 'you phone up a number –'

'I know what faxes are,' said Dorothy. 'I mean, that's how you communicate?'

'I want us to get onto e-mail.'

Dorothy gazed at Allegra's dark head, bent over a page of sums. She thought: is this what has been happening to the world, all these years?

The ground floor of Erin's house had been knocked through to make one big room. They ate in the dining area at the back.

217

It was painted dark red and smelled faintly of joss-sticks. The walls were hung with tribal fabrics.

'Was it like this when you moved in?' asked Dorothy.

Erin shook her head. 'I knocked down the wall, there. Put in the fireplace.'

'It's quite a job.' Dorothy, who knew about building, had to admire the woman. She didn't like Erin; they had nothing in common and she suspected that Erin found her suburban – invisible, really – just someone who happened to be in her house. Female solidarity obviously didn't extend to senior citizens from Purley who didn't wear jewels in their nostrils. Erin had offered her no word of sympathy about the break-up of her marriage. Maybe she thought that men were so contemptible that Dorothy was well out of it. Dorothy had no idea what went on in Erin's mind, she hadn't met anybody like her before. But she could see how Maddy was drawn to her – there was something inspirational about her, something fiercely independent. Maybe Dorothy could learn to be like that too, one day. One day in the distant future. It seemed impossible to contemplate at the moment. Oh, she had put on a brave front to Gordon but she was terrified. Who wouldn't be? Where, for example, was she to stay after these couple of nights with Maddy? Back to Prudence? Connie in Harrow? Soon she would run out of friends.

'She built the kitchen too,' said Maddy, 'designed it and everything. Would you like some more rice?'

'My dad designs houses but he never gets any work,' said Allegra. 'It's because people in Britain are design-blind.'

Erin shook her head. 'He's too authoritarian.' She turned to Dorothy. 'Aziz comes from a high-caste family. He treats his clients like untouchables. That's why he's hardly got any.'

'He's nice!' said Allegra. 'Mum doesn't like him coming here.'

'He has a bad effect on you,' said Erin. 'You're upset for days afterwards.'

Allegra wrinkled her nose. 'Only because you're so horrid to him.'

218

'He's very aggressive.' Erin tossed back her hair. There were crescents of studs in her ears; they winked in the candle-light. 'It stems from weakness and fear. He's out of touch with his feelings, that's why he's so angry.'

'Perhaps he's angry because he never sees his daughter,' said Dorothy. 'She is his daughter, after all. She hasn't got another father. However faulty he is.' Suddenly she was filled with despair – at the faxes, at the world. 'And I know it's none of my business, but I don't think we should be talking about him like this in front of her.'

There was a silence. Maddy turned to Erin. 'She's right.'

Erin stared at her. 'What?'

Maddy leaned over to the little girl. 'Have you finished? Go and have your bath.'

Allegra slipped from her chair and left the room.

Maddy said to Erin: 'Mum's right. You always slag him off in front of her.'

'What's the matter with you?' Erin demanded.

'She shouldn't hear her father criticised like that.'

'You can talk!' Erin snorted. 'You're always criticising *your* father.'

Dorothy interrupted: 'Actually, she's been surprisingly nice to him recently.'

'Forget mine.' Maddy stood up and started collecting the plates. 'It's not fair, Erin, that Allegra's always out on Sundays. You do it on purpose. It's not fair on either of them. You're the one who's being authoritarian.'

Erin glared at her. 'Maddy, what is all this?'

'She has a right to see him, otherwise she'll never trust him, she'll end up in women's groups slagging him off. And he has a right to see her.' Maddy scraped the rice back into the bowl. 'You really can be very bossy, Erin. Who says yours is the best way to bring up a child? Most of the time you're working or off somewhere giving interviews or shut away in your stu–' She stopped. 'My bedroom. In fact, *I* see more of Allegra than you do nowadays.' She paused, her face flushed.

219

Erin raised her eyebrows. 'Do you feel better now?' she asked.

'I'm sorry.' Maddy stood up. 'I just think Mum has a point, that's all.'

Dorothy picked up the plates. 'Why don't I take them into the kitchen?'

'It's all right, I'll do it,' said Maddy. 'I do all the washing-up anyway.'

She went into the kitchen. Erin got up and followed her. Dorothy sat down again. She gazed at the ruined remains of the meal.

Erin closed the kitchen door behind her. 'What was all that about?' she hissed.

'It's true.' Maddy dumped the plates into the sink. 'I've been meaning to say it for weeks.'

'But you only dared to now your mother's here. You're such a coward, Maddy. You attack me like that but you haven't the guts to tell her you're gay.'

She swung round and left the room.

The rise in the divorce rate must do wonders for the sale of sofabeds. Dorothy lay, tucked-up, in Erin's living room. A draught came through the crack in the window-shutters. She thought: I can't afford to fall out with my hosts. I'm at their mercy.

Outside, a dog barked. She was somewhere in Hackney; she didn't know where. Some kids walked past in the street. One of them chanted: 'Paul's Mum picks her bum.' What were they doing out at this time of night?

Maddy, wearing a long T-shirt and socks, came in to say goodnight.

'I'm certainly putting my foot in it nowadays,' said Dorothy.

'It's not your fault.'

'Used to be your dad's speciality, didn't it? Putting his foot in it.' Beneath the duvet Dorothy shivered; she shoved her fingers into her armpits to warm them up. 'Oh, I do miss him.'

'I know.' Maddy – gruff, embarrassed – leaned down and rubbed her mother's shoulder. 'I didn't mean to – you know – take his side or anything. The other day. I don't want to take anybody's side.'

Dorothy cleared her throat. 'Don't let it put you off . . . what's happened to your dad and me. Marriage is – well, wonderful really. And you'll find the right man.'

Maddy reached towards the lamp. 'Shall I switch this off?'

Dorothy nodded.

'Night night,' they both said, at the same time.

'So this little boy says, *I'll show you mine if you show me yours.*' Robert pulled on his cigar. Their guest, a neighbour called Derek, nodded encouragingly through the smoke. Robert took a sip of brandy. 'So he pulls down his trousers and she says, *Oh, is that all?*'

It was half past twelve. Louise thought: he's bored rigid by Derek; why does he invite him to dinner?

'She says, *My Daddy's got two of those.*'

'Two?' Derek guffawed.

Robert nodded. 'She says, *A little one like that, which he pees with, and a big one the au pair brushes her teeth with.*'

They roared with laughter. Louise stood up. 'I'm off. Night, Derek.'

'Terrific nosh, as per usual.' Derek looked at his watch. 'God, work tomorrow. Better toddle.'

Robert leaned over and refilled his glass. 'Come on, have a nightcap.'

Louise glanced at her husband, and left the room.

Alone at last, Prudence and Stephen had made love. They

221

slept. When they shifted their position, moist animal smells were exhaled from the sheets. Outside, in the one-way street, a lone car passed.

Suddenly, Stephen sat up.

'What is it?' Prudence asked.

'I keep thinking the house has caught fire.'

She sat up and sniffed. 'Can't smell anything.'

'Not here. At home.'

She paused. 'Oh.'

'I keep thinking something's happened to the boys and I can't get to them.'

'They're fine.' Her voice was sharper than she had intended. 'Go to sleep.'

Maddy lay in Erin's study. She couldn't sleep. She gazed at the shrouded bulk of the Apple Mac.

The door opened. Allegra crept in, and climbed into bed with her. 'Don't quarrel with Mum,' she whispered. 'Don't leave us.'

'I won't . . . It's all right.'

She hugged the little girl. The fax bleeped.

'It's Dad!' Allegra pulled away and got out of the bed.

'Not at one o'clock.'

The machine started to hum. Maddy switched on the light. They watched the paper slide out.

Allegra pulled it off. The fax was addressed to Erin. She gave it to Maddy.

'It's from her agent in New York,' said Maddy. 'They've sold the paperback rights.'

'How exciting.'

'Don't be sarky.'

'When her book comes out she's going to get even worse.' Allegra climbed back into bed.

'Only a month to go.'

Allegra sighed. 'Just wish it was from Dad.'

222

*

The front door slammed. Robert came upstairs.

Louise lay there. The moonlight slanted through the window, silvering her pile of magazines. She said: 'Why do you stay downstairs nowadays until you know I'm asleep?'

'You're not asleep, are you?'

He went into the bathroom and closed the door. She lay there, alone in the big brass bed.

The moonlight shone through the window; it shone onto Imogen's brow as she lay asleep. Outside, somewhere near the church, an owl hooted. Down below, the gravestones slanted towards each other as if they were whispering. Below them lives had been stopped at forty years; at fourteen. In the vases daffodils had withered into little screws of paper. Their lives had been the shortest of all.

Imogen lay sleeping. She had already reached sixteen; she had got this far. Nothing had hurt her yet, not truly hurt her. She lay, her fist pressed against her mouth, sucking her knuckle. She had slept like that since she was a baby.

Three

'What are we going to do about Mum?'

Maddy, Louise and Prudence sat in the caravan. It was like the old days, except now the positions were reversed – it was they who felt like parents. It seemed so late in the day for their parents' marriage to explode. Sometimes it struck them as thoughtless; after all, they had busy lives of their own.

Their father was gadding about like a twenty-year-old, bopping till dawn for all they knew; none of them had seen him for weeks. He was back at work, upsetting their mother by turning up at the office. Dorothy had become a loose cannon, wreaking havoc wherever she landed. She was temporarily housed in a bedsitter in Prudence's street but she was still dangerously at large, descending on them for evenings when she angrily slagged off their father and cross-questioned them to see if they had had any contact with him. She still hadn't found a permanent place to live; she couldn't decide where to go.

'It's like King Lear,' said Prudence. 'Except this time its Mrs Lear. Who's going to have her next?' She looked at Louise. 'You've got off lightly so far. Isn't it time you pulled your weight?'

Louise had always had it easy – looks, children, money, wistaria-burdened house with five bedrooms. It didn't seem fair, but then nothing seemed fair where Louise was concerned.

'I can't,' said Louise. 'She's got to be in London.' It was true. Dorothy still hadn't found anyone to run the office.

Imogen came in and sat down. Her face glowed. She thwacked her riding crop against her jodhpurs. 'You hiding from Jamie's friends?' she asked.

They nodded. Even in the caravan they could hear the thud-thud of music from the house.

'They're so infantile,' drawled Imogen. She seemed, these past weeks, to have grown out of Jamie's contemporaries.

'We're trying to decide what to do about your granny,' said Louise. She explained the situation. 'She sees your grandad every day, it's like rubbing salt into the wound. She'll never start to recover or begin a life of her own.' She picked up a cigarette butt. 'Has your brother been smoking in here?'

Imogen turned to Prudence. 'Why don't you get your boyfriend to run the office? After all, he's run one before.'

The three women gazed at her. There was a smudge of mud on Imogen's nose. Despite this, she looked impressive. Imogen could be surprisingly practical – even, on occasion, inspired. It was she, after all, who had suggested that Stephen work for Gordon in the first place.

'He can work in the office,' she said, 'and leave Granny free to look for another husband. She doesn't look too bad, for her age. And then she'd be off your hands.'

So Stephen joined Kendal Contractors as office manager, a position more suited to his capabilities than that of a labourer. On a blustery day in February The Birches was sold, the yard cleared and the office shifted to new premises in Herne Hill, near Frank's place. Dorothy dumped the last of the files on the desk and kissed Stephen on the cheek.

'Good luck. You'll need it.' She gave him the keys. 'I'm off.'

'Where?'

She patted her handbag. 'Put this in the bank.' It was her cheque for half the house. 'Then I'm off to the hairdressers. Then I'm treating my friend Connie to a slap-up dinner in the

225

West End and later I rather fancied one of those male stripper places.'

'You're not!'

'No, but I could, couldn't I?' There was a glazed, hectic look to her. She gestured at the piles of cardboard boxes. 'Rather you than me.' She put on her coat. 'Bye Frank, bye chaps.'

And she stepped into the waiting minicab and sped away.

The magnitude of what had happened over the past two months still stopped Gordon in his tracks. It seemed extraordinary that something as abstract as love could result in such monumental physical upheavals. Thirty-three bags of rubbish had been pulled from his house and loaded onto refuse trucks; the furniture had been crated up, loaded into lorries and locked into a depository in Croydon. The caravan had been hauled along twenty miles of motorway and heaved into position at the Old Vicarage. A new family, with their own furniture, had been lumberingly installed in The Birches. Stephen travelled to Herne Hill every day. Dorothy had moved into a rented room near Prudence; people had no doubt been trudging up and down those stairs lugging carrier bags and cardboard boxes.

A mere smile had started this – a spark of recognition, a stirring in his loins. This seemed both terrible and miraculous to him.

He accepted full responsibility. Gordon was a decent man – oh, he was boastful and impatient, he had his faults. But he was basically a good person who had done a deed that had shocked himself as much as anyone else. Now the house was sold his family map had been redrawn. New territories had been created and new alliances formed. He wanted to make peace with his daughters. He was nervous, however, about getting in touch with them. They were busy dealing with Dorothy; she was the one who needed their support. He had been cheered by Maddy's show of solidarity in April's flat

226

but suspected that this was just a momentary act of rebellion; Maddy had always been out-of-kilter with the rest of them. The situation was too raw to test his youngest daughter's support, just yet.

So he busied himself with work. It was strange no longer to hear his old ally Dorothy on the phone or to see her face when he dropped in at the office. Instead, Stephen sat there, painstakingly learning all the procedures that he and Dorothy had taken for granted. It was strange travelling to a new office – in fact, on several occasions he had found himself heading towards Purley.

It was liberating, however, to get rid of the house. Dorothy had said that she was glad to get shot of it. Maybe, despite her bitterness, she too felt liberated. It felt unnatural that he couldn't ask her. That, and so many other questions that popped into his head. She was his oldest friend; he couldn't just switch her off. He missed her, and he could tell nobody this. How daft that you could love somebody else and still miss your wife! Perhaps everybody felt this; he didn't have a clue. Men his age didn't have these sorts of conversations.

The Sunday after the house was sold he took April out to lunch. They went to a restaurant in Maidenhead, overlooking the river. The couple at the next table gazed at them; it was envy, of course.

April opened the menu and yawned. She had just come off a week of night duty.

'Why don't you give up your job?' he asked. 'Let me take care of you.'

'I don't want to give it up.' Her face appeared over the leather binder. 'I like it.'

'You told me you're just a glorified skivvy.'

'Yes, but it's glorified. It's what I've always wanted to do.' She pointed to the menu. 'I'll have the avocado and the pheasant. I know I complain about it but so do you, about yours. That's why people live together. Well, one of the reasons. It's cosy complaining.' She put down the menu and smiled at him. She wore a demure white blouse he hadn't seen before; she still had clothes he hadn't yet seen.

He said: 'I want to buy you a house. How about it? How about renting out your place and moving in with me, somewhere nice.' He put his hand over hers. 'You deserve it.'

She gazed out of the window. The river was grey and swollen. 'Everyone who doesn't live in Brixton thinks that everyone who does is longing to get out. Actually, I like it.' She smiled at him. 'Let's not rush things. We're happy as we are, aren't we? You're such a restless bugger.'

It's a funny thing about love. The same words can be an accusation or a verbal caress. Words are like tofu: their taste comes from the emotions that drench them.

Gordon looked at April. She picked through a bowl of nuts, searching for the cashews. She put one into her mouth.

In her white lacy collar she looked like a gospel singer. He said: 'Right enough. I'll do whatever you want,' because what he really wanted was to kiss her.

But he was unconvinced. He wanted to look after her. He wanted to be in charge.

At the end of the month Erin's book was published. Prudence held a party in her flat. Dorothy helped with the preparations. She needed tasks to anchor herself. She felt she was spinning into space, dizzy with loneliness. She needed to get a grip.

'Haven't you got any more baking trays?' she asked Prudence irritably. If only sadness were as appealing as it sounded. In fact, it makes those suffering from it quarrelsome and egotistical, distempered and intolerant. Dorothy knew that she mustn't alienate her daughters; they were all she had. But as she laid out the onion bhajis she felt herself prickle with hostility – towards the guests, who would no doubt be contented and handsome, towards Erin whose book she didn't like the sound of, towards the very fact that they had to have vegetarian food, which struck her as self-righteous. She knew she was being unreasonable. She knew that even her daughters had only a limited reservoir of tolerance, but the very fact that she now had to be nice to people – she was a guest in their homes, she was beholden to them – only increased her bad temper.

She carried a plate of crudités into the living room. 'Your father's not coming, is he?'

'Of course not,' said Prudence. 'You think I'm an idiot?'

'He'd love to show up and ruin it for me.' Dorothy dumped down the plate. She was a tanker, run aground on the rocks. Her sides were split open; out of them seeped poisonous oil.

The guests arrived – a lot of people Dorothy didn't know. They did indeed look handsome and contented; there was a sheen to them. Some of the women wore suits.

'So you're Prudence's mother,' said one of them. 'I've heard so much about you.'

What: that I'm an abandoned wife? Her gaze flickered around the room, searching for Gordon to rescue her.

He wasn't there, of course. She was so stupid. Her eyes filled with tears. It was the blasted cigarette smoke. What could she do with these old habits, how could she slough them off? How did anyone do anything?

Prudence tapped her glass. The room fell silent. 'People say that publishing isn't a risk-taking business any more, that new novels are hard to promote unless they're written – or not written, as the case may be – by a TV personality or stand-up comedian. Well, Erin Fox is not a household name – yet. But listen to these reviews.' She read from a piece of paper. '*Marie Claire* said *A stunning debut*. The *Guardian* said *Compulsively readable, a raunchy trans-global romp through the female psyche* . . . and there are plenty more where they came from. So, please raise your glasses to *Playing with Fire*. We played with it and – look! – we haven't got burned.'

There was a murmur of laughter; the clink of glasses. Dorothy was standing near Stephen. A man turned to him. 'Here's to you too, old cock.' He raised his glass. 'I hear you're working for a builder, eh? Doing their paperwork.' He grinned. 'Need all your editing skills there, I bet.'

'What do you mean?' asked Stephen.

The man grinned. 'Making things vanish, nudge-nudge.'

Stephen laughed. Dorothy stared at him. She turned to the man. 'Not all builders are crooked, you know. Certainly not our firm.' She turned to Stephen. 'Thank you for standing up for us.'

She collected an empty plate and took it into the kitchen, where Maddy was pouring out some grapefruit juice. She dumped the plate on the draining board. 'How could Prudence live with such a weak man?' she demanded.

'Don't spoil things!' hissed Maddy. 'It is Erin's party.'

Dorothy looked at her daughter. 'That used to be your department.'

'What did?'

Dorothy said: 'Oh, it doesn't matter.'

The Literary Editor of the *Sunday Times* flicked his fag-end into the fire. Prudence flinched. Couldn't he tell it was gas?

Her room was packed with people. Between the heads she could see Stephen talking to Erin. She wore the same tribal dress she had worn to that dinner party all those months ago. *At least he didn't have trouble with one erection.* What a fateful party that had been! Maddy had fallen in love, she had become a lesbian. Now she had moved home and started a new career. Their father had fallen in love, again with the most unexpected of people. Their parents had split up, their home sold and their childhood packed into crates and locked up in Croydon. Stephen had left his wife and come to live here, with her. She thought of the absent Louise. Only she had remained untouched, her charmed life sealed off from the mess everybody else made of theirs.

Prudence passed round the samosas. She was a practised host, she liked giving parties. This was a business affair, however, and the presence of her mother made her uncomfortable. In the old days Maddy had been the troublemaker but love had changed her. She was proud of Erin's book, she had somehow entered into Prudence's life.

'It is a wonderful novel, isn't it,' Prudence said to the man from *Kaleidoscope*.

'I'm going to sue you,' he said. 'It's ruined my sex life. My girlfriend brought it to bed every night for a week.'

Prudence laughed. 'Maybe we could market it as a contraceptive device.'

She moved away, looking for her mother. She didn't trust Dorothy; she had become so unpredictable – weepy, aggressive, manically cheerful. Dorothy was passing round a plate of quiche. Her hair was tinted a redder shade nowadays. She wore her suede waistcoat and emerald-green slacks; she looked like a brassy woman who picked up men on cruises. Behind the bold front, however, she seemed to have disintegrated. Prudence realised, standing there, that she didn't know her mother at all. She wasn't a separate person; she was half of Prudence's parents. Was she mean or generous, for instance? Was she a sensual person, or basically inhibited? Prudence didn't have a clue. Her mother's identity had drained into her husband, he was the dominant person and had bullied her into a shape of his making. What on earth was going on in her mother's head?

'Are you okay?' Prudence asked. 'Are you enjoying it?'

'I'm fine.' Her mother smiled – a sweet smile, Louise's smile. Her mother was scattered into all of them.

They were interrupted by a woman with a crew-cut who worked for Channel 4. 'Erin Fox is a real star!' she sighed, her cheeks blazing.

'She is, isn't she? We've got great hopes of her.' Prudence thought: there's a substance to Erin, an inner conviction, that's why people are drawn to her.

Prudence found her handbag. She rummaged in it and took out her cigarettes. Lighting one she realised: this is the first time I've smoked in front of my mother. Is it because I've finally grown up, or that now she's a weakened vessel I just don't care?

231

She drew the smoke into her lungs. Standing, jostled by her guests, she bade a mental farewell to her mother. For Dorothy had now become a person, incomprehensible and contradictory, loosed into the world; a woman for whom Prudence felt the weight of responsibility.

Dorothy went into the bedroom. Allegra sat on a pile of coats playing with her Game Boy.

'I've been looking for you,' said Dorothy.

'I don't know any of these people,' said Allegra.

'Nor do I.'

'I'm fed up with vegetarian muck,' said Allegra.

'So am I.' Dorothy smiled at the little girl. 'Get your coat.'

'This is much more fun,' said Dorothy.

Allegra, her mouth full, nodded. They were sitting in a place called Costas's Burgers and Kebabs, opposite Clapham Junction station. Allegra was eating a double burger and chips. She was small for her age; she looked as if she needed fattening up.

'She your granddaughter then?' asked the man behind the counter – a large, moustachioed Greek.

Dorothy shook her head. 'I've just borrowed her.'

'We've borrowed each other,' said Allegra.

What a tenuous link they had, she and this little girl. They were sticks, tossed by a storm and washed up together on a beach.

'Where does your daddy live?' she asked Allegra.

'In his office.'

'His office?'

Allegra nodded. 'He's lived there since Christmas but he's not supposed to. It's against the regulations.'

'Hasn't he got a home?'

Allegra shook her head. 'His wife chucked him out.'

'He's married?'

Allegra tore open a ketchup sachet with her teeth. 'She's a cow. She's got these horrible children.'

Dorothy's head spun. 'Whose children?'

'Someone she met before Dad.' Allegra squirted ketchup over her chips. 'Anyway, Dad and her bought this house, it was all falling down, and he did it up really nicely. It took him ages, years and years. And then, when it was finished, she said she didn't love him any more. She chucked him out and her pottery instructor moved in. Dad's really bitter.'

'I'm not surprised.'

'He's trying to get her out. He's spending all his money on lawyers.'

'Does he have any other children of his own?' Dorothy asked.

'No. Only me. And he hardly ever sees me.'

'But he sends you faxes.'

Allegra nodded. She speared a chip with her fork and put it into her mouth.

'Do you want to see him?' Dorothy asked.

Allegra nodded.

'Do you know his phone number?'

Dorothy felt invigorated as they got into the car. Everyone else broke the rules; why shouldn't she? She felt sorry for this Aziz man, he had sounded nice on the phone. He had been thrown out of his home too, just as she had. She drove through the littered streets. The world seemed full of such cruelty, such selfish brutality. Why not mend two of the broken pieces?

She drove north, across Waterloo Bridge. She knew she was interfering, but what the hell. Erin thought she was taking Allegra home, and would baby-sit her until they returned from the party. If she found out – too bad.

Dorothy had found the place in her *A–Z*. She drove to Kentish Town and parked the car in a turning off the high street, next to a closed Magnet showroom. Allegra took her hand and led her up an alleyway. The greasy cobbles shone in the lamplight. It was cold; the wind whipped a plastic bag into the air.

'He lives here?' she whispered.

A voice called: 'Hello, Sunshine.' A man sat in a doorway. Allegra said, 'Hello.'

'How's my little girl been then?'

'Fine.'

For a mad moment Dorothy thought that this was Allegra's father. Nothing would surprise her any more. The man lifted a can of lager to his mouth, toasting them. 'Light o'my life!'

'He's always there,' whispered Allegra. She led Dorothy to a doorway at the end of the alley and rang the bell.

Aziz's office was a high-tech sliver of concrete and glass. He opened the door, hugged Allegra and led them up a spiral staircase into a room. It had a drawing-board, a computer and a settee. Allegra pointed: 'That's where he sleeps.'

Another sofabed, thought Dorothy.

Aziz was charming. He was a courtly, formal man, dressed harmoniously in russet and ochre. He poured Dorothy a glass of wine.

'Everyone was sucking up to Mum so we thought we'd come here.' Allegra went to a cupboard, opened it proprietorially and took out a computer game.

'I shouldn't be doing this,' said Dorothy, 'but I have.'

'I'm very grateful.' He didn't look authoritarian; rather the opposite.

Allegra slotted the game into the computer and sat down on the floor. Dorothy said to Aziz: 'Are you getting enough to eat?' She stopped, blushing. 'I'm sorry, you just look so thin.'

'I've always been like this.' He smiled, but his beautiful, dark eyes were tragic. She longed to ask him questions. Did he know, at the time, that Erin was just using him to have a child? Had he been in love with her? He looked a private sort of person, however. Besides, what business was it of hers?

'Allegra's very talented, isn't she?' she said. 'I've heard her on the clarinet.'

234

They chatted for a while. It felt stagy sitting there under the bright light – the non-grandmother and the absent father, connected by the thinnest of threads. But then aren't we all? she thought. Everything can snap, just like that.

She felt that she should leave Aziz alone with his daughter. She felt like a gooseberry, tagging along on a date, but where could she go? Allegra, sitting on the rubber floor, seemed engrossed in her computer game.

'It's just nice having her here,' said Aziz, reading her thoughts. 'Not just on a Sunday.'

'It's not fair, is it?' Dorothy blurted out. 'Any of it.'

He shook his head and gazed at a bowl of lemons. They were the only fruit in the room. Dorothy wondered if this was a lone man's lack of housekeeping talent or whether Aziz was going to use them in some Indian way.

He said: 'You've caught me at a bad moment, I'm afraid.'

'Maybe we should go –'

'No – don't. I'm glad you came. It's just – I've lost a client, and frankly there aren't many of them around nowadays. Too many of us chasing too few jobs.'

'I know.'

'Do you?' he asked.

'I've seen plenty of architects go bust over the years.' Oh dear, that sounded tactless.

'And my wife – ex-wife . . . well, Mrs Hammond, to be perfectly honest –'

'Dorothy.'

'Dorothy – let's just say I feel exploited, one way and another. But can a man say that? Oh no, because it's women who're the exploited sex.' He lowered his voice. 'Erin – then my wife – they've both used me for what they can get out of me. And because they're women they can bloody get away with it, if you'll excuse the language.'

'Men can use woman too,' said Dorothy.

'Yes, but everybody knows about that.'

'It's still not fair.'

'So when's life fair?' He ran his fingers through his hair

and gazed at the lemons.

'Don't be so sad, please!' she said.

He raised his head. 'Tell me, what's there to be so happy about?'

She thought: this is what I've joined – this mess. Tears of pity sprang to her eyes – for herself, for Aziz, for all of them. For Allegra, who tonight struck her as the ultimate victim of it all.

She leafed through *Blueprint* while Allegra helped her father cook his dinner – there was a microwave and a sink in a cupboard. Afterwards, Aziz walked them to the car.

Allegra got in and fiddled with the radio knobs. Dorothy turned to Aziz. 'Why did Erin want a child?' she whispered. 'She hardly ever sees her. I've stayed there, I know.'

Aziz gazed down the street. An empty bus passed, lit like a ghost bus. 'Erin's a control-freak. That's why she's written a novel. She's invented herself like a character in it. She's really a suburban girl, did you know? Her father's a chartered surveyor in Watford.'

'That true?'

Aziz nodded. 'She fantasised herself a role as a mother. It was just another image. And the mother of an exotic, mixed-race child too, what could be better? Unfortunately, in this case, there were other people involved.'

'Maybe we all do that.' She thought: I fantasised that I was happily married. I concocted my own lies too.

The next day Erin went off on a publicity tour. She was going to be away until the end of the week, giving interviews and readings around the country. Her book seemed set to be a roaring success; the reviews so far had been ecstatic and for days the phone had been ringing with journalists wanting her views on everything from *in vitro* fertilisation to the Middle-East crisis.

Dorothy and Maddy drove Allegra down to the Old Vicarage for the day; it was half-term and Imogen had promised the little girl a ride on her horse. While Louise cooked lunch the two women went into the garden. The air smelled fresh and clean, as if the world had been rinsed. In the paddock Imogen led the horse around in a circle; Allegra sat there, rigid, clutching Skylark's mane.

Maddy flung herself onto the grass and lay full length. 'You shouldn't have taken her to Aziz's, you know.'

'I know,' said Dorothy. 'But I did.'

'It's all right. I won't tell.'

Dorothy sat down on the bench. 'She wants to live with him.'

'How could she? It's his office.'

'I know. What a mess.' The sun warmed Dorothy's face. She closed her eyes. 'A man that night, in the café, he asked if I was Allegra's grandmother. I thought, *What if I tell him the truth? If I said, No, she's the daughter of an Indian man who was just used for his sperm, and my daughter's lesbian lover.*'

There was a silence. In the flowerbeds the daffodils, enquiring trumpets, appeared to be listening.

Maddy addressed the sky. 'How did you know?'

'Oh, I've known for years.'

Maddy sat up. 'You have?'

'I knew you weren't interested in men. And that only left one option.' Dorothy gave a shrill laugh. 'Unless it was going to be Alsatians.'

Maddy picked at the grass. 'Did *everybody* know except me?'

'I'm tired of lies. I've been lying to myself about all sorts of things, it seems.'

'Like what?' Maddy looked up at her, for the first time.

'Oh, being happily married.'

'You were.'

'Apprently it died long ago. I just didn't want to notice.'

'That's Dad's excuse to make himself feel better.' Maddy tugged at the grass. 'So you don't mind?'

'Why should I mind? As long as you're happy.' Dorothy looked at the bent head. 'You are happy, aren't you?'

237

Maddy didn't look up. 'Of course,' she said.

Lunch was high-spirited; the conversation in the garden seemed to have cleared the air. They ate slabs of lasagne that Louise had left in the oven too long because the rabbit had escaped again; it had taken them half an hour to corner him and heave him, kicking and hissing, back into his cage.

Louise looked at their scratched wrists. 'We look as if we've made a mass suicide pact,' she said.

Dorothy shook her head. 'He's not going to get off that easily.'

'I think you ought to get another husband,' Imogen said.

'Already?' Dorothy helped herself to fruit salad. 'I don't want another husband. One was enough.'

'But won't you get lonely?'

'Who did you have in mind?'

Imogen jumped up and fetched the local paper. She pointed to the front page. 'Look – Mum got this article printed about the shop. She got hold of this journalist.'

'He's going to find me a husband?'

Shaking her head, Imogen leafed through the pages. 'I'm looking for the Lonely Hearts.'

'This is very kind of you,' said Dorothy, 'but I'm perfectly all right.'

Louise took the paper. She fished in her handbag and produced a spectacle case. 'Look, I've had to get reading glasses. I'm getting old.' She turned to Maddy. 'It'll be your turn next.' She put on the delicate, gold-rimmed glasses. They made her instantly look more intelligent. She peered at the Personal column: '*Clairvoyant and psychic – confidential and friendly guidance . . . Egg donors needed for infertile couples, phone Assisted Conception Unit . . . Qualified plumber* – whoops! Wrong column.' She peered closer. 'Look. *Widowed gentleman, 63, seeks lady for companionship* – there you are. There's lots of them.'

'You just want to get rid of me,' said Dorothy. 'Marry me

off so you needn't worry about me any more.'

Imogen took her grandmother's hand and pulled her to her feet. She led her upstairs, into Louise's and Robert's bedroom, and flung open the wardrobe.

'First, you've got to revamp your image,' she said. 'You can borrow some of Mum's clothes. She never wears them.' She riffled through them, rattling the hangers, and pulled out a silk blouse. 'You'd look great in this.' She pulled out a dress and held it against her grandmother. 'That's just your colour, look!'

Dorothy stopped smiling. She looked at herself in the mirror. Suddenly she was back in the bedroom at home, twirling round in front of Gordon. She turned, and saw his face changing.

'What's the matter?' Imogen was a warm, impulsive girl. She flung her arms around her grandmother.

'I'll be all right in a minute,' said Dorothy. She patted Imogen's head and put the dress back in the wardrobe. *Sweet sixteen*. She remembered Imogen's birthday party. Gordon tapped his plate for silence. She remembered Imogen's gasp, when she saw her horse ... the magical moment that had stilled her family.

'I hope you'll be happy,' she said.

'Oh, I am.' For a moment Imogen was tempted to tell her what had happened, how she had been kissed in Blackthorn Wood and how the world was transformed. It was easier to confide in her grandmother than her parents. But she didn't speak, and the moment passed.

They left for London when it was getting dark. Louise watched the tail-lights disappear round the corner. She watched the headlights reappear, beyond the church, and illuminate the lane as her mother's car drove towards Beaconsfield. Soon it would be swallowed up in the darkness, then emerge into the arc-lights of the M40, a time-traveller plunged into another day. Soon Robert would be returning in the other direction. Sometimes it seemed that he had indeed been travelling through time-zones to reach her, so distant did he seem nowadays.

She went back into the kitchen and gazed at the dishwasher. It was grinding away as if it, too, found the whole business wearisome. The phone rang.

It was Robert, calling from work. 'Got a breakfast meeting,' he said. 'Think I'll stay in town tonight, I've got to take some clients to dinner. I'll kip down at Henry's place.'

She told him about the Lonely Hearts ads. 'Immy bullied Mum about it. The young are so conventional, aren't they? They think marriage solves everything. Anyway, Mum's promised to look in the London papers.'

'Wow. Your mother doesn't waste any time.'

'She's in a what-the-hell mood.' Louise paused. 'So am I, actually. I think I'll look in them, too.'

'What's that supposed to mean?'

'Why are you always staying away? It's been twice this week.'

'Darling.' His voice was patient. 'Do you really think I want to spend the evening with somebody who, battling against strong competition, must hold the title for the most boring man in the world? And his crimplene-clad consort? You really think that?'

Louise put down the phone. She felt deflated. Robert was good at that.

The house was empty. Imogen and Jamie had gone out and wouldn't be back until late. When Louise was alone the darkness outside seemed a solid presence. She pulled down the kitchen blinds. She went into the living room and drew the curtains. Last night's ashes lay heaped in the fireplace. She fetched the coal-shovel and started to clean them out. Lonely, lonely heart, she thought, and felt feverish with self-pity.

Later, she took the dog out. It was a still, moonless night. Next to the churchyard wall the lane was lit by a single lamp.

She walked a few steps, breathing the air. Suddenly, Monty growled.

'It's all right, it's only Rocky.' She bent down to pat Tim's arthritic spaniel. Tim stood by the lamp-post, hunched in his anorak. 'Sorry,' she said. 'You gave me a fright.'

Tim's face was narrow; the children called him the Weasel. In the lamplight she saw how his hair was thinning. Away from his shop, his domain, he looked smaller. She had noticed this before.

Tim indicated her house. His glasses flashed as he turned. 'I saw that he wasn't there.'

'Who?'

'Your husband. His car's not there.'

She swallowed. 'You look awfully cold.'

'Louise, I have to talk to you.' He cleared his throat. 'I can't bear it any longer. I've always thought, how could a woman like you possibly be interested in me, someone who's not worthy of washing your feet –'

'Tim –'

'– but then, well, you've been coming round to see me so often recently, I thought to myself – does she really care about this campaign, or could I dare think –' He twisted the dog lead round in his hand. 'Could such a woman, such a goddess –'

'Tim, please – '

'No, hear me out. I've been wanting to say this for years, five years, since I saw you for the first time, getting out of your Volvo –'

'Oh yes, the Volvo!' she said wildly. 'Funny how you forget a car the minute you get rid of it –'

'And then, that day in March, remember? When the bag broke and we picked up the potatoes and you put your hand on my arm –'

'Did I?' She stared at the wall; its stones were sweaty in the lamplight. At first she'd thought Tim was drunk but now, with a sinking heart, she realised he was sober.

'Your eyes were so sad, and I thought, nobody realises how

241

sad she is. And then at the fête, when my photograph won first prize –'

'What did I do then?'

'You don't remember? You kissed me.'

'Did I?'

He took her hand and pressed it to his lips. 'I love you. I would die for you.'

'Tim, I can't – you can't – '

Monty pressed his nose into Tim's crotch. Louise put her hands around the dog's shoulders and heaved him aside. This gave her an excuse to stand further away.

'I've tried to start a new life here.' Tim's voice shook. 'After – you know, after it happened. When me and, you know, when we came here and set up the shop, we were trying to start afresh. But it was no good, Louise. It had all finished by then.' He stepped closer. 'To tell the truth they could bulldoze the shop tomorrow, I don't care. My only life is with you.' He took her hand and stroked her fingers, one by one. 'I want to make you happy, we both deserve it, Louise. You're horribly neglected, how could any man do that?'

'It's not true –'

'Is there any – just the smallest – chance that by some miracle you could feel the same? Or maybe, one day, feel you could?'

An owl hooted. She thought: I'll never be able to step into the shop again. Then pity rose up again and engulfed her.

'Tim, you're married, I'm married –'

'Can I hope?' He spoke urgently. 'Please just tell me that. Please give me something to live for!'

A car approached. Louise sprang back. Headlights dazzled them; the dogs barked.

The car slewed to a halt. 'Hi, Ma!' called Jamie. Doors slammed; music thumped out. Jamie and Imogen shouted goodbye to their friends.

The car drove off. When Louise turned round Tim had disappeared, swallowed back into the darkness.

'I'm ravenous,' said Jamie. 'Got any supper left?'

242

'What were you talking about?' asked Imogen. 'With the Weasel?'

'Dad says he's the sort of person who mends his specs with sticking plaster.'

'He doesn't!' snapped Louise. 'You snobs!'

'She laid her down under the banyan tree,' read Erin. *'She laid her on the sand. Her blood pounded. She moved down Roxanne's body, sniffing it like a dog on heat. She pressed her lips into the thicket, tonguing the red berry, the rose-hip hidden amidst its thorns. How sweet were the cries of her beloved!'*

Maddy opened the door. The bookshop was crammed with women. They gazed at Erin as she sat, reading her novel. Maddy squeezed her way through.

'A man approached. He slapped his bullock with a stick. Roxanne hurriedly pulled the cloth over her nakedness. "Aren't you proud of us, my love?" asked Eve. "Aren't you proud of your beauty?"'

Maddy wasn't listening. Her bladder was bursting. She had been working all day in the bush-free garden of a locked-up house. One of the disadvantages of the job was its lack of lavatorial facilities. She remembered her father, in one of their rare moments of closeness, describing the ingenious and often revolting arrangements that builders made when caught short.

'Is there a loo here?' she whispered to the woman standing next to her.

'Ssh!'

Maddy tried to concentrate. *'Come with me, my dearest, let's swim . . .'* said Erin. Maddy knew what was coming next. Erin's book both embarrassed and unsettled her. She looked round at the audience. The conversation with her mother, the week before, had affected her profoundly. If her mother knew, then it must be true. Maddy was a lesbian; she had been born that way. All her life she had felt that she hadn't belonged in her family and now she knew why. She belonged here, amongst these uncompromising women who lounged against the bookshelves. No longer did she feel inferior to Louise and Pru; she had her own proud identity now.

And how proud she was of Erin! She felt very much in love with her that evening; she had hardly seen her all week and she missed her. The audience's attention charged up Erin; she glowed. She wore her nipped-in satin jacket and a tie; her hair was slicked back with gel. She looked like a plumaged bird compared to the drab sparrows of her devotees.

They burst into applause. Erin moved to another table to sign books. Maddy eased her way through the crowd.

'Hey, this is a queue, you know.' A woman with a shaved head glared at her.

Maddy joined the queue. It shuffled forward. Eventually she arrived at Erin who sat there, her pen poised.

She looked up. 'Darling. How did I sound?'

'Great,' said Maddy. 'I've got the van outside. I thought you'd like a lift home.'

'Sweetheart, I can't. I've got to go out to dinner with the Waterstone's people.'

'But I've bought some supper. You said you'd be home tonight.'

Erin smiled. 'Oh dear. You sound just like a wife.' The woman behind them tittered.

Maddy turned round and pushed her way through the crowd. Tears stung her eyes. She pushed open the door and stepped outside, into Notting Hill. She hurried down the street, her bladder bursting, her heart bursting. She got into the van and drove home.

Embarrassment is the tyrant of the young. It eases its grip with age. That was what Dorothy told herself as she sipped a glass of wine with her first date. His name was Raymond. Such a nice man, that was what made it worse. Her embarrassment, unlike that of the young, was not just on her own behalf but on his, too. It was a cosmic pity for the two of them. They sat in a pub in Holborn. Buses passed outside. In them she glimpsed people with whom she wished so strongly to change places that her body ached.

Raymond took out a photograph of his wife. 'She passed away last spring,' he said. 'She was a wonderful woman.'

His skull was blotched with liver spots. His skin was papery; when he put away the photo his hand shook. While Dorothy had been married, men had been ageing. She supposed that she had been ageing too. Was this what she looked like? This man mirrored not just her own loneliness – indeed, a loneliness that seemed to engulf the world – but her own mortality. She wondered if he were looking at her with horror and thinking the same. In a long marriage neither partner grows old; their wrinkles are visible yet not recognised, for both people remain at some indeterminate age – not the age when they first met but some blurred stage in between.

'I play golf, for my sins,' he said. 'Do you enjoy any hobbies?'

'Well – I used to play badminton.'

'How interesting,' he replied. 'When was that?'

'At school,' said Dorothy.

There was a silence. She could sense his desperation; she could smell it, coming off his body. He was frightened of dying alone.

Prudence and Stephen were not alone in the flat; her mother had long since gone but Kaatya remained. Kaatya was a guest who could not be removed; her ghostly presence was a gas, poisoning the air. It was getting worse. Prudence had never seen her; she had only heard her voice on the phone, harsh and foreign: *Can I speak please with Stephen?* That she hadn't learned such a simple English sentence by this time seemed insulting. From remarks dropped by Stephen she had clues to his wife's appearance – black-haired, like their sons, and inclined to wear startling clothes she had picked up in Oxfam shops. In Prudence's imagination Kaatya was beautiful, as unknown rivals always are; as time went by her beauty

245

increased and by now, fuelled by Prudence's jealousy, she was dazzling. She had wide, sensual lips, like the women in the *Heartbeat* books that Prudence published. Prudence's own mouth was small. She rolled her own cigarettes – how rollicking and carefree that sounded! She drove a battered 2CV which she was constantly scraping – Stephen at that very moment was struggling with the latest insurance claim. She was volatile and creative; Prudence felt, by contrast, pinched and dowdy. A lusty woman, she could drink Stephen under the table. She was physically powerful; once, on holiday in Greece, she had picked up a sheep and put it on a wall to take its photograph. Prudence, torturing herself, pictured Kaatya in bed with Stephen, vigorously manhandling him. He had lived with Kaatya for fourteen years, six of them married; they must have made love thousands of times – in Dulwich, in Amsterdam, on countless holidays in hotel rooms and under canvas – probably, from what she had heard of Kaatya, in the open air. Prudence felt sick.

Even Kaatya's many faults – her ruthless selfishness, her slovenliness, her lack of interest in anything remotely intellectual – even these faults, emphasised by Stephen no doubt to make Prudence feel better, only deepened her jealousy. They made Kaatya horribly real, as if she were there in the room. Besides, if his wife were really so impossible, why had he stayed with her?

Prudence had confessed none of this to her sisters; she felt demeaned by it. She knew she was obsessed; she could stand aside and watch herself with a repulsed detachment. How could she presume to possess his past? It was none of her business, his relationship with his wife. Didn't he tell her that he loved her, that living with Kaatya had been a sort of madness? She knew, however, that he couldn't have been that stupid. For many of those years he must have been happy with his marriage. If she truly loved him she wouldn't hope that he had been miserable, would she? Ah, but it was painful. When reminiscing about the past, he tried, tactfully, not to mention Kaatya. She stiffened, however, as if the

246

conversation might detonate; however carefully he trod, the sudden 'we' exploded in her heart.

She knew she had to take action. The day came one Saturday in March. Stephen had taken the boys down to Chichester to stay with his mother. Prudence showered; she made up her face with care. She knew this was stupid. For one thing, she probably wouldn't see the woman; even if she did, she had no intention of revealing her own identity. She dressed herself in her artiest clothes – black velvet leggings and a boldly patterned sweater she had bought on impulse years before and never worn.

She drove towards Dulwich. Half the roads seemed to have been dug up. She sat in a traffic jam, waiting at a temporary traffic light. Was this a sign telling her to go home? She thought of all the things she should be doing on a Saturday morning – reading manuscripts, collecting the dry cleaning. Ahead of her was one of those Toyota monster-jeeps, the sort that Louise drove. It belched exhaust smoke. How superior it seemed, how huge and armoured! Louise was safe in her marriage. Louise had children – something that Kaatya had shared with Stephen and that was a tie deeper than marriage.

The cars shunted forward. Prudence thought about her mother's outbursts about April. *'She's not even that attractive!'* Her mother's jealousy seemed pure and fine – seemed utterly understandable – compared to her own curdled sickness. April had stolen Gordon's heart and thrust her mother into the wilderness. Three months earlier Dorothy had been running a business and living happily in a large house in Purley. Now she was alone, issuing forth from a rented room to meet strange men in wine bars. This could be considered exhilarating – she was free, she could do anything, at last she could live for herself. Prudence had told her mother this, with false cheer, as if she were really capable of dispensing advice.

She parked at the top of Agincourt Road and turned off the engine. Her heart thumped, just as it had all those months ago when she had sat there, looking at Kaatya's and

247

Stephen's cars. It was March now; the trees were bare and she could see the house more distinctly. Even from this distance she could see that there was no Citroën parked outside. Maybe Kaatya had gone out. On the other hand, the car could be at a garage, being repaired. She looked up at the roof. It, too, had been repaired, by her father's firm. Had Kaatya arranged this to lure Stephen back, or simply to upset him?

Prudence lit a cigarette. Her hand shook. She thought: I just need to see her. The image of her had been building up for eighteen months; just a glimpse of her would surely prick the boil and release the poison.

Half an hour passed. Prudence sat there, inert. She didn't even play the radio. Maybe if she sat there long enough these big Edwardian houses would be neutralised; the street would revert into being a comfortable, anonymous place, one of thousands of similar streets throughout London. Perhaps she could persuade herself to feel sorry for Kaatya, the abandoned wife. Perhaps – who knows? – Kaatya would emerge from the front door arm-in-arm with another man.

Prudence was imagining this when the front door opened and a woman came out. It was unmistakably Kaatya – who else could it be? From this distance all Prudence could make out was a blur of black and white, with red legs. Kaatya walked off in the opposite direction.

Prudence got out of the car. She hurried down the road, drawing nearer. Kaatya carried a hold-all. Like a film star, she was shorter than Prudence had imagined – in her mind Kaatya had grown powerfully tall. She was wearing a fake-fur coat, red leggings and boots. She had a mass of black hair. Prudence could almost inhale her scent. Kaatya strode across the main road, narrowly missing a car. Prudence followed her.

Down past the parade of shops stood an industrial building. Kaatya disappeared into it. The sign said *The Old Brewery Fitness Centre*. Prudence read the price list, pinned to the doorway. *Membership £250 per annum.* Stephen had paid that. He paid for everything. Throughout their marriage Kaatya

248

had never earned a penny; she was too disorganised. She was one of those arty women who bought large amounts of equipment on their husband's credit card and never finished anything. It was one of Stephen's many complaints that just made Kaatya seem more attractive – impulsive, creative, highly sexed.

There was an alleyway beside the building. Prudence walked up it and gazed through the window.

The room was filled with women. She spotted Kaatya straight away. Kaatya wore a shiny green leotard. She was thin, with small breasts; even from this distance the nipples were visible. Her stomach was so concave that her pelvic bones jutted out. She stood, swinging her arms first one way and then the other. She twisted her body, rotating her hips as if balancing a hula-hoop. Those same hips had rotated beneath Stephen. She wiped her forehead, revealing black hair in her armpits. She had that loose-jointed look of someone who is at ease with her body.

Prudence watched her with a close, ardent attention. Kaatya moved to the music. She had dark eyes; there was a haunted, mid-European look to her. Oh, she was handsome all right, but not in the way Prudence had imagined. By now her body was shining with sweat. She lay on the floor and parted her legs; she opened and closed them like scissors, making love to the air. Prudence, too, was sweating. She felt strangely aroused. She and this woman had shared the same body; they had both been entered by the same man.

Kaatya clambered to her feet; she turned and spoke to the woman next to her. Prudence felt a surprising tweak of jealousy. She wanted Kaatya to speak to *her*. What was the matter? Was she a secret lesbian? Erin said that true desire was no respecter of gender; when she loved, the sex of her beloved was irrelevant. Prudence had thought this was hogwash – just Erin's way of getting two for the price of one – but then she remembered her schoolgirl crushes, the hot flush of them, the jealousy and rapture.

Prudence turned away. She walked back to the car. Seeing

Kaatya hadn't solved anything; in fact, it had made it worse. For Kaatya was a person now, flesh and blood. She could no longer be spirited away.

'I'm fortunate to have travelled,' said the man. 'I've a collection of book matches from all the major capitals of the world. For service I would recommend British Airways but for legroom the Swiss.' He gazed at Dorothy through his pebble glasses. 'To be frank, Mrs Hammond, I'm looking for long-term commitment on a loving basis.'

Dorothy must have managed to make her excuses because now she was leaving. She didn't remember how she did it, maybe she had behaved oddly, she couldn't recollect.

It was a dazzling day, the first true day of spring. She crossed the Cromwell Road. To her left reared up the Natural History Museum. She had taken the girls there once, when they were small, way back in another century.

She bumped into somebody. 'Sorry.' She recrossed the Cromwell Road. Where was she going? Where was she supposed to go, for the rest of her life?

It was then that she saw the van. It was parked outside a hotel. Somebody was carrying a bush, holding it like a baby. She settled it into a tub on the front steps of the building. It was Maddy.

A jolt of pleasure shot through Dorothy. In the split second before she'd recognised her daughter she had seen her as a stranger would: a square woman – had she put on weight? – with cropped hair, dressed in army trousers and an old jacket. A woman who was desexed by her shapeless clothes. She worked, oblivious to the passers-by, pressing earth around the shrub.

Dorothy hurried across the road. 'Maddy!' she called. There is something romantic about glimpsing someone familiar, even one's daughter, in an unfamiliar neighbourhood.

Maddy straightened up. 'Mum. What're you doing here?'

250

'Can you stop for a moment?'

They sat in the hotel bar. The walls were hung with pictures of slaughtered birds. Maddy had washed her hands but there was still a raw, outdoors look to her.

'Have a glass of wine,' said Dorothy.

'I don't drink.'

'Keep me company, just for once.' Dorothy looked at her daughter. 'Keep me company. Please.'

Maddy ordered a glass of wine. There were two reasons why she didn't drink. She didn't like the taste, and if she did drink, it immediately went to her head.

'I've done four, now,' said Dorothy.

'What do you mean, you're done for?'

Dorothy nodded. 'I'm done for. I've met four of them.' The muzak was playing the Tom Jones song *It's Not Unusual*. She liked Tom Jones, a fact that her daughters had found hilarious. 'One of them was a scout-master who lived with his mother. I think I want to die.'

'There must be someone out there,' said Maddy.

'Who needs men? You don't.' Dorothy stopped. 'I mean, who needs anybody?'

'I do.' Maddy took a sip of her wine.

'But you've got – I mean – where's Erin?' She looked around, as if Erin might come through the door. The barman rubbed a glass.

'At a conference,' said Maddy.

Dorothy waited. Silently, she urged Maddy to confide in her, but she didn't want to pry. Besides, she didn't like Erin and if one doesn't like the person concerned one's questions seem more intrusive.

'She's famous now,' said Maddy. 'She was on TV last night. Did you see her?' She took another gulp. 'She's changed.'

'How?'

'She just has.' She drained her glass. 'Shit, I'm drunk.'

Dorothy suddenly asked: 'What are we going to do?'

'Have another go. You can do better than Dad.'

'You think so?'

251

'Dad bullied you,' said Maddy. 'He kept you down. I used to listen to him eating. And then he'd light up before we had finished. He was a pig.'

'He wasn't.'

'Actually, I like him better now. At least he's done something unexpected.'

'I know you do,' said Dorothy tartly. 'But what about me?'

'I told you, you're well rid of him. He's a control freak. Remember our holidays, when he planned everything with the map and we had to go exactly where he said. He had a bloody timetable!' She ate a crisp. 'He bullied you and you let him.' She hiccuped. 'It takes two to be bullied.' She hiccuped again. 'It's sort of an unhealthy pact.'

Dorothy waited. Her daughter didn't continue. 'Maddy –' she began.

'Try one more,' said Maddy. 'Go on. Just for luck. Just for you. Whatever. Let's have bloody one of us being happy. You seen Prudence lately? She looks terrible. Let's one of us be happy. Lou's the only one who's got off scot-free.'

Louise had told nobody about the incident with Tim. She didn't want to humiliate him by making him into a story. She could imagine, only too well, Robert's reaction. Since it had happened, the week before, she hadn't been to the shop. She thought how ironic it was that Tim's declaration had deprived him of her custom.

It was a beautiful day. The hedgerow was starred with celandines as if somebody had flung coins there. There was a breezy largesse to the air. She wondered what it must be like for Tim and his wife to witness this yearly renewal, when the one thing they had loved was stilled. She walked past the churchyard. The headstones leaned together like teeth loosened with age.

Children's shouts floated from the primary school down on the green. Louise loved children – in fact, she wished she had had more of them – mothering came naturally to her. She had been at her happiest when Jamie and Imogen had been babies. Now she helped six-year-olds learn to read, taking them, one at a time, out of the class. That morning, gazing at Sophia Wilmott's bent head, she thought about Tim. He had no daughter to love, her blond hair scraped back into pigtails. Louise had never suffered, not really. Tim's grief was too vast to comprehend. Perhaps – who knows? – it was the cause of his startling declaration. What on earth could she do? It had never crossed her mind that he harboured a secret passion for her. From now on, if she were friendly he would take it as an encouragement; if she were businesslike he would be hurt.

'Goblin,' she said, pointing to the sentence. *'Wimbush the Goblin was the saddest goblin in the wood.'*

That evening Robert announced that he wouldn't be home the next night, he had to go to Walsall.

'Again?' she said. 'What are you doing in Walsall?'

'Markham Brothers, remember? The brake linings? We've got a board meeting first thing in the morning. Somebody has to work around here.'

'Want to swap? I spend the whole time slaving away, cooking for your bloody friends, keeping this place nice.' Her voice rose peevishly. 'I helped three children learn to read today, not that you'd be interested.'

She walked round the room snapping on the lights. Getting older, she realised, meant saying things one never thought one would say. *When I was your age,* she said to the kids. *You don't know how lucky you are.* The sentences were waiting, like her reading glasses, until she put them on without even thinking about it.

She stopped at the window. 'I wish I'd had more children.'

'God, isn't two enough?' he asked.

'I wouldn't feel so alone.'

In the old days Robert would have put his arms around her. Now he sniffed and looked at the grate. 'Has the cat been peeing in the fireplace again?'

She gazed at the window. Her husband, standing in the lamplit room, was reflected back. When she moved closer to the pane he vanished. All she saw was the darkness outside.

'At least somebody loves me,' she said.

'Who?'

She turned round. She bent down to stroke the dog. 'You do,' she said to Monty.

Robert collapsed into the armchair. 'I'm sorry. Things have been, well, a bit fraught at work.'

'You sound like somebody on TV,' she said. Later, she realised why.

His name was Eric. He listed *Wining and Dining* amongst his recreations. He described himself as *Vintage, certainly, but not Premier Cru*. He said on the phone that he would like to take her out for dinner and at first Dorothy hesitated. What if he was boring? What if they realised they had two more hours to go?

He must have sensed this. He said simply: 'I'm tired of eating alone.'

'So am I,' replied Dorothy. He gave her the address of a restaurant in Holland Park. 'How will I recognise you?' she asked.

'I'm not very memorable,' he replied. 'So you can always forget about me afterwards.'

The restaurant was called Archie's. This sounded like the sort of egg-and-chips place that had brought on her husband's heart attack. At first glance it did indeed look functional – bright lights, plain wooden tables partitioned off like stables. She was relieved that it wasn't overly romantic.

Eric, rising to greet her, said: 'Don't be misled. It takes itself very seriously. They pour balsamic vinegar on their mashed potatoes.'

Eric was a small, rather feminine man. He said that he adored cooking; in fact, with his bald head he resembled a hard-

254

boiled egg. He said that he had always cooked for his sons. Now that they had grown up, and his wife had died, he sometimes rallied himself by making spectacular meals-for-one.

'But it's not the same, is it?' He pointed to the menu. 'The fishcakes are good, do you like fish?' He moved his finger down the page. 'This is their speciality, it's got roasted peppers on top. If you choose first I can order something different and you can taste mine, if you like.'

If Gordon had said this it would have sounded like bullying. Eric, however, simply seemed enthusiastic. She relaxed. He was a chatty man, at ease with women. She thought about Gordon. All his life he had been surrounded by women, but he still stayed resolutely male. Nothing had seeped in; he was waterproofed.

Eric told her about himself. He had worked as an industrial designer and retired the year before. He had two sons, one a vet and the other a teacher. He spoke of them with the teasing affection of someone who took love for granted. 'John, the oldest, he's the cautious type. He's the only person I know who straps himself into the seat-belt in taxis.'

The food arrived. She told him about her daughters. 'Louise is married, two children, a boy and a girl, they live in a lovely house in the country. Prudence is the career girl, she's in publishing, in fact she's an editorial director at Unimedia, have you heard of them?'

'And the other?'

'Madeleine's led an interesting life – Canada, Africa – she's been all over. She's the adventurous one, the independent spirit.' She stopped. She pushed a piece of fishcake around in its sauce. She looked across at Eric. Under the clownish dome his face was frank and enquiring. The wooden partitions boxed them in like a confessional. Beyond, she heard the murmur of voices and rattle of cutlery.

'Actually, that's only partly the truth,' she said.

'What do you mean?'

'It's easy to tell you things like that. Boring, isn't it?' She gazed at her side plate. Vegetables lay there; stripes were

255

seared into their flesh as if they had been branded. 'The truth is – well, Louise's husband bullies her, like my husband bullied me. She's got everything anyone could want, she's been blessed from birth, but I don't think she's happy. My second daughter always wanted children but now it's probably too late. She's living in sin with a man who's run away from his family and she doesn't look happy either. And Maddy's always been difficult. Her first word was *No*. Now it turns out she's gay.'

'Really?'

'I'd guessed but it's still a shock. She's living with another bully – what do my daughters want, to live with their father? Her girlfriend's too busy to care for her own daughter – for my daughter, too. So there you have it.' She picked up the peppermill and ground it over the fishcake. 'I've learned more about my daughters in the past three months than in the past thirty years. I don't know why I'm telling you this, you're a complete stranger.'

He smiled. 'Maybe that's why.'

'Maybe.'

He smiled. 'Try this.' He offered her a piece of pork on his fork. She opened her mouth, like a baby bird, and ate it. She felt a curious sensation, as if, after a long winter, she were thawing.

She told him about her childhood, how her father had worked in the haulage business all his life; how he had seated her beside him in his cab and driven her around Britain. How she had felt the monarch of all she'd surveyed. 'The roads were so empty then. They rolled away ahead of us like the road to Oz. I loved that film. It was as if I saw my life ahead of me, I was going to conquer the world.' They were drinking coffee now. 'There's a Peggy Lee song – have you heard it? – called *Is That All There Is?* In one of the verses, she's taken to the circus, when she's a little girl, and she asks that. My husband played it, he liked Peggy Lee. Is that all there is? Well, it wasn't, not for him.'

Eric said: 'One day I'll tell you about my wife. We were

256

happy, by and large. Other people thought so, no doubt. But it was more complicated than that.' He stirred the cream into his coffee. 'When she died, oh, I grieved of course. I still do. But I also felt a shameful feeling of freedom.' He looked up. 'I've never told anyone that.'

'So we're quits.'

When they got up to leave her body felt weightless. Maybe it was the wine. They walked to the door. Passing one of the partitions she glimpsed a familiar face. It was Robert. He was talking to someone she couldn't see.

She opened her mouth to call out. A waiter said: 'Excuse me, please.' She moved aside for the steaming plates. And then Eric held her elbow to guide her to the door. She thought: I don't want Robert to be a part of this, not just now.

And they went out into the street.

'Gosh, Mum, I've read about Archie's in *Harpers*,' said Louise. 'You are getting trendy.'

'Aren't I just?' said Dorothy. 'I had fishcakes with lemongrass. They were delicious.'

'Leaving Dad's done wonders for your education. Watch out – lemongrass one minute, cocaine the next.'

It was the following evening: Friday. Dorothy had driven down to Wingham Wallace for the night. 'I was quite an adventurous cook once,' she said. 'When we were first married. But your dad didn't like things messed around.'

'So what was he like?'

Dorothy had a hangover. She gazed at the dog basket. It was lined with the old tartan blanket they had used, long ago, for picnics. She felt the past detach itself and drift peacefully away. 'It was like meeting an old friend who knew exactly what I was talking about. I feel about thirty.'

'You look about twenty. Was he nice? Did he make a pass at you?'

'Goodness, what an old-fashioned expression.'

'Go on, did he?' urged Louise. 'You mustn't let them get

257

too far on a first date.'

'I'm sixty-three.'

'*I* can't remember what a first date was like either,' said Louise.

They laughed. Later, Dorothy remembered that moment in the kitchen. The smell of roasting meat, the laughter. Louise questioning her as if their positions were reversed and Louise was her mother. The relapse into girlish confederacy. Even Monty joined in, wagging his tail and sweeping the letters off the dresser.

'He fed me,' said Dorothy. 'I've spent my life feeding everyone else.' She felt poised at the brink. It was such a lost sensation that it took her a while to identify it. She had forgotten the sheer, breath-taking adventurousness of it all – the *will-he-phone?* The *what-shall-I-say?* He had said: *One day I'll tell you.* What did that mean, that he wanted to see her again?

A car arrived. The door opened and Robert came in. He brought in a gust of cold air. 'Hi ,Dorothy.' He dumped down an overnight bag and kissed her on the cheek. He kissed Louise. He seemed in a good humour. Dorothy smiled at him, for he was included in her happiness.

Louise took the ice-tray out of the freezer. 'Mum's been telling me about her date last night.' She pressed out the ice; it clattered into the glasses. 'She's getting very upmarket. She went to that trendy place in Holland Park. Archie's.'

'Oh yes?' Robert turned away to stroke the dog.

Dorothy should have realised then. Robert never stroked the dog. But she rattled on: 'At last I've been somewhere that's trendy enough for you. What did you eat?'

Louise unscrewed the tonic bottle. It hissed. 'What do you mean?' she asked.

Dorothy smiled at her son-in-law: 'I meant to say hello but a waiter got in the way.'

The tonic had sprayed Louise. She wiped her hands on her sweater. Then she said to her husband: 'I thought you were in Birmingham.'

258

PART FOUR

One

The collapse of Louise's marriage was spectacular. Imploded, it sank to its knees; it sank in a cloud of dust as if detonated by dynamite. The sight was awesome. For those who were jealous of this fortress – and there were many – there was a shameful thrill to its demolition. Even her sisters, who were basically nice women, who loved Louise, even they felt a brief frisson, though they admitted it to nobody. *It's not fair!* Maddy used to wail. *Lou's got off scot-free.*

Now the balance had shifted. At the beginning, her sisters tried to reason with her but Louise surprised them with the ferocity of her reaction. 'The bastard!' she cried. 'The pig! Know how long it's been going on? Six years. Since he dumped us out here.'

That first weekend, when it all blew up, Robert disappeared back to London. Her sisters drove down on Saturday. Like news of a death, it obliterated their plans; they forgot what they were supposed to be doing. Jamie and Imogen had gone off for the day; they still didn't know that anything was wrong.

'It's me who's been stuck out here, raising the kids, servicing his bloody life!' said Louise. 'Like a pit-stop, that's all I've been. And all this time he's been shagging this – this woman.'

Dorothy said: 'I'm sure he still loves you. He's always loved you. Men have these, well, these peccadilloes.'

Louise glared at her mother. 'What's got into you all of a sudden?'

'It's just that – it happens,' replied Dorothy. 'I should know.

Robert says he doesn't want to break up the family. Why don't you forgive him?'

'Whose side are you on?' Louise demanded.

'Go away somewhere quiet, the two of you, and talk it over.'

'I don't want to talk it over.'

Outside it was raining. The four of them sat round the blow heater; nobody had the energy to get in some wood and light the fire. The house already felt unloved; despair had settled on it like dust.

'Please, Lou,' urged Prudence. 'Think of the children.'

'I have thought of the children,' replied Louise. 'That's why I've been fucking stuck out here for six years.' She spooned sugar into her tea; her hand shook. Unhappiness had coarsened her looks; her hair hung lankly. 'I'm going to divorce him. I'm going to sue him for every penny, for every freezing, chilblained day I've spent digging up bloody potatoes so he can show the place off to his bloody friends.'

'Louise, calm down.' Prudence sat beside her on the arm of the chair. 'We've got to think how to tackle this.' She indicated Dorothy. 'Mum and I, we've been through this. Join the club.'

'I don't want to join the fucking club,' said Louise, and burst into tears.

Dorothy stared at the grill of the heater. There was something arid about its hum. 'If only I hadn't seen him. It's all my fault. I've come barging into your lives like a bull in a china shop.'

'I'm glad I know,' said Louise. 'It all makes sense now.'

Maddy and Prudence gazed at her. Despite their equivocal feelings towards Robert the crisis shocked them deeply. Their parents' break-up was bad enough, but this was the destruction of an ideal. When people closed their eyes to picture a marital haven, it was the Old Vicarage they saw. How could Robert do this to their sister? It was as if he was committing adultery with their dreams. He had soiled them.

'How could he?' wondered Prudence. 'And with someone

who's nearly fifty too. And not nearly as beautiful as you.'

'Pru!' said Maddy.

'Oh, sssh . . .' said Prudence. 'This is no time for political correctness.'

There was a pause. They gazed at their wrecked sister. 'How could I have loved him?' sobbed Louise. 'How could he have lied to me?'

Prudence passed her a Kleenex. She suddenly had a sense of *déjà vu*. On Christmas Eve their mother had sat sobbing in this very same chair. *I hate him! How could he do it?* She had sat there repeating the same words, for joy and sorrow call forth the same worn phrases from those experiencing them – phrases, like pebbles, washed up by the storm of human emotions and worn smooth by handling.

Her name was Deirdre. She lived in Essex, where her husband owned a garage. He was a compact, pugnacious man called Graham Frye; he had come to Robert's firm with plans to expand his business. This was seven years ago, when Robert and his family were still living in Chelsea. His children were children then and his marriage the envy of his friends. Louise had class, the class that comes with her kind of ethereal beauty. That she was a builder's daughter was neither here nor there, for Robert's City friends, brought up in the melting-pot of the seventies, came from a variety of backgrounds that would have been unthinkable in the old days. If anything, Louise's working-class roots only added to her allure, for unlike many of his friends' wives she seemed content to play a subservient role in Robert's life, caring for the children, creating a home and cooking the sort of cordon bleu dinners which their wives had neither the time nor the goodwill to cook themselves. Where Louise came from, women knew how to be women.

Robert's appreciation of his wife's qualities had not stopped him from having a series of affairs, fleeting ones dating from when the children were small. He had all the

261

qualifications for this: a lack of morals, a strong libido and, more potent than this, a devouring sexual curiosity that was almost infantile in its intensity. He was also a restless man, easily bored, and keeping secrets gave him a thrill. In other words, he was a classic philanderer. Until then, however, nothing had threatened the solidity of his marriage.

Robert had travelled up to Colchester to check out Graham Frye. He remembered that day – grey, damp, no sense of the momentous within it waiting to be released. Frye's garage was a sprawling place – workshops, a showroom; he had the Saab agency. It was situated next to the Stour estuary and he had already expanded into boat repairs. His scheme, for which he was seeking planning permission, was to go into partnership with a local businessman to build a marina. 'That's where the future lies,' he said, 'leisure.'

It was an ambitious plan which needed a large capital investment. Robert was an adventurer; he had always been attracted by small men with large vision. Even then his firm was dominated by pension schemes and management buyouts, and it was to become more so. Robert was considered a maverick, a wild card – brilliant, but needing to be kept on a leash. Frye's plan attracted him with its riskiness and by the end of the morning he had made up his mind to recommend it to his board.

It was then that Frye's wife came in, carrying a tray of coffee. They were sitting in the office. The window was open; outside was a squealing commotion of gulls.

'Sorry it's late,' she said. Her voice was low and melodious. 'I had to go to the post office.'

'This is my wife, Deirdre,' said Graham.

She put down the tray and shook Robert's hand. She was a full-breasted, mature woman, with soft brown hair. She wore a cream blouse and silky cardigan; she had that indefinable look, rare amongst the English, of wearing expensive underwear. She was by no means beautiful but she looked at ease with herself, something he had only found in continental women. He found out later that she was half-Irish, half-

262

French. She looked at his shoes. 'I see he's been dragging you through the mud. Are you cold? Shall I close the window?'

Robert shook his head. He felt at peace, as if within his body his organs had settled into their proper places. He felt that all his life he had been waiting for this woman; it was as simple as that.

Maybe he exaggerated, with hindsight. Maybe it didn't happen all at once. She said, later, that she had found him unsettling. 'This wolfish man. I thought, *I can't trust him. I thought, Under his clothes this man is thick with hair, like an animal.*' She said that she had sensed him sniffing her and she hadn't liked it.

That was later, much later. They didn't sleep together for over a year; she wouldn't let him. She was married; she was a devout Catholic. He wore her down; when he wanted something badly he always got it, in the end. Finally, when they became lovers, it seemed the most natural thing he had ever done in his life. She was the warmth in his heart; she was his woman, his soul-mate. From the begining, he didn't feel that he was being unfaithful to Louise. In fact, it was the opposite; when he was with Louise he felt unfaithful to Deirdre. She understood him; she healed the broken pieces of his past. She loved him unequivocally, the way his mother had never managed – his flaky, inadequate mother – and in a way that made his relationship with Louise, despite the children, seem flimsy and shallow-rooted.

They went on like this for years. Deirdre refused to leave her husband and he had to accept this. For a man of his character, he was remarkably patient. But Deirdre made him a better person – he told himself that he was even a better husband to Louise. That she never found out somehow sanctioned it too, as if it were blessed by God. He saw Deirdre maybe twice a week; they had snatched afternoons together, the odd night in London. The rest of the time he sleepwalked – pleasantly so – and nobody seemed to notice. Deirdre was simply there, in the fabric of his life, keeping him sane. Until a year ago, when things began to change.

On Sunday night Louise's sisters and mother left. Robert returned. He looked so terrible that, just for a moment, Louise pitied him. The next morning he drove Imogen to the airport; she was going to France on a school study trip, she would be away until Easter. Jamie, too, went away, up to York for some Open Day at the university; he was going to stay away for a couple of nights with some friends who were in their first year. Still neither of the children knew, or seemed to guess, that anything was wrong.

Robert and Louise were alone in the house. They closed themselves away from the world like wounded animals. He didn't go up to London; he took the week off work. If she could have felt anything, she would have felt gratified by this. They closed themselves off from the sunshine which mocked them at the windows, showing up the dust. The weather was suddenly beautiful, outside in the world where life seemed to go on as if nothing had happened. The holidays had started. At the school, an Easter Fair was being prepared; Louise should have been helping. The local cubs tramped along the lane outside the house, whistling.

Indoors, the dirty cups piled up in the sink; the phone went unanswered. Louise and Robert wandered unwashed, pale as ghosts. They sat in their dressing-gowns, like invalids, drinking whisky as the sunlight outside slid around the garden and finally sank behind the church. They talked, round and round in a repeating loop. They talked but it exhausted them, for there seemed nothing to say. With the death of love their words had perished.

Louise's anger had drained away. Robert didn't love her; he loved another woman more. He tried to explain; he tried to be kind. 'She's older than you. She's not nearly as beautiful. She's not even that clever or amusing.'

'You really think that helps?' asked Louise.

They sat hunched in the kitchen. The cat brushed against Louise's legs, miaowing for food.

'When did you stop loving me?' she asked.

'I never stopped. I've always loved you – been fond of you –'

'Fond!'

'Nothing's changed,' he said. 'None of this changed what I felt for you.'

'*You* changed,' she said. 'The past few months.'

'That was nothing to do with you. You must believe me.'

'I don't believe anyone any more. I'm too tired.'

'Lou – we can get over this –'

'You love her more than you love me. There's nothing more to say, is there?' Louise looked at him. 'That's the awful thing.'

She sat there, numb. What *had* they ever talked about? Twenty years of marriage dissolved away; all those words, what had they been? Just words; a heap of ashes. She wished she could feel something but all she felt was sick. If she were alone she could try to catch up with the shock of it but Robert was there, trying to be kind, like a poisoner rubbing her with anaesthetic as he administered the lethal injection.

Her head throbbed. What she was going through, it had happened to so many people she knew; it had even happened to her mother. She had comforted them with such blind and patronising ignorance. She had read countless articles about it in magazines but nothing had prepared her for how it felt. She had had no idea.

Nor could she have guessed how Robert would behave. For during those terrible days he was indeed kind to her – gentle, even. He ran her a bath. It wasn't like him but then neither of them was recognisable to the other. He was like a stranger with whom she had nothing in common except the lumber of family life. A corner of her brain wondered what he was like with this other woman – she couldn't bear to call her by name – was this pale, solicitous man the Robert whom *she* knew? Did he run *her* baths, was that where he had learned it?

Louise lay in the water. She lay there for a long time, until

265

it grew chilly. Her body already looked uncherished, like that of an elderly woman. Her pubic hair looked like an anachronism, like a powder puff left on the dressing-table of somebody she didn't know. For the first time in her marriage she had locked the bathroom door. She and Robert had become modest with each other, undressing separately, putting on pyjamas and lying in bed without touching. Neither of them had moved to another room. They needed the simple, animal comfort of another body lying next to their own, breathing deeply as it pretended to sleep through the interminable night.

In the mornings Robert brought her a cup of tea, as he had done years ago, before the children were born. They were alone, as they had been at the beginning. The house was so silent that she thought that, behind the closed doors, the rooms must be stripped bare. No teenagers inhabited them, they had never played their horrible music, it had all been a dream. She had dreamed a family for herself, and now she had woken up.

She went downstairs. Even this was exhausting. She realised that it was Wednesday morning; two days seemed to have passed. 'What are we going to tell the children?' Asking a question exhausted her too. 'What are we going to do?'

'What do you want to do?' Robert stood, looking out of the window.

'You want to live with her, don't you?'

He didn't move. She looked at the back of his dressing-gown – maroon and black stripes, she had bought it for him at Liberty. Outside, in the morning sunshine, steam rose off the roof of the stable.

'You're a born cheat,' she said. 'You learned it at your mother's knee. But this isn't just cheating, is it?'

He shook his head.

'If we –' She stopped. She couldn't say *separate*. 'If you go, she'll leave her husband?'

He nodded. 'She didn't want to break up our family. She's rather religious.'

266

Not too religious to shag you, Louise would have said, if she hadn't been so tired. 'We'd better do it then. I'm not going to fight. Fighting for your marriage – what's the point, when the battle's lost? We'd better do it. Sell the house, do it. We can't possibly go on now.'

Robert stood there. She heard the drip of the tap. After he spoke, that moment was imprinted on her memory for ever: Robert's striped, towelling back, the view of the church spire through the window – the view she had gazed at as she had prepared a thousand meals for her family to eat.

Finally, he spoke. He didn't turn round. 'Louise,' he said, 'there's something I haven't told you.'

Night had fallen. Louise was sitting in the garden. She had sat there for some time; she couldn't go back into the house, not with Robert in it. She wore her overcoat but still she shivered. Over by the shed, the rabbit shifted around in his hutch.

Behind her, in the house, a window slid open. She willed Robert not to call out. After a moment, the window slid closed. Through the hedge she heard the horse. Skylark moved around in the meadow; she tore at some grass, the ground reverberated as she trotted off. She, too, was restless tonight. It was as if the animals had sensed that something had happened.

It was still Wednesday. It seemed inconceivable that it was still the same day. Over and over Louise thought: *so that was why he was being so nice.* She looked up at the church. It was lit from within; they must be preparing it for Easter. In the stained-glass window angels blew trumpets around the body on the cross; they looked as if they were on fire. Louise had never prayed, she hadn't been taught to. She had stepped inside the church simply to show it to her guests. She thought: if I believed, He would be an avenging God, He would punish the wicked in the flames of hell. He would watch them perish and then He would hold me in his arms, my

267

Father, and give me comfort. If I believed in God I wouldn't be alone.

She wasn't alone. Someone was watching her.

Louise turned her head slowly. A figure stood in the garden, half-hidden by the yew hedge. It was a woman – a large woman, in pale clothes.

Louise turned away. In the house the dog barked, once, and was silent. Her heart thudded. If she sat still, maybe the woman would disappear. It was that woman, of course, Deirdre. She was standing there, waiting for Robert. If Louise pretended that she hadn't seen her, maybe the woman would take him away.

The horse whinnied. The lights were switched off in the church. It stood there, a black bulk, its spire rearing up into the sky. Couldn't Deirdre wait? Maybe she had some sadistic impulse to watch the death-throes of the marriage she had helped to destroy. Louise held her breath; across the lawn she could almost hear the woman breathing.

Maybe Deirdre couldn't stay away. She had come here to spy on them. Prudence said that she had driven to Stephen's house, once, just to sit there looking at the windows. Maybe the woman thought that Robert wasn't going to leave, could that be possible?

Louise felt furious. How could Deirdre dare to come here? She got up from the bench and walked across the grass. The figure was rooted to the spot, like a piece of garden statuary. Louise stepped up to her.

She was a fat woman. She wore a pale jacket, a skirt and wellington boots. There was something familiar about her but it took Louise a moment to recognise her. It was Margot, from the General Stores.

Louise asked: 'Are you all right? What are you doing here?'

'I want to talk to you,' said Margot.

'What's happened?'

'I know everything,' said Margot. 'About you and my husband.'

Louise stared at her. Margot's face glimmered in the moon-

268

light. A broad face, her hair curly and somehow inappropriate, like a wig. Louise hadn't seen her for months.

'What about your husband?' Louise tried to remember what had happened with Tim but her brain felt scrambled. She heard a noise. She turned; the back door had been opened, a beam of light shone into the garden. Robert stood there. 'We can't talk here,' she whispered.

Louise slipped behind the hedge and across the gravel. She made her way around the back of the stable, to the caravan. Margot followed her. Louise opened the door. Margot's face was blank, as if she were sleepwalking. She didn't seem to find it odd that Louise hadn't invited her into the house.

The street lamp shone through the little window. Louise sat down on the stool. Margot seemed to fill up the cramped interior. She sat down on the bed, breathing heavily from the walk.

'I found out about you, you see,' said Margot. 'Do you want to know how? Are you interested? Stop me if I'm boring you.' She stared into Louise's face; her gaze was unnerving. 'Something happened to me today. You wouldn't understand it but I'll tell you all the same. The sun was shining, you see, and I felt something happen. I don't know if you know about – the thing that happened, or if you care, it probably means nothing to you –'

'Oh, I do care, I'm so sorry –'

'– but for the first time in six years I felt this unusual sensation, so unusual I'd forgotten what it was. Most peculiar. I felt as if a weight was lifting, a glimmer of light at the end of the tunnel, call it what you will. It was hope. A tiny glimmer of something almost approaching happiness.' She shifted her position; the bed creaked. Still she didn't take her eyes off Louise's face. 'I'm only telling you this so you'll know what you've done to me.'

'What have I done?'

'It's our half-day closing on Wednesdays. I thought, *We'll have a barbecue. Look, it's a sunny day!* I thought, *Tim will be so pleased.* He's suffered, you know, you wouldn't believe. I thought, *I've got some chicken pieces and a packet of sausages. I'll set out the barbecue, out the back, and we'll do something nice, just for us.* So I went to the shelf and pulled out a sack of charcoal. And that's when I found them.'

'Found what?'

'The photos.'

'What?'

'Of you.'

Louise froze. Her throat closed up.

'He says he loves you.' Margot's voice was flat. 'He's not up to much, Mrs Bailey, but he's all I've got. How can you take him from me?'

'But I haven't –'

'What a greedy woman you are. You've got everything and now you've got my husband too –'

'I haven't!' said Louise.

'Seems to me, you see – seems to me a little bit unfair,' said Margot. 'You probably don't think so, people like you probably don't even notice –'

'You think I've got everything?' Louise leaned forward; her knees bumped against Margot's. 'Shall I tell you the truth? My marriage has just broken up, that's what's happened.' She wiped her nose with the back of her hand. 'My husband's leaving me, he's fallen in love with somebody else, he's been in love with her for years. He was only staying with me until the children were old enough for him to go, except I've found out so he's going now. He's fond of me. That's what he said. He's fond of me and I've looked after the children.' She pushed her hand through her hair. She looked around the caravan – the tiny cooker, the flowery curtains. In the lamp-light it seemed sinister, a goblin parody of normal life. She looked up at Margot. 'Shall I tell you something else? Something he told me today? He's stolen all our money, too. He's cheated me over that as well. Last year he took out a loan against the security of our house, and do you know what for? To bail out this woman's husband. His business is going bust, poor thing. So we've paid for it. *That's* how much he

270

loves her. We've paid for it and we haven't got a bloody penny left. Nothing belongs to us – the house, any of this.' She gestured around wildly. 'It's all gone. It's all nothing.' She looked at Margot's expressionless face. 'I don't know why I'm telling you this.'

'Because I don't count,' said Margot bitterly.

They sat in silence. Far away a dog barked. Maybe it was Monty. Her house seemed to have drifted away, she couldn't imagine ever going back into it now.

She looked at Margot. She seemed too old to have had a child; maybe she and Tim had married late. Maybe they had both been married before. Louise didn't know anything about them. Margot was right; until that moment in the lane she had hardly thought about them.

Margot said: 'Sometimes, the first few weeks, I'd wake up and think – oh, she'll be late for school.'

Louise gazed out of the window. The sky seemed paler. Maybe they had sat there for so long that it was already morning.

'What a fucking mess,' she said.

Two

Jamie told Imogen when she got back from France. He didn't seem unduly upset.

'They're splitting up,' he said. 'Dad's got some slag in Essex.'

Imogen burst into tears.

Jamie looked gratified. 'Chill, sis,' he said. 'Everybody's doing it.'

Imogen slammed the door of her room and threw herself on the bed. Her heart was breaking. She had read the words so often and now it was happening. Part of her stood back and watched these histrionics – herself flung on the bed, her face buried in the pillow, making noises as if she were being sick. Part of her thought: when I see Karl I'll throw myself into his arms and burst into tears and he'll comfort me. She thought: now I can't show off my tan from France, it will seem too trivial.

She thought all this and yet she was dying. Her mother knocked on the door and came in.

'I wanted to tell you myself,' she said. 'Oh, Immy . . .' Already she looked like a single parent – peakier, more battered. She wore her old gardening trousers though she hadn't been gardening. She sat down on the swivel chair. It swung round in a carefree way; she stopped it with her foot.

'I hate Dad,' said Imogen, wiping her nose on her sleeve. 'How could he? I'm never going to see him, ever again.'

'Don't, darling. It'll only make it worse.' Her mother pushed back her hair. She had large hands, dry and reddened from looking after her family. 'Don't be angry with him. He feels terrible too.' She paused. 'The bastard.' She tried to smile; it was a poor effort.

'Is he going to move out?' asked Imogen. 'Are we going to stay here? What's going to happen to Skylark?'

'I don't know. Nothing's worked out yet.'

Imogen swung her legs round and got up. She looked at her suitcase. When she had packed it, a week ago, what a sad little squit she had been! 'When's he back?'

'The usual time,' replied her mother. 'He wants to take you both out.'

'Why?'

'For a meal. To talk to you.'

'You must be joking.' Imogen left the room.

'Darling, wait . . .' her mother called out weakly.

It was three in the afternoon. Imogen fetched the bridle. She went out into the meadow. During the past week the field had become furry with grass; dandelions were flowering and the hedge was misted with green. How stupid nature was, pushing up the plants, blind to everything!

She caught Skylark. When the horse tried to pull away she jerked her head back roughly. She saddled her up.

Every Tuesday, Karl shod the horses at the Valley View Stables, where Imogen had learned to ride. It lay five miles away, across the A40 and out towards Whitton.

She thwacked Skylark with the crop. The mare, surprised, jerked forward. They set off at a trot. Her mother ran out of the house but they had gone.

The clouds were torn open; rods of sunlight poured out of the gap. The countryside was bathed in molten light. Imogen thought: nothing is beautiful any more, it's all ruined. She kicked Skylark's swollen flanks; how fat her horse was becoming, what a slug! Skylark broke into a canter. The track was stony; Skylark stumbled but Imogen kicked her on. She thought: I will never be happy, ever again.

It was four-thirty when she arrived at the riding school. It was the Easter holidays and the place was full of kids. Karl's van was parked in the yard. A little girl led Crackerjack, a skewbald gelding, out of his loose-box; her face wore that look that small girls have when they are anywhere near a pony – bossy, proprietorial, as if they were responsible not just for an animal but for the whole country. Imogen had been like that once; how funny. She dismounted. This place had once been her heaven on earth; now she gazed at it with detached pity.

Jackie, the owner, emerged from the tack-room.

'I was just passing by,' said Imogen. 'I've got a message for the blacksmith.' She felt like a hologram, a ghostly presence floating over this place.

She tied up Skylark next to the watering-trough and loosened the girths. Karl was working in the next yard; she heard the rat-a-tat-tat of metal against metal. She felt her past slipping away. She walked in a trance, towards the hammering of her own heart.

'First it's my grandad, then it's my own fucking father,' she said.

They were sitting on a bale of straw. With his knuckle, Karl wiped a tear from her cheek. 'You poor bugger.'

Despite her misery she felt proud to be sitting next to him. The blacksmith, with his curly black hair – it had grown. How jealous the girls must be! Sure, Imogen was crying, but no doubt they thought it was a lovers' tiff, something way beyond their feeble little lives.

'I just had to tell you,' she said.

He picked white hairs off her jodhpurs. The insides of her thighs were stuck with them; her legs felt sweaty from riding.

'I must look horrible,' she said.

'You've got a great tan.'

She smiled weakly. She urged him to respond in the way she wanted. If he disappointed her she would be utterly alone. Despite her passion for him she hardly knew him at all; she saved their moments of intimacy for when she was alone. In real life she saw him once a week, on Thursdays, when he came to the village pub to play chess with his mates Spider and Baz; she sat next to him like his girlfriend and afterwards he chastely kissed her goodnight. The rest of the time she daydreamed about him so intensely that when she saw him again she blushed.

He said: 'When I've finished up I'll drive you home.'

Her heart thumped. 'Really?'

'Get them to stable your pony. There's no way you're riding back. It'll be dark in a while and we don't want anything to happen to you, do we?'

He touched her cheek. She felt very close to him just then. He had seen her cry; he had comforted her. They had negotiated a hurdle together, far higher than the hurdles she had jumped with Skylark.

'She's not a pony, by the way,' said Imogen. 'She's a horse.'

In the van, she said: 'I don't want to go home, ever.'

He said: *Come and live with me.*

He didn't. He said: 'Come on, I'll buy you a drink.'

They stopped at a pub. She phoned home. Her mother answered.

'It was getting dark so I've left Skylark at the stables,' she said. 'I'll be home later.'

'How are you getting back?' asked her mother.

'Sandra's here. Her parents'll give me a lift.'

She put down the phone. Emboldened by her lie, she gulped down the rum and coke that Karl put in front of her. 'I want to do something exciting,' she said.

'No you don't.'

'What do you think I am, a sissy?'

'Sissy!' He laughed. 'Oh sooper-dooper.'

'Stop making fun of me. You're always making fun of me.'
He ruffled her hair. 'You're a sweet girl.'

'Stop patronising me!' she shouted. The couple sitting next to them turned to stare. She didn't care; for once, she didn't care about anything. 'It's not my fault – my school, my stupid bloody family, any of it! You think I'm just a little squit. Well, fuck you!' She stood up.

He put his hands on her shoulders and pushed her down in her seat. 'I'm sorry. Have a crisp.'

'A crisp. Oh, that'll make everything all right.'

He grinned. Her insides turned to liquid. They had quarrelled! He bought some more drinks. She took one of his cigarettes. He lit it for her; she inhaled deeply and blew the smoke through her nostrils without choking. *Ruddles*, said the beer mat. What a ludicrous word!

'Who mates for life anyway?' she asked. 'Certainly not badgers.'

'Hey, I never saw your photos.'

'Elephants do.' Her head swam. 'But who'd want to be an elephant?'

'You're a funny girl. Know that?'

'Funny, ha-ha? Or funny she should be locked up?' She drained her glass and held it out. 'Go on, get us another.'

When they got up, she staggered; he took her hand. The pub seemed to be suddenly full of people. As she pushed her way through them, holding his hand, she felt as proprietorial as the girls with their ponies. She felt the solemnity of the drunkard. *I'm his woman*, she thought.

In the van, Karl kissed her. She buried her face in his jacket and smelled the horse-sweat. Wedged against the gear-stick, she pressed her body against his. He stroked her breast, kneading it through her sweater. The van smelled of burned hooves – an acrid, singed smell, the smell of her hair shrivelling when she and Jamie had played with matches. She kissed Karl more deeply, burying her fingers in his hair. *I love you*, she told him silently. *The world is burning, all those bones burning, the hair shrivelling, bugger the lot of them.*

He disentangled himself and started the engine. 'I'm taking you home,' he said.

'No! I'm not going home, ever.'

'Yes, you are.'

'Take me somewhere exciting.'

He pulled out of the car-park. 'Okay,' he said.

He drove through the dark. How long had they been in the pub? Hours? He drove for some time in silence. She kept close to him, shifting sideways when he changed gear. Some time later he pulled off the road; ahead of them, a gate was illuminated in the headlights.

They got out of the van. He climbed over the gate and held out his hand. She grabbed it and jumped down. He led her up a rutted track. She thought: this darkness, we're always stumbling through it together. She thought: how sweet we were when we went to watch the badgers. She giggled.

It was a moonless night, she couldn't see much. When they reached the top of the hill, however, she could discern the orange glow of London. The immensity of it! She thought how pitiful her parents were, their little lives.

He said: 'Feel this.' He took her hand and laid it on a stone wall. 'It's a church. St Cuthbert's.'

'Cuthbert,' she giggled. 'You can't have a saint called *Cuthbert*.'

They stepped over some rubble. The place was open to the sky; she could sense this, by the air. The holiness had evaporated; it was just a husk.

'Know when this was built?' he asked.

'Don't know, don't care.' She took his hand and closed it with hers. Her heart was bumping; could he sense it? 'Let us pray,' she chortled. 'Let us pray that my father rots in hell.'

She thought: I've left my horse behind; I've left it all behind. I'm spinning in space, up above the carcass of this church, up into the corrupt sodium sky.

She knelt, pulling Karl with her. He practically fell. She pulled him close, his knees pressed against hers.

'Our father,' she said.

'Forgive us our traspisses – trespers –'

'Trespasses,' she corrected. 'As we forgive them that trespass against us . . .'

'For thine is the kingdom –'

'Blah blah,' she said.

'Amen.'

He kissed her. Toppling over, he gripped her shoulders to steady himself. She realised, with gratification, that he was even more drunk than she was. They lowered themselves to the ground. She extracted a piece of metal, it felt like a bedspring, from under her hip and flung it away. She squeezed her eyes shut and surrendered herself to oblivion. It was chilly; she thrust her hands inside his jacket, feeling his flesh through his shirt. Karl's tongue explored her mouth; his breathing quickened. Awkwardly, hoisting himself on one elbow, he tried to unclip the side fastening of her jodhpurs. She did it for him. His hand slid inside her knickers. She gasped. It was so strange to have another finger there, where only her own had been. She parted her legs, as much as her position would allow. His finger slid inside her.

'Is that nice, sweetheart?' he muttered. He had never called her *sweetheart* before. His finger moved inside her; he pressed the fleshy part of his palm against her pubic bone. Heat spread through her. 'Aah, you're wet,' he murmured. His breathing grew hoarser. He pushed his finger in and out. 'I've got nothing with me,' he gasped in her ear.

'I'm on the Pill,' she whispered.

'Yeah, but still –'

She stopped him. She moved her hand down to the front of his jeans. She rubbed the bulge there. He groaned louder. What power she had! She rubbed harder. He shuddered, trembling.

His hand guided her to the zip; with difficulty she pulled it down. His finger stabbed frenziedly inside her, faster and faster. Then suddenly he pulled it out. She lifted her bottom; he pulled off her jodhpurs and knickers. She helped him.

278

He laid her down. She felt him shifting as he pulled off his jeans. Then he moved on top of her. He licked her ear and her neck; Boyd, her rabbit, did that to the does when he was preparing to mate. Karl's breath rasped in her ear. He positioned her, spreading her legs beneath him. He did this in an expert, workmanlike way. His penis nudged her belly as he moved her to one side, where the ground was softer; it bumped against her thigh. He wedged her legs wider apart with his knees; then he took his penis and pushed it into her.

Imogen yelped. She pressed her fingernails into his cold, shockingly bare buttocks as they clenched and unclenched. He thrust inside her, his hips moving as if they were oiled. She squeezed her eyes shut and pictured Boyd, gripping the furry rump of a female, juddering. Karl was mating with her. His movements quickened; he shoved his hand under her and pulled her rhythmically against him. She tried to move with him; she wanted him to think she had done it before. Then he groaned, loudly, and gripped her in a spasm. She felt him pumping inside her, waves of pumping, a warm flood of it. Then he loosened his grip, exhaling. He lay on her, a dead weight.

So that was it. She had done it. A bird screeched, that eerie cry of their badger night. After a moment his breathing grew more regular. He kissed her forehead and drew back.

'I shouldn't have done that,' he said.

'It was sooper-dooper,' she replied. His face was a pale glimmer above hers. She couldn't see if he smiled.

'Look at them,' said Jamie. It was Saturday morning. Tesco was full of mums and dads with their brats. 'Look at them, the sad fuckers.'

Jamie and Trevor were unloading vegetables. Trevor lifted up a cucumber; he hoisted it to his shoulder, took aim and made a machine-gun noise. The effort exhausted him. He leaned against the shelves, coughing his smoker's cough.

'Let's blow the place up,' said Jamie. 'It's time we did something exciting.'

Trevor emptied a box of carrots into the display trough. One of them fell on the floor. It was a good size. He picked it up and looked at Jamie. 'Want to take this home for your mum?' he asked. 'Think she needs it?'

Jamie laughed. He felt vaguely sick. He had told Trev about his parents splitting up. *'My Dad's a bit of a lad too, just like yours.'*

'Heard the one about the little boy and the little girl?' Jamie flung bags of potatoes into the trough. 'She asks to see his thing and so he shows her and she says, "Is that all?"' He told Trevor the rest of the joke. Trev grunted; the nearest he ever got to a laugh. 'I got it from my dad,' said Jamie.

Just then, when he looked down the aisle, he saw someone familiar. It took him a moment to identify the person; he looked different out of context. It was the blacksmith. He pushed a trolley. A child sat in it; another child, a little girl, walked alongside, picking her nose. With them was a woman. She looked at a piece of paper in her hand and said something to the blacksmith. He nodded obediently and fetched a bunch of bananas from the shelf. The woman frowned, shaking her head. He went back and fetched another one.

He used to live with somebody, Imogen had said, *but it's all over.*

Jamie felt a curdled satisfaction in his stomach. The slimy git, he thought. They're all at it.

'Want to go out tonight then?' said Trev.

'Only if it's somewhere exciting.'

'Up to London.'

'We haven't got any wheels.'

'Oh, that can be arranged. No problem.' This was a long conversation, for Trev.

'How?'

Trevor told him.

Robert had cancelled his Saturday tennis game and disappeared to London. Maybe to Essex. Louise didn't know. Her husband now had an official other life; he no longer had to lie. He said he would be away overnight. Maybe he was making arrangements to move in with this woman. A second marriage was being dismantled. Louise felt a brief wave of sympathy for her fellow-cuckold, the husband. Maybe he was suffering as much as she was. Then she stopped. Christ, the man had been living off her! She, Louise, had been bled dry to keep his business alive. Didn't he and his wife know where the money was coming from? Hadn't they thought to ask? The lies, the treachery . . . She had shared a house for twenty years with a man who had betrayed her, who had stolen her and her children's future from them. The panic returned; it felt like a blanket being shaken out in her gut.

She hadn't told the children about the money. She had told nobody. Her children had enough to deal with as it was. Their reactions, this past week, had been painful to watch. Imogen had been tearful and volatile. 'I hate you!' she had shouted at Robert. 'How could you do this to Mum?' She had shut herself in her room, or disappeared on long rides. She was deeply upset but at least it showed. What would happen, however, when she learned the whole truth?

Jamie, on the other hand, was more unsettling. He feigned indifference – in fact, feigned it so well that it was convincing. He spoke to his father quite naturally – off-hand, cool. 'I've always wanted to get out of this dump anyway.'

On Saturday night both the children went out. Louise wandered restlessly from room to room. She gazed at the dead fireplace and the read magazines. She couldn't eat. She felt more alone than she had ever been in her life. For forty-two years she had been accompanied by others, by her parents, sisters and then by children, by her husband. Outside, the wind blew, whistling along the telephone wires. She couldn't bring herself to break the silence and switch on the TV.

Just then the phone rang. It was Rosemary Giddings, a woman who lived in the village. 'Can you and Robert come to dinner next Thursday?'

Louise gathered her wits. The news hadn't leaked out yet; to everybody else, her life with Robert was carrying on as usual. At some point she had to put a stop to this and come out with the truth. Just now, however, she couldn't bear to speak it, especially to a woman she disliked.

'I'm sorry, we can't.' She made some excuse – Robert going away, maybe. Later, she couldn't remember because then Rosemary said: 'By the way, have you heard the latest gossip? Margot Minchin – you know, at the shop – she's packed up and gone. She's left poor old Tim.'

What happened next was something that Louise confessed to nobody as long as she lived. Even when she and her sisters had grown old, when events had lost their sting and been shaped into stories, even then she told nobody what took place on that Saturday night, in that spring when her life was disintegrating.

Soon after the phone call she changed her clothes. She watched herself pull on her red woollen dress, the one that clung to her breasts; she watched herself from a distance. She put on her coat and walked down the lane. It was nine o'clock. In the darkness the hedgerows rustled. The village green was ringed by scattered, lit windows; she felt as if she was out at sea and the land was somewhere she would never reach.

A light shone above the shop. She rang the bell. She waited. Tim appeared in the gloom of the shop. He unlocked the door.

'Can I come in?' she asked.

He looked startled. She hadn't seen him since that night in the lane. She stepped into the shop. He closed the door.

She thought: I'm dreaming this. He has taken photos of me. He's a sad, creepy man. Robert calls him the Trainspotter.

But Robert was no longer there; he was only an amused voice in her ear. And as for the photographs – just now they seemed no more or less bizarre than anything else that had happened during these past two weeks.

'I'm just making some tea,' said Tim. She followed him upstairs. She had never been in the flat before. Cilla Black chattered on the TV; an electric fire was pulled out into the middle of the carpet. The remains of supper was on the table. In the kitchen a kettle whistled.

'I heard what happened,' said Louise. 'I'm so sorry.' She looked around; there was something missing. 'Has she taken the dog?'

Tim nodded. He turned down the sound of the TV.

'She told you about me and my husband, I presume.' Louise tried to laugh. 'We're sort of in the same boat, aren't we?'

Tim wore his old blue tracksuit. There was a growth of stubble on his chin; it made him look surprisingly raffish. She urged herself to find him attractive. He wore an unfamiliar pair of gold-rimmed glasses. Maybe he just wore them at home.

'Do you mind me coming here?' she asked.

He shook his head. He took her coat and laid it over the back of the settee.

'I just felt so lonely,' she said.

'Are you warm enough? I could switch on the other bar.'

She shook her head. He went into the kitchen. She heard the clatter of crockery. On the TV, a blonde girl sat on a sofa, holding hands with a young man. They simpered soundlessly. The children were addicted to *Blind Date*; they liked sneering at the couples. So did Robert.

Louise smoothed down her dress. There was a ladder in her tights, on the knee. She hadn't seen it when she had pulled them on. She was eighteen years old again, sitting in a strange room, her insides fluttering. On Tim's supper plate lay the remains of a pork pie.

Tim came in, carrying a tray of tea things. As he lowered it the cups shivered.

283

'You haven't got anything stronger, have you?' she asked. 'I've been drinking whisky like there's no tomorrow.' She stopped – what a strange expression to use.

'Of course.' He fetched a whisky bottle and two glasses. He stood still, looking at her. 'I can't believe you're here.'

She smiled. 'Nor can I.'

'Water?'

She shook her head, took the glass and swallowed it in one gulp. 'I feel really shitty. It wasn't me she left for – I mean, because of me?'

'No. Of course not.' He refilled her glass. 'It was nothing to do with you.'

'Can you sit down?' she asked. 'You're making me nervous.'

He sat on the settee, his knees pressed together like a virgin. How thin he was; how sloping his shoulders! Through his glasses he gazed at her. She imagined removing them and putting them on the table.

She moved across and sat down next to him. 'I just wanted to be here,' she began. 'What you said to me that night – well, it was so lovely. Just to hear words like that.' She recrossed her legs. Her tights made a faint, rasping sound. 'It was so nice of you.'

'What do you mean, nice?'

'I thought about it a lot afterwards. What you said.'

'You did?' He raised his eyebrows.

'So I came here.'

He put his glass on the table. 'I think you should go.'

'It's all right. I don't want to.' She touched his hand with her forefinger. 'You see, I don't have to any more.'

'No, but I want you to.'

There was a silence. Louise fixed her eyes on the TV screen. Cilla Black giggled soundlessly.

'You're making a bit of a fool of yourself, aren't you?' Tim got up. He straightened the ornaments on the mantelpiece. 'It really isn't very nice. I expected better of you.' He turned to look at her. 'I don't terribly like being used, you know. Even by someone as delightful as yourself. Do you really think you can come in here and – it's not very nice.' He moved a china dog. His voice was trembling – from anger, she realised now. 'I suppose you want to pay your husband back, it's some sort of tit-for-tat, something like that. So you snap your fingers for poor old Tim. I wish I could oblige but I really don't want to. Strange though that might seem.' He picked up her coat. 'I think it would be best if we forgot this ever happened, don't you?'

Louise found it difficult to stand up. Her legs seemed to have liquified. Finally she got to her feet.

'I think I'll stick to the photos, if you don't mind.' He held out her coat. 'I know it's pathetic, but at least I'm not doing anybody any harm.'

It seemed a mile, the journey down the stairs and across the shop. Finally, she reached the door. Tim unlocked it and held it open.

'I'm sorry,' she said, and stumbled into the darkness.

Until that Saturday night Jamie had committed no crime. As a child, he had eaten a Kit-Kat that his friend had stolen from the shop near their school in Chelsea. He had smoked dope, and planned to smoke a great deal more when he travelled around Europe that summer. His mother, in her haphazard way, had tried to instil some morals in him; his father, never. In October he was going to study psychology, which would no doubt acquaint him with the criminal mind. But he had never truly entered this area of human activity.

Ah, but how easy it was! He sauntered, with Trevor, past the parked cars. Trevor had straightened up; he looked purposeful, professional – more concentrated somehow, as if his molecules had bunched together. He seemed to know, intuitively, where to strike.

And now he did it. There was a grace in the way he stopped beside the Escort and looked around. He looked as if he had been bred for this moment, like an athlete when he steps onto the track. It was dark; the street was empty. He fiddled with the door and then they were in. The interior was tidy; it smelled of pine deodorant. *Travelling salesman*, Jamie thought. Then he thought: *a Crime Victim.*

The engine roared into life; the very roar sounded lawless. They were off. Jamie was flung back. He hadn't buckled himself in; you didn't hot-rod a car and then strap yourself into a bloody seat-belt.

They drove out of High Wycombe. An oncoming car flashed them.

'Lights!' hissed Jamie.

Trevor, who was stoned, fumbled at the dashboard. The headlights flared. Now they were speeding through an illuminated tunnel, hedges high on either side. They were plunging down a plug-hole; somebody had pulled the plug and they were off, spinning down.

'Wicked!' Trevor snorted.

Exhilaration swept through Jamie; his balls tightened. He felt alive, down to his fingertips. What power! You broke in, you roared off, you just did it! He forgot everything: the confusion and the anger, sod it all. They roared past the darkened bulk of Tesco; they gave it the finger as they passed. The speedometer inched up ... 80 ... 85 ... 90 ...

Jamie shouted: 'This is better than sex!' His few couplings, even they were blown away. Trevor was careering towards London. How glamorous he seemed, now, as he sat at the wheel! Jamie felt like a swooning female, Trevor's date for the night. He clutched the door-handle as they swerved around a corner.

And then something happened. Later, he couldn't remember what caused it. He was stoned, too. But now a gate was rearing up in front of them and splintering like matchsticks. Trevor cackled like a maniac.

'Hey, watch out!' yelled Jamie.

A sea of mud rushed towards them. Jamie rammed his hands against the dashboard. He ducked. The car slewed to a halt.

Trevor giggled. He crashed the gear into reverse. The wheels spun.

'Abandon fucking ship!' he shrieked.

Jamie flung open the door. 'Women and children first!' He half-toppled into the mud.

He watched himself with curiosity as he picked himself up. See, like a cartoon character, he too sprang up, unharmed. He seemed to be in the middle of a ploughed field. He and Trevor ran, in great leaping strides. He turned to look at the car. The twin rods of the headlights shone in the darkness. The lit interior looked oddly homely.

'Come on, dickbrain,' said Trevor. They stumbled across to the gap where the gate had been. Jamie picked his way through the planks of wood; he slipped in the tyre-ruts. His knee hurt; it must have hit the dashboard.

They ran up the lane, over the brow of the hill. Jamie paused for breath. The sky was suffused with the orange glow of London. Below lay the lights of a village. It was Wingham Wallace; he was only a mile from home.

The next week Louise went up to London to see her father. They had arranged to meet for lunch in a restaurant near Marble Arch. Why Marble Arch? She didn't know; her father inhabited a new territory now.

As she walked down the street she gazed irritably at the passers-by. What a lot of them there were, jostling and hostile. Until recently she had enjoyed coming to London. Now it seemed a place filled with strangers who cared nothing for her and who had homes of their own to go to. All her life doors had opened and the sunshine flooded in; now they had slammed shut. Or, to be accurate, they had closed quietly and regretfully. *I think you'd better go now*, Tim had said.

She passed a bookshop. *Playing with Fire* was displayed in the window. She hadn't thought about her sister and Erin for what seemed like decades, nor about her mother who had seemed so rejuvenated by the man from the small ads. Louise was closed off from other people's lives; grief and bitterness had sealed her away from the world, which now seemed insolently heartless. *Fuck you*, it brayed at her.

Her father looked indecently well. He looked years younger than she felt. He wore a yellow pullover; he looked as breezy as a golfing pro.

'Patch it up,' he said. 'Come on, Lou. Tell him you forgive him and give the bugger another chance.'

'Funny. That's just what Mum said.' She gazed at the menu. 'You didn't try to patch it up, remember? We came round and pleaded with you, you didn't listen to a word we said. You just bailed out.'

'But you've got kids.'

'We're kids too. Just grown older. It still hurts, you know. You bailed out from all of us.' She looked at the pasta. *Fettucine . . . linguine . . .* It was all the same stuff, flour and water. 'You made us feel our childhood was all pretend, you were just waiting to leave.'

He looked chastened, just for a moment. 'Is that why you came to see me? To tell me this?'

She shook her head. 'I want to ask for your help.'

'Funny way to go about it. More Maddy's line.'

She thought: I've lost my charm. It's so tiring being charming. She took a breath and told him what had happened. 'He transferred all this money from our account. I never look at the bank statements, I hadn't a clue what was happening.' She paused. 'Robert's ruined us. I don't know what to do. I'll have to sell the house but I don't own it any more, so that doesn't help.'

Her father listened but in a detached way, as if she were reading the news on the radio. He mouthed words of sympathy. He said: 'You poor love. I never trusted the bloke, you know that. Remember when he wrote Imogen's homework for her and she got an A? What a way to bring up a kid.' He said this but he seemed miles away.

'I just wondered . . .' She paused. 'If you could lend me some money.'

288

Gordon rubbed the side of his nose. He sighed, and gazed at her across the table. 'My love, I don't believe that's possible. Not now.'

'What's happened?'

He leaned down, lifted up his briefcase and snapped it open. He passed her an estate agent's leaflet. 'Had my offer accepted yesterday.' He pointed to the photograph. It showed a large, red-brick house. 'April wasn't so keen at the beginning but I wore her down. When I want something I'm a persistent sod. Like it?'

He couldn't keep the excitement out of his voice. Louise thought: what a monster he is. She thought: happiness, like grief, makes monsters of us all.

'Wandsworth,' he said. 'Well, Wandsworth borders. Ten minutes' walk and you're on the Common.'

She looked at the photograph. 'It's huge.'

'Maybe I'm a bit mad, but aren't we all? There's a touch of subsidence, scared people off, but that's no problem.' He took the photo and gazed at it as if it were his new-born child. 'Trouble is, love, it's cleaned me out. Cashed in my pension, redeemed my policies, the lot. I could manage maybe a couple of thou, but I think you're talking about a few more big ones than that, right?'

She nodded. 'Just a few.'

She snapped a bread stick in half. She thought: happiness has stolen my father away from me; he has entered another life now, where he has no need of me. My whole family has other lives now. So that's that, then. I'm on my own.

After work, Prudence went to see her mother. Dorothy was still living in the bedsitter, a few houses away on the other side of the road. There was a studenty feel to the place – attic window, Baby Belling. Her mother was dressed up for a night out with Eric.

Dorothy seemed to have shed ten years. She wore a blue silky dress pulled up on one shoulder with a clip; it was somewhat vulgar but there was a bounce to her nowadays that suited it. Prudence felt haggard and ghost-ridden.

Dorothy uncorked some wine and poured out two glasses. 'Hungarian Hárslevelü,' she said. 'My latest tipple.'

'Since when did you know about wine?'

Dorothy blushed. Prudence knew that her mother wanted to talk about Eric but there seemed no room for that just now. Her mother had a glazed look to her; the sheen of happiness. 'What are we going to do about Lou?' Prudence asked.

She really wanted to ask: what am I going to do about me? As they talked her mind wandered. Gazing at the striped wallpaper she thought: a new woman has broken up my sister's relationship. It's an old one, a previous one, that is breaking up mine. She said: 'I don't know what to do about Kaatya.'

Her mother paused, the glass halfway to her mouth. 'Kaatya? What's she done?'

'You know about jealousy. Tell me about it, tell me what to do. I went round there the other day. I saw her. I thought it would make it better but it only made it worse.' The pipes gurgled; another tenant was running a bath. It seemed the loneliest sound in the world. 'It's as if she's living with us – in his voice, in the air . . .' Prudence had nobody else to ask. Maddy wouldn't understand; Louise had her own problems. She certainly couldn't confide in Stephen. 'It's as if they're still married. They *are* still married. I thought I was such a sensible person, but she's there like a ghost.'

'Even sensible people believe in ghosts,' said her mother. 'That's what's so frightening about them.'

'What – sensible people or ghosts?'

Her mother laughed. She said: 'Meet her. Ask yourself round for a cup of tea. Maybe she's feeling just the same as you are. Anyway, whatever she's like, it couldn't be worse than your imagination. You poor dear.'

You poor dear. Her mother never talked like that. She had acquired a new vocabulary along with her wardrobe.

Prudence left. She waited on the kerb for the traffic to pass. Suddenly, she wished for a grown-up's hand to slip into hers. She thought: my parents are no longer parents. I have lost them for ever.

She hurried across Titchmere Road. By the time she reached her front door she had made up her mind.

On Saturday morning Robert left home. His loaded BMW scraped the gravel as he pulled away. It was three weeks since Dorothy had detonated the explosion. Since then events had taken on a momentum of their own; both Robert and Louise were helpless. He was moving into a rented flat in London. His mistress would no doubt join him there; nobody had asked.

There was something ignominious about his departure. No big scenes, no tearful send-off. Only Louise and the dog watched him go. It was as if, now it had been decided, everyone just wanted him out of the house, like one of their less popular weekend guests. Louise listened to the engine fading into the distance for the last time. Oh, he would be back to help sort out the house when it was sold, but it was today that he was leaving his family for good. Louise thought: he's a rat deserting a sinking ship. Robert had never possessed moral courage; in the past he had cheerfully admitted this.

She went into the living room and sat down. Then she thought: maybe he's courageous to go. What was going to happen to him? There were gaps on the shelves; Robert had taken some of his books. The rest remained. *You never read a book. Not unless it's heavily disguised as a copy of* Options.

Imogen came into the room. She sat down on the arm of the chair and stroked her mother's hair, like a daughter in a stage play.

'Don't cry, Mum,' she said.

But it was no good; Imogen started crying too.

*

291

Imogen found Jamie in the caravan. He was sitting in a fug of cigarette smoke reading *Viz*.

'How could you?' she cried. 'How could you just sit here? Mum's in a terrible state.' She glared at his bent head. His shoulders shook. It took her a moment to realise that he was giggling. 'Jamie!'

He pointed to the page. 'You read *Ted and his Giant Testicles*?'

'What's the matter with you?'

He looked up. 'Matter? Nothing.'

'She needs you! All week you've done bloody nothing. You've hardly even been here – gadding off each night with your horrible friend.'

'So where were *you* on Thursday night?' he asked. 'A little birdie told me you were getting slaughtered at the Bull's Head with your hunky blacksmith.'

'I wasn't getting slaughtered. I was just there for an hour or two. It was Karl's chess night.'

'How sweet.'

He turned the page. She looked at his soft, fair hair – it had been like that since he was little. 'You aren't even interested in what's happening!' she said.

'Well spotted.' He turned the page. 'Personally, I don't give a flying fuck. They can all go to hell as far as I'm concerned, except Dad'll probably shag himself to death first.'

'Know something? You're getting to sound just like him. Way you're going, when you get married you'll be just the same as Dad –'

'Think I'm going to get married?'

'– lying, cheating, selfish, cynical,' she said. 'You've got a cruel streak, just like him –'

'You're so sad.' He fished for his cigarettes. 'Grow up, sis. You know bugger-all about blokes. If it's got a hole, we poke it.'

She flinched. 'That's disgusting. Some men aren't like that.'

'Oh no?'

'No!'

'You are a-fucking-mazing in your fathomless ignorance.' He flicked his lighter. It didn't work.

'You're a truly warped human being,' she said.

He flicked his lighter again. 'Shit.' She noticed, with surprise, that his hand was shaking. He said: 'So blokes aren't like that, eh? Know who I saw your blacksmith with last Saturday? In Tesco?'

'Who?'

He paused. 'Oh, never mind.'

'Who, you little prick?'

He looked at her. She would never forget the expression in his eyes – a blank, hectic satisfaction. It chilled her to the bone. 'Only his wife and kids, that's who.' He raised his eyebrows. 'Didn't you know?'

Three

It was a long way – ten miles. Imogen rode over Westcott Ridge; she skirted Blackthorn Wood and rode down through the hamlet of Little Wallace. She emerged onto the main road. Skylark, with her horse sense, knew something was wrong. She flinched at the traffic; when a lorry passed, she skittered sideways, banging Imogen's leg against a bus stop. A car, thumping music, hooted; Skylark jerked forwards, throwing Imogen back in the saddle. They galloped along the verge, past a litter basket which had vomited its rubbish – Skylark shied at that – past the chicken farm with its prison huts and chimney. The sky boiled with clouds; the wind whipped her face, stinging her eyes.

TETBURY MAGNA 2 MILES. She turned left, up a lane. Skylark's shoulders were lathered with sweat. Imogen's thighs shook as she rose to the trot; thud, thud, her bottom hit the saddle. She looked at her jolting watch; it was 5.30. She had been riding fast for two hours. Her legs ached; her arms felt as if they were being pulled out of their sockets.

She had never seen Karl's house. She had never phoned him there; only on his mobile. She thought of his tongue in her mouth; his penis moving inside her. *We're just animals. Animals with clothes on.*

The sky darkened; dusk seemed to have descended, though there were still hours of daylight left. As Imogen rode into the village she felt profoundly weary. Ahead of her stretched the rest of her life. How did anyone manage; what was the point? She realised, with surprise, that it was only a few hours since her father had left; it seemed to have happened in another century. During these past two weeks a hand had pushed her across hostile borders, one after another, sending her reeling into foreign lands.

14, Riverview Close. She rode over a bridge; it was hardly a river, more a scummy stream knocking with cans. Riverview Close was a small estate of council houses. Her father would have described them as slovenly, but she wouldn't be listening to her father any more. They were set around a green of trampled grass. A dismembered car sat in the middle. Suddenly, Imogen longed to be home, back on her own village green, its church clock rewound back to when she was twelve and her mother hummed in the kitchen. When everything was safe, and Monty lumbered to his feet when he heard the sound of her father's car.

Toys littered the grass outside number 14. She heard the faint sound of a TV. There was no van parked outside.

Between her thighs, Skylark took a long, shuddering breath. She coughed – a bronchial, human cough. Imogen dismounted. Her legs had turned to jelly.

So he wasn't home yet. She led her horse behind a scouts' hut, out of sight. The place had been vandalised; its windows were broken and its door hung open. Imogen tied up her horse. She wiped her nose on the back of her glove; she was past crying now.

'I didn't know him at all,' Louise said. 'My own husband. That's what's so terrifying. Margot, who ran the shop, we talked the other night and I felt more intimate with her than anyone. That's gone now. She's gone. But twenty years – it's all nothing. Isn't that terrifying?'

Prudence, down the line, offered words of comfort. Louise thought: oh, but I miss him! Where will I find anyone else who will make me laugh?

'Know something?' asked Louise. 'Sometimes I wish Mum hadn't told me, that I'd never known. We could just go on like before. Anything would be better than this.' She gazed at Robert's slippers, lying on the carpet. Imogen had given them to him for Christmas but he hadn't taken them with him. 'If only she'd kept her mouth shut. Mum's made such a mess, hasn't she? Blundering into our lives and messing them up – you and Stephen, Maddy and Erin.'

'Why don't you blame Dad?' Prudence said. 'It's Dad who started it.'

Louise gazed out of the bedroom window. The church spire reared up, its clock stopped at 3.15. It had been broken for years. 'If only we could turn the clock back. If Dad hadn't had that heart attack.' She paused. 'You're not free tonight, are you? To come down and have some supper?' How swiftly the balance had shifted between them; she was now the person seeking company. 'Jamie's going out but Immy will be here.'

'Oh dear, I wish I could,' replied Prudence. 'Thing is, we've got to go out to dinner.'

We. The world was full of 'we's. Louise was no longer anyone's first priority. Weak with self-pity, she put down the phone.

Stephen had brought home a pile of paperwork. He sat at the dining table, staring at it. 'My respect for your mother grows every day,' he said. 'I've never worked so hard in my life.'

Prudence nodded. 'You always had somebody else to do it for you.'

He opened a bulging folder. 'What's the worst torture, filling out a VAT return or having to read a manuscript by Jeffrey Archer?'

She laughed. 'Want a drink?'

He looked up. 'You look very nice. What've you done to your hair?'

'Just – you know – washed it.'

'We going out tonight?'

Prudence fetched the gin bottle. 'We've been asked out to dinner.'

'Where?'

'At your wife's.'

Stephen stared at her. 'What?'

'I thought it was time we – well – got together. Seems silly, never meeting. So I phoned her up –'

'You phoned up Kaatya?'

'And she invited us round for supper.'

It was six-thirty. Karl still hadn't returned. Imogen was sitting in the hut; through the broken window she could see his house. A child had emerged, briefly, and pushed a stick around. Then a woman's voice had called it in.

Outside, the sun was sinking. It shone against a blind bedroom window, patched with cardboard, in Karl's house. Imogen shivered. She thought of the cottage where she and Karl lived in their future, the farmhouse in the fold of the hills. She felt as if a hand had thrust into her throat and pulled out her insides. She didn't know why she was waiting – to see him arrive, to make sure he really lived there? To torture herself even further? She remembered the badgers appearing, the hiss of his indrawn breath. *I love him I love him I love him . . .*

The inside of the hut had been wrecked. The sign for *Scouts and Cubs Fixtures, Tetbury Magna* was sprayed with graffiti – ALLY WINGATE LIKES IT UP HIS BUM. Styrofoam shapes, the sort that cradle electrical equipment, lay around like ice floes. In Antarctica the ice floes were breaking up; the ozone layer was splitting open like a wound and the whole world was melting.

Imogen heard the sound of an engine. She looked out of the window. Karl's van drove up and parked on the kerb.

It happened so fast, the next thing, that she had no time to think. She stumbled out of the hut and shouldered aside Skylark, who stood in the way. She ran around the building and hissed: 'Karl!'

It was too late. He was walking into the house. She

297

retreated behind the hut. Her legs gave way; she leaned against the wall.

She leaned there for a moment, until the hammering in her heart eased. There was nothing she could do now; she had to ride home. It was getting dark, too. Maybe she would be killed. She would be thrown from her horse and die a lingering death. He would weep at her graveside.

At some point during this she became aware of raised voices. A woman was shouting – a high, hysterical yelling. A baby was crying. Imogen peered around the edge of the hut.

'You've been screwing her, haven't you?' screeched the woman. She bundled Karl out of the front door. 'You fucking bastard!'

Karl tried to remonstrate with her; Imogen couldn't hear the words. He put his hands on the woman's shoulders. She pushed him away; he staggered back.

'Fuck off! Fuck off to her, the little bitch, she can fucking have you! Fuck off and don't come fucking back!'

Imogen stood there, paralysed. She felt the heat rise up to her face. Her mouth dried.

For a moment she couldn't move; she felt dizzy with joy. Then she darted forward. The van was parked a few yards away, its rear doors facing her. She ran across the grass, pulled open the door handle and jumped into the back.

There were four of them in the car – a brand new Carrera. According to the window sticker, its owner had visited *The Okehampton Shire Horse Centre*. Jamie, veteran of one car-theft, had joined the big boys. These consisted of three neighbours of Trevor's, residents of the same estate, who had lifted the Carrera from the car-park behind the Rickmansworth Supersaver. Jamie sat sandwiched between two of them. The bloke on his left seemed to be called Edge. Or was it Egg? The other one was overweight and had a heavy cold. Jamie kept his mouth shut, in case they mocked his accent. He offered round cigarettes.

'My Dad fucked off this morning,' he said and instantly regretted it. Nobody was interested.

Trevor sat, hunched, at the wheel. He was driving towards London; they were going to a gig in Brixton. Trevor had shaved his head; though it was growing dark outside, he wore shades. There was a pimple on the nape of his neck. *Headlights!* Jamie wanted to say, but he didn't dare.

Karl, grating the gears, drove out of the village. For a moment Imogen didn't dare speak. If she surprised him he might crash the van. Besides, she wanted to relish this moment, to savour it to the full and store it for ever.

Wedged against his portable anvil, she sat hugging her knees. In the darkness she gazed at the back of his head. If she leaned over she could touch it. She thought: he's left his wife for me. For ME. He loves me and we can live together for ever. If it weren't for Skylark, tied up back in the village, we could carry on driving for ever.

He swerved around a corner. She steadied herself. The horseshoes shifted in their box. Where was he driving – to her home, to pick her up? Ah, but she wouldn't be there! Imogen grinned; she gazed at the tools, murky in the gloom. She would leave school, good riddance, she was never going to get good grades in her A levels anyway, not as good as Jamie's. She would run away with Karl and live with him in his van, toiling at his side. They would visit horses together and at night wrap themselves in his blanket.

Karl slowed down. She couldn't see where they were; maybe he was going to stop at a pub on the way. The poor darling must be upset. But she would let him visit his family; she would be magnanimous.

She leaned forward to tap him on the shoulder. She stopped. She heard the blip-blip-blip of his phone. He was punching in a number.

She smiled. He was phoning her house! Her mother would answer: *I'm afraid she's not here; who's that speaking please?*

'Shirley? It's me.' Karl spoke into the phone. 'She's found out . . . yeah . . . the shit's well and truly – what? Yeah . . . Be with you in five minutes . . . Me too, sweetheart.'

Trevor drove down the slip road and slewed onto the motorway. Jamie craned his neck . . . 85 mph . . . 90 . . . The arc-lights were lit, flaring against the setting sun. They replaced the dying day with their own eerie daylight. *For the natural order is oe'r thrown, the elements in a rage . . .* Funny to think he'd done his A levels, got an A, too. His Dad had toasted him with Bolly.

'Seen me skins?' The big bloke on his right was rummaging in his pocket. Trevor passed him a packet of Rizlas over his shoulder. Jamie thought: we're going to smoke dope. In a stolen car. Years ago, his dad had taken him on the Big Dipper; poised at the top, Jamie had squeezed his eyes shut, waiting for the drop. Ah, the plunge! Down he had plummeted, leaving his body behind.

'Did the shop in your village last week,' said Trevor.

It took Jamie a moment to realise that Trevor was speaking to him. 'You what?'

'So it's spend spend spend.'

'You mean – you broke in?' asked Jamie.

'No, we did not break in,' replied Trevor, as if addressing the retarded. 'He was in his little store room out the back.' He put on a baby's voice. 'Easy-peasy.'

The van stopped. Karl switched off the engine. The door slammed.

Imogen was hunched in the back, her hands pressed into her eyes. She heard a murmur of voices – Karl's and a woman's. Her ears roared.

The voices faded. She pressed her fingers into her eye-sockets. She waited, frozen. The van made small ticking sounds as the engine cooled.

Finally, she unlocked herself. Her limbs were numb. She leaned over and opened the door, just a slit. Outside was blackness. For a moment she thought it was the middle of the night, but the blackness was pine trees, a dense forest of them. She climbed out of the van. A path led through the wood to a cottage. It was the cottage you would find if you left a trail of bread. It stood alone in a clearing. Karl and a woman opened the front door. Light flooded them. They went in and closed the door behind them.

Imogen was running blindly. Branches whipped her face; how silent was the floor of the forest! She felt as weightless as if she were dreaming, but it wasn't a dream, not any more. Night had fallen early; the roof of the forest shut out the light. She ran over the springy bed of pine needles, willing herself to wake up: none of this had happened, she was lying in bed at home and she could begin all over again.

She stumbled into a ditch; she picked herself up and ran on. Her breath rasped; her lungs felt as if they were scoured out with a red-hot poker. Somewhere, nearby, a large creature lumbered away; she heard the crash of the undergrowth.

She never knew how long it took her to force her way through the wood. After a while she emerged onto a path. It was truly night now; the sky had caught up with the forest. The path was simply a lessening of the dark. It forked and she turned left, for no reason, and stumbled along; the ground was deeply rutted. On either side stood a black wall of trees. Men stood behind them, watching her. If she hesitated they would step out. If she turned, she would see them following her.

Imogen started to cry. She shouted silently: *I want my mummy!*

Jamie was adrift in a forest of bodies. He had lost sight of Trevor and the others. A wave of people pushed him; he was rammed against a pillar. The music hammered into his brain; in the strobe lights faces mouthed at him, black holes splitting

301

open and closed. He stood there, not stoned enough, not nearly, and knew that Egg and the others, even if they saw him, wouldn't be bothered to recognise him. He shut his eyes but all he saw was Imogen's face – only that morning, wasn't that strange? *Only his wife and kids, that's who.* Her face collapsed; it melted with tears, like wax. You could do that to somebody – easy-peasy. Put your hand into the till and steal it all away.

Jamie leaned against the pillar. He felt his life sliding away beneath him, pulling him down as if somebody was tugging the carpet.

How far had she walked – one mile, six miles? Imogen was walking along a lane now, the tarmac thankfully hard under her feet. A car approached behind her; she pressed herself into the hedge. Thank God the car didn't slow down; perhaps they didn't see her. As it drove past its headlights flashed on a sign: TETBURY MAGNA 1 MILE.

She walked around the corner. Ahead of her was the pub she had ridden past earlier; it was lit up now with fairy lights. She walked past and was plunged into darkness again.

She hadn't expected Skylark to be there. She had presumed that her horse, like everything else, would have been stolen. But there she stood, her head drooping, dozing in the darkness. Imogen pressed her nose against Skylark's neck; the fur was clotted with dried sweat. She stood there for a moment, breathing in her horse's scent.

'My darling,' she said.

Then she tightened the girths and mounted her. She glanced at Karl's house; the rooms blazed with light. She pulled Skylark's head around and rode off.

Jamie pushed down on the bar of the Fire Exit doors. He found himself in an alleyway. It was cold; it had started to rain. He walked into Electric Avenue. They had parked the car outside a butcher's shop.

302

The space was empty.

Jamie looked at his watch. It was 10.30. They had left him, just like that. They probably hadn't noticed his absence.

Jamie stood there. Humiliatingly, his eyes filled with tears. He was alone in a city that cared fuck-all for him. What could he do?

He walked past a roaring pub, past the shuttered shops. He emerged onto the high street and made his way towards Betterspecs. Its interior was lit like an operating theatre – rows of glasses inspecting him in his pathetic state.

He went up to the side door and rang the bell. There was no reply. He rang again.

He heard a window slide open above him. He stood back and looked up. A face loomed down from the top floor.

'I'm looking for Mr Hammond!' shouted Jamie. 'He lives here!'

'They've gone,' said the face.

'Where?'

'Dunno. They moved out this morning.'

And the window slid closed.

Louise had phoned round Imogen's friends. None of them had seen her. She had even phoned the riding stables in case her daughter had left Skylark there, as she had the week before. It was 10.45.

She sat in the kitchen, cradling a mug of coffee. Outside, it had started to rain. Her hands shook. Where was her husband now that she needed him?

Finally, she picked up the phone. On the pegboard was pinned up the list of emergency numbers which until now she had never needed to call.

She dialled the number of Beaconsfield Police Station. 'My daughter hasn't come home. She rode off on her horse – oh, hours ago. This afternoon.' Louise burst into tears. 'I don't know what's happened to her.'

Jamie had five pounds in his wallet. He stood in the rain in Brixton High Street, waiting for a taxi. Cars sped past, splashing his legs. It was chucking-out time. Gangs of youths sauntered past. They turned to stare at him. Maybe they thought his face was wet from the rain.

His father was somewhere in this city but Jamie had no idea where. How desperate he must be, to want to see his father! Jamie was sobbing now, loud sobs and he didn't care who saw him. He was freezing cold; the rain had soaked through his jacket. He wanted to be home, tucked up in bed. He wanted it so badly he thought he would burst.

Finally, he flagged down a taxi. He told the driver Prudence's address. Aunty Pru would take him in; she would look after him. You could rely on Aunty Pru; she always remembered his birthday, she always stayed the same. Her flat was cosy. As the cab drove towards Clapham he wiped his nose and thought: she'll make me hot chocolate, like she did when I was little and we came back from the pantomime. She'll tuck me up in her sofabed and everything will be all right. He thought: I might even make this into a funny story, omitting the fact that the car was stolen. We can laugh at Trevor and his really sad friends.

The heater warmed his face. For the first time in hours he started to relax. Aunty Pru would understand; she knew what it was like to be lonely.

The taxi stopped in Titchmere Road. Jamie paid the driver; he only just had enough money. The cab sped off into the night.

Jamie rang and rang the bell. There was no reply.

Kaatya was rolling a joint. She did it expertly; Prudence watched her busy fingers. It was 11.30 but they had only just finished supper. Kaatya seemed to have a casual attitude to both the timing and preparation of food; the vegetable risotto had turned into a sort of porridge.

How strange it was to be in Stephen's house! It was like stepping into the most familiar yet strange of dreams, like stepping through the looking-glass. They sat in the kitchen, under bright strip lighting. The room looked like a workshop; half-assembled collages were stacked against the cupboards. Nobody could accuse Kaatya of over-zealous clearing-up for her guests.

Kaatya had dressed up and yet not dressed up at all. She wore a shrunken striped jumper and what looked like a child's pleated skirt. Plastic teddy bears hung from her earlobes. She wore tartan tights on her thin, bony legs; no shoes, just red socks. Prudence found her oddly attractive. Under the bright light there was a pallor to her skin; there were dark smudges under her eyes and her large mouth looked blurred, as if it had been bruised by kissing.

'I'm glad you came here,' said Kaatya. 'I know in here –' She pointed to her chest '– when I like somebody. I trust my feelings.'

'I don't.' Prudence laughed. 'Mine are far too frightening.'

'You have powerful feelings, I can sense that.' Kaatya licked her Rizla. 'It's all this English shit. The English, they're so constipated.' She stabbed the joint at Stephen. 'When I came to England and I meet his friends, they are like schoolboys, schoolboys with grown-up brains, how proud they are of their brains! If they have a feeling, you know what they do? They go to the bookshelves and look up the word in the, the, you know –'

'Dictionary,' said Stephen.

Kaatya nodded. 'That thing.'

Stephen said to Prudence. 'She thinks we're emotional cripples, the walking wounded. Perambulating thesauruses –'

'You see?' said Kaatya. 'What's he talking about?'

Stephen was enjoying this. He looked from one woman to the other, urging them on. 'Go on, Prudence, stick up for me.'

Prudence said: 'I think words create feelings. Once you have a word for it, you can recognise it and then you can feel it.'

305

'Bullshit.' Kaatya lit the joint. 'So how come you have just one word for love?' She inhaled, deeply, and passed the joint to Prudence. 'Explain that, please.'

Prudence put the joint between her lips and drew in the smoke. She hadn't done this for twenty years; she had forgotten the sensation. The smoke hit her lungs, for a moment she couldn't breathe. Then she felt her brain shaking loose, like a bunch of flowers released from their rubber band. Maybe Kaatya was right – what use were words, when you thought about it? Maybe she thought too much. Warming to Kaatya, she indicated Stephen. 'He's not that inhibited. You should have seen him at our office party.' She kicked off her shoes and laughed. 'Emotional constipation's not the phrase that springs to mind.'

Kaatya said: 'He was drunk, right? He gets sorry for himself when he's drunk, you find that?'

Prudence nodded. 'Maudlin's the word.'

'Maudlin?' snapped Kaatya. 'There you go again. What's maudlin?'

'I was unhappy!' said Stephen. 'I'd just left my wife!'

He was drunk, of course. They all were. He looked flushed and excited by the two women in his life, sitting there opposite him. 'Nobody understands me,' he said.

'Don't be maudlin,' said Prudence. 'Some people would envy you.'

Throughout the evening, Prudence had felt her position shifting. Sometimes she felt like an eavesdropper, listening to Stephen and Kaatya's well-worn complaints. Stimulated by her presence, the two of them re-enacted their old battles. Sometimes she felt that it was Stephen who was the onlooker and that she and Kaatya were confidantes, giggling together. *They're ganging up on me!* her father used to say. Ah, but the voltage tonight! She felt dizzy with it.

Kaatya leaned through the smoke. She touched Prudence's wrist. 'I'm glad you came here. All this time I've been thinking what do you look like.'

'Did you?'

With her finger, Kaatya traced the veins in Prudence's wrist. 'See, we're just flesh and blood. That's all.'

Prudence took another drag of the joint. 'When I was little, me and my friend Janine said we'd cut ourselves and mingle our blood. She did, but then I copped out.'

'Copped out?' asked Kaatya.

'I didn't dare.'

'Ah, but you dared to come here tonight. What did you want? To see if I was flesh and blood, too?' She took Prudence's finger and laid it on her own wrist. 'We must know each other and love each other. Only then will we all be happy. We can be like sisters – blood sisters.' She pointed to Stephen. 'He's the blood between us. In us, here.' She moved Prudence's finger against her vein. 'It doesn't separate us, you understand? It brings us together.'

'You've always been there,' said Prudence. 'All this time, since I've known him, you've been there.'

'Is that true?' asked Stephen.

They ignored him. 'I'm a woman, just like you,' said Kaatya. She put Prudence's hand on her breast. 'See? Just the same.'

'Steady on, Kaatya!' said Stephen.

Prudence's hand cupped the breast; she felt it through the matted wool of the jumper. She blushed and took her hand away.

'We have pains each month,' said Kaatya, 'we have suffered childbirth –'

'I haven't,' said Prudence.

'– we know things he knows nothing about.'

Stephen stood up unsteadily. 'I think we should go. She's getting carried away.'

'You can't drive,' said Kaatya. 'Stay here.'

The boys were away for the night. They had the house to themselves.

'Let's go to bed,' said Kaatya.

'Kaatya!' Stephen exclaimed.

Prudence's heart hammered.

Kaatya turned to Stephen. 'You can stay here.' She laughed. 'Can't he Pru? I can call you that?'

'My sisters do.' Prudence stood up in a trance. Kaatya's fingers laced through hers; they were thin and strong.

'We leave him to wash up,' whispered Kaatya, leading Prudence to the door.

'Wait!' Stephen stubbed out the joint and followed them.

The rain bucketed down. Imogen rode blindly through the darkness. She was soaked to the skin. She felt no sensation except terror; she was no longer even capable of crying.

They were trotting along some lane. No lights through the rain, nothing. She had no idea where Skylark was heading, she had long ago lost her way. Her hands were frozen to the reins; she rose up and down on the sodden saddle, somebody had wound her up like clockwork, soon all life would expire from her but still she would rise and fall, thudding on the wet leather. Images swooped close and fell away . . . her primary school playground in Chelsea, blazing sun . . . the pebbles on the beach at Brighton . . . She was riding up into the sky, through dissolving bands of the past, she was on her rocking-horse, rocking across the heavens in a Chagall painting . . . how bright the suns were, twin suns, how dazzling in the darkness!

The noise grew louder, the lights bloomed. Something huge was approaching from behind. The ground shook. For a second, the lane ahead was lit as brightly as day – a fence either side, the startled faces of cows. Behind, the thing thundered up like a black tidal wave, rising to engulf her . . .

Imogen yanked the reins, pulling her horse into the side. The noise was deafening now, the lights blinding. Skylark reared up. Imogen felt her body loosening from the saddle, in slow motion. Her foot was caught in the stirrup. She slid over Skylark's shoulder.

Skylark reared again, skittering backwards. Imogen was

thrown into the ditch. The Tesco lorry roared past and was swallowed up into the darkness.

Later, when she sobered up, Prudence could scarcely believe what she had done. That night in their bed existed in a separate dimension, as lurid and weightless as a pornographic film. You stepped into the street, into daylight, and behind you the door swung shut, closing away the secrets you had shared with strangers so briefly in the dark.

It was Kaatya's matter-of-factness that took her by surprise. The woman was so earthy, so straightforward. She took off her clothes and climbed into bed.

'We sleep, we have fun. Whatever you want, you're the guest.'

'Are you always so hospitable?' asked Prudence. She sat on the bed. 'Have you done this before?'

'Kaatya's done everything,' said Stephen, emerging from the bathroom. 'Not all of them with me.' He was wearing pyjamas. 'I'm keeping my jim-jams on.' He laughed, but Prudence could tell he was excited. His eyes glittered as he looked from one of them to the other.

He's thinking: timid old Prudence, she won't dare. Prudence smiled at him and unbuttoned her blouse. She thought: even my sisters have never done this. Swiftly she pulled off her tights and skirt and climbed under the duvet. She kept her bra and knickers on.

'You are cold?' asked Kaatya, plumping up a pillow for her. 'You want me to make the electric blanket?'

'I'm fine.'

'Here – you sleep next to me.' Kaatya moved over, to give her room. 'In my home village, when I was small, I snuggled like this with my brothers and sisters.'

'What about me?' Stephen stood beside the bed.

'You sleep next to Pru. She's your woman now.'

Stephen climbed into bed. It was a king-size bed but it was still a tight fit. Prudence lay sandwiched between them. She hardly dared breathe. Kaatya switched off the light. They lay there in the darkness.

Kaatya laced her feet around Prudence's. 'Mmm, your feet are so warm. Stephen's, they were always like ice.'

'They still are.'

'All the blood is in his brain, you see,' said Kaatya, 'busy making new words.'

'Come on, warm me up then,' said Stephen. His cold foot joined theirs.

'Ugh, take it away!' yelped Kaatya.

'Come on, girls, look after me.'

'We're not girls,' said Kaatya. 'He still never learns, even with you?'

'He's been cosseted by women all his life.'

'Hey, I am here,' said Stephen.

'Tell me something, Pru,' said Kaatya. 'His secretary, what was her name –'

'Monica?'

'Yes, Monica. She buyed the boys' birthday presents for him?'

Prudence nodded. 'Once or twice.'

'You know how I guessed?' said Kaatya. 'Because they were so good.'

Prudence laughed. Stephen said: 'Want to start telling each other about my inadequacies in bed?'

'I'm just talking to my new friend,' said Kaatya. 'I like women. Oh, I wish they had dicks.'

'My sister's a lesbian,' said Prudence. 'She seems to manage all right without them.'

'I try, several times,' said Kaatya, 'but it's not the same. Even a dick like his is better than nothing.'

'Hey!' said Stephen.

'She's only joking.'

'Kaatya doesn't know how to make jokes,' he said. 'They don't teach them in Holland.'

Kaatya kicked him. She missed.

'Ouch!' cried Prudence.

'Oh, I'm sorry.' Kaatya stroked Prudence's cheek.

The three of them lay there in silence. The rain flung itself at the window. The school-dorm playfulness vanished as abruptly as it had begun. Prudence felt Kaatya's warm skin, her jutting hip-bone, pressed against her on one side. On the other side she felt Stephen's familiar bulk, but how strange in this bed, in unfamiliar pyjamas! She wondered what he was feeling; she had no idea. Aroused? Disturbed?

Stephen's hand stroked her belly. 'I'm so sorry for everything,' he murmured. Prudence wondered: who is he speaking to, me or Kaatya? Which of them was the odd one out? He shifted close; his hand moved over, she could feel his arm moving as he stroked Kaatya's belly. 'I never wanted to hurt either of you,' he said. 'You're both wonderful women.'

Kaatya turned and curled herself around Prudence. She stretched her arm across Prudence's breast and stroked Stephen. 'You love us both, don't you?'

Stephen nodded; his cheek grazed Prudence's face.

'Love us both, then,' murmured Kaatya. She kissed Prudence's shoulder. 'Kiss her,' she said.

Stephen's finger turned Prudence's face towards his. He kissed her on the mouth. As he did so, Kaatya ran her hand down Prudence's back. With one hand Stephen pulled down his pyjama bottoms. Kaatya guided Prudence's hand down to his penis.

'Don't hide from us,' murmured Kaatya. 'Don't be shy.' She cupped Prudence's hand, with hers, under his balls. 'Don't you know us both?'

His breathing quickened. So did hers, or was it Kaatya's? Prudence could no longer tell whose body was whose . . . where did she end and they begin? Stephen's penis pressed against her pubic hair. Fingers guided it into her. He moved on top of Prudence. His buttons rubbed against her chest as he thrust in and out. Prudence spread her legs wide; she felt the heat, spreading up her body. Was it she who was moaning? She turned her head; Kaatya's lips were on hers, Kaatya's wide, soft mouth. Stephen's arm pulled Kaatya

311

against them; she moved with them.

'Isn't she wonderful?' Kaatya gasped. 'What a woman, no wonder you wanted her.' She took Prudence's hand and pressed it between her own legs – how wiry and damp her hair was! Prudence didn't dare move her hand but now Kaatya was moving it for her, rubbing it against her wet inner flesh, against the knob of her clitoris. She came almost immediately, gripping Prudence's hand between her thighs. She cried out – a high, strangled cry. Stephen was still thrusting inside Prudence but now Kaatya's hand was helping him. Stephen grew frenzied; he made a loud, moaning sound Prudence had never heard before. She held his buttocks but Kaatya's hand was already there, flat against him. Her finger was inserted into his anus, pushing in and out. So that was what did it! Prudence had never done that; it seemed to drive Stephen into a paroxysm of pleasure. She left Kaatya to it and tried to concentrate on her own satisfaction but it was too awkward, with the two bodies, and now Stephen, with a loud, shuddering cry, ejaculated inside her.

He lay there, trembling, his face buried in the pillow. Kaatya murmured: 'Men, they don't understand do they?' She pushed down her hand between their bodies. Stephen moved aside a little for her; his penis slipped out. Her fingers rubbed Prudence so expertly that within a moment Prudence cried out, half-sobbing. She twisted her head away from Stephen and rested it against Kaatya's shoulder. Kaatya's hand remained there, cupping Prudence's bush; her secret pulse throbbed against Kaatya's fingers. A tick-tick, like a car when the engine has been switched off.

Stephen shifted slightly. His hand joined Kaatya's between Prudence's thighs. It lay there, heavy and male. 'Isn't she amazing?' he murmured sleepily.

Prudence thought: which *she* does he mean?

It took Jamie two hours to walk from Clapham to Hackney. He walked through Saturday night into Sunday morning. His boots leaked; his feet were soaking, he was soaked to the marrow. The areas of London through which he walked were unknown to him until he reached Parliament Square. He made his way to Trafalgar Square, along the Strand and down Fleet Street. Then again he entered unknown territory.

He walked north. He knew a little about orienteering because, for one brief, embarrassing year, he had joined the scouts. He walked along the main roads because there were traffic signs to guide him, looming up above his head: SHOREDITCH 1 MILE, HACKNEY 2 MILES. He felt himself dwindling. He was just a speck, floating alone in the world. He had left his life behind, he had lost his own self. He had walked through the barrier of loneliness; with each jolting footstep he was passing further into an existential nothingworld that possessed no signposts.

HACKNEY ½ MILE. He walked past shuttered shops, past derelict premises. Lorries splashed him as they passed. SAINSBURY'S; WHERE GOOD FOOD COSTS LESS . . . Once he had stacked shelves, wasn't that quaint?

He saw a lit window. *BeeGee Cars: Drivers Wanted.* He opened the door and went into a minicab office. Under the strip light, two men sat smoking behind a desk. The room smelled of a million dead cigarettes. He asked them the way to Romilly Street. One of the men gave him directions. *Left here . . . right there . . .* 'You all right, mate?' The man seemed to be swaying backwards and forwards, like a cardboard cutout anchored by his feet. Soon he would fold over entirely.

Jamie was outside now, walking the last few streets. Left and then right . . . right and then left? . . . And now he saw the sign: Romilly Street.

He walked up the road. It was 2.20. The houses were dark; it looked as if nobody had ever lived in them. Behind a front door a dog barked two short barks and was silent. Jamie had no idea of Maddy's number; it was a miracle that he had remembered the name of the street. He gazed at the houses, shabby in the sodium light. If he couldn't find Maddy he would die.

And then he saw the van: *Fox Gardening Services*. His aunt was here, somewhere. He thought: my aunts are the only people who can save me. Parents are useless. He inspected the houses. Window-boxes, wouldn't hers have window-boxes, seeing as she lived with a gardener? But several had window-boxes; even a trellis. The front doors danced up and down, they were performing a musical routine.

He shouted, 'Maddy!' His voice felt hoarse with disuse. 'MADDY!' he bellowed.

The sound echoed down the street. He was disintegrating into pieces. He would either lie down in the road or float away.

'MADDY!' So this was what happened when you went mad.

Lights were switched on. Windows slid open. The street of the dead came to life.

'Jamie!' Maddy leaned out of an upstairs window. He had never been so pleased to see anyone in his life. 'Jamie, what's happened?'

A moment later the front door opened. Maddy opened her arms – Maddy, who never hugged. She put her arms around him. He laid his head against her dressing-gown.

The phone rang. Louise, sitting in the living room, grabbed it.

Maddy's voice said: 'Don't worry, he's here.'

'What?'

'Jamie. He's soaked through but he's all right.'

Jamie? Didn't she mean Imogen?

'He's walked miles,' said Maddy. 'Pru wasn't in and he couldn't remember where Mum lived but he's fine –'

'But where's Imogen?'

'I've tucked him up in bed,' said Maddy. 'Didn't you know he was in London? I think he's upset about his dad. We had a good talk about fathers. I told him I didn't always get on with ours either –'

Louise wasn't listening. Her ears had picked up another sound. It was so faint she must be imagining it.

314

'. . . I tried to explain about Robert,' Maddy was saying. 'I wanted to say what a shit he was but I suppose he *is* Jamie's dad. Anyway, he's fine. I'll put him on the train in the morning . . .'

It was the sound of horse's hooves. Louise flung down the phone, rushed to the window and flung open the curtains.

The outdoor light was on, illuminating the gravel drive. Monty barked. The clop-clop grew more distinct.

Louise stood there, frozen. The sound grew louder. Skylark appeared, a grey shape in the dark. She trotted up to the front door and stood there, snorting. She shook herself.

Her saddle had swung around; it hung upside down on her belly. The horse stood there, riderless, in the rain.

PART FIVE

One

April had wanted a man to take care of her. She had got tired of bailing men out, of mopping them up – she had enough mopping up at work. She had got tired of their anger and remorse, of telling herself lies: he'll be different with me, I can change him. *I'll* be different with *him*. Dennis had been the last in a line of men she could now see in perspective. Some radar had attracted her towards the hopeless cases, and them to her.

Then along had come Gordon. He had swept her up; she had been powerless to resist. He had bulldozed through her guilt, he had bulldozed through her desire for independence. He had bulldozed through the disapproval of her family and friends, for he was an unexpected object of her affection. Her mother was no longer speaking to her. She had, however, spoken the truth to Jamie that night: she was simply devoted to him. She should have felt worse about what she had done, but, like many people who spend their time caring for others, April was ruthless in her personal life and, besides, Gordon had insisted that his marriage was dead. She was a robust person who lived for the moment; Gordon was, too: they answered this in each other.

And now he had bulldozed her into giving up her flat and moving in with him, and she had agreed with only token resistance. He was going to take care of her, this balding, stubborn, endearing man, and she sloughed off her past life just as he did his. She had even given up her job.

If it all felt unreal, she blamed it on the move. She knew no-

317

body in Wandsworth; nor did he. Maybe that was the reason why he had wanted to move there. The house was enormous. She walked from room to room, her footsteps echoing. Neither Gordon nor she had many belongings; he had relinquished most of his possessions. Their packing-cases barely filled the dining room.

Gordon had bought the house on impulse. He had rushed through the whole business – contracts, completion – in a couple of weeks. She had rented out her flat. The speed of it all made her feel rocky. This place needed a lot of work but he had fallen in love with it, he had plans. *Only a palace is good enough for you, my love.* This bossy, selfish generosity was Gordon through and through.

She couldn't, however, picture their life here yet. That first morning, Sunday, she dumped a bag of rubbish in the front garden. It had rained during the night but now it was a beautiful morning, fresh and green, and the neighbours were out in force. They vacuumed their cars and painted their front doors. She felt as if she had arrived in Noddy's Toytown, a place of primary colours and innocent activity. It was utterly alien to her. A child, walking past, stared at her until its mother pulled it away.

Gordon was in the kitchen, making coffee in her espresso machine. He enjoyed this; it was his ritual to make their breakfast. Outside, the overgrown lawn was surrounded by bushes whose names she didn't know. Some of them were flowering in the sunshine. She and Gordon were isolated in a sea of alien bushes and neighbours; they clung to their small rituals as they began their life together.

Later, she remembered her feeling of dislocation. She had come on a long journey; Gordon didn't know the half of it. He didn't ask her questions about herself, he wasn't interested in her past, anybody's past, in fact; he wasn't a curious man. She watched him plugging in her toaster for the first time, for their first breakfast in their new kitchen. She wondered if he had been the one who had made breakfast in his old life; she had never asked him. Was it because it was too painful to

318

think about those years he had spent with his wife, or was she simply as incurious as he was? She knew nothing; she had lost sight of herself.

Later that morning, they drove down to Buckinghamshire. Louise had asked them to lunch. April was pleased about this, of course; his daughters seemed to be thawing towards her. Maybe this was simply due to the passage of time and the fact that, from what she had heard, their mother seemed to be sorting out a new life for herself. Maybe, now that Louise's marriage was breaking up, she herself felt adrift and needed her family around her.

Whatever the reason, April was curious to visit the Old Vicarage. She wanted to see Jamie again, whom she had liked. She had dreaded this first visit but the fact that Louise's life was now in a mess made it easier. She had never met Louise – she had missed her when she had visited Gordon in hospital – but by all accounts Louise was the least intimidating of Gordon's daughters.

She was unprepared, therefore, for Louise's horror when she opened her front door. 'My God, I'd forgotten you were coming,' she said. 'I'm sorry.' For a moment April thought she was going to close the door in their faces. 'The place is a pigsty . . .' Louise began, and burst into tears.

They went into the kitchen and sat down. Louise wore an old tracksuit; her hair was pulled back in a rubber band. April passed her a Kleenex.

'I've been up all night,' sobbed Louise. 'I'm sorry. You see, Imogen's only just come home.'

'What's happened?' asked Gordon. 'She's been at one of her parties?'

Louise shook her head. Joltingly, the story came out. How Robert had left home the day before, and how Imogen had ridden off nobody knew where and had been thrown from her horse in the middle of the night.

'It took her, oh, hours to walk home. She's gone to bed. She's all right – a bit bruised . . . exhausted of course.' Louise said that the doctor should be dropping in later that day to

319

check her over.

'Shall I just pop upstairs?' asked April. 'Shall I look at her, would you like me to?'

When April came downstairs, thoughtfully, twenty minutes later, Jamie had arrived from London. He too had had an eventful night, tramping across the city in the pouring rain. Gordon seemed put out that all this had been happening and nobody had told him.

'You've got your own life now,' said Louise. 'Anyway, what could you have done?'

'I rang your bell in Brixton,' said Jamie, 'but you'd moved away.'

April thought: Gordon has detached himself from his family now, he has cut adrift. Doesn't he realise? She looked at the three of them, slumped around the kitchen table. She said: 'Why don't you go into the other room and I'll rustle up some lunch?'

So that was what she did. Upstairs, Imogen lay, a ticking time-bomb, while down in the kitchen April yanked open the freezer and shoved frosty packets into the Aga. Gordon, who hated sitting around doing nothing, came in and tried to help but she sent him away.

She chopped up a cucumber. Suddenly, she was flooded with happiness. She had been launched into the hot centre of Gordon's family, into the middle of a crisis. They needed her! She would take care of them.

When they returned to the kitchen, an hour later, April felt as intimate with their lives as with the contents of their cupboards. She tossed the salad and put the bowl on the table.

'You're so kind,' said Louise. 'That's what we needed, a nurse. A cook.' She carried a bottle of Bollinger. 'I've found another case. Let's drink the lot!' She poured out the champagne; it frothed over the glasses. April guessed that it had been her husband's job to do this. 'I may have lost everything

320

else but at least I've got my children back. Isn't that all that matters?' She turned to April and raised her glass. 'Welcome to the Hammond family,' she said. 'And all who sail in it.'

'Join the shipwreck,' said Jamie.

On Thursday, in her lunch-hour, Prudence drove to Chelsea. She had arranged to meet Maddy. Stepping out of the traffic fumes she entered a garden. She brushed past a beech hedge; its leaves were such an intense green that she felt breathless, as if she had been sucking lemons. She suddenly longed for a garden of her own; all her adult life she had lived in flats. She longed to step out onto the grass in her bare feet. She closed her eyes. A child, its hair flying, came running towards her.

Maddy was planting out a tray of zinnias, handling them as tenderly as if they were babies. It was only May but her face was already tanned from working outdoors. She wiped her hands and produced packets of sandwiches wrapped in foil. How was Erin? Prudence asked. Working on a new book. How was Allegra? Fine. Far away the traffic roared. Prudence's own desultory questions sounded as distant. They fell silent. Maddy wasn't the sort of person who felt the need to make conversation.

Prudence swallowed the last mouthful. She lit a cigarette. She said: 'Something extraordinary happened last Saturday. The night Jamie came to your house. I want to ask your advice.'

She told Maddy what had taken place. Maddy was the only person in the world she could tell. Her sister had the un-shockability of the pure at heart; she had no prurient interest in the murkier reaches of human behaviour. When Prudence finished, she just said: 'Gosh.'

'The thing is – I found her … thrilling. I don't know whether it was because – you know – Stephen was there.' She laughed lightly. 'You see, I've never had a lesbian experience before.'

Maddy poured coffee out of a Thermos. Prudence

321

struggled on.

'Remember when you told me about Erin? You said you didn't know if you were gay, or you'd just fallen in love with her.'

'Did I?' Maddy passed her the plastic cup. 'I've only got one, we'll have to take turns.'

'Maybe I am – well, gay. Underneath.'

'Of course you're not.'

'Well, anyway – now I'll know what you're talking about.'

'It's not what you do.' Maddy took the cup. 'It's what you feel.'

'I told you – it felt wonderful.'

'I mean, what you feel about Stephen.'

Prudence gazed at the freshly dug earth. A robin flew down and pulled out a worm.

Maddy said: 'I bet he just did it to turn himself on.'

'No,' said Prudence weakly.

'Sounds like he was using you,' said Maddy. 'I should know, I speak from experience.'

'No. That's not true.'

Hadn't he been reluctant at first? *I'm keeping my jim-jams on.* Prudence's head spun.

'Nice kinky sex, three in a bed,' said Maddy. 'Bet he couldn't believe his luck.'

'It wasn't like that!'

'Every middle-aged bloke's fantasy.'

'Don't be so hostile,' said Prudence. 'Not today.' The worm was too fat; it twisted in the robin's beak. Why did Maddy always say the thing one didn't want to hear? Her first word, apparently, had been 'No'.

'Why did you ask me then?' said Maddy. 'If you didn't want to know?'

Prudence drove back to the office, past Canary Wharf. The glass buildings glinted in the sunlight; they flashed a warning.

How did she feel? Angry with Maddy, for a start. How could she say such things?

I should know, I speak from experience. Prudence parked the car. She thought: what had Maddy meant by that? Did she feel used, too?

Maddy yelped. She had pricked her finger on a rose thorn. She pushed the cushioned underside of her fingertip, pressing out the drop of blood. It emerged, a bead, from her interior. If she went on pressing she would make a necklace.

If she fell asleep, what would happen? Bloody nothing. Maddy didn't believe in fairy stories. By the time she'd been born her mother must have got tired of reading them. Her back ached. She straightened up. Sucking her finger, she put away her tools and drove towards Hackney, through the clogged rush-hour traffic. Louise was the fairy-tale princess and look what had happened to her.

Maddy felt her family breaking up under her feet. She was losing her balance. When she'd lived abroad she had considered herself independent. Only now did she realise how much she had relied on them to be there, safe and unchanged. A solid family to rebel against and come home to, for despite her adventurous life she had still felt like an adolescent, resenting the very people she needed.

She wondered why she had been so abrupt with Prudence, who, after all, had come seeking her advice – an almost unheard-of occurrence. Was it because Prudence had muscled in on her territory?

She picked up Allegra from her clarinet lesson. As they drove home she said: 'You're lucky, being an only child.'

'Why?' asked Allegra.

'When you're the youngest everything's been done before. They've worn the clothes. They've ridden the bike. Everything you've got is second-hand. So you try to be different.' She shrugged. 'Then you find they've done *that*, too.' She turned left into Romilly Street. 'They thought I was going to be a boy. They would've called me Buddy, after Buddy Holly.'

'Who's he?'

'*Then* I would have been different.'

Allegra wasn't listening. 'Look.'

Two cars and a BBC van were double-parked outside their house. The front door was open. A crowd of kids had gathered, leaning on their bikes.

'Oh God,' said Allegra. 'It's the TV.'

They got out of the van. A man carrying a walkie-talkie barred the front door. 'Sorry, love. We're filming.'

'We live here,' said Allegra. Clutching her clarinet case she slipped through.

Maddy pushed her way into the hall. The house was full of men shouting at each other. 'Bob, where's the bloody masking tape?' Cables ran up the stairs.

Maddy was exhausted. Her back ached, she was filthy. When she went upstairs she found the bathroom door locked. Behind it, somebody flushed the lavatory. The landing was crammed with people. One of them was bellowing into a mobile phone: 'Get Tanya to bike them over, pronto!'

Maddy looked into Erin's study. The light was dazzling. Erin sat at her word processor. She wore her red velvet jacket; a girl dusted her face with a brush.

'Excuse me, sweetheart.' Somebody moved Maddy aside.

Someone shouted, 'Quiet please! We're going for a take!'

'And . . . ACTION.'

Erin sat in the blazing light. She was a goddess, worshipping at the altar of herself. As Maddy watched, something snapped. All her half-lies, all her efforts to fool herself. They snapped and she was released.

She turned and pushed her way to the bedroom. A woman sat on the bed. She wore a black suit and was talking on the phone.

'Get out,' said Maddy.

'I beg your pardon?'

'Get out of my bedroom.'

Maddy was packing her bag now, opening drawers and

shoving in clothes. Allegra came into the room and stood beside her.

'You're going, aren't you?' she said. 'Like all the others. I knew you would.'

'CUT!' somebody called.

'Where are you going?' asked Allegra.

'I don't know,' said Maddy. 'I'm not leaving you. Just leaving her. I'm sorry.' She looked at Allegra's face – a dusky triangle, wide eyes and pointed chin. It was hard to believe she belonged to Erin at all. Maddy felt a pain in her chest.

Allegra fingered the mirrored bedspread. 'She wouldn't notice if I went either.'

A voice said: 'Is that her little girl?' A man came into the room. He said to Allegra: 'Come along, sweetheart. Let's have you in the shot.'

Five minutes later Maddy stepped out of the front door. Nobody, except Allegra, noticed she had gone. At the top of the street she turned. The BBC van looked like a fire engine, its hose running into the house. She thought: nothing will put out Erin's fire. It will devour everyone else, but it will never devour her.

Prudence stood in the kitchen, her back to Stephen. She addressed the calendar on the wall. 'You never really left her, did you?' As she spoke, she wondered why all the show-downs in her life took place in kitchens. 'You just used me to revive your marriage.' Or cars.

'That's not true,' he said, but he didn't move nearer her.

May 29 was ringed in Pentel, with an exclamation mark. It was Stephen's birthday, but now they wouldn't reach it together. There were months left after that. Then another calendar and another year.

'When you said *Isn't she amazing*, who did you mean?'

'What?' he asked.

'It doesn't matter.'

'Prudence, listen –'

'You used me. Both of you did. Maybe you didn't realise, but it doesn't really make any difference, does it? Your marriage was the real thing, all the time.' She moved to the window. 'I was just a sex-aid, when you had run out of all the others.'

'I loved you – love you. It's just . . .' His voice broke. 'I miss my boys.'

There was a silence.

'And your wife,' she said. 'You don't like her, but you love her.'

He said: 'I'll always love you.' The words dropped like pebbles; the four words everybody dreads to hear.

He was slipping from her; he had been for months. It was night, but next door's garden was floodlit. Their cherry tree was in blossom. The branches were burdened with it, like snow; they looked as if they would break. Beneath it stood a child's climbing frame. She longed for Stephen to leave.

He didn't put up much of a fight, her darling, weak lover. Late that night, he packed the bags he had dumped five months earlier on her office floor. She phoned for a minicab.

Love . . . she thought. Love . . . LOVE . . . *love* . . . His wife was right. Funnily enough, as she didn't speak English so well. There should be words for the different kinds of love he felt. Everyone felt. She thought: *I'm the word person but she's beaten me at my own game.*

Outside, in Louise's garden, the magnolia had shed its petals. The lawn was white with them, as if snow had fallen. It was late Saturday afternoon but the church clock had stopped years earlier at 3.15. Soon it would be Saturday evening but neither Louise nor her children had plans to go out. Jamie and Imogen lounged on the sofa, watching a *Blackadder* video on the TV.

Louise sat down on the window-seat. When they had bought the house she had imagined herself sitting here doing tapestry; in fact, she had never sat on it at all until now. The bookshelves were emptier; Robert had been down to collect more of his stuff. He had moved, with the woman, into a flat in Dollis Hill. *Dollis Hill*. My God, thought Louise, he really must love her.

Her sisters' love-affairs had broken up; they were alone now, like herself. For the past week, Maddy had apparently been sleeping on the floor of a friend's house, one of the mysterious friends her sisters had never met. The three of them were casualties of love. Its failure had made them familiar to each other, sisters again; they were no longer altered by those with whom they lived. She longed to be near them.

'Do you mind moving back to London?' she asked.

'Mind? You must be joking.' Jamie tipped the tube of Pringles; the last one fell out. He put it into his mouth. 'When can we leave?'

'What about you?' she asked Imogen. 'You don't mind us selling Skylark?'

Imogen shook her head. 'Think I can ever trust her again?'

'We won't have much money,' said Louise.

'Why not?'

She paused. 'We just won't. We'll have to rent a flat. I'll have to find a job. Things'll be different from now on.'

'Can we live in Brixton?' asked Jamie. 'It's wicked.'

'We could always live in the caravan,' said Louise. 'People have been happy there, in their own little way.'

She looked at Imogen. Her daughter was inspecting her fingernails as if she might find gold beneath them. Imogen had been quiet lately. She had actually been helping around the house. Louise found this alarming; was Imogen suffering from delayed shock from the accident?

Jamie stood up.

'Hey, you're in the way,' said Imogen. He was blocking the TV screen.

He said: 'If we're leaving, I think someone else should, too.' He went to the door. 'Come on, you lot.'

He went into the garden. Treading on the fallen petals, they followed him to the rabbit hutch. He pulled down the latch and opened the door.

327

'Come on, Boyd, old bugger,' he said. 'Bugger off.'

'He'll eat the plants,' said Louise.

'They're not ours any more.' Jamie squatted in front of the cage. Boyd sat hunched in his corner, growling. 'You a man, or what?'

'He's a rabbit,' said Imogen.

Jamie lifted him out. It had been a long time since he had picked him up. Boyd, taken aback by this, froze. Jamie lowered him onto the grass. 'Off you go. Forget those home commitments, all that responsibility. Wasn't it boring in your little hutch?' Still the rabbit didn't move. Unnerved by the prospect of freedom, he sat there, his ears twitching. 'Go on, go forth and multiply,' said Jamie. 'Shag thyself senseless.'

Boyd hopped a few feet. He stopped and sniffed the air. Then he started nibbling the grass – it was long and lush, nobody had cut the lawn for weeks.

Louise straightened up. She put her arms round her children. They were no longer her kids; they were two large allies for the short amount of time she would have them, because soon they too would be gone. She felt strangely exhilarated.

'Let's celebrate. There's still some Bolly left.'

'I'd like some lemonade,' Imogen said.

'Oh, diddums,' said Jamie.

They had run out of lemons. Louise jumped into her Space Cruiser and started the engine. She remembered Imogen's birthday, how Robert had driven off to look for lemons. Why had he been away for such a long time? The past, that once-smooth landscape, was now planted with mines of this kind.

On the dashboard a light started winking. Brake fluid? Oil? Robert had dealt with all that. She had so much to learn but just now she didn't care. She had the children and Robert had lost them; there was a sick satisfaction in this. Today she didn't care about anything, even seeing Tim for the first time since that humiliating evening.

She stopped outside the General Stores and jumped down. The shop was closed. She looked at her watch: it was 5.10.

328

Arnold, the publican, was watering his hanging baskets. 'He's packed up and gone.' He jerked his spray bottle at the shop. 'Last Thursday.'

'Tim?' asked Louise stupidly. 'Why?'

'Came to our village for some peace and quiet, you know he's had a rough ride. Well, he said the vandals were the last straw.'

'What vandals?'

'Stealing cars, you not heard? Been a spate of it round here. Then a few weeks ago somebody emptied his till. That did it.'

Louise gazed at the shop window. The blinds were pulled down. Stuck to the glass, however, was the banner. SUPPORT OUR VILLAGE SHOP. Its colours had faded in the sunlight.

She walked back to her car. She thought: I tried to save him. I did, in my own blind way.

Being alone now, Maddy and Prudence drew closer to each other. Released from the constraints of disliking each other's partner – a vocal dislike in Maddy's case and an unspoken one in Prudence's – they felt more intimate with each other than they had for years. That Prudence had introduced Maddy to Erin deepened this; so did their shared lesbian confidences. And then there was Allegra. Maddy loved the little girl and felt responsible for her. Erin had always neglected her daughter and now only took her to photo-opportunities.

Maddy and Prudence decided to take her out on the sort of jaunts they would have taken their own children, if they had had them. On a Sunday in late May they took her on a river trip to Greenwich. Aziz accompanied them. They made a curious, reconstructed little family.

Prudence hadn't met Aziz before. She was charmed by his elegaic good manners and sorrowful eyes. He looked like a prince who had been stripped of his inheritance. They watched him leaning against the rail, his arm around his daughter.

'His life's such a mess,' said Maddy.

'Join the club.'

'He feels betrayed.'

'Don't we all.' Prudence laughed. 'Stephen betrayed me with his wife, Robert betrayed Louise with their money and Erin betrayed you with her own ego.' She flung back her head. The clouds raced above her.

'You're good with words,' said Maddy. 'You've always made sense of things.'

'Oh, words are easy.'

Aziz joined them. Prudence pointed out the Unimedia building, glittering in the sun as they slid past. 'That's where I work.'

'Carl Zinich built that,' he said. 'We were in partnership when we started out.' He pointed out the other buildings and told her the names of their architects. 'César Pelli, Richard Seifert . . . Know how many square feet of office space is lying empty over there? Docklands is a monument to developers' greed. I want to build wonderful spaces for people to live in.' His voice warmed up. 'We put people into little boxes, they get so lonely, like rabbits in their hutches. I want to create big, flexible spaces that absorb our comings and goings, that have privacy and conviviality. My family's house in Bombay, it was a living organism, aunts, cousins, it welcomed them all in, very Chekhovian . . . wouldn't people be happier living in big, loose arrangements, a sort of non-family version of mine?'

'Our father's a builder,' said Prudence. 'Did you know? Not grand, like those architects, but he had ambitions, too. Ambitions for us. So he worked and he worked until he could buy a big house in Purley, mock-Tudor, all that. Trouble was, by then he had given us the education to sneer at it.' She laughed. 'I'm sure your house in Bombay wasn't like that.'

'Oh no? So why do you think I left?'

She smiled. They drifted down the Thames, through the hazy sunshine. They were flotsam, bumping together in the current.

They ate a picnic on the hill, up by the Observatory.

London lay spread beneath them. The buildings seemed to be exhaling, exhausted by the burden of those living within them. The Canary Wharf building rose into the haze, the light on its pinnacle pulsing in the sunshine.

Prudence gave Aziz a sandwich. 'It's so strange.' She pointed to the knapsack Allegra wore on her back. 'Maddy and I, we could pack one of those and just go anywhere.'

'Don't go!' said Allegra.

'We're not going to.'

Maddy said solemnly: 'You think you can leave it behind, but you take your baggage with you.'

'It's just an alarming thought, that's all,' said Prudence.

'Shall I tell you when I was first truly afraid?' asked Aziz. 'I said to my elder brother, *Look at that beautiful yellow balloon* and he said, *Ah but your yellow may not be mine. How can you tell we're really seeing the same thing?* I suddenly felt utterly alone.'

'You think you can rely on words,' said Prudence. 'I used to think that, when I was little. Then I looked closely at the newspaper and it was all little dots. I felt terrified.'

'It's okay,' replied Aziz. 'They're computer-typeset now.'

Prudence laughed. She said: 'When my parents split up the past sort of disintegrated. Back into the little dots.' She turned to Allegra. 'Even at my age that happened.'

'Mine weren't parents to begin with,' said Allegra.

Aziz brushed grass-clippings off his trousers. 'Don't blame me for that, my darling.'

Prudence flung herself back onto the grass. She stared up at the sky. 'Let's all go to India and live in a big house with a veranda. Let's pack our bags and go. Nobody'll miss us.' How huge the sky was, above the suffused city. 'Let's all see the same colours. Let's live together because we like each other, not because we're related. Wouldn't it be fun?'

'Yes,' said Allegra.

Maybe the seed was sown that day. Later, Prudence remembered that conversation on the hill and her vision of a communal life – serene, companionable, unmuddied by sex.

Herself, her sister Maddy who had been lost for so long, the lonely child, and the refined, pedantic man who brushed grass-clippings off his linen trousers. Maybe they had as good a chance as any of being happy.

And they were happy that day, the four of them. After lunch, Prudence took them to the Unimedia building, the security guard let them in, and while she showed Aziz around its empty, marble spaces, Maddy and Allegra travelled up and down in the lift, mouthing at each other in its glass lozenge. They went into her office and she made them some tea. She gave Allegra some children's books; she gave Aziz a book on landmarks of modern British architecture which she had recently published. As he leafed through it she gazed at his shiny, blue-black hair. A feeling of pleasure spread through her; she always felt this when she watched people reading.

And then the peace was shattered. 'I suppose we'd better go,' she said, stacking the cups on the tray.

'I'm not,' said Allegra.

They looked at the little girl sitting on the carpet.

'I'm not going home,' she said. She unclipped her knapsack and took it off. Dumping it on the carpet, she opened it and showed them what was inside – pyjamas, a pair of knickers, her Barbie ballerina.

'I'm coming to live with you,' she said, looking from one face to another. 'If you won't have me, I'm running away.'

'Ally!' said her father. 'Don't talk like that.'

'Why did Mummy have me if she doesn't want me? She never watches TV with me, she never does anything, she's always doing something else.'

Prudence, staring down at her, had a sense of *déjà vu*. Stephen had stood on that very spot, his bags heaped on the floor. *I've left them. Can I come and live with you?*

Maddy sat down next to Allegra. 'Of course she loves you.'

'*You* know what she's like,' said the little girl. 'She doesn't love anybody except herself and her beastly book.'

'Come on, darling.' Aziz stretched out his hand.

332

Allegra grabbed her knapsack and ran out of the room.

They chased her, their footsteps clattering on the stairs. Down and down she ran, they glimpsed her dark head as she turned the corners. Finally, down in the lobby, Maddy cornered her. She had ducked behind a tub of ferns. Maddy took her arm and led her out. 'Come on, darling,' she said.

Prudence felt a jolt. She had never heard Maddy call anyone *darling* before. All her life Maddy had worked with children and she had never had one of her own.

In silence they drove Allegra back to Hackney. Aziz sat with her in the back. When they arrived in Romilly Street she had fallen asleep against his shoulder.

On Saturday Louise's sisters and mother came down to clean up the Old Vicarage as if preparing a bride for the highest bidder. They arrived together in Prudence's car. In the lane, a man was hammering up a FOR SALE sign; though this was inevitable, it was still a shocking sight; it always is.

Louise tried to greet them warmly. On a good day this would have felt like a show of female solidarity, womenfolk rallying round and rolling up their sleeves, but today there seemed something pitiful about these four abandoned women. She could picture herself and her sisters ending their lives alone, a cat on each of their laps. Jamie was the only invigorating masculine presence, dragging down a bag of rubbish from his room.

'What's happened to the shop?' asked Dorothy, getting out of the car. 'We stopped there for some rubber gloves – I thought, Lou won't have enough rubber gloves – and it was shut up.'

Louise explained about Tim and Margot. 'They had a daughter, you see. She died from meningitis six years ago. They came here to start a new life. Village shop, sounds so idyllic.'

Jamie lowered his bag to the ground. 'They had a daughter?'

Omitting her own role in this, Louise recounted what had happened. 'So she went first, and finally he left. He said the local vandals were the last straw, smashing up scouts' huts, stealing cars, that sort of thing.'

'What?' Jamie was looking at her curiously.

'Then somebody burgled his shop. That did it. And he left.'

Dorothy looked at the house, at the heavy buds of the wistaria hanging over the porch. 'Even here, in this beautiful place,' she said. 'You'd think you'd be safe here.'

'Nothing's safe,' said Louise. 'If I've learned anything, I've learned that.'

'Don't, Mum.' Jamie shifted his weight from one foot to the other.

Dorothy turned to him. 'Those hooligans, they're probably your age. I blame it on the parents.'

Jamie hauled away his bag of rubbish.

They set to work washing woodwork and clearing out cupboards. They sorted things into piles for the Help the Aged shop in Beaconsfield, reducing the Bailey family past to jumble. '*If in doubt, throw it out*,' was Dorothy's motto and she muttered it as she rummaged through the hall cupboard, flinging out child-sized wellington boots and frayed espadrilles, flattened like biscuits. Having already cleared out one house that year she was ruthless but Louise felt the same way and left her to it.

She and Prudence started on the marital bedroom – *splendid master bedroom with en suite bathroom and extensive views*, according to the estate agent's brochure. Prudence, standing on a chair, opened the top of the wardrobe and pulled out a cardboard box. It was filled with baby clothes – dungarees, Babygros. 'Why did you keep these?'

Louise, busying herself, didn't reply.

Prudence blushed. 'It's a bit late now,' she said, and dropped the box on the floor.

'Have you heard from Stephen?' Louise asked.

Prudence shook her head.

In the *en suite* bathroom Maddy was polishing the taps with an old silk stocking she had found behind the towel rail. 'Never had a jacuzzi,' she said, looking at the bath. 'Never done lots of things. I'm going to start a new life.'

'Me, too,' said Prudence. 'So how do we begin?'

'Search me,' said Maddy.

Jamie came in and gave a carrier bag to Maddy. 'Allegra might want these. My old computer games and things.' He paused, and turned to his mother. 'Do you know where Tim's gone?' he asked. 'The man from the shop.'

Louise looked at him sharply. 'Why do you think I should know?'

'Only asking,' he said, and went out.

Thoughtfully, Louise stuffed her old magazines into a rubbish bag. Had Jamie overheard something? Had he been around when Margot had come to the garden? No, he'd been in York.

'When I've finished this, shall I help Immy with her room?' asked Prudence.

Louise shook her head. Imogen had been shut in her bedroom all morning. 'She says she's doing it herself.' She lowered her voice. 'She's been very quiet lately.'

Just then they heard Imogen's door open. Footsteps hurried past them to the bathroom. The door slammed shut. They heard the muffled but unmistakable sound of vomiting.

Louise dumped down her magazines and hurried into the corridor. She listened. How violent the retching sounded, as if Imogen's inside were being torn from her. Maddy joined her, clutching her bottle of Brasso. Even the dog padded upstairs and stood there, his tail waving to and fro.

The lavatory flushed. They heard the sound of running water. The door opened and Imogen came out, her hair wet. She stopped and leaned against the radiator. She looked as if the knots within her body had been loosened; at any moment she would slide to the floor.

Louise brushed back the hair from her daughter's fore-

335

head. 'Darling, are you all right?'

'Not really,' said Imogen. 'I'm pregnant.'

They sat on Louise's bed, a row of them. Jamie and Dorothy had appeared, drawn there by Louise's cry of horror.

'Who is it?' asked Louise. 'Who's the father?'

'Karl.'

'Karl?'

'The blacksmith.'

'The *blacksmith*?' Louise felt dizzy, as if she were watching them all suspended from the air. 'How do you know? Are you sure?'

Imogen nodded. 'I did a test this morning. April sent me the kit.'

'*April*?' Louise stared at her daughter.

'April?' snapped Dorothy. 'How does she know?'

'I'd missed my period. I was worried.'

Louise said: 'So April's known all this time?'

'It's only three weeks,' said Imogen.

'Why did you tell April?' demanded Dorothy.

'She was here,' said Imogen. 'She's a nurse.'

'I know she's a nurse!' barked Dorothy.

Louise said: 'You told April before you told me?'

'Louise! Mum!' Prudence frowned at them. 'Is it so important, about April?'

'I'm sorry.' Louise put her arm round her daughter's rigid shoulders. 'When did it happen? Have you been – seeing him – a lot?'

Imogen shook her head. 'I hate him.'

There was a silence. Outside, horses clopped down the lane. Skylark whinnied from the field. She was answered by another whinny. For a mad moment, Louise imagined the horses telling each other the news. Soon it would be all round the village.

Imogen said: 'He's married. And he's got a girlfriend. Not me. Another one.'

Nobody spoke. They sat side by side on the brass bed. They gazed at Imogen, who picked at the skin around her fingernails.

'When was this?' Louise hooked her daughter's wet hair behind her ear. 'My poor love. Was it when you heard about Dad and me, or before that?'

Jamie said: 'I bet it was when you left Skylark at the stables. I always thought that was funny.'

Imogen said: 'I asked for it. It was my fault, really.'

'Course not,' said Maddy. 'It was his. Shall we go and kill him?'

'It was our fault,' said Louise. 'Your father's and mine. Oh shit.'

They sat there on the bed; beneath its covers Imogen had been conceived. Louise still couldn't take it in. She closed her eyes and it replayed itself in normal life. Imogen, emerging from the bathroom, said, *I must have eaten something funny last night*, and they carried on with their cleaning.

Prudence was talking. 'What do you want to do, Immy?'

'What do you – oh. Keep it, of course.'

'Darling, you're sixteen!' said Louise. 'You're still at school.'

'I hate school. I'm hopeless at everything. I'd rather have a baby.' Imogen raised her head; her face glowed. 'When'll I feel it kicking?'

'This is completely insane,' said Louise.

'I'll love it,' said Imogen.

'You can't possibly keep it.'

'Why not?'

'Because you're too young.'

'I'd like to be a mother,' said Imogen. 'I'd be good at that. I want a baby more than anything in the world.' She looked at her two aunts. 'Can't you understand?' They didn't reply. 'I want something to look after, that's mine.'

'It's not a rabbit,' said Louise.

'You never cleaned them out anyway,' said Jamie.

'You've got your whole life ahead of you,' said Louise.

'So has the baby,' replied Imogen.

This silenced them for a moment.

Then Jamie said: 'You told anyone? Like at school?'

Imogen shook her head. 'Only April.'

'April!' Dorothy snapped. 'I can't believe –'

'Shut up, Mum,' said Louise.

There was a silence. Dorothy, who was sitting in the arm-chair, gazed at the row of them. There was a smudge of dirt on her cheek. She wore the daisy-patterned apron she had worn for years. 'If she wants to keep it, she should keep it. We'll rally round, Imogen, love. I think it'd be lovely to have another baby in the family.'

They stared at her. 'Mum!' said Louise.

'Goodness!' Dorothy laughed. 'Gordon'll be a great-grand-father. He won't like that.'

'Is that all you can think about?' Louise retorted. 'Come to think of it, this isn't my fault. It's yours. If you hadn't opened your stupid mouth about Robert none of this would have happened. I wouldn't be selling the house, Imogen wouldn't be pregnant –'

'Lou,' said Prudence. 'That's not fair.'

Louise turned to her sisters. 'You two probably wouldn't have split up and been so unhappy.' Something snapped. She glared at her mother. 'Now you're alone you want to make us all helpless and dependent, you want to put the clock back and make us all single again, make us back into your little daughters!'

'Lou –' began Prudence.

'You want to blame me for everything?' demanded Dorothy. 'What about your father, why don't you blame him? He started all this.'

'Do shut up, both of you,' said Maddy.

'Why do children blame their parents for everything?' asked Dorothy bitterly. 'Why can't you grow up and blame yourselves? You'll be blaming me for the dead daughter of your shopkeeper next.' She appealed to the room in general. 'You educate your children and what do they learn? How to attack their parents.' She paused, breathing heavily. 'Anyway, I'm not trying to get you back. I've had quite enough of all that, thank God. The reason I came down today, apart from trying to help, was to tell you I'll be off your hands soon.'

'Why?' asked Prudence.

'Eric and I are getting married.'

They stared at her. Even Imogen stared.

'Married?' whispered Louise.

'Well, when I get divorced.'

Suddenly they all burst into laughter.

Two

It took Jamie a whole morning to reach Tim's flat. He knew the address, he had got it from Arnold, who ran the pub, but once he arrived in London he had to take the tube to Bounds Green, then a bus, and finally found himself in the outer reaches of London, almost off the *A–Z*, out beyond the North Circular Road which hummed in the distance.

It was a sunny Saturday, a week since he had heard the news about Tim and about his sister, a child snuffed out and a child begun. As he walked up the street he felt strangely confident. The old Jamie would have been embarrassed by what he was about to do but now he had crossed the threshold into adulthood. He was the man of the family now. He walked past the rows of semis and modest blocks of flats. This was where people lived, the sort of place where he himself might soon be living with his family; how fortified they had been by their good fortune but now the barriers had melted and he had joined the human race.

This was how Jamie put it to himself, for the nobility of his plan created sonorous words in his head, like a gong being struck. Petty considerations – what would happen, for instance, if Tim wasn't at home – seemed irrelevant. Life consisted of massive events, how liberating this was! The harm he had done in the past dissolved, he was going to put it right, he was a better person now. He felt happiness filling him like warm soup. He hadn't felt so happy for months.

Jamie found the place at last. It was a small, purpose-built block of flats opposite a children's playground. Two boys rode their bikes round a dried-up paddling pool. A row of poplars shivered and swayed, their silvery leaves applauded him as he rang the bell.

Tim opened the door. It was odd seeing him away from his shop, like seeing one of his teachers in Beaconsfield, looking like a normal person. Tim blinked through his glasses.

'I'm James Bailey – you know, I used to come to the shop.'

'My goodness. What are you doing here?' He let Jamie in. They went upstairs and into a room. It was sunny. Some sort of historical costume lay on the floor.

'Caught me doing my mending,' said Tim. 'Would you care for some coffee?'

Jamie shook his head. 'I just – well, dropped by. I heard what happened, you know, with the shop.'

'What do you mean?'

'That you were robbed.' Jamie's confidence drained away. 'Well, I've managed to get some of the money back. 'He fished in his jacket and took out the envelope. He gave it to Tim. 'So I brought it back to you.'

Tim took the envelope, opened it and looked at the notes. On the wall a cuckoo flung itself out of its clock and squawked.

'Why?' asked Tim.

'I know it's probably not enough. But at least it's something.'

Tim sat down heavily in an armchair. Its stuffing was bursting out like brains. Jamie sat down in the other one, facing him. He thought: my father would never do this. Look, I'm a separate person.

'How did you get it?' Tim asked.

'I can't really say,' said Jamie. 'It doesn't matter.' It was, in fact, his accumulated earnings from Tesco. He had saved it up to go travelling around Europe in the summer.

Tim removed his glasses and rubbed the bridge of his nose. He was wearing a Pizza Express T-shirt. Maybe he had got a job there; Jamie never found out. Tim looked at him, his eyebrows raised. 'Your family's always trying to give me things.'

341

'Who? What sort of things?'

'It doesn't matter.' Tim smiled. 'A case of *noblesse oblige*.' He leaned across and gave back the envelope. 'In this case, too, I feel I must refuse.'

The envelope lay on Jamie's lap. It was a windowed one, a business one, from his father's desk.

'Call me old-fashioned,' said Tim, 'but my instinct is to serve.'

'Is that why you had a shop?'

Tim shook his head and pointed to the costume. 'Hence my loyalty to the Royalist cause. We're re-enacting the Battle of Wallingford next week. Probably seems silly to you, a lot of middle-aged men sloshing around in the mud, but in fact it's rather satisfying.'

'Why?'

'If I didn't do it – who knows? – I'd probably go and do something silly.' He paused. 'I mean really silly. Like bashing something up. Like your friends.'

'They're not my friends.'

'And then where would we be?' Tim gazed down at the costume, lying between them. There was a bald patch in the middle of his hair. 'At least I know whose side I'm on. Everything else, it's not that easy.'

'Please take it.'

Tim shook his head. 'To tell the truth, young man, I'm glad she's left. My wife, I mean. I think she is, too. We couldn't cope any longer. I won't go into details. I'll just say that bereavement is not endearing. I hope you'll never have cause to discover that.' He stood up. 'So keep your money. Enjoy it.' He paused. 'Live.'

Jamie stood up. They stood there for a moment, formally. Feeling a hot, guilty relief, he put the envelope back into his pocket. Now he could go Inter-railing with Max and Chris from school.

Tim stepped over the costume. It was laid spreadeagled on the floor, as if its Cavalier had vaporised. 'Something I found comforting, though you might not think so, it's something I read. That the living are just dead people who have not yet taken up their posts.' He escorted Jamie to the door. 'It's not as gloomy as it sounds. You're a nice kid. Remember what you said in the shop? Well, I hope your life is long and sweet.'

Jamie went downstairs and let himself out into the street. He felt light-headed – so light-headed, that, if nobody had been there, he would have jumped onto one of the swings and pushed himself up, up into the dazzling blue sky.

The Amersham Horse Show was in full swing. In a roped-off enclosure jumps had been erected. A girl on a chestnut horse cleared the double-hurdle and cantered off. *'Number 26, clear round!'* boomed the loudspeaker. In another enclosure smaller children stumbled to the finishing post in the egg-and-spoon race. Tethered horses whinnied to each other across the sea of cars; the air smelled of dung and exhaust smoke and the aroma of sizzling frankfurters. Vans had flung open their flanks to reveal items for sale – saddlery, soft drinks, china ornaments of famous stallions.

Louise and her sisters, avenging furies, strode through the crowd. Karl was here; Imogen had told them so. Louise looked at the row of horseboxes, their opened ramps littered with straw. A teenage girl sat there, jodhpured legs apart, munching a sandwich; she fed the crust to her pony which was tethered beside her. Tears stung Louise's eyes – tears of rage and grief. That should be Imogen, sitting there in the sunshine. But Imogen was at home; she no longer rode, she had lost her nerve – besides, she was scared of losing the baby. Her youth had been stolen from her.

The three of them walked towards the far ring where a crowd had gathered. Louise thought: this time last year we were a happy family. Now strangers are tramping around my house, opening the cupboards, standing in front of the windows, looking at my view.

'What are you going to do when you see him?' asked Prudence.

343

'Castrate him?' asked Maddy.

Louise shook her head. 'I don't know.'

'I just want to see what he looks like,' said Prudence.

At the time they had no plan. Louise had no intention of telling the blacksmith that he had made her daughter pregnant; the thought filled her with horror. What happened next filled her with horror, too, in retrospect. She would never have managed it without her sisters' presence. For they regressed, that mad day, into the giggly plot-making of their childhood.

The Young Farrier's Competition was in progress. A man held a megaphone. It was John Suttler, Louise knew him, he ran the riding stables with his wife.

'. . . points against the clock,' he was saying, explaining the rules to the new people who had drifted towards the ring. Louise and her sisters peered through the crowd. A bent figure stood in the ring, hammering a shoe onto a large black horse.

'That him?' whispered Prudence.

Louise shook her head. *He can take my shoes off any day.* How flippant she had been, how insouciant. She watched the blacksmith at work. She thought how all these years she and her children had been playing on a beach with their backs to the water, oblivious to the tidal wave that was rearing up behind them, higher and higher, poised, ready to engulf them.

When Karl walked into the ring she had made up her mind. As she watched him, it was Robert's face she saw. He grinned at her: *I like sex with women, too.* Beside him hung the upturned horseshoe, its luck spilling out. Louise looked across the grass at Karl. His hair was oiled flat like an otter's; he wore his leather apron slung around his hips. She pictured him on top of her daughter. A bay horse had been led into the ring; the clock clicked 1 . . . 2 . . . Karl got to work.

Louise squeezed through the crowd. How charmingly she smiled at John Suttler, oh, she could still charm. He gave her the megaphone and above her the clouds scudded and below her feet the earth turned, for she was clearing her throat and speaking into the mouthpiece loud and clear.

'Let's have a big hand for Karl Fairlight, a rising young blacksmith from Tetbury Magna. Karl is married with two small children but that hasn't stopped him pursuing his main career . . .'

Karl straightened up. Louise, appalled at what she was doing, stopped. Maddy grabbed the megaphone from her – Maddy, the brave one, who didn't care. Prudence whispered the words into her ear and loudly Maddy repeated them.

' . . . you see, ladies and gentlemen, Karl is a bit of a stallion himself, he has a very high score in that respect. If it moves, jump it, that's Karl's motto, so if he visits your home we would advise you to keep your wives and daughters safely tethered up indoors.'

A hush fell. Across the showground the loudspeaker boomed but the crowd was stilled. They stared at Maddy. Their heads swivelled round; they stared at Karl. He hadn't moved.

The three sisters escaped to the car. They slammed the door and exploded into laughter. They laughed so hard they thought they were going to be sick. As they drove off, bouncing over the grass towards the exit, Louise thought: what the hell. After all, in a few weeks I'll be gone for good.

By the time they had pulled into the main road the incident seemed so unreal they could hardly believe they had done it. Already it had taken on the patina of a myth.

Prudence, driving, patted Louise's knee. 'Let's stick together. We make a great team.'

That Saturday was the last day of Gordon's life. If they had known it, his daughters wouldn't have been at the horse show, humiliating a blacksmith. If they had known, they would have made their peace with him and no longer blamed him for breaking up their family, for by now they had learned the havoc that love can wreak. Maddy would have told him what she had been planning to say, one day – that he wasn't entirely to blame for her misery when she was growing up. That his disappointment was understandable, for she had burst from her old skin like a butterfly and she too could look back on her old self, an atrophied chrysalis all those years, with bemused pity. That Erin, for all her arrogance, had solved her, and for this she would always be grateful.

His other daughters, what could they have told him – that they loved him? They hadn't told him this since they were children, maybe not even then, though they had signed their letters *lots of love, all my love* – how easily such words slip from the pen. Neither of them felt anything as simple as love but it must be lying there hidden, surely it must. If they had known he was going to die the wind would have blown away the topsoil and revealed the rock beneath, wouldn't it? Louise, caught in the present, was still hurt by his refusal of help when she most needed it. If she had known, that Sunday lunch when he'd visited her with April, she would have forgotten her own distractions: after all, Imogen had survived.

But they were caught in the present, in the myopia of the moment. Nobody more so than Gordon himself, a man of impulse, who seldom reflected on the past or anticipated the future. That was his wife's department, and it was something he missed, had he realised it, when in the company of April. He also missed the past itself. Though it was exhilarating to start afresh, Dorothy was his *aide-mémoire* for his adult life, the early struggles in Chislehurst, the raising of their girls, the world events that he was frequently too busy to heed; without her presence, he felt, at times, drifting and untethered.

This particular morning, this Saturday, he was buying a new lawn-mower and cursing his recklessness in leaving the old one back in the shed at The Birches. If he had known, he would have taken April to Paris, or at least taught her the words of the song which now she would never sing.

And if she had known, April would never have spoken to him the way she did when he came home. He unloaded the

346

car. She followed him out into the garden. The nameless bushes challenged her – prune us, don't prune us, you haven't a clue, have you? She thought: why are we weighing ourselves down with a house, with *things*? With all these things? He's done this before; why is he doing it all over again? The dry rot, the tasks. The building of a home only to find that its occupants have fled.

The scent of roasting meat drifted through the hedge; next door was having a barbecue. The woman laughed shrilly. April had only met her once, when she'd been coming home with some shopping and the woman had asked her: 'Excuse me, do you work here? I'm desperate for a cleaning lady.'

Gordon was tearing open the box. He never undid things, he always tore them open. Today, because she was feeling out of temper, this annoyed her. She said: 'I'm feeling homesick, Gordon. I want to go back to Brixton.'

He straightened up. 'What, to live?'

She didn't nod, thank God, though this was the answer in her heart. She was unhappy in Wandsworth. She missed her friends, she missed the late-night shops, she missed her job. She had realised this, with a sinking sensation, over the past week. Thank God she didn't speak the truth.

'You don't like it here?' he asked.

'It's fine. I'm sure it'll be fine.'

'You having second thoughts, about me?'

'Of course not.' Thank God she said this, too, though in fact she was having doubts. Not about Gordon, exactly, but the reality of their life together. But nobody ever knew this. She said: 'I just feel a bit like one of those plants, pulled up by the roots. I don't like being dependent on a bloke. I want to get some agency work.'

He put his hands on her shoulders and gazed into her eyes. 'You do whatever you want, my love. You saved my life, know that?' He smiled but she could see he was upset.

'I just fancy – you know – seeing some of my mates, maybe having a bite.'

'Your wish is my command,' he said. 'Sod the lawn. Had

347

forty years of mowing the lawn.'

She had intended, in fact, to go alone. Later, she was grateful that he had misunderstood her, for it had saved his feelings being hurt.

Ah, but if he had been a more sensitive man – if he had understood her and stayed home – if that had happened, might he still be alive?

So they went to Brixton later that day and had a coffee in the market. They dropped in on her friend Carole, who ran the hair salon in Second Avenue, and when Carole's last client left they bought some wine and went back to her place, where her husband cooked them a curry. Beverley dropped by, the friend who had told April about the earlobes, which hadn't worked because Gordon had resumed smoking but which, on the other hand, had worked because it was his earlobes that she had first touched, apart from nursing touching, and it had been his earlobes that had switched on their electricity. The evening gathered momentum, as Saturday evenings do when one is not living in Purley, or Wandsworth, and soon another couple of people dropped by and then somebody said: 'Let's go dancing.'

'Me?' said Gordon. 'I'd look a right nincompoop.'

But he went, willingly, and as they walked to The Fridge he flung back his head and looked at the stars, bright even in the sodium light, and he turned to April and ceremoniously kissed her hand. *'Hey there, you with the stars in your eyes,'* he sang, and she knew he was drunk but then so was she. She fell in love with him again that night – it wasn't just in retrospect – she loved this stubborn, sentimental man, and then they were inside, under another galaxy of pulsing lights and she shouted at him: 'Better than a hottie, eh?'

He didn't hear, the music was too loud. She took his hand and led him onto the dance floor. His last words, shouted at her over the noise, were: 'Oh well, you only live once.' But she didn't hear them, they were drowned by the music.

348

The music thumped, it beat through three hundred shared heartbeats. It thudded through their skulls, through their pulsing, jointed bodies, the miracle of them. *Don't they know what a miracle it is? No matter what an idiot someone is, how selfish or stupid, still their bodies go on digesting, pumping . . .* April and Gordon, who were both guilty of selfishness, and more besides, drew closer. *However bad we've been, our bodies always forgive us. Heart-breaking, isn't it?*

He took her in his arms. For a moment they danced together, cheek to cheek, heart to heart, the proper way to dance, the way they'd danced when he was young.

And then he fell and she was sliding with him to the ground.

She wrestled his collar open. Hunched over him, bumped by the legs of other people, she opened his mouth with hers. Before Gordon died his lover left him; she was replaced by April the nurse, the April he had first loved.

But all her professional skills, great though they were, could not save him now.

Three

That Saturday, for Dorothy, was one of the bad days. Her rage against Gordon had a life of its own, it flared up unexpectedly like the inflammation from a gunshot wound where the bullet has not been removed. It existed alongside her new-found contentment with Eric, and she kept it quiet. Her marriage had not been kindly dismantled. Gordon had torn it open like the lawn-mower's packaging; he had cut the knots he couldn't untie, removed the contents and left her to cope with the rubbish. What could she do with all the stuff that filled her head?

Eric had come to lunch. He had brought his road map with him; they were looking at possible places to live in the country. 'What about opening a tea shop?' he suggested. 'A little business, something to keep us busy.'

A watercress farm? It was April, she was sure, who had told Gordon that story. *You wouldn't believe what happened to April last night.* She remembered him sitting up in bed, his eyes bright.

Dorothy felt sick. How could she start a new life when her old self was raw and unfinished? Later that afternoon, when Eric left, she dialled Gordon's number.

His machine answered. *'We're not at home . . .'* How easily one *we* had replaced another! She ignored the fact that exactly the same thing had happened to her. The machine played a moronic, electronic version of 'Greensleeves' and beeped.

'Gordon,' she said, 'Dorothy here. Are you going to go on burying your head in the sand or will you meet me and talk?

350

Maybe you haven't even heard about Imogen or the various other things that have been happening to your family whilst you have been otherwise engaged. Maddy's out of work, Louise and your grandchildren will soon be homeless. D'you think if you just keep your eyes closed these things will go away? Please phone me at your earliest convenience.'

That night Louise phoned her father. She was sitting in Robert's study. His framed print of Charterhouse had been knocked sideways by somebody pushing past his desk. Strangers moved over her house, herds of them; they ground their cigarette butts into her lawn. She gazed at the picture of Robert's old school. It was a boring print; she had never liked it. Why had he left it here; was he putting childish things behind him?

'*Gordon Hammond here. We're not home at present but if you want to leave a message for me or April please speak after the beep.*'

She was pleased. It was easier to leave a message on a machine. How much simpler life would be if you never had to speak to a living, breathing person.

'Dad . . . Hi. Hope you're well. Maybe April's spilled the beans already, she's known for a while. Just to say, remember Immy's birthday? You said she'd beat her aunts to it? Well, you were right. In January you'll be a great-grandfather. Hope it doesn't make you feel too old . . . Lots of love. Bye.'

When she replaced the receiver Louise immediately regretted the message. How abrupt it had sounded! But she couldn't undo it now.

Two days passed before April could bring herself to listen to the answerphone. She replayed the messages. They rolled off her like drops of mercury. What did any of it matter now? She paused for a moment. Then she pressed OGM Play.

'*Gordon Hammond here. We're not home . . .*' She thought: typical Gordon, putting himself first. Her eyes filled with tears. She pressed Eject. She took out the tape and put Gordon's voice into her pocket to keep for ever.

The coffin slid into the furnace. The curtains closed the little show that was Gordon's life. They paused halfway, as if hesitating; then they made up their mind and swished together, swinging gently. Gordon had not been a religious man, he hadn't had time to believe in God. He slid into the unknown to a recording of *Bali Ha'i*, his favourite song from *South Pacific*.

His daughters, to their surprise, shuddered with tears at this point. Until then they had coped. They sat squashed together, passing each other tissues. Robert, who had arrived late from work, sat behind them. Afterwards, they drove back to the house in Wandsworth, where, in the half-decorated dining room, April had laid out food and drink.

It was a strange gathering, for they had regressed back a step. Eric and Deirdre were not present; nor were Stephen and Erin, ghosts who had briefly entered their lives and vanished. Their family had reverted to its original cast of characters, to how they'd been before everything had changed. Yet the room was filled with people-shaped spaces – those from the past and those who would be the future. And the largest space of all was the space that had been Gordon.

They stood around awkwardly. Louise passed Robert a glass of wine. 'How's Dollis Hill?' She looked at him warily. 'Are you happy there, in your own little way?'

'Can we be friends?' he asked. 'Please?'

Prudence, munching a chicken leg, was talking to her mother: 'What sort of little business?'

'Something in the country. Something Eric and I can do together.'

Imogen said: 'Why don't you take over the village shop?'

They turned and looked at her.

Outside, the sun came out. Buttercups were flowering

amongst the tall grasses that nobody had cut. April opened the french windows. Dorothy came up to her. 'I was just wondering – did he hear my phone message? Was he upset?'

April shook her head. 'No, it was me who killed him. By asking him to dance.' She refilled Dorothy's glass. 'Shall we get pissed?'

'Shall we?'

'One day he told me he wanted his ashes to be scattered in the Lake District,' said April. 'Where you courted. He said you would know the place.'

'Did he?'

April nodded.

Just then there was the sound of hammering. It came from upstairs. They fell silent.

'It's Gordon,' said Robert. 'He just had to finish fixing that skirting board before he left.'

'No,' said Jamie, 'he's knocking at the Pearly Gates. *Let me in! I've been hanging around here for bloody hours.*'

'I think he's in heaven already,' said Imogen, 'and he's starting to sort it out.'

'You're right,' said April. 'That was his idea of heaven.'

'He's saying *I'll get the lads in . . .*'

'*Got a nasty damp patch there, must be all those clouds . . .*'

'*Roll over, Beethoven, got to get to work . . .*'

They laughed. The atmosphere thawed, for funerals can be surprisingly boisterous occasions. April explained that it was a local plumber hammering away upstairs, but Imogen, her head cocked, was listening to the tattoo of her blacksmith, who in her case had died whilst creating life.

April put on some music. Robert pushed back the table and took his daughter in his arms. Frank the foreman grabbed Dorothy and April kicked back the rug and led Jamie into the middle of the room. They danced, and then the song changed and Robert took Louise into his arms. They had always danced well together. Robert pushed Louise's hair back from her face, which weeping had washed bare, and after a while she relaxed in his arms and moved with him around the floor.

353

And then they all stopped and drank a toast to Gordon, who had had the last dance of all. April tapped her glass for silence. Later, when they thought of her, this was the image they remembered – April ablaze in a red satin suit, her hair pulled back with silver clips; a woman who radiated life.

She said: 'I just want to tell you I'll be packing up tomorrow. You can have the house, it was never really mine, to tell the truth, it never felt like it. I've got this friend, you see, she's matron at an old people's home, it might sound funny but I prefer nursing old people –' She stopped. 'Maybe it's not so surprising. Anyway, she's asked me to join the staff so –' She pointed to the table. 'Eat, drink and be merry – be merry, please, Gordon would have wanted that.' She smiled. 'And one day, who knows? If you need me, I'll be waiting for you.'

Four

A year had passed. It was a cloudless Saturday in May and Maddy was working in the garden. Neither she nor her sisters had liked the shrubs; they had seemed sooty and lifeless, atrophied in somebody else's past. She had pulled them out and now she was planting a herbaceous border. She lifted the plants from their pots, cradling their matted roots. Each plant she willed into its new home. A blackbird sang from the flowering cherry; the petals drifted onto the grass like snow.

At the end of the garden stood the caravan. Inside it, Allegra sat doing her homework. The caravan was her secret place, its dwarfish furniture absorbed her hopes and dreams as it had absorbed those of her almost-aunts. She was happy here, living in Wandsworth with her almost-family. For they had earned her love through loving her, rather than bearing her, and it was her mother now who arrived on Sundays, as Aziz had used to do, to take her out.

Aziz considered it Chekhovian; the three sisters living in a house that sopped up outsiders like a sponge. People drifted in and out – Jamie's friends from York, Aziz, who spent most evenings there. He and Prudence had a tender, cautious understanding; they treated each carefully, like breakable china. Maybe one day they would move out and live together but this present arrangement seemed charmed for they were alone, yet not alone, and the presence of children released them from their spinsterly habits.

Imogen and her baby were lying on the grass. Imogen, like Allegra, was doing her homework. In a month she would be

355

taking her A levels. Aziz was drawing up plans for their new kitchen and Prudence was unpacking her weekend's pile of manuscripts. This studious atmosphere was broken by the baby's yells. Louise dumped down her shopping, went outside and scooped up the baby in her arms. She held her, swaying in the sunshine.

Prudence picked up the manuscript. *Home Truths* by Erin Fox. She sat down in the armchair and turned to the first page.

'*Once upon a time there were three sisters – Isobelle, Effie and Vida . . .*'

Prudence looked out of the window. Louise twirled the baby round and round in a snowdrift of petals.

'*Isobelle was the sweet one, the pretty one, the good little girl who wanted to grow up and have babies . . .*'

Outside in the garden the little Louise sat playing with her dolls. How gold her hair shone in the sunlight! She tucked up her favourite doll, Mary-Belle, in a tea-cloth and laid her on the grass . . .

'*Effie was the bookworm, the clever one. And Vida? Vida was the tomboy . . .*'

The blackbird's song echoed down the years. Out in the garden, Maddy, square and determined, trundled her bulldozer across the grass. She drove it over Pru's open Enid Blyton book – how Prudence yelled! She drove it over Lou's doll, except it wouldn't go over, it pushed the doll along the ground – how Lou screamed! . . .

On the green, the kids were playing football. Their yells drifted through the open door of the General Stores, where Eric was serving a customer four portions of his salmon and spinach roulade. The shop was thriving because the inhabitants of Wingham Wallace were busy, achieving people; they commuted to London, they worked in PR, they had Agas but no time to cook in them and so they flocked to the shop, where they purchased Eric's delicacies and served them at dinner parties, passing them off as their own, or ate them, exhausted, in front of the TV and washed them down with one of his New World sauvignons, for he had an excellent stock of wine. At last they had a shop which understood them, they said.

Dorothy was selling stamps to the new occupant of Louise's house, a woman to whom she had taken an instant dislike. The woman asked: 'Tell me, did your daughter have any trouble with rabbits?'

'Rabbits?' asked Dorothy, giving her some change.

'We're simply overrun with the things. Had the garden done, cost a fortune, and they're eating it down to the ground.'

'As I remember, she did have a troublesome buck,' replied Dorothy, 'but God knows what happened to him.'

It was dark when Prudence finished the manuscript. Supper was over. Aziz had lit the fire and the others were sprawled around the living room watching TV.

'. . . *So the three sisters lived happily ever after. Or so they thought, for they didn't realise that this was just the beginning.*'

She laid down the last page. Maddy looked up. 'What's that you've been reading?'

'Erin's new novel.'

'Is it any good?'

Prudence shrugged. She got to her feet and went over to the fireplace. She fed the manuscript, page by page, into the fire. The flames leaped, illuminating her sisters' faces as they turned, briefly, to watch. Then they turned back to the TV. Monty, lying on the hearthrug, thumped his tail.